MW00965843

To Err Is Human

The cover stained glass photograph is taken from the collection of the State Museum of the History of St. Petersburg, Russia
Vladimir Knyazhitsky, photographer

To Err Is Human

A Novel

Elizabeth Murtaugh

Writers Club Press
San Jose New York Lincoln Shanghai

To Err Is Human
A Novel

Writers Club Press
an imprint of iUniverse.com, Inc.

For information address:
iUniverse.com, Inc.
5220 S 16th, Ste. 200
Lincoln, NE 68512
www.iuniverse.com

ISBN: 0-595-19468-0

Printed in the United States of America

Good nature and good sense must ever join;
To err is human; to forgive, divine.
Alexander Pope (1688–1744)

Acknowledgements

I am grateful to my sisters, Agnes Fiedler, Margaret Egan and Catherine Martin for their review of each chapter of this book as it was written; to my son, William Murtaugh and nephew, Jay Amberg for critical editorial advice; to my daughter-in-law, Susan Murtaugh, for copying services; to my friend Janice Westler for my photograph and especially to my daughters Mari Connors and Katherine Murtaugh for valuable assistance in getting the book published.

CHAPTER I

An amazing amount of ordinary life drains off like spring rain into some deep reservoir of oblivion but this frigid January day is one Sue Carney will never forget. She will always remember vividly the people she will meet for the first time this morning and the reception for the Cardinal in the evening. Because of what happened, the whole day will become part of her conscious history forever.

The weather itself is memorable. She stands at the baptistery window listening to the ten o'clock chimes and absorbing the wonder of the winter scene. An abundant fresh snow had fallen during the night but in early morning the temperature had plunged to zero. Now the whole world outside is crisp, clean, sparkling under clear sunlight and a brilliant blue sky. The enormous spruce in the island of the circular driveway holds its load of luminous snow in absolute stillness. The silent shadow of the tree, drawn so simply into the dazzle of the drifted snow, moves Sue deeply. Her heart expands with the song of the carillon. Oh yes! "Joyful, joyful we adore thee!"

A moment like this when her soul tingles with the glory of God is not unfamiliar to Sue but she knows this morning that some portion of her joy is due to the fact that Father Paul Rossi will be conducting their scripture discussion. He is a young priest, perhaps forty, certainly not handsome but tall and attractive in a rugged sort of way. He is quiet, reserved, and intelligent. Some parishioners complain that it is not easy

1

to know him well. Sue, however, is aware of how carefully he observes people and how attentively he listens to them. He is a man she has come to love in the short time he has been at St. Francis de Sales parish.

He had arrived last August as a total surprise. Three years ago when Monsignor Fiedler had retired, the Cardinal had been so slow in appointing Father Foley, their present pastor, that parishioners feared they might never get one. With the current shortage of priests, there had been no hope or expectation that an assistant would be assigned to them. Even though Father Rossi retains some jobs at the Chancery and is downtown almost every weekday, they feel that his presence is precious. He is, after all, an endangered species.

Sue, who sees him often because of her position as Minister of Care in the parish, has developed a delightful rapport with him. Their conversations are seldom long and often had in passing. Still, they share the same perspective on church issues and the same insights into people and events and this has created a bond between them.

Although their views are far less compatible, Sue's husband Fred and Father Rossi have developed a friendship of their own. It amuses Sue to recall the intensity of their political discussions, their heated scrimmages over social issues. Feeling vindicated by a Republican revolution in Congress, Fred tends to attack with heavy conservative clout, to ram theories home with a rigid righteousness that drives Sue up a wall. He grows excited. High color invades his earnest face. But Father plays it cool. He is like an experienced tennis player who gives the ball ample time to bounce before smoothly slamming it into his opponent's court. She loves it that he is unperturbed by Fred's intransigence. She loves the tolerant teasing glimmer in his eyes when he parries Fred's pummeling with humorous quips. She loves the calm, resonant timber of his voice when he quietly presents an argument. Most of all, she loves it that he understands Fred who, for all his adamant objections to taxation and welfare, has yet to pass up a real life beggar on the street.

An occasional dinner with Father has become part of their routine and on a couple of occasions they have taken him along on picnics with their three little girls. When Sue thought about these barbecues on the shore of the lagoon with the woods a blaze of color and the Indian summer wind singing through dry leaves, she remembered the thread of excitement and exhilaration that ran through them. It became difficult to sort out her feelings. Was her heart exalted because of the enchanted autumn day or because Father Paul, this man whom she admires, was striding along the woodland path holding her youngest daughter by the hand?

"Maybe it was a little of each," she said to Monsignor when she went to talk to him about her uneasiness in this new relationship.

Monsignor had been for so many years the pastor of de Sales that parishioners still think of the church as his and continue to consult him about their problems. They have a fierce loyalty and affection for this scholarly wisp of a man who loves the liturgy and who often in the evenings plays his violin in his study. Sue has a special fondness for him and complete confidence in his advice.

"I was thinking I should take a job teaching at the Academy, " she said. "The nuns have offered me the sophomore religion class for next semester."

"But Susie, you're doing wonderful work here in the parish and you've often told me you love it. Why would you quit?"

"Well, I'm trying to tell you, Monsignor, that I think there's a bit of chemistry going on between Father Rossi and me. Maybe I should just clear out."

Monsignor raised his thin, tent-shaped eyebrows thoughtfully. In his gentle way, he asked Sue a number of questions. "Did Fred share her friendship with Father? Was there a genuine friendship of mutual interest and respect? Had her friendship with Father affected her relationship with her husband?"

"No, it's not like that. Fred is home base, you know that. Fred and I are forever. It's just that there's this attraction…"

"Well, Sue, I don't think you're exactly making history. All of us are human and such attractions crop up from time to time. You say you enjoy Father Paul's low-key humor and I must say I do too though we are exposed to little of it at the rectory. By dinner time he's often tired and preoccupied. Priests have to work so hard these days. So I think it's a good thing if he lightens up a little with you and Fred. And your little girls may be a precious thing in his life very much as your family has always been in mine. But beyond the fun you enjoy with him, Sue, can you tell me what you think of him as a person. What is your deepest impression of him?"

Sue thought a moment before she answered. How could she adequately express her sense of Father Rossi's serious dedication to God? Finally she said, "Look, this is going to sound corny but I'll say it anyway since it's what pops to mind. When we were children, the nuns used to tell us heroic tales about the martyrs, how St. Agnes when she was only thirteen was beheaded for her faith by the Emperor Diocletian. And they would pose this terrible question: Would you be willing to die for your faith? I've never been certain that I would but my deepest impression of Father Rossi is that he is a very committed and resolute Christian. He is a man who would die for his faith. That's the best way I can describe my sense of him."

"And you would never want to get in the way of his vocation as a Catholic priest?"

"God, no. That's what I've been trying to tell you."

"Well, Sue, you must make your own decision, of course. You are far closer to your situation than I am. But my best judgment is that this friendship between you and Father Rossi may well be a gift from God. It may be a source of encouragement to both of you in your spiritual lives."

Monsignor went on to speak eloquently of the many saints who had shared such friendships, dwelling at some length on the relationship between Saint Francis de Sales, their patron saint, and Saint Jane de Chantal who had a deep love for each other. "Their sense of union was steeped in their love of God," he said. "They loved each other in God and for God. So pray often for Father Rossi, Sue. Hold him in your heart before your loving Father in heaven and all will be well. Do you understand what I am saying?"

It was late on a rainy afternoon and growing dark in the little apartment that the pastor, Father Foley, had constructed in the office wing of the rectory for Monsignor's retirement. Sue got up to switch on a couple of lights. Although he had hesitated, reaching for a word here and there, Monsignor had been as clear and articulate as he had always been and Sue understood him well. Still, she found it embarrassing to express how deeply she was moved by his conception of a friendship in God: So she simply said, "Yes, I get the idea."

Monsignor's smile at this reply lifted the myriad fine lines in his thin face giving him a look of elfin delight. "I knew you would. And I'll spare you lectures about prudence and discretion. I would guess you have an in-bred knack for all those Convent virtues."

"Not the seductive type, eh?"

"Hardly, but a natural beauty nevertheless."

Sue did not bother to deny this. It was what everybody said. It made life very simple that her short, dark hair was naturally curly and her fresh Irish complexion needed no make up. Sometimes for a party, she used shadow and mascara to highlight the perfect shape of her violet eyes, but usually she did no fussing whatsoever.

"I brought you a couple of detectives," she said as she was leaving. "A new Lawrence Saunders and *Deep Gold*, a riveting sea treasure hunt by Jay Amberg." Mystery stories weren't the most important interest Sue and Monsignor had in common but they were part of what bridged the generation gap between them.

Now, her heart gladdened by the splendor of the day and the prospect of a morning in the company of Father Rossi, Sue waits at the baptistery window for the others to arrive. It was her idea to have the scripture meeting here since it is Saturday and the school is closed. She is pleased with her choice. This room which leads into the chapel had been designed as an entrance hall. It is spacious and well proportioned with a high ceiling, lofty leaded windows and a marble floor. When it was built it had seemed like extravagant space waiting for its purpose to be invented. Eventually it had been converted into a parish library. Books now line the inner walls adding warmth to elegance.

Monsignor had built the baptistery in 1968, the year Sue was born. Back then it had been known as Fiedler's folly, a classic architectural achievement that many thought unnecessary. There had been pro-longed wrangling at the town hall over the height of the tower which exceeded limits set by a community determined to maintain its village ambiance. However, after several witty skirmishes with town officials, Monsignor had won the day.

The whole parish complex, the school, the rectory, the convent, the old stone church that dated back to the time when Lakewood was a farming community, clung to an incline that made a leisurely descent toward Forest Road and Lake Michigan. The baptistery stood at the summit and when lit at night made a shining sacramental statement in the dark sky. Villagers had long since changed their minds about it, had claimed it as their most distinguished landmark.

Father Rossi is the first to arrive at the baptistery this morning. Opening the door, Sue accosts him playfully. Noting the path he has ploughed through the snow all the way from the rectory, across the parking lot and up the driveway, she says, "You would be the first to destroy our virginal winter scene!"

"I had just that same feeling as I trekked over here, that I was tres-passing on an immaculate Eden, scarring an innocent and perfect world. My sin, my apology. I see you got the commentaries."

"No problem. Alverno mailed them right out."

Sue is thinking how wonderful he looks, how much more vital and rested than when he arrived last summer. The cold has raised color in his sallow—Sue prefers to think of it as off-olive—skin. His light blue eyes, a surprise in his otherwise dark visage, are alive, alert. She thinks for a moment that he looks handsome but then judiciously reconsiders. Nose too Roman, chin too jutting. But he does have wonderfully thick black hair and absolutely perfect teeth. Someday she will find the word to describe his smile.

People arrive, stamping snow from their boots. Although not everybody knows everybody else, there is friendly chatter, an air of camaraderie that excessive weather can create even among strangers. When they have all tossed their jackets on the couch and poured themselves a cup of coffee at the counter they pull up to the table and are ready to begin.

Sue observes that Father does not sit at the head of the long, rectangular table but rather in the middle. To be more one of them? He begins with a prayer that the Holy Spirit will enlighten them in their study of St. Luke's Gospel, that there will soon be an end to the wars in Alvarado, and that God will bless the parishioners and priests of their parish on the Feast of St. Francis de Sales and the ninetieth anniversary of the founding of the parish.

Actually, the feast of St. Francis had been yesterday but observation of it had been moved up to accommodate Cardinal Cardone who is coming to offer an evening Mass in celebration. A visit from a Cardinal is an unprecedented event and Sue has been busy for several days with arrangements for a reception to be held in the gym following the Mass.

"I don't suppose we kiss his ring these days," she remarks.

Father smiles. "I think that went out with Vatican II. Actually, the Cardinal is a very simple man. He likes to be considered your brother Joseph as he often says."

To begin the meeting, Father Rossi suggests that each person give a brief biographical sketch and share with the group his or her reason for signing up for the scripture course. "Let's begin with Jo," he says.

Jo looks a little alarmed at this unexpected request. She has been a friend of Sue since they first met in the third grade, a bright competent little person with a deep aesthetic sense which Sue particularly values in her. But looking at her now Sue sees her suddenly as perhaps the group does, an extremely thin, tired, nervous woman anxiously twisting the top button of her blouse.

"I'm Jo James," she says. "I've lived in Lakewood most of my life. My two boys are in St. F's School. Currently, I'm working weekdays at the Thrift Shop. I decided to take this course because my life is in a state of flux and I feel a need to get back to basics."

State of flux, thinks Sue, is a minimal way to express what is going on in Jo's life. She has recently been separated from her alcoholic husband, is trying to straighten out the bewildering financial mess in which she finds herself and to cope with the problems of her sons who are certainly a couple of disturbed kids. Sue had been instrumental in getting her counseling at Family Service where she was offered a job at the resale shop which supports it. Sue knows Jo could do a lot better than sorting second-hand clothes but needs time before tackling something more challenging.

"Aren't you the Jameses who have that beautiful decorating shop on Elm?" someone inquires.

"Had. It got to be too much for us so we sold out."

"Such an attractive shop. It's a shame you had to let it go."

"I know."

Perhaps to terminate this conversation, Father Rossi says, "Boyd, why don't you go next?"

Sue takes quick inventory of Boyd Harris whom she's never met before. A yuppie type with blown-dry hair and an expensive sweater, probably hand-knit in Peru. A chunky body and chubby face, a little like

Newt Gingrich. Probably paleoconservative. Possibly quite smug. He says their home backs up on the lagoons, that he has two sons in college and two daughters at Lakewood High and that his wife, Winnie, is in real estate. So Winnie, that redheaded dynamo, is this dull man's wife! Life is full of surprises.

Boyd goes on to say that he had worked with Central Airlines but the company folded just before Christmas. He is between jobs as they say and is here today because Father, whom he's known for some time, has persuaded him to come. "Winnie's the Catholic in the family," he says. "This is new territory for me."

"That's great," says Sue. "You'll bring a fresh perspective." She quickly revises her first impression of him. Maybe not smug or even dull. Maybe depressed, having a mid-life crisis, scared to death he will lose his super house or worse yet, become dependent on his over-achieving wife.

"A close-out like Central can be pretty devastating," she says. "I hope something turns up for you soon."

She is about to begin her own sketch when there is an interruption, someone at the door. She gets up hastily to open it. It turns out to be Jens, the maintenance man, with an electric heater Monsignor has sent over thinking that in this weather the library might be chilly. Actually, with the sun pouring in the east windows, it is fairly comfortable but added warmth may be welcome for the older people.

Sue finds an extension cord so that the heater, a veritable antique, can be brought closer to the table. Father Rossi gets up to help but Jens will have none of it.

"You think I can't plug in a cord?" he says. "You think I am too old or something?" His tone is surely, rude. After he leaves, Sue says, "Well! What was that all about?"

Father Rossi shrugs his shoulders. "Who knows? I think maybe I'm on Jens' list of the rejected. Father Foley tells me that sometimes he stops talking to people and they never know what they've done to offend him, but in this case I can make a guess. You know, he really is getting old and one day last fall when he was struggling to rake a whole avalanche of oak leaves on these extensive grounds, I suggested to Father Foley that he hire a Mexican team, not permanently of course, but just now and then to help out with heavy projects. Well, when the team came in with all their sweepers and blowers breaking the sound barrier, Jens must have thought his job was threatened. He was so angry with Father Foley that Father finally said, "Hey, look, it wasn't my idea. Why don't you talk it out with Father Rossi?"

"He always was a sad, alienated character," Sue says. "And it doesn't help that he's such a huge, homely hulk. The kids all call him Frankenstein but he and I have always been friends, maybe because we both love gardening."

Sue senses that this digression is going on too long and quickly launches into her own biography. She winds up by saying, "My husband, Fred, is a pediatrician, a real expert in case anyone is in the market for a children's doctor. And the reason I joined this group was to see that Father Rossi here doesn't lead us into heresy. You've got to watch out for these bright, creative types."

"Ah ha!" exclaims father. "A Vatican spy!"

"He looks pretty orthodox to me," volunteers the young woman on Sue's right. "He's even wearing a Roman collar."

"I promise not to be so formal again. Today I have to go down to the Chancery when we're through here. Pixie, why don't you tell us a little about yourself?"

Pixie! What a perfect name for this woman with her blond bangs, sharply trimmed sideburns and small, tilted nose. A warm apricot color blooms on her round cheeks.

"Well," she says, "I'm Patricia Bergman and I come from a town you never heard of, it's so small. I mean, it's outside of Grand Rapids, Minnesota and I bet you never even knew there was a Grand Rapids in Minnesota. My husband and I just moved here from St. Paul. He's a lawyer with a big firm, Craddock and Delaney. Maybe you've heard of it?"

"A very fine firm," Boyd assures her.

"Well, this man from Craddock and Delaney who had some cases with Bill got him a job in Chicago and I must say the North Shore is a big adjustment for me. There's so much money around here and I would guess it's very materialistic compared to how I grew up. I worry about my son, Roger—he's in the first grade—about his growing up here. I mean, Bill bought this big brick house on Forest Road, a lot bigger than we need really and across the street is this twenty-room mansion on Lake Michigan that some Mafia character lives in. I keep wondering what kind of neighbors they'll be for Roger. And then I know there's all this cocktail drinking and drugs and we even saw some murder on TV, some crazy woman who shot up the school children."

Sue realizes that this young woman is suffering some displacement anxiety and hastens to reassure her. "That wasn't in our village but of course the case got wide publicity just because it occurred on the North Shore where such things seldom happen. There hasn't been a murder in Lakewood since 1904. Believe me, Pixie, Roger will be just fine here. Our schools are tops and it's really a very peaceful community with everything you could possibly want for children. You'll love it when you've settled in."

"Well, I know I'm a little nuts about wanting it right for Roger. You see, I almost lost him at birth. I mean, we both almost died and they…"

Again there is someone at the door and conversation is cut off as Sue goes to answer it. The woman waiting there is wrapped in a raccoon coat that reaches to her ankles. She is nevertheless shivering from the cold.

"Do come in and warm up," says Sue.

"Yes, do." Father Rossi has also risen to greet the latecomer.

When she thought about it later, Sue realized that the entrance of this stranger into the quiet of their ordinary morning was pretty theatrical.

Right now, as she offers to take the fur coat, she is too occupied observing details to make any general assessment.

The young lady sheds her coat with a casual shrug and emerges from its luxurious folds like a butterfly from its chrysalis. She is wearing a tangerine knit suit with a brief, mid-thigh skirt. An exotic silk scarf circles her neck and drifts down the whole length of her long, tightly tailored jacket. Knee-high leather boots and a cocoa-colored derby perched daringly over one eye completes her ensemble. Not exactly your usual Saturday morning suburban outfit. In her jeans and baggy sweater, Sue feels suddenly quite seedy.

A whiff of light perfume floats behind this woman as she walks past Sue and extends her hand to the priest.

"You are Father Rossi? I am so pleased to make your acquaintance, Father. My name is Elena Esquivel. I come from Spain."

Elena's voice is low and husky but projects well like that of a trained actress. Her accent is light but her speech has peculiarities. She places heavy emphasis on the word "Spain" and Father repeats it after her as though she has mentioned an improbable place. Which of course, she has.

"Spain?"

"Yes, Spain. We arrive only this week past. I see the notice in the Sunday bulletin but I mix the hour up. I am sorry to be tardy."

Sue notices that all the time Elena is talking she continues to hold Father's hand. She is looking directly into his face in a way that seems too bold and personal to suit Sue. After all, she has just met him and he *is* a priest. She quickly lays the raccoon coat on the couch and goes to stand beside Father. To protect him, she thinks jokingly, but also to get a good look at Elena's face.

Not beautiful, Sue decides. Nose a bit hawky, forehead very broad. But an unusual face with dark eyes set wide apart, straight well-defined brows extending almost to the hairline, a sensuous, sullen mouth accented by a heavy coat of tangerine lipstick. Her glossy black hair is drawn smoothly into a bun at the nape of her neck. Close up like this, Elena looks younger than Sue had first thought. Twenty maybe, certainly not more. Spoiled, Sue is sure. Passionate is a guess she would bet on.

"This is a beautiful parish you have," Elena comments. "Is it not what Americans call the plum?"

This is something Sue might tease Father about herself, but she resents the bold and hostile insinuation she senses in Elena's husky voice. What is she trying to imply? She thinks Father seems uncomfortable and is glad when he winds up this conversation by saying it is a parish with a wonderful spirit and wonderful people and hopes she will like it.

Boyd offers his seat to Elena and draws up a card table chair for himself. When Father inquires about where they left off, Sue reminds him that they were about to hear about Roger's difficult birth.

"I'll spare you the details," Pixie says. "The good news is that we both survived. The bad news is that I had to have a hysterectomy. I mean, it really killed me to know that I couldn't have any more children and practically ever since we've been trying to adopt one. I guess if you already have a child, you're way down on anyone's list. So one reason why I joined this group is because Father here has been so good to Bill and me. He's using his influence at Catholic Charities to see if we can have a little boy they have in their care. He is a special case and may not have to go through regular channels. Is that how to explain it, Father?"

"It's an unusual case and while I can't promise Bill and Pixie anything, I am trying to see if they can have this child. Surely they would be wonderful parents for him. The boy was abandoned on an airplane flying in from Mexico City, evidently stowed aboard and strapped into a paid-for seat. He must have been given Dramamine or something similar because he slept the whole trip. I was sitting across the aisle and never noticed him. Some passengers had wondered about him but it wasn't until the plane landed that it became obvious he had been abandoned.

"There was a lot of debate about what to do with him, consultation with the airline management etc. But when I offered to place him in the care of Catholic Charities, everyone was relieved. This happened last summer and every effort has been made by the Archdiocese and the airline to trace the boys' origin without any luck whatsoever."

Sue was immediately intrigued by this story. "How old is this child?" she inquired.

"Hard to say exactly. He tells us that he's three but judging by his general physical development, they think he may be closer to four. He's a bright little fellow but hasn't been able to supply us with any hard information. He misses his 'Bapa' but that doesn't give us much of a clue. Well, I think we'd better move on. Pixie, had you finished?"

"Well, I just want to say that the other reason I joined this group is because I thought Bill and I ought to stick close to the church down here. And it was the right thing to do because already this group makes me feel very much at home, like I really have some friends. So maybe you'd all pray that I can have this little boy. The trouble is not just all these complications but also with my husband. He's a gung-ho American type and he's a little leery about adopting a foreign child. But Father says when he meets Juan there'll be no problem for Bill. He's pretty Caucasian looking, if that's the right word."

Self-introductions continue around the table: Sister Thomasita, a formidable retired principal whom Sue's generation had dubbed "Tank" and a few parishioners with whom Sue is familiar. When it is Elena Esquivel's turn, she says little and addresses all her remarks to Father Rossi.

"My husband and I are only just married. He is with Citicorps. You know Citicorps?"

"I guess we all know Citicorp."

"And I take this course because I want to learn more about dear Jesus." Elena lowers her eyes demurely. Her lashes, thick and heavy with mascara, flutter slightly. Why do I think she's more hypocritical than humble? muses Sue. After all, she did brave the cold to get here.

Father gives a very informative introductory talk on St. Luke who wrote his gospel between 70 and 90 AD. Listening to his interesting presentation, Sue wonders if perhaps he has taught at the Seminary. How little she knows about him really and how much she looks forward to learning more. He assigns the first two chapters of the gospel for their next meeting and they all adjourn. Sue cleans up quickly and zips herself into her down jacket.

"Anybody need a ride. Elena? You looked like you may have walked this morning."

"It is only the four blocks but I do not know how cold is the zero."

"I'll take you home. I live just a few doors from here so I'll go get the car and be right back to pick you up. You wait inside. Father, are you coming?"

"I have to set up for a baptism tomorrow, a double header. The Murphy twins. You go on, Sue."

Outside, the snow squeaks under Sue's boots. She sees Pixie striding ahead of her and calls, "Hey Pixie, need a ride?"

"Thanks, but no. I have to drop something off at the rectory. Bill is picking me up there at noon."

"Just noon now," Sue exclaims as the chimes send the sweet sound of the Ave Maria floating across the arctic scene. The hymn is still playing when Sue pulls up to the baptistery entrance. Elena, swathed in fur and carrying a large tapestry bag with horn handles, comes out promptly.

"My needlepoint," she explains, climbing into the car. "I wasn't sure. Is it polite to sew at a meeting?"

The simple question makes Elena, this self-assured perfect-looking person, seem more human. Sue decides that she really should make an effort at friendship.

"I think it might be okay," she says looking at the bag curiously. "Are you making seat covers?"

"Nothing quite so ambitious. Just a pillow slip."

"I'd love to see it."

Elena starts to withdraw her work but her needles catch in other contents of her bag and she has to open it wide to straighten things out. Sue catches a glimpse of chaos inside the bag's voluminous depths: bright yarns tangled with a white cord, bottles, cosmetics all jumbled together. Elena grasps a hairbrush and shoves it out of sight. She seems excessively flustered that such disorder has been viewed by anyone. Hastily, a little petulantly, she tries to explain.

"I use this bag to travel on the plane. At the house there is no one to unpack so this morning when I find I am late, I just throw in my needle-point and come." Still embarrassed, she holds up a patch of her work for Sue to see.

"I love that leaf pattern," Sue exclaims with genuine enthusiasm. "Those autumn colors are gorgeous. It's going to be stunning!"

How could Sue guess when she drops Elena off at her house around noon on the rescheduled Feast of Saint Francis de Sales that the disorderly interior of the girl's tapestry bag will come to haunt her, that the vision of its curious jumble of contents will recur in her dreams and cause her times of trepidation. At the moment everything seems ordinary enough, even exotic Elena standing like a fur-clad Russian princess in the knee-high Siberian snow of the sidewalk waving a wobbly goodbye. All so ordinary it's a wonder she remembers later either the bag or the girl's tremulous smile

CHAPTER II

The mood at the reception for Cardinal Cardone is jubilant. Mass had been beautiful and the singing astonishingly so. Sue is uncertain whether choir and congregation had been inspired by the feast day or were showing off for their visitor. In any case, the crowd is coasting on a high as they sip wine and wait for a chance to talk with the Cardinal.

"Three of anything but the shrimp," Sue says leaving her three daughters at a table loaded with appetizers. Duties accomplished, she joins Fred who is visiting with old grade-school friends at the entrance to the gym. Sooner or later at any parish function, this group gravitates toward each other for a hilarious reunion. Although their paths have diverged and few of them see each other socially, they have this in common. They have all remained in Lakewood and they all go back a long way together.

A lot of backslapping and teasing is going on as Sue arrives but she notes that Jo James and Mike O'Connell, the local policeman, break up an earnest conversation to greet her. Maybe some problem with one of Jo's boys? Mike had been Jo's childhood sweetheart and is still as handsome and affable as when he was the school's basketball star. He's been an extraordinarily loyal friend to Jo.

"Here's Sue!" he exclaims. "Now the gang's all here. Even Winnie Harris breezed by on her way to sell the Cardinal a choice piece of real estate."

"You've got to be kidding."

"Absolutely not. That old Ballard house on the bluff with eleven bedrooms and two kitchens is on the market, a real lemon, but Winnie thinks it would make a great retirement home for antiquated priests. Incidentally, she was looking for you. She wants to tell you that she simply adores your décor here in the gym."

The friends all laugh heartily at Mike's perfect imitation of Winnie's exclamatory habit of speech. Sue is giving them a graphic description of her struggle to get Ellen, her seventh-grader, out of jeans and into a dress for the evening when Father Foley interrupts.

"Sue, do you know where Father Rossi is?"

"No idea. I haven't seen him around here and I didn't spot him at Mass either. Maybe he was in the congregation."

"I don't think so or he would have helped with Communion. He never turned up for dinner. Nora was all upset because of the extra place sitting there empty. You'd think he might have called. Do you know what his plans were?"

"He was going downtown after our meeting this morning. But I know he planned to be back for dinner. Have you tried the Chancery?"

"Been trying off and on for hours. Saturday, of course. Nothing but the answering machine."

"Well, anything could happen to a car in this weather. He's probably stalled on Eden's somewhere." Sue recognizes Fred's let's-look-on-the-bright-side voice but she is far from reassured.

"He wasn't driving. He was going to catch the 12:20 train."

"Look," says Mike. "This sort of thing happens all the time. People are delayed for good reasons no one can imagine. We get hundreds of calls a year at the police station, people worrying their heads off and in the end it turns out to be nothing. I'm sure Father Rossi will turn up any minute now. But if you like, Father, I can check out the hospitals."

"Do you think that's necessary?" Sue can tell that Father Foley's mind is elsewhere, on the Cardinal and the big event he is engineering here in the gym.

"Wouldn't hurt to make the calls."

Mike, always eager to be of service, hurries off to use the phone in the principal's office. Saying "Let me know if you find out anything," Father Foley returns to his guests. Sue stands alone with Fred, her mind racing, trying to recall everything Father Rossi had said that morning. She can think of absolutely no reason for his absence.

"I know something's happened to him," she says.

"Possibly you're right. It's certainly out of character for him to stand the Cardinal up for dinner. But I don't think there's a damn thing we can do except wait until there's some news."

"I know what I'd like to do. I'd like to go up to the baptistery where we last saw him and check it out."

"I don't see much point in that. What could we possibly find?"

"Who knows? Maybe a clue. Maybe he took a phone call there and wrote something down."

"It's a crazy idea but we'll go if you want to."

The wind feels like sharp knives assaulting them as Sue and Fred leave the gym and head across the parking lot. A clear sky and white snow cover make the night extraordinarily bright, something to marvel at had there been leisure to observe it, but Sue is in a hurry. She pulls her wool scarf across her face and puts her arm through Fred's. Together they stride rapidly toward the lighted tower. She welcomes the shock of the frigid air and the brittle silence that surrounds them. The cold calms her, helps to relieve the apprehension that has gripped her. Still, the walk seems interminable. When they reach the circular drive where the blue spruce broods in the starlight, she takes a deep breath. They are almost there.

It had been such a hectic day that Sue had never returned the baptistery key to the rectory. Holding her mitten in her mouth, she digs it out of her pocket and opens the door. She and Fred feel along opposite walls for the light switch. He finds it first and suddenly the dark room is flooded with light from a chandelier suspended in the center of the hall.

Sue's first impression is one of dismay at how different this place looks at night. Its lovely windows that had held the morning light are now blind and black. Yet it is only seconds before she sees Father Rossi lying on the floor at the far end of the room. She runs forward quickly but stops before she reaches him. She claps her hand over her mouth so that she will not scream. She has seen death before. She recognizes the awesome rigidity of bone, the waxy, plastic flesh, and she knows it is too late. Too late to help him, too late to do anything. Too late, oh, God, too late!

"God damn it anyway. What the hell is going on here? How could this possibly have happened?" Fred is swearing vociferously. He is down on his knees feeling the pulse in Father's throat but Sue knows this is an unnecessary ritual. She stands quietly watching him.

At first sight of Father, something sharp and cold, a knife, an icicle, pierced her heart causing incredible pain, an anguishing ache that made her gasp for breath. She is stunned, paralyzed. But she knows this will not do. Death has its own requirements, incontrovertible demands it makes on the living. When her mother, after an exhausting battle with cancer, died at home in her own bed, Sue knew she must put her heartache on hold, knew there were things that must be done. She must withdraw her hand from the one growing cold in hers, must summon the doctor, must call her brothers, must select the casket, must order the ham and get the good cups down from the top cupboard. And now the knowledge of things to be done anesthetizes her heart, numbs her wound, leaves her detached, steady, preternaturally calm. Tense and alert like one who is awakened by a strange sound in the dead of night, she is observing the death scene with dry, sharp eyes.

Father Rossi is lying on his side facing the counter so that only his right profile is visible. One leg is drawn up at the knee, the other stretched out with the electric heater turned over on it. The cord of the heater is caught around the shoe of his right foot. A glass coffeepot is overturned on the floor next to him. A smell of scorched cloth hangs in the air.

Sue goes immediately to unplug the heater and returns to find Fred down on his haunches scanning the corpse with narrowed eyes. The position he has struck with his buttocks balanced precariously over his heels is one most humans could not hold for more than a minute but Fred can maintain it indefinitely. Poised in this miraculous squat, she has seen him supervise his small daughters' floor games, bury tulip bulbs, remove spots from the dining room rug. She thinks of it as an intimate, domestic position requiring blue jeans and privacy.

To watch Fred, the medical doctor, in his good trousers hunched over Father Rossi's dead body seems somehow ludicrous. She wishes he'd get up. She has things to tell him. She feels annoyed until she happens to notice under the strong light of the chandelier a little thinning in the cowlick at the crown of his head. Fred has sandy hair that curls softly when Sue can persuade him not to have it cut too short. To find for the first time this almost imperceptible beginning of a bald spot in her husband's head of hair saddens her. How suddenly he seems vulnerable to age and death. She is relieved to see how effortlessly he rises from his crouching position and begins to circle the body viewing it from all sides.

"Well," he says, "we'll have to assume it was electric shock that killed him. They were giving warnings on the TV just last week about never taking a heater into the bathroom with you, so, I suppose if he were wet that heater could generate enough shock to kill him. I figure if the cord were plugged in, it would have been taut enough to trip him."

Fred reaches down to remove the heater from Father's leg, but Sue instantly stops him. "Don't touch anything," she says in a shrill, strained voice that makes Fred look up at her in surprise. Aware that she has startled him, she adds more gently, "Please, just don't touch anything."

Fred catches a slight tremor in her tone and comes quickly to take her in his arms. He holds her close for a moment. He is a big man, very solid and strong, and whenever he embraces her, Sue is aware of his physical power, the fortifying feel of his hard, muscular body. Tonight she rests her head on his chest and clings to him. He is so sturdy, a stout oak she can safely lean against. She feels the lump in her throat thicken, feels moisture gather in her eyes. Grief is grabbing hold and in the secure warmth of Fred's arms, she is yielding to it until she remembers that there are facts to face and things to do. With deliberate determination, she wriggles free of his embrace and looks directly into his face. It touches her to discover that there are tears in his eyes. That Fred is easily moved to tears by tragedy had impressed her in their early friendship and Sue still appreciates this unexpected sensitivity in her husband, a man of more common sense than sentiment.

"I'm so damn sorry, sweetheart," he says. "He was such a good friend."

"I know. Fred, can you tell how long he's been dead?"

"Several hours I would guess."

"You can't be specific about the time?"

"I'm not exactly a mortician, Sue. Why is the time so damned important?"

"Because I know he has been murdered."

"Murdered! Sue, honey, that's a bit far fetched, isn't it? I'm afraid what we've got here is one God-awful accident."

"It's the fishiest accident I ever saw. He would have to have tripped on the cord, completely lost his balance, spilled the pot and somehow pulled the heater over on himself. What are the odds against all that happening simultaneously? And besides, Father was no klutz. You'd know that if you'd ever seen him on the basketball court with the kids. There is no way I could buy a picture of him messing everything up like someone in a stupid comedy act."

"It wasn't stupid, Sue. It was a sudden freak accident that could have happened to anyone."

"Not to Father Rossi. I'm telling you Fred, I *know* he was murdered."

"Sue, you've had a hell of a shock but hang on to your good judgment, sweetheart. How could you possibly know a thing like that?"

How could she know? Intuition maybe, that swift and sure apprehension of a situation which often bypassed her conscious mind. She had always known some things with a mysterious and inexplicable certainty: that there was a good loving God, for instance, although her contemporary world gave little evidence of his presence, or that she would marry Fred long before he ever asked her out, in fact while she was still falling in love with other men. But there must have been unnoticed reasons for these important convictions in her life and Sue now sought desperately for clues to make her firm impression of murder rational.

"There's no liquid in the coffee pot." She mentions this to Fred with some relief that she has spotted objective evidence of wrongdoing.

"So?"

"The pot isn't turned upside down but only lying on its side. If it actually fell that way, it wouldn't be empty. There would still be some liquid left in it. And besides, don't you think it's strange that it failed to break when it crashed like that on a marble floor?"

"And that proves a murder? Come on, Sue darling, let go of such a distressing idea. Things are bad enough as they are. I think I'd better go fetch Father Foley but you needn't battle the cold again. Will you be okay here alone?"

"Alone is fine with me but be sure to bring Mike back with you too. What we need here is the police."

In the awesome silence that follows Fred's departure, Sue thinks she can hear her own heart beat. The heat snaps on and the sudden sound of it breathing in the ventilators startles her. She begins to circle the room, scrutinizing everything carefully. Her eyes ache from the strain of her diligent attention. She finds little but misses nothing and finally includes the chapel in her search. There, lying in preparation on the altar are the candles and the white linen for tomorrow's baptism, probably the last things Father touched before he died. She brushes them lightly with her fingers before returning to the library where she draws up a chair for a lonely vigil with his body.

She feels numb, cold. Still, it is with great love that she sits looking at her friend, at his dear dead face with its less-than-perfect nose. She would remember every detail for a long time to come: the single eye staring at the wall, the chin jutting high above the Roman collar, the awkward, out-flung arm. At last she reaches in her pocket for her rosary and begins to pray. But she can feel no resignation as she had when her parents died. Any consoling sense that it was all in God's hands eludes her. God had not done this.

Her voice is barely audible when she murmurs, "Oh, Rossi. Couldn't you have been quicker or more wary? How could anyone as smart as you succumb to such a crummy plot. I just know that some Judas has done this to you and I promise you I'll find him. I'll find him and see that he gets his."

CHAPTER III

Mike arrives before the others. A bitter draft blows in the door with him and he hastily closes it behind him. He pushes back the hood of his jacket and is about to greet Sue when he catches sight of Father Rossi's corpse.

"Good God," he exclaims. "How could this happen to such a great guy?"

"You knew him well, Mike?"

"From church, of course, but also he came down to the station a couple of times to pick up Gerry James when Jo was working and couldn't get him. Gerry's really been messed up since Jo and Tim separated. He keeps getting into trouble, no big time stuff but graffiti at the railroad station and twisting street signs, things like that. Father took time out to have a long conversation with me about the kid's problems. What I really liked about him was his genuine concern for Gerry."

"Your own is pretty nice."

"That's nothing. Jo's an old friend. But about this accident here. Fred says you have some questions about what happened?"

"I definitely do."

Sue is eager to share her concerns about Father's death with Mike. Although she still sees him primarily as an old friend, the kid who always kept the crowd laughing with his anecdotal humor, she hasn't failed to notice the professional manner he has developed in recent years. He has put on weight, has assumed an air of authority which impresses her. Right now he is regarding her seriously, attentively, and Sue is sure he will not dismiss her observations as Fred had.

But before she can present Mike with the incriminating details she has marshaled in her mind, Fred and Father Foley arrive. Father is breathless as he hurries through the door and strives hastily toward the end of the room where his assistant lies on the floor. Sue sometimes mentions to her friends that their pastor could pose as the monk in a wine or cheese ad. His round, balding head looks as though it has been tonsured and his substantial stomach is shaped somewhat like a tulip bulb. But this image doesn't cross her mind tonight. She notices instead that his face and head are a bright pink. She finds herself hoping this is from the cold rather than hypertension. His face is contorted now with what Sue judges to be mixed emotions: pity for his poor dead priest but also anxiety about the difficulties this death might place in his path.

Father Foley is a practical man in his early fifties. He has only in recent years been given his own parish and likes things to go smoothly. He is fond of saying that life is what happens when you've made other plans but this insight never becomes operative wisdom in his daily existence. His adjustments to unexpected events are often slow, fretful and agitated. Surely he would not have scheduled a death on the night of the parish celebration with Cardinal Cardone and Sue, feeling sorry for him, wonders how he will deal with it.

But Father Foley's first reaction is one of a priest who understands the sacred importance of death. Almost his first words are, "I'd like to anoint Father Rossi."

This strikes Sue as irrational, as part of the surreal sequence of this strange evening. The sacrament of anointing is administered for the healing of the sick or to give spiritual strength to the dying. It is possible to anoint someone if there might still be life in him but Father Rossi has been dead for more than half a day. Still, it occurs to her that her pastor does not know when Father died and she decides not to tell him.

Father Foley appears to be an ordinary man, often brusque and business-like with none of Monsignor's ability for spiritual inspiration and, although not unkind, none of Father Rossi's immediate and intense compassion. Yet Sue knows that he has a profound understanding of his role as a priest. To bring the grace of God to his parishioners through the Mass and the sacraments, to be the unimportant instrument through whom the loving kindness of God is channeled to others is to him the significant meaning of his ordination. And if he wants to confer the last sacrament on Father Rossi, she is not going to deny him that privilege.

"We can turn Father over now so that you can anoint him," Fred says. "Sue didn't want me to touch anything until you got here but if you think you've grasped the picture, we can move him now."

"What's to grasp?" Father Foley says. "It's very obvious what happened. The poor fellow tripped on the cord and tangled with the heater. An idiotic death very much like Thomas Merton's accident with an electric fan some years ago."

Thomas Merton had been a famous Trappist monk whose spiritual writings inspired a whole generation of Christians. The similarity in the deaths of the two priests is striking but Sue does not dwell on this. She does not wish to delay the anointing but feels that she must demonstrate a few things to Father Foley before anything is touched.

"Look, Father," she says. "Before they move Father, I want you to observe the odd position he's in. If he had tripped on the cord as everyone is suggesting, how could he have landed on his side like this? Wouldn't he have fallen straight ahead?"

"It might be hard to judge with any precision how a person would fall," Mike suggests. "I agree, his position is a little strange but hardly beyond the realm of possibility."

Now Fred removes the heater from Father Rossi's leg, revealing a bad burn on the exposed skin between his sock and trouser. When he and Mike turn the body on its back, a gentle gasp like a whisper of wind rises from the watching group. On the left side of Father Rossi's face is a fiercely discolored bruise that runs from his blackened eye across his temple and into his hairline. Sue shudders when she observes the extent of this injury. She watches Fred trace the course of the bruising until he finds on his scalp the wound that has caused it.

"He must have hit his head on the corner of the counter when he fell," Fred says.

"Maybe and maybe not." Sue too has dropped to her knees. Gently, with infinite tenderness as though Father could still feel the pain of her touch, she is probing the wound for herself. Buried in Father's thick hair, there is a gash the size of a fifty-cent piece opposite the eye and directly above the ear.

"This seems to be circular rather than rectangular or triangular as one would expect if he hit the corner of the counter," she says. "And why no blood?"

"The wound isn't deep. I think the blow just caused all this bruising immediately before he died."

Father Foley has placed his stole around his neck and taken the oil for the anointing from his pocket. He listens to their speculation with growing impatience. "It's obvious the poor fellow hit his head on the way down," he says. "I hope Fred is right that he died quickly. Now, if you don't mind, I'd like to anoint him."

Kneeling by the side of his assistant, Father Foley traces a little cross with the oil on Father Rossi's forehead and on the back of his hands. Sue notes that all signs of his hurried impatience have vanished, that he who tended to live life at an accelerated pace has switched gears to enter this prayerful moment with quiet concentration. This does not surprise her. At early morning Masses, he lifts the host at the altar with this same suspension of exterior distraction, creating by his own stillness an awed sense of presence in the sacred bread which he holds in his plump hand. Despite some obvious faults they find in him, parishioners appreciate the reverence with which he offers their Masses.

Now as he prays that by this holy unction and by his most tender mercy, the Lord might forgive Father Rossi whatever sins he may have committed, Sue finds consolation in the earnestness with which he conducts this final ritual. When he has finished, and they have murmured Amen, Father Foley lingers on his knees for a moment, then pats Father Rossi on the cheek. This is the surprise, this brief, affectionate, moving gesture of farewell. So he too had loved him.

"Was Bob Cudahy at the reception?" Father inquires as he struggles to his feet. Bob is the local undertaker who handles most of the Catholic funerals in the village.

"I didn't see him," says Sue, "but that doesn't mean he wasn't there. It was a big crowd."

"Well, let's track him down. We might as well get things underway."

Sue is alarmed as Mike moves swiftly toward the phone on the counter to put in the call. She feels that events are moving out of her control, that the opportunity to present her case for murder is slipping away, that no one has given it serious consideration. She clears her throat and assumes the authoritative stance she uses when subbing in the seventh grade classroom. She needs to get everyone's attention.

"Look, Father, we have to discuss what really may have happened here before Bob Cudahy arrives." Her voice is firm with a cutting edge of command to it but this fails to impress her pastor.

"You mean some nonsense about this not being an accident? I think that's ridiculous. An accident makes perfect sense to me."

"You may be right," Sue says politely, "but it doesn't entirely make sense to me. There are a lot of unanswered questions. Look, it took almost no time for Father to line up the few things he needed for the baptism tomorrow and they are there in the chapel all set to go. Why, then, didn't he leave immediately for the train station? Why set up the heater and start making coffee? And why did he fail to notice that there was no coffee since I had taken it home with me? And when he plugged in the cord, why did he set the heater a few feet away from the wall so that the cord would be in his own way? And why did he attach this extension cord which he never used in the other socket? And having just plugged in the heater and bypassed it on his way to the washroom for water, why was he so careless in tripping on the cord on his return trip? We've all noticed the strange position in which he landed, but another question is why the water spilled down his trousers soaking them instead of spilling ahead of him as he went down. Wouldn't it be logical to extend his hands to break his fall? And why is there no liquid in the pot?"

As she mentions this once more, she sees Fred and Mike exchange a glance. She remembers suddenly how Reverend Mother at the Convent had taught her pupils that nothing was quite so rude as exchanging glances, nothing so cutting or demeaning. She appreciates the truth of this now because the look her husband and old friend give each other implies quite clearly that they think Sue is temporarily off her rocker, that, upset by Father Rossi's death, she is drawing wild conclusions from a little liquid left in the bottom of a container.

"Nobody can entirely account for accidents," Fred says. "My aunt fell on the sidewalk last week and injured her knee. She's uncertain whether she tripped on a crack or turned her ankle or slid on some gravel. She went down so fast, she can't be sure what happened. I think something similar happened here."

Sue can't see what Fred's aunt has to do with anything. "But what about my questions?" she insists.

"I don't think they're very serious questions," Father Foley says. "Even if we can't account for every last detail, it is obvious what occurred. I think the rest of it is all idle speculation."

"Maybe, but I want you to speculate a little further. Let's say it's just past noon and everyone has left the baptistery. Father has laid out the things for the baptism when someone comes to the door. There is almost conclusive evidence that someone was here. I straightened the chairs this morning and I'm absolutely certain that they were all lined up evenly at the table. But I found two chairs pulled back at this end as though someone had used them. It is very probable that Father and some other person sat here to complete some business. Between these two chairs, I found this." Sue reaches in her purse and produces a gold pen. "It's no ordinary bic. It's an expensive pen with the name of an insurance company engraved on it so we may be able to trace it. I'm dead certain there was nothing on that table when I left this morning. I also found a pair of leather gloves on the sofa. I'm less sure about them. They may belong to someone from the study group. Also, at the rear chapel door, I found a pair of heavy galoshes but I think those may belong to Jens."

"Sue, I can't believe that finding a few things left around the baptistery somehow proves a murder." Father Foley speaks with a familiar finality which Sue knows is supposed to cut off further discussion but she stubbornly persists in finishing what she has to say.

"Let's say that Father and his visitor finish some kind of work here at the table and now, having missed his train, Father suggests that he show his guest the chapel. The two move down to this end of the room when suddenly and quite unexpectedly, the visitor hits Father on the side of his head, a serious blow that knocks him out. You have seen what a vicious hit it was. He may have used some kind of weapon which created the circular wound on his scalp. The murderer then pours water on Father's legs, plugs in the heater and arranges it so it is touching the wet exposed portion of his leg. All very neat and quick."

"And very amateur," comments Fred. "I can't imagine anyone planning a murder like that."

"Maybe he was an opportunist, not a planner. Suddenly here was his chance and he took it. In fact, that probably had to be the way it was. Nobody could have known ahead of time that the heater would be here."

"For God's sake," interjects Father Foley. "Who on earth would want to kill Father Rossi? Why would you think you had to invent a cock-and-bull story like this to explain his death?"

"Because an accident leaves too many things unexplained."

Fred's sandy brows are knotted in a frown of disdain and disbelief. "Come on, Sue," he says impatiently. "The question of who would want to kill him seems greater to me than a few unexplained details."

"But details are always the clues to a murder, aren't they? And who the murderer may be is always a mystery. I know that someone killed him."

"How can you possibly know such a thing?" Father Foley is growing impatient.

Bob Cudahy, the funeral director, has slipped so quietly into the baptistery that no one notices him until the draft of freezing air from the doorway reaches the group. Father Foley, obviously relieved by his arrival, takes this opportunity to close out further discussion.

"To me," he says, "it is perfectly obvious what happened here and I want all of you to listen to me carefully. That Father Rossi's death was anything but an accident is a notion that should never leave this room. Speculations about a murder could cause all kinds of trouble in the parish and possibly create a scandal in the village. If the media were to get hold of it, they'd never let it go. I'll announce the death at all the Masses tomorrow and perhaps it would be best not to mention it until then."

Sue agrees to this, it makes good sense, but she is reluctant to let the matter end here. She watches Cudahy, an elderly, discreet little man, carefully observe the corpse. His initial reaction of shock is almost immediately replaced by professional scrutiny. He turns to Father Foley and says very softly, "It looks like someone took a sledge hammer to the poor fellow, but if you want an open casket, I can promise a good job on his face."

Now Sue knows she must move promptly. "Before things go any further," she says, "I think I should empty the contents of Father's pockets."

"Sue, if you don't mind my saying so, I think you're out of your mind." Father's voice is sharp. He has reached the limits of his patience.

"Look, Father, there may be some papers in his pockets that need attention right away. It wouldn't hurt to look through and see."

"I can't believe you're serious about this."

Bob Cudahy looks from Father to Sue and understands immediately that an impasse has been reached. He is accustomed to dealing with people in distressful situations and he quietly suggests that he will reserve all the contents of Father's pockets and deliver them to Sue if that is agreeable to Father Foley.

Fred puts his arm around Sue's shoulder. "If that's okay with Father, I don't see any reason why we should hang around here while they remove the body. Let's pick up the girls and go home. Maybe Mike would join us when he's through here."

With coat collars turned up against the cold, Fred and Sue thread their way quickly through the parking lot. As they are approaching the school entrance, a car door slams behind them. In the stillness of the deserted lot, the sound startles both of them and they quickly wheel around to see a tall young man coming toward them.

"I'm Bill Bergman," the stranger says. "I just came out to get my wife Pixie's sweater from the car. She wanted to wear a silk dress to the reception but it's a little cold for that tonight."

"So you're Pixie's husband!" exclaims Sue. "I'm Sue Carney and this is my husband, Fred. I met your wife just this morning at the scripture group."

"How really good to meet you. Pixie mentioned you when I picked her up this morning. Is something going on in the baptistery tonight? I notice all the lights are on."

"Baptism tomorrow," says Sue. "The Murphy's little twin sons. Fred came along to help me set up for it."

The three of them head hastily for the school door, eager to be out of the cold. Perhaps because they became such good friends later or because his sudden appearance cut an incisive image in her mind, or because he was an extraordinarily handsome man, Sue was to remember vividly this first meeting with Bill Bergman, to hold a clear picture of how he looked standing there in the bright winter night: the wiry texture of his close-cropped hair, the Mediterranean blue of his deep-set eyes, the sophistication of his beautifully tailored winter coat. So this was Pixie's husband, Mr. Gung Ho America. She found him delightful.

CHAPTER IV

"Bergman seems like a great guy," Mike observes when a short time later they relax around the fire at Sue's home. "He mentioned that law firm he was with but I didn't quite catch it."

"Craddock and Delaney," Fred replies as he sets a tray of drinks on the table and hands Mike a beer. "A prodigious outfit. He couldn't do much better than that."

"I guess that's what I liked about him. Here he is some big-shot lawyer but he talks to you as one professional to another. Not everyone takes an interest in our local police station."

"He's got a cute wife too. They'll be a nice addition to the parish." Sue welcomes the glass of Chablis Fred offers her. The discussion at the baptistery has left her uneasy. Although she knows that Father Foley intended no disrespect, his cavalier dismissal of her view of events has irritated her. She would feel more comfortable about her own conviction if Fred had shared it, but he seems determined not to consider the possibility of murder. It is a relief to let go of it for a while, to watch the flickering blue flames licking the oak log and to engage in some every day small talk.

"I remember some great parties in this house when we were kids," Mike says. "I'll bet your mom would like what you've done to the old place. You've managed a marvelous update but retained all the charm.

"Sue is less certain than Mike that her mother would approve the changes she has made in her old home but she had been determined to gradually convert it to her own style. Several years ago when she left Boston to stay with her mother during the final months of her illness, she and Fred had no intention of returning to the Chicago area. Yet one thing had led to another. Fred had been offered a partnership in the new Lakewood Medical Center, their daughter Ellen had loved de Sales School and didn't want to leave, and Sue had revived old friendships. Perhaps the clincher came when the long row of lilacs along the driveway bloomed just as they were trying to decide on future plans.

It was a spring day shortly after her mother's funeral. The family had decided to put the house on the market and Sue had written an ad for the *Lakewood News*. She read it aloud to Fred. "Historic frame Victorian near schools and transportation. Spacious living room with fireplace, dining room with built-in cabinets. Library, sunny breakfast room, large remodeled kitchen, five bedrooms, two baths, screen porches, hardwood floors, bay windows, lovely garden." Sue sighed. There were so many things she loved about the old place. "Am I listing too much?" she inquired.

"Sounds perfect to me," said Fred. "Let's buy it."

Easier said than done but somehow they had managed it. Eventually, as Fred's practice developed, Sue had taken up her mother's wall-to-wall carpeting, refinished the floors and invested in oriental rugs. She had replaced the heavy chintz drapes with mini blinds, hung Boston fern in the dining room windows and placed a ficus in the living room bay. The look was light and airy and Sue loved it.

"Did Jo help with the decorating?" Mike inquires.

"Well, I knew exactly what I wanted but she did suggest that deep tile color for the library and everybody thinks it's knock-out."

"She's got talent and taste for sure. I thought she looked very wan at the party tonight though. Do you suppose she's got financial problems as well as Tim's drinking to cope with?"

"Well, as you know, Tim sometimes indulges in illusions of grandeur. I think when all those yuppies were making money hand over fist in the stock market, he took out a second mortgage on the store and made some risky investments that boomeranged. I don't know exactly what happened but the shop had to be sold to pay off debts."

"I guessed as much though Jo only talks to me about her kids. She's so loyal to that damn bastard husband of hers."

Sue looks at Mike curiously, at the angry scowl on his usually amiable Irish face. Mike is not critical by nature and seldom uses strong language. The venom with which he spat out the word "bastard" surprises her. She knows it is packed with under-surface significance and she finds herself trying to understand its meaning. Mike's wife had divorced him a few years before and moved to California with their only daughter. He seldom sees them. Had he somehow rekindled an old flame? Could it be that after all these years he was still in love with Jo?

"I remember when she married him, " Mike says. "I tried to be happy about it. Tim seemed perfect for her, such a gentleman, and God knows I understood that she was out of my league. But all he's ever given her is grief."

"He doesn't mean to. He's just got this terrible addiction. But you're right. He does give her a hard time. She told me just this evening that although Tim only has visiting privileges with the boys on Sundays when she is home, he showed up this morning at their basketball practice. Evidently he was in control while he was at the gym but when he got home and discovered Jo was attending a meeting with Father Rossi, his anger was savage. Jo says his rage on such occasions can be terrifying."

"All because Jo was attending a meeting?"

"I think he's been very angry with Father Rossi. He thinks Father talked Jo into the separation, which is not true, although he did approve it. He just doesn't want to believe that Jo would choose the separation herself. The boys said that as soon as they mentioned Father Rossi, he began throwing things and cursing like crazy."

"So Father Rossi had been counseling Jo. I'll bet she'll miss him."

"He was a great help to her. Poor old Monsignor never heard of tough love I guess but Father Rossi was more familiar with the Alanon program. The separation is very hard for her. She keeps worrying about what may happen to Tim but she's hoping it will jolt him into facing the reality of his problem. I guess a lot of us will miss Father Rossi."

"You weren't really serious about thinking someone may have killed him?"

"There was some evidence," Sue says defensively. "But Fred won't even open his mind to the possibility of murder. He really won't even consider it."

"Listen Sue," Fred's response has an edge of anger to it. "Has it occurred to you that maybe the reverse is true, that you haven't given the accident explanation a chance? You seem to want to believe in this gruesome notion you've concocted."

Sue feels uneasy and anxious again. Is there some truth to what Fred is saying? Mike, whom she had counted on to agree with her, had failed to back her up. Father Foley too had failed to give her scenario any credence and he had asked a question to which she certainly had no answer. Who would want to murder Father Rossi? For the first time, at home now and removed from the scene of the shocking events of the evening, Sue begins to wonder if she might possibly be wrong. The phone is ringing and when Fred goes to answer it, she sips her wine thoughtfully.

"Well, I certainly was serious about it," she says, "but maybe…"

"The shock of finding Father on the floor must have been pretty awful for you. Anyone might jump to conclusions walking into something as distressing as that."

Fred has returned to the living room and is busy turning the huge log in the fireplace. He does this adroitly and with great know-how. He may have a frustrating habit of approaching ideas with a closed mind, but when it comes to a husband's household chores, Sue cannot fault him.

He is expert at building fires, carving turkeys, digging garden beds and making repairs. Her father and brothers had been inept with their hands, dispirited and given to under-the-breath cursing when things failed to work for them. Her whole notion of masculine traits had to be revised when Fred came along. And maybe now she should make some revisions, reconsider her assumptions about Father Rossi's death.

"Who was that on the phone?" she asks.

Fred puts the tongs back on the stand and turns to face them with a puzzled frown on his face.

"It was Bob Cudahy. He says there is a bruise on the calf of Father Rossi's leg similar to the one on his head."

"What do you make of that?"

"I'm not sure but he could hardly have hit his leg on the counter."

CHAPTER V

The brief zero spell was an aberration in what turned out to be the warmest winter in the memory of Lakewood residents. By Thursday a thaw had set in. Dark water raced in the gutters and only small white aprons of snow remained tied to the north side of houses. Driving back from the nursing home where she had brought Communion to the Catholic patients, Sue consults her watch. Eleven thirty. Just time enough to track down Jens before meeting Mike at her house for lunch.

She is running late because, toward the end of her hospital rounds, a wizened little woman with a gaping mouth like that of a hungry baby bird grasped her arm and held her riveted to the bedside. From her vacant mouth poured a piteous garbled question. "Will he crumb engine?" Will be crumb engine?" Her intense anxiety flowed like lava into the cramped, disordered room.

Gently Sue freed her hand and taking the woman's false teeth from the glass where they were soaking on the bedside cabinet, rinsed them at the closet washstand.

"Here," she said. "Let's get these in so I can understand what the problem is."

The woman inserted her teeth herself and then, turning beady eyes on Sue, cried in a wild, wavering voice, "Will he come again? Will he come again? Sue sighed. Who would come again? Christ? A long-dead husband? A negligent 65-year-old son? But perhaps it didn't matter. She sat patiently by the bed holding the old woman's hand in her own. She was acutely aware of this patient's dry parchment skin, her bird-light bones and the sluggish blood which coursed slowly through her blue, protruding veins. This hand with its long history of skilled usefulness and its present fragility seemed like a sad metaphor of old age. She gave it a loving little squeeze.

"Yes," she said firmly. "He will come again. You can be sure of that. If not today then certainly tomorrow. Here now, let's brush your hair before he arrives."

Now Sue parks in front of church and reaches in the back seat for the galoshes which had been left in the chapel on the day of Father Rossi's death. Her search for Jens is brief. She finds him mopping the vestibule of the church and her first glimpse of him saddens her. His heavy, loosely knit cardigan is stretched tightly across his massive shoulders emphasizing how stooped they have become, how sharp the bony blades. Why had she not noted before the degree to which age has eroded his Herculean strength? Father Rossi had been aware of it when he recommended the Mexican gardening team. Should Jens, she wonders, still be doing work like this?

Her conversation with him leaves her troubled to say the least. The boots are his all right. He was apologetic about leaving them in the baptistery. But when she inquires why he happened to leave them behind on such a snowy day, he gives no explanation. His eyes, sunken deep in his big face, simply shift.

He had been at the baptistery shortly after his lunch at the Sidewalk Café where he and a couple of local workmen often had hamburgers together. No, he had seen no one, no one at all, not even Father who must have been there dead or alive. He refuses to look at her but keeps glancing at the floor, first at the section that his mop had left damp and shining and then at the remainder still stained with slush. He acts distracted, even guilty, but guilty like a child caught creating disorder in a sacrosanct place. "Sorry, Mrs.," he says. "I shudda put 'em in the closet."

"You know Jens would never have killed Father Rossi," Sue says to Mike when they are seated in the sunroom eating the corned beef sandwiches she had picked up at the deli. "But he knows something. He really was acting very strange."

Bob Cudahy had been unable to find Sue at home in the few days following Father Rossi's death. At the funeral yesterday he had given Mike a manila envelope with the contents of Father's pockets to deliver to her. When Mike called, Sue had invited him to lunch to examine these items with her. Fred would have joined them, she explained, but he had to be out at Children's Memorial where a young patient was scheduled for a fourth shunt operation. He had, however, gone to the funeral parlor on Sunday to examine the wound on Father's leg. He found a bad burn, probably inflicted by some electrical device which he couldn't identify. The wound was round, perhaps an inch and a half in diameter and surrounded by the same bruising they had observed on Father's face. At Sue's insistence, he had reported his findings to Father Foley.

"Father couldn't seem to get it through his thick skull that there might be some connection between the burn and a murder," Sue said. "He refused to report it to Captain Vogel, so the funeral went ahead without any investigation."

"Did Fred make the same connection you've been making?"

"Well, he admits the burn is an odd manifestation he can't account for, but he assumes there's some reasonable explanation short of murder. To tell the truth, Mike, he's been so concerned about this spina bifida child who is being operated on today that he can't seem to think of much else. I guess you're the one who'll have to report all this evidence to Vogel."

Sue is surprised and disappointed at Mike's hesitant response. He looks dismayed by her request but then makes a valiant effort at humor. "Can't you visualize it, Sue? I go into Vogel's office and announce that a tipped-over heater electrocuted Father Rossi but he had a couple of additional burns that Sue Carney thinks indicates that he was murdered. God, he'd waste me. Vogel can make you feel ridiculous. He can really reduce you to a heap of ashes. I can just hear him. 'So, I suppose this priest had some big insurance policy his nephews were willing to polish him off for? Or some jealous prelate wanted his enviable position at the Chancery? Or he got mixed up in some local Lakewood drug warfare? C'mon, O'Connell! Come up with some plausible motives or get the hell out of here. I've got work in the real world to do.'"

Captain Vogel was noted for his sharp sarcasm and ordinarily Sue would have been amused by Mike's excellent imitation of his belittling manner. Today she scarcely smiled. Was her case really so easily dismissed?

"But if you told him all the strange circumstances?"

"Look, Sue, if you can come up with more convincing evidence, I'll be the first to report it to Vogel. In the meantime, if I can help in any way, just say the word."

Obviously, Mike isn't going to change his mind and Sue lets it go for now. "Okay," she says, "Let's see what we've got in the envelope."

"Not much there, I'm afraid. I checked out the pen you mentioned and there is no Bennington Insurance Company in the Chicago area. I suppose it could have come from anywhere but right now its no lead. Here, in his wallet, there's just the usual stuff, some cash, a couple of charge cards, some frequent flyer coupons, and a check for $100.00 made out to Father by a Boyd Harris. Then there's a ring with several keys, a handkerchief, some foreign change and these." Mike is placing everything on the table and now adds a little heap of stones, mostly oval in shape and gray in color. "Odd," he says. "They're not particularly beautiful or unusual. Why would he save them?"

For the first time since Father Rossi's death, Sue's eyes fill with tears. Rubbing her finger over the cool surface of the stones, she says, "Can't you see how thin they are? They're skipping stones."

The stones are like a fragrance, a melody that has the power to resurrect a scene from the past. Vividly she recalls the day Father had joined them for a family picnic at the beach to celebrate Jennifer's sixth birthday. It was growing late, the bluff was in deep shadow, they had packed up to leave and were all standing at the water's edge when Father sent a stone skipping far out past the sandbars. Once again he showed Jennifer how to hold the stone, how to swing smoothly from her waist. Suddenly she shouted, "Look! Look! I hopped one!"

He picked her up then and after noisy congratulations, held her quietly as together they gazed across the water toward the horizon. It was a hazy evening, warm, without wind, water merely murmuring as it lapped the shore. The setting sun had tinted the still surface of the lake in delicate shades of light lavender and silky salmon and pink so pale and exquisite that Sue was sure it had never existed in the world before. Peace and poetry held them spell-bound for a brief moment. Then Jennifer, with an urgent need to express her exhilaration, to run, to race, to dance on the sand, squirmed to get down.

"I'm so happy I could explode!" she exclaimed. And Father Rossi, smiling at the others, said, "You know what, Kitten? I think we all are." Sue finds her purse on the floor next to her chair, extracts a Kleenex and blows her nose.

"I think he was saving those stones for Jennifer. I'll keep them to give to her. His death was hard for all the girls but particularly devastating for her. She can't seem to get it through her head that he won't be coming back or that we can't go where he is."

"Good idea. Death is so tough for kids. These might be a kind of farewell present for her. It doesn't look like they're much of a clue to a murder, but what do you make of these?"

Sue examined the coins Mike spread out on the table. The inscriptions seemed to be in Spanish. "Perhaps Mexican?" she guesses.

"Maybe. You could take them to the bank and find out. And maybe you'll want to stop in at Charlie's and get a set of these keys made for yourself before you return them to the rectory. Never know when you might want to get in somewhere."

Is he teasing her about being a sleuth? Probably, but she decides to take him seriously.

"Not a bad idea," she says.

"Now here are some papers that might have some kind of significance, though I doubt it. There's this application for adoption signed by William and Patricia Bergman dated that same day, the Saturday on which he died."

"We heard about this adoption at the Scripture meeting that morning." Sue explains. "Pixie must have given him the application and he was taking it down to Catholic Charities to deliver personally. Maybe I can see that it gets to Monsignor because Father Foley will be much too busy to follow up on it. And here's a notice for the church bulletin announcing the St. Luke study group for the Saturdays in February. Father Foley has asked me to take over that group. I guess I can do it but it certainly won't be the same."

"I'll bet you'll do a bang-up job," says Mike. "Maybe even I will come. It would be a good chance to check up on all your suspects."

"You don't really think any of those people are suspects, do you?" Sue's tone is incredulous.

"If there really was a murder, they are certainly suspects," says Mike. "They're all innocent until proven guilty but you better consider them suspects nevertheless."

"Do a sort of legal double-take? Here is this good friend discussing Luke's infancy narrative with us but I'm to keep a sharp eye out because he might turn out to be Herod?"

"Something like that. Does that bother you?"

For a moment Sue is silent, watching the run-off from the roof drip past the paned windows of the breakfast room. It looked like the investigation of Father Rossi's murder was going to be largely her responsibility with only sideline help from Mike and she was beginning to realize that it might be a very distasteful and uncomfortable job. Still she is absolutely committed to it no matter what it might involve.

"I don't have to like it," she says. "But I'll manage. What's this letter about?"

"It's written to an Adele Adabeau together with a check made out to her signed by Paul Rossi. Maybe you should just read it for yourself."

As she read the letter, Sue was already connecting the check for $100.00 made out to Father by Boyd Harris with this check for the same amount to Adele Adabeau.

Dear Adele,

Enclosed is a check from our mutual friend who hopes it may be a little help toward Twinkie's tuition. I think he's doing all right although he is quite discouraged that he has not yet found work. I hold both of you in my heart before God, asking him to be near you and to give you strength in your present hard circumstances.

Sincerely in Christ,

Paul Rossi.

"What's the address on that envelope?" she asks Mike.

"4625 South Hampton."

"Wouldn't that be in St. Felicia's, our partner inner-city parish? Not that there's necessarily any connection."

"I guess so. I wonder who the mutual friend could be?"

"I have a distinct hunch that it's Boyd Harris. At our study group meeting Boyd mentioned that he and Father were old friends. He also said that he had been laid off when Central Airlines went under at Christmas and had been unable to get work. But Adele Adabeau, who on earth is she?"

"A serious girl friend, I would guess. You don't send money for tuition to strangers."

"Not possible. Boyd told us he was married to Winnie Harris and had kids in college and at Lakewood High."

"Being married to Winnie doesn't rule out a girl friend. At any rate, you ought to find out. Perhaps since this letter was ready to be posted, it doesn't have to be returned to Father Foley. You could hand deliver it to Ms. Adabeau on the pretext that you wanted to inform her of Father's death in person."

Sue is hesitant. "Do you really think this is any of our business? I mean, what possible connection could it have to a murder?"

Mike shrugs his shoulders. "No apparent connection, but it's a piece of the puzzle concerning Father's last days and if I were you, I'd look into it."

"Okay, I'll ask Father Foley if I may deliver it. Then I could bring it out there in my capacity as Minister of Care. Tomorrow I'm scheduled to tutor at St. Felicia's. A group of us drive down there every Friday and I could easily swing over to Hampton and see if this Adele is home. Now, what about this last item here?"

"A letter to Senator William Harrington and it just says, 'Enclosed are the dates and names you asked for. See you for lunch on February 5th. Thanks for giving me an hour of your valuable time.' And here's the enclosure."

Sue skimmed it quickly.

March 12, 1987   Pedro de Cesaro, a priest, shot dead in his country parish.

December 24, 1989 Antony Evangelides, Bishop of San Cristobal, shot dead in the Cathedral confessional on Christmas Eve.

February 2, 1995 Elizabeth Sullivan and Jean O'Donnell, American missionary nuns, raped and shot dead on the steps of their convent.

November 28, 1998 Felix Rodriguiz, Amada Jullio, Ignatio Sapienze, Pablo Parra, four Dominican priests, Francisco Perrone their housekeeper and her daughter Maria shot and killed at the University of San Cristobal.

"This hardly exhausts the list but they are the best known cases."

"Priests and religious killed in Alvarado," says Sue. "Father's last prayer on the day he died was that peace negotiations would begin soon in Alvarado. He was probably trying to persuade Harrington to vote against more aid for the military down there."

"But I thought we were supporting the military to prevent a Commie takeover."

"I know. That is the Administration policy and Fred used to back it up one hundred percent but Father Rossi gave him a very different slant on it. I guess D'Astici and his death squads never stuck to just fighting Communist guerillas. They are out to eliminate anyone working toward legitimate reform for the poor as this list proves. Fred and Father used to have some hefty debates on U.S. aid and arguments about what was really going on down there." Sue smiles remembering the heat and vigor of those arguments.

Mike glances at his watch and begins gathering papers together. "I'll reseal this and maybe you can return it to Father Foley to take care of," he says. "I've got to leave in a few minutes to police the parking at the Henderson's, some big tea for the historical museum. It's one of those mansions on the lake with a winding downhill approach, a real traffic nightmare. But before I go, was there anyone in particular in that study group that you ought to be thinking about?"

"Maybe Elena. Elena Esquivel, this young Spanish woman who arrived late. She seemed to have some kind of chip on her shoulder. Her manner with Father was really bizarre. She had an opportunity to do him in while I was getting my car to pick her up. But of course, that's really insane. She would never have had the strength to knock him out like that."

"Women learn great jujitsu tricks these days. Some Spanish version just might be lethal."

"Why do I get the impression you're teasing me?"

"Not really, Sue. If I were you, I'd keep an eye on everyone who was present that day and take notes on anything significant that turns up. And if I can help you in any way, just let me know."

"Maybe you could do something for me. Could you check to see if Jens has a prison record?"

"Jens?"

"Yes, you know at the Cardinal's Mass, he mentioned in his homily that Monsignor used to spend his day off each week visiting the prison in Joliet and that he sometimes found jobs for ex-convicts. I remember rumors years ago that maybe Jens was one of his former prisoners. Could you check it out for me?"

"I'll try. If I can't do it, I'll find someone who can. Any other clues you picked up in your conversation with Jens?"

"Nothing really except that his behavior was strange."

After Mike leaves, Sue searches through her purse to find the dog-eared prayer card Jens had given her. He said he had found it in the baptistery chapel floor on the day of Father Rossi's death. On one side of the card was a simple Celtic cross and on the other the A.A. Serenity Prayer. She had made a quick decision that it was not necessary to bring this much-used card to Mike's attention.

CHAPTER VI

Although St. Felicia's is an integrated parish, white members tend to be older people who have remained in the neighborhood while younger families moving in are black. The school children, little girls in navy jumpers and boys in dark cords and white sweatshirts, are mostly black and so are the three fifth grade boys Sue is instructing in reading.

Teaching demands all of her energy and concentration. It seals out the rest of the world as though it did not exist. On the drive into the city she had been preoccupied with concern for Boyd and Winnie Harris but now there is no crack through which worry can penetrate.

When Mike suggested Boyd might have a serious girl friend, she had rejected the idea out of hand, but the suggestion jogged her memory. Almost immediately she recalled an incident which Father's death had totally erased from her mind. On the Friday afternoon before that fateful day, she was polishing candlesticks in the sacristy when she was startled by a loud voice coming from Father's office down the corridor. She recognized it immediately. Winnie's voice was unmistakable and carried well at any time but now it was raised in anger and had a shaky, hysterical quality to it that Sue found frightening. She was embarrassed to have overheard it and left the sacristy by way of the church so she could not possibly be seen by Winnie. The voice, still trembling with rage, followed her into the sanctuary. How could she have forgotten such a troubling incident and what might it mean in connection with Boyd?

Tutoring at St. Felicia's takes place in the cafeteria, several groups at separate tables huddled over their work, the room filled with the hum of lowered voices. Sue's students are easily distracted. They tend to fidget and yawn and quibble among themselves. They are all tough cases. Vision problems and dyslexia have been ruled out and IQ's are better than average. Sue, up against an invisible wall of boredom and lack of motivation, is determined that before the year is out, these kids are going to read at the national level or better. She had risen early that morning to type a news article in caps for them to read. Now she spreads the sports page with pictures in front of them.

"Here we have some flash cards with all the words you need to read this article about last night's game," She says.

"But we already seed the game," complains Lamont.

"If you know all these words," Sue continues, "you could be a sports writer some day and cover all the games from one end of the country to the other."

"Not me," says Lamont. "I'd rather play. That's where the money is. But the real money is in drugs. One time my cousin…"

The name of Lamont's game is diversion, resistance and diversion. The whites of his eyes widen wickedly in his dark face whenever he launches into one of his street stories intended to fascinate his friends, shock his teacher and postpone reading forever. The degree to which Sue loves this skinny little kid with his smart talk and wild imagination is ridiculous. Once she had thought it strategic to listen him out, but she knows better now. Interrupting, she announces that the flash cards will be a basket ball game. Lamont will keep score. Each word a student gets right will be a basket.

Miraculously, the scheme works. Although the article is more difficult than the story assigned in their text, each boy reads part of it with prompting from the others when hesitations grow too long. In the car now, following Sister Terisita's directions to Hampton Court, she thinks it was worth all the preparation. Although she knows there will be ups and downs, she feels there has been a breakthrough, a real victory. This didn't happen every week and she is elated.

Hampton is a picturesque little enclave that runs for a few blocks along the Illinois Central tracks. The row of small Tudor structures makes the street look like an illustration in a Dickens novel. The dinginess, the peeling paint and cracked stucco, even the soot on the mounds of melting snow in the parkways seem mitigated by a sense of old world charm. Finding the address she is looking for, Sue pulls up to the curb. Her car is the only one parked on the entire block. Except for some small children floating coke cans in a muddy puddle, the street is deserted.

Adele Adabeau's house seems in better repair than neighboring ones. The door and window panes were recently painted in a subtle carmine color. An elderly lady, gracious and garrulous, with fine wrinkled skin like a withering white petunia, answers the bell and directs Sue to an outdoor wooden stairway at the rear of the house. Climbing to the second floor, she notes the dead garden beds in the small back yard and the row of willows that screen off the railway tracks. A Christmas wreath still hangs on the door at the head of the stairs and on the landing stands an old fashioned wicker doll buggy. Saying a prayer that all will go well on this visit, Sue knocks on the door.

"Adele Adabeau?" she inquires of the black woman who opens it. She had anticipated a white person and now finds herself absorbed in detailed impressions of the woman who stands in the doorway. A neat, modified Afro, dark liquid eyes, rich brown skin with polished highlights on broad cheek bones and a wide forehead, a prominent mouth sensuously shaped make this an attractive woman in anybody's culture.

"Yes," she says in a soft voice. "I'm Adele. Can I help you in some way?"

"I'm Sue Carney, the Minister of Care from St. Francis de Sales parish in Lakewood. My pastor, Father Foley, asked me to bring you this letter from Father Rossi. He wanted me to deliver it in person because we have sad news about Father."

"Sad news?" Adele's voice is concerned. "Won't you come in please and tell me what has happened."

She leads Sue through a small, spotless kitchen into an immaculately white living room. A large mahogany bookcase, the size of an ordinary fireplace, serves as focal point. Over it hangs a large print of Roualt's Christ. The deep stained-glass colors of the picture and the shiny spines of the books provide the only color in the room. The rest is white: the walls, the twin leather love seats on either side of the bookcase, the cotton rugs on the dark hardwood floor. In the far corner, suspended from a large skylight, a Boston fern hangs like a chandelier over a glass-top bamboo card table.

Someone else might have played up the quaintness of this small attic apartment with its sloping ceilings and dormer windows. Sue thinks it says something special about Adele that she opted for simplicity. Her immediate impression is that Mike is wrong about Boyd being a boy friend. Only two chairs are drawn up to the table. There seems no place here for a man to put his feet up and make himself comfortable. It looks like the home of a single, female parent. Still, she is determined to remain open minded and alert.

When they are seated across from each other on the love seats, Adele asks about the news of Father Rossi and Sue tells her about the accidental death in the baptistery. She explains that he had many friends in the parish who were saddened and shocked by this sudden loss and since Adele too was a friend, Father Foley wanted the news brought to her personally.

"Yes, it is better to hear it this way," says Adele. "And you were very kind to come. In a way, Father was a good friend although I did not know him well. I am an airline hostess and last summer on a flight from Mexico, a little boy was deserted on the plane. I had seen a native woman bring him aboard but had not noted that she departed before we took off. Perhaps this was because a man, unrelated to the child, was seated next to him and he did not seem to be alone.

"Father was seated just across the aisle. I remembered him from other flights to Florida and knew him to be a kind person, so I enlisted his help. It was a coincidence that we both knew the manager at Central airport, I in a professional way, but he, as an old friend. We took the little boy to his office and together we debated about what to do. I offered to bring the boy home with me, but since I had a flight the next morning, it was decided that it was better for Father to take him to Catholic Charities. Of course, I could not forget that little boy.

"Father and I were in touch during the investigation that followed. Occasionally, he brought the little fellow to spend a day with me here and once he took my little daughter and me to the zoo with him. That is how we knew each other."

Sue listens intently to Adele's story. It is told with a straightforward sincerity and composure that impresses her, but it requires concentration to follow it. While Adele speaks English fluently, she has a slight accent that makes careful attention necessary. Questions race through Sue's mind. Frequent flights to Florida? She knows Father occasionally flew down to visit the Archdiocesan partnering mission of Chilpancingo Chilapo in Mexico, but frequent flights? And was Boyd the manager at Central Airways? Is there cover-up intent in Adele's identifying their relationship as professional? But for the moment, she circumvents her curiosity to ask a simple, friendly question.

"It must be hard to arrange for your little girl if your flight schedules are irregular. I often wonder how mothers manage when they are working."

"I'm not working presently. I was laid off at Christmas time and am still trying to find another job. But when I was flying, Miss Harris took care of Twinkie for me."

"Miss Harris?"

"Yes, she is my landlady who lives downstairs. She is a lovely person, a retired school teacher and very fond of children. She has been a real blessing in my life." Sue is due back at school to pick up her friends in less than half an hour. She knows she has little time to spare and so decides to take a plunge.

"I know a Boyd Harris in our parish," she says. "He also worked at Central and was laid off at year's end. It's a long shot, but I wonder if he might be related to your land lady."

Adele smiles widely in astonishment. "But yes," she says. "What a small world it is! Boyd Harris is Miss Harris' nephew. He is the man whom Father and I consulted about Juan. Several years ago when I was expecting Twinkie, he arranged with his aunt to have this apartment renovated for me. His aunt had just retired and did not wish to move but could no longer afford the house without more income, so it was a happy arrangement for both of us. Mr. Harris is a considerate man, is he not?"

"Sounds like he is. I only met him recently but I have known his wife, Winnie, for years. She's a very successful real estate woman in our community."

"I'm sure she is a fine person."

Sue is certain she detects a little acid edge to Adele's smooth voice when she mentions Winnie. But how can she follow up on it? Instead, she asks Adele about her accent and discovers that she had immigrated from Haiti several years before. Life had been difficult enough when she left the country but now she is concerned for her family there in an ever worsening economy. The conversation shifts to Adele's youth, the Convent she attended there and her current need to find work.

Sue soon forgets about time, about the purpose of her visit. The mellow, soothing quality of Adele's voice, her quiet self-possession, the way her polished nails perfectly match her coral angora sweater all enchant Sue. She enjoys few things more than making a new friend. She takes great delight in exploring those initial little rivulets of conversation which eventually lead into the main stream of another's life with its unique fascination, its special joys and problems. She is thinking only of

Adele, not of her original desire for information when she says it must be terribly hard to lose one's job.

"It may have been a blessing in disguise," says Adele. "I did secretarial work in Haiti but when I came here, I spoke no English. A secretarial position was out of the question. Through a friend, I found a job with Central Airway and was glad to get it. But I should not have stayed with them so long. Now I am brushing up my typing and taking a computer course. The unemployment compensation is seeing us through but it is hard to keep up Twinkie's tuition at St. Felicia's. It is terribly important that she stay there so I hope it will not be impossible to find work. Jobs have been very hard to get."

"I know, but your French must be a great asset. Have you thought about a position where you could use your language skills?"

Adele seems interested in this suggestion and Sue agrees to shop around and see if anyone knew of possible employment for her. As she is leaving, she picks up a framed picture of Twinkie from the top of the bookcase. The child does not look like her mother. She has a round, cherubic face, lighter skin, softer ringlets, more mischievous eyes.

"What a darling little girl," Sue exclaims. "She must be the same age as my Jennifer. Does she look like her father?"

"A little, but perhaps mostly like my sister who is a nun in Haiti. Her auntie is so pleased with the resemblance."

Studying her photograph carefully, Sue is willing to concede that maybe the fun-loving eyes resemble those of some distant aunt in Haiti but the rest of the child's face bears a stunning similarity to someone much closer to home. Sue is somewhat shocked, reluctant to accept the evidence before her eyes. Still, she remembers a line from Father Rossi's letter to Adele, "I hold your hard situation in my heart before God." If he had not been judgmental, need she be?

Consulting her watch, Sue says she has to run but will stop by next Friday to let Adele know if she has come up with any job opportunities.

When they part at the door, she has a satisfactory feeling that they are already good friends.

Chapter VII

At the foot of Adele's narrow, wooden stairway, a black man steps aside to let Sue pass. She senses that he is observing her as keenly as she is him. He wears a dark raincoat over a business suit: is thin, neat, with well-trimmed hair and highly polished shoes. He is not a handsome man but his features are sharp, memorable. He is probably in his late thirties.

His car, a white Camaro, is parked behind Sue's. Slush has soiled the fenders but the top of the car is shining as though it had just left the shop. She examines it carefully but it never occurs to her to look at the license plates. It is only later, when she has picked up her friends at St. Felicia's, that she wishes that she had.

As she is pulling out of the pock-marked parking lot next to the school, avoiding what puddles she can, she notices a white Camaro idling in front of the church. The distance is too great to identify the driver but later, after she has pulled onto the Dan Ryan Expressway, it seems to be following her two or three cars behind. Even after she gets on the Kennedy Expressway, she can spot it dodging in and out of the traffic.

The women who tutor with her on Fridays are all old friends. Coming home they are often tired and conversation dwindles to a comfortable silence. Sue is not crazy about expressway driving and is grateful for the quiet. She does not need to become distracted trying to spot the driver of the Camaro.

"Dotty, are you awake back there?" she inquires. "I think an old boy friend of mine is following us in that white Camaro a couple of cars behind us. If he pulls up closer, see if you can get a look at him, okay?"

"No one ever had as many old boy friends as you. I'll see what I can see."

"I'd appreciate it."

In a few minutes the Camaro edges into a position just behind them in the adjoining lane and Dotty starts to laugh.

"A very sophisticated old boy friend," she says. Very black with Hollywood sunglasses.

"All I wanted to know. From a distance I thought I recognized him."

The car follows them from the Kennedy onto Edens. All the way to Lakewood, she can spot it weaving in and out of the traffic behind them. But when she turns east on Trent Road to approach her own village, the car remains on the highway. Sue takes a deep breath of relief.

She had thought that the man at the foot of Adele's stairway was possibly her husband. He had looked like a serious black yuppie, a professional or business man, and seeing him had dampened suspicions she had about Adele's current relationship with Boyd. But perhaps he was not related to Adele at all. Her ride home had unnerved her. Who was this man and why was he following her?

She stops at the house to refill the bird feeder, water plants and put on a load of wash before going to Potter's Electric. Ellen greets her with a vehemence and animosity to which Sue feels she will never become accustomed. Nothing anyone ever told her about teenagers had prepared her for the recent change in attitude of her oldest daughter. Once a gentle little girl who adored her mother and enjoyed her company, she now aggressively disapproves of everything Sue does or says. Right now she is exploding with righteous anger when asked to sit with Jennifer.

"Mom! That's not fair. It's just plain mean. Sarah gets to go to her friend's house but I'm hung up here with this brat all day long."

"Okay, okay," Sue says wearily. "I'll take Jennifer with me. But I don't ever, I mean ever, want to hear you call her a brat again, do you hear?"

As soon as Sue walks into Potter's, she realizes that she is probably in the wrong place. The shop is loaded with TV's, radios, vacuum cleaners, fans, irons but she sees nothing that could conceivably have been the instrument that inflicted the burns on Father Rossi's body. Fortunately, she runs into Pixie Bergman and her little boy, Roger. Quite inadvertently, Pixie presents her with another avenue to work on.

"I'm looking for a hair dryer," Pixie says. "We lost one whole carton of things in the move from St. Paul and my hair dryer must have been in it. I keep hoping it will turn up but I guess it's not going to. I've been looking terrible ever since I got here, so today's my day to treat myself to a new one."

Sue stands back a bit to examine Pixie's sunny short bob. "You mean your hair could look better than it does? I don't believe it."

"Wait 'til you see me blow-dried. It's a major improvement."

Roger and Jennifer who know each other from the first grade at de Sales are examining radios while their mothers visit. There seems to be a contest about whose father has the biggest model. Watching them for a moment, Pixie smiles.

"I'm so glad they've become friends. Jennifer is such a great little girl."

"She's a dream child," sighs Sue. "I wish I could pickle her so she would never get to be thirteen. Pixie, I hope we can get together soon. Do you think you'll be coming to the Scripture meeting tomorrow?"

"I'll be there. I really feel awful about Father Rossi. I guess we were the last ones to see him alive."

"That reminds me. I asked Father Foley to give your application for adoption to Monsignor Fiedler. He'll probably be calling you soon about it. You'll love him and I think he will be a great help to you and

Bill. Oh, and speaking of Bill, do you suppose in a big law firm like his there might be a job for a secretary who is fluent in French? I know this well-qualified Haitian woman who badly needs a job. Would Bill think I was crazy if I called him about it?"

Whenever Sue promised to check around for something, she did a thorough job of it. She mentioned it to absolutely everyone she talked with because you just never knew. She found this worked more often than not.

"I'll mention it to Bill," Pixie says. "And of course you can call him. He'd be glad to hear from you."

The only hair dryer at Potter's is an expensive one with extra high power and four settings. The women decide that perhaps Pixie can do better at the drug store. Each, with a child in hand, waits at the curb for a chance to cross the street.

The enormous old elm in front of the bank had been taken down in the fall. Standing there, Sue is aware of the vacuum its removal has created, how naked and exposed the street seems without it, how the sun falls without shadow on the stark brick of the bank building. Perhaps in the spring the village will plant a new tree but it will be a generation before it can spread its branches as graciously as the old one had. Engaged in a sad reverie for the loss of the ancient elm, Sue suddenly spots a white Camaro parked in front of Lakewood Shoes directly across the street from Potter's. It's flanks are splattered with the day's slush but its roof gleams in the lingering winter sunlight. The car is empty. She hastily looks up and down the block but the driver is nowhere in sight.

"It really shook me up," she reports to Fred a little later. Fred drinks a beer at the kitchen table while she pares an eggplant and chops onion for a ratatouille, his favorite. She finds it wise not to cut back on dinner when she has been gone all day or he will start in how she is trying to do too much. She has no desire to relinquish any of her activities; certainly not tutoring Lamont and his buddies.

"There have to be thousands of Camaros around." Fred says. "I don't see how it could possibly be the same one."

"That's what scares me. It *was* the same one and if he got off Eden's at the next exit, he would have to have known where my house is. He parked around here somewhere and then followed me to the village. It gives me the willies to think about it."

"But I'm trying to tell you, Sue, that it wasn't the same car. There are a lot of Camaros around. Just look in the parking lot at Mass next Sunday."

"I'd know this particular car anywhere," insists Sue. "It has a brand new shine on top where the splatter has not reached. I've got the license number here and I want you to check it out for me."

Fred takes a big draught of his beer and looks at her in amusement. "Can it wait 'til tomorrow?" he asks. In a way, it relieves her anxiety that Fred refuses to take the incident seriously. He examines the package on the table as though nothing heart-thumping had happened to her.

"What's this?" he asks. "A Gillette Supermax Pro 1400?"

Before Sue can explain that it is a hair dryer, the phone rings. It is Bill Bergman calling to say that just possibly there might be a job for her friend at Craddock and Delaney. A secretary with language skills was needed from time to time. Only a few days ago, a fellow lawyer had mentioned difficulties in some transaction because they had no one truly knowledgeable in French. Perhaps she could tell him something about her friend so he could recommend that the firm interview her.

Bill has what Sue's mother would have called a good telephone voice: resonant, clear, and pleasant. It affirmed her first favorable impression of the handsome man she had met just a week ago in the school parking lot.

"Bill!" she exclaims. "How great of you to call. The woman I mentioned to Pixie is in her early thirties. She's had secretarial experience but recently has been employed by Central Airlines. She's been brushing up on her skills and taking a computer course at her local public school.

She's attractive, very presentable and courteous, and my guess is, very responsible. She grew up in Haiti and was educated by the nuns there so, of course, her native language is French. But you understand, Bill, Haitian means black."

Sue wants no misunderstanding about Adele's race that might lead to later disappointment.

"Black might be a plus," Bill assures her. "I think the firm is interested in affirmative action whenever they can find qualified people. What about references? Have you known her long, Sue?"

"Not very long, but she's an exceptionally fine person. I'm a very good judge of character."

"I can believe that. See if you can line up some references and I'll get right on it next Monday. I'll get back to you as soon as I know anything."

Sue, tired and still anxious about her unnerving drive from the city, is warmed by Bill's call. It lifts her spirit and restores her faith in a normal safe, friendly world. Fred has disappeared into the living room where Sarah has cornered him in a game of scrabble. Even when he's exhausted as he is tonight, he seldom says no to Sarah. She is a plump, good-natured ten-year-old with copper tinted curls like her Dad's and an extravagant devotion to him. Sue wanders in to oversee the game and tell Fred about Bill's offer.

"I really like those Bergmans," she says. "That was very generous of Bill to call and when I saw Pixie at Potters, she was so friendly. Do you like them too, Fred?"

"Bill seems like an intelligent man but I'm not so sure about Pixie. She looks like a dumb blond to me."

"Daddy," giggles Sarah. "That's not nice."

"A very cute blond," says Sue. "And I'd say naïve, not dumb."

"Naïve!" exclaims Fred. "The very word. That'll take me one more space than navy."

He and Sarah resume their game. Sue returns to the kitchen to put the meat loaf in the oven. As she adds a little basil to the ratatouille, she is wondering if it is worth the hassle to insist that Ellen set the table when the phone rings again.

Mike apologizes for calling at this hour. He knows that she is probably engaged in some engrossing gourmet cooking, but he has just received interesting news that can't wait. She'd better brace herself. Is she ready?

"Ready," she agrees, smiling at the sense of dramatic conspiracy he has managed to convey. "What's up?"

"It's Jens. I got his prison record for you just a few minutes ago." Mike pauses briefly, managing to create further suspense.

"Well?" Sue grows impatient.

"He was convicted of manslaughter."

"Manslaughter! This seems incredible."

"Yes. Evidently he killed his wife back in 1948."

Chapter VIII

The next morning is overcast, the sky smudged with a charcoal cloud cover that denies light to the beautiful baptistery windows. As she switches on the chandelier, Sue tries to put the brilliant dazzle of the previous Saturday out of mind. To remember the joy with which she had awaited Father Rossi's arrival and the hope that had filled her heart for a spiritual friendship with him is almost unbearable. But if her mood is now as subdued and sad as the somber winter day, she is determined not to succumb to it. She has work to do. Still, it takes an odd bit of courage to fill the coffee pot as though it were not the same vessel that had been treacherously poured out the week before, to forget where the body had lain on this same cold marble floor.

She is glad when Mike arrives. They had spoken only briefly the night before but had agreed to meet here before the scripture meeting began. As soon as Sue pours each of them a cup of coffee, they commence exchanging notes.

Mike explains that he had found it impossible to get downtown to look up Jen's police record so he had called Bill Bergman and asked him to do it. He was sure a smart guy like that would find a way to get access to the information and he had indeed obtained it promptly.

"Was that smart, asking someone in the parish?" Sue says.

"He hasn't been here long and doesn't know Jens. But I did ask him to be discreet."

"Well, just so Jens' record doesn't leak out. It certainly makes him a prime suspect. I was stunned when you told me last night that he had murdered his wife and I'm really angry with Monsignor. He had no right to hire a criminal for a job where school children are involved on a daily basis. I suppose he thought he was being charitable but it seems to me to be just as irresponsible as sending one of those pedophile priests to another parish when he has already molested a child elsewhere. I think the first thing we should do is see that Jens gets fired."

"Hold on, Sue, not so fast. I know the possibility that Jens may have killed Father Rossi is one hell of a frightening thing, but we really don't know what it is all about. I suggest you have a visit with Monsignor and see if you can get a rundown on the circumstances surrounding the murder."

"Okay, I'll stop in there on my way home. And in the meantime, maybe you can report all this to Captain Vogel so the police can get going on an official investigation."

"Sue, I can't do that. The fact that Jens committed a crime forty years ago doesn't prove that a murder was committed last week. That we have a likely suspect makes it more believable to me but it sure wouldn't impress Vogel. The evidence is as weak as ever. Let's work on it a while longer and see if we can't turn up something to make a stronger case."

Sue finds this response frustrating. She wishes Mike were more completely convinced, more committed to the pursuit of justice. She has a feeling that he may have been going along with her because he likes to be the nice guy, always accommodating, and then was surprised when Jens' record turned up a murder. Sue needs Mike's know-how and she asks impatiently if he shouldn't be doing something right now, maybe taking fingerprints before the meeting begins.

"Jens' prints would have been on the heater in any case," Mike reminds her. "He was the one who carried it into the room. It really wouldn't prove anything to find his prints on anything."

"Except maybe one of these," suggests Sue, showing him the hair dryer she had purchased the day before. "Fred says the coils in this just about exactly match the burn wounds on Father's head and leg. What do you make of that?"

Mike throws back his head and laughs. "I think it hysterical. That's the craziest murder weapon I ever saw. You aren't serious, are you?"

"Fred thought is was a big joke too. But, let's face it, something inflicted those burns and it may well have been one of these."

"Well," Mike says. "that certainly doesn't let any female suspects off the hook."

Sue runs the cord of the dryer through her fingers, folding it in order to return it to the box when suddenly she remembers her glimpse into Elena's bag as she was driving her home the previous Saturday. There, tangled up with her needlepoint, had been a white cord identical with this one. She had been curious about the cord at the time, wondering what sort of electrical gadget one might need on a flight from Spain. Still, though she finds this possible clue startling, it seems so slight and so remote that she does not mention it to Mike.

She tells him instead that when she had returned Father's belongings to Father Foley, she had been unable to find out much about Father Rossi's work at the Chancery. He had been attached to the Propagation of the Faith Office, but Foley didn't have the impression that he was involved in fund raising. He knew he had to travel occasionally, possibly to missions in Central America. This might tie up with the fact that the bank had identified the coins in his pocket as from Alvarado. It might also account for the frequent flights to Florida that Adele had mentioned.

"Foley can't believe we're still pursuing this case," she says. "He saw no reason why we should search Father's room or be allowed to examine his files in his downtown office. He was quite satisfied that none of this investigation was necessary. His parting shot was that if we decided to exhume the body, the police department would have to pay the expense."

"Typical. You don't think he protesteth too much?"

Sue smiles. "I had his key to the baptistery and besides, no pastor kills an assistant these days."

When Sue relates the story of her visit to Adele, she tells Mike she is fairly certain Adele had an affair with Boyd several years ago and that Twinkie is very probably his child. Her picture looks like him and there was no evidence of another father around. The fact that Boyd's aunt had been helpful in the situation when the pregnancy occurred tended to cement her conclusion. Adele seemed like a moral, even quite a religious, person but perhaps was extremely lonely and vulnerable when she was new in this country and who knew what may have been happening in Boyd's life.

"Can you be certain about the child just from a picture?" Mike is skeptical.

Sue smiles. "Pretty certain. My mother provided me with a reliable course in family resemblance. Every time one of my brothers brought a new baby home for the holidays, she would hold him on her knees and give him this prolonged examination. 'His hairline is exactly like Grandfather Egan's' she would exclaim. I remember when Sarah was born, she said, 'Don't let Fred's coloring fool you. This child has our cheek bones. I'd recognize her in a whole nursery full of babies.' So I learned to observe features carefully and to trace them to their origin in the family. Twinkie has Boyd's head shape, his forehead and the same round cheeks, also an identical indentation in the chin. Her color might fool you but not me. Still, I can't guess what Boyd and Adele's current relationship is."

Sue adds that she thinks the situation is dead end as far as their investigation is concerned. Neither Boyd nor Adele strike her as murderers and what would their motive be in any case?

"What about Winnie?" muses Mike. "Winnie strikes me as a real killer."

"Oh, come on Mike. How do you add that one up?"

"Well, Father's letter to Adele indicates to me that there is some kind of on-going relationship. If Winnie knew of the situation and thought Father might reveal it or was encouraging it or recommending a divorce, she would be furious with him. No one who threatens her social status would be safe, I'd guess."

Sue laughs at this ridiculous hypothesis. "That won't hold water," she says. "You know Father would never encourage an extramarital affair nor would he recommend a divorce, particularly with Boyd's four children involved."

"You're right. I can't figure Winnie in this case. But she *is* a killer! I was in the Jewel the other day in the pickle and peanut butter aisle and two aisles over I could hear Winnie buttonholing some parishioner about putting her house on the market. You know how that brassy, breathy voice of hers carries. She says so all the store can hear, 'I don't know how you *live* with three children and only one bathroom.'"

Sue smiles at Mike's perfect imitation of Winnie's voice. She thinks about the contrast between it and Adele's calm, modulated tone: about Winnie's tall, bony body, her narrow face and large teeth, her bright red, perfectly groomed bouffant hair-do, her overwhelmingly social manner. She sighs, remembering how frequently Winnie's aggressive friendliness gets under her skin. Still, she is not going to let Mike get away with a derogatory description of her.

"You just have it in for her because she's a successful business woman," she declares loyally. "Winnie probably makes more money than most men in Lakewood."

"I'll give her that. But if I were you, I'd keep an eye on her. Don't rule her out. Have her show you a few condos or something."

"I can think of better things to do with my time."

When Sue tells Mike about the car following her the day before, she tries to make light of it. With a good deal of humor, she recounts the nightmare she had during the early morning hours in which a Camaro was trying to force her off the road into a mile-deep canyon. "It was terrifying," she says. "I woke up in this awful sweat, trembling like a leaf and hanging on to Fred for dear life. Of course, two minutes later, he rolled over and was snoring again, but I never got back to sleep at all."

Mike is more concerned about the incident than Fred had been. He thinks Sue's dream is classic Jung and right on target. The man following her was probably trying to push her off the road, that is, scare her off the case. Otherwise, he would hardly have been so obvious, so much in evidence. On the other hand, though, who even knew she was investigating Father Rossi's death? Fred was probably right. There are a lot of Camaros around. Sue finds this easy reassurance unacceptable and at her insistence, Mike calls the police station and tracks the license to a downtown Budget Car Rental. They have to leave the mystery there because people are beginning to arrive for the meeting.

Elena is one of the first to show up. She is wearing tight black stirrup pants and a long black and white argyle sweater with an enormous black cowl collar, a sophisticated outfit but one far more appropriate than her get-up of the week before. Sue thinks she is less carefully put together and far less assured and assertive. She expresses great distress over the death of Father Rossi. Why did God allow such dreadful things to happen? Why should a good priest have to die? Why should this saintly man have been taken from us while drug lords and thugs survived? Her voice trembles. Tears well up in her dark eyes. Was this all Hispanic hyperbole or was she as sad as she seemed? For someone who had met Father Rossi only the week before, her grief appears excessive.

Sue decides it will be wise to allow a brief period for the group to express their shock at Father's death. Then she firmly leads into the meeting with a prayer to the Holy Spirit. Surprisingly, it is Boyd who raises an interesting question in the discussion of Luke's infancy narrative. He had watched Joseph Campbell's TV series on mythology and remembered his suggestion that Luke's account of the birth of Christ had been taken from Greek myths concerning virgin birth. Was it possible, Boyd wanted to know, to view the virgin birth of Jesus in this way?

Sue puts the question to the group and then sits back to see how various members handle it. The differences between conservative and liberal frames of mind, the ways in which strongly held ideas shaped people's lives always fascinates her. Was it something in their chemistry or their genes that made them committed traditionalists or open-minded thinkers, that fueled their hatred of Communism or their love of social causes? Or was it all education and environment, the family you grew up in?

Because Boyd is not a Catholic, his question is received with more respect that it might otherwise have been. Nevertheless, Sister Thomasita immediately demonstrates that her old nickname of 'Tank' is no misnomer. "A myth? The idea is preposterous," she snorts, smashing into it with dismissive scorn. "Hadn't the angel announced that Jesus would be conceived by the Holy Spirit?"

Mike, with a wicked twinkle in his eye, tells Sister that he has read a reliable scientific article, which asserted that Christ must have had a human father, that to be a human person required two sets of genes. Elena, up to this point quite withdrawn, responds heatedly that God could have supplied male genes without getting them from Joseph or anyone else. Sue is amused that Mike's teasing has aroused such ardent feeling. She suggests that they are veering off track in talking about genes. She initiates a discussion of myth as the purveyor of profound meaning that turns out to be a valuable part of the meeting. Jo seems to understand immediately.

"Even as a child, fairy tales had a lot of meaning for me," she says. "I'm always annoyed when people imply that they are a waste of time for children as though there were no truth in them."

Pixie Bergman, who originally seems threatened by Boyd's question, is now interested and making an effort to understand. "Like what fairy tales?" she asks.

"Like *The Frog Prince*," says Jo. "The truth that faithfulness and love will restore the ugliest frog to his true, noble nature."

The Frog Prince, thinks Sue, is probably the story of Jo's life, of her years of devoted effort to restore Tim to sanity and sobriety. But she knows Jo won't want to go into further explanations so she invites each one of the group to state as well as they can what the birth of Christ means to them. Some answers are theological: some are simple, from the heart and very touching. All agree that their feelings about the mystery of the Incarnation, about God's entrance into the human race as a helpless newborn, are really beyond telling.

As the meeting winds up, Mike congratulates Sue on her handling of it. "For a while there," he says, "I was holding my breath. I thought they were going to cheat me out of Christmas. But in the end, it seems like the carols have had it right all along."

The expensive leather gloves left on the couch the week before turn out to be Boyd's. Winnie had given them to him for Christmas. Although it had been bitter cold that day, he had not missed them because he had an old pair to which he was attached in the car. But when he reached home, Winnie immediately noticed that he was no longer wearing his gift. She was leaving to show a house—even in that zero weather—and said she would stop by the baptistery to pick them up. When she got there, no one answered the door although she kept banging and banging on it.

"She was terribly annoyed about the whole episode," says Boyd with a whimsical smile. "My carelessness with her gift and the fact that no one responded to her knock. She's going to let Father Foley know in no uncertain terms that he should install a door bell here in the baptistery."

"I'm sure he'd be glad to do so if Winnie wants to pay the bill," says Mike. "So I suppose it was about 12:30 by the time she got back here."

"Just about, I would guess. Perhaps by that time, poor Father Paul was already dead."

"Maybe or maybe not," says Mike giving Sue a nudge with his elbow.

Sue asks if she can drive Elena home and the girl is pleased to accept her offer. Once in the car, she begins again to mourn Father Rossi's death. What a tragedy that his life was snuffed out when his future was so full of promise. He seemed to be exceptionally intelligent and talented. Surely he would have been a Cardinal one day had he survived. Again, there is that emotional tremor in her voice. Had Sue known him long? she inquires.

"Only since August when he was assigned here, but he became a good friend of my family. We miss him a lot."

"Yes," sighs Elena. "I can understand."

When they draw up in front of Elena's house, Sue asks if perhaps Winnie Harris had found it for her. It is a lovely, large Spanish stucco with a red tile roof and tall narrow windows set far back from the street. A formal avenue of evergreens leads up to an arched entrance. Sue knows that Winnie has a certain genius for matching houses to people and this seems like it might be the perfect home for the Esquivels.

"It was the first one she showed Gabriel," says Elena. "and after looking at several others, he agreed it would be fine for us. But the previous owner, an old widower who had done no decorating for years, neglected it. Gabriel says that the interior is entirely up to me but I really have no notion what to do with it. Could you come in, Sue, and maybe give me some ideas?"

"I would love to," says Sue who finds this challenge almost irresistible. "But I have to stop by to see Monsignor Fiedler and then I must get home. Fred will be chomping at the bit."

"Oh, please come in for just a minute. Just for a quick look around so you can be thinking about what I should do. I really don't know where to begin."

Sue senses a certain desperation in Elena's voice, a reluctance to let her go, a helplessness with the task Gabriel has assigned her. Her self-assurance of the week before seems to have deserted her entirely. But after all, she is very young and alone in a strange country.

"Okay," agrees Sue. "But I really can't stay long."

As they start up the walk, Phil, a long-time Lakewood postman, comes whistling along. Sue greets him cheerfully and as Elena's hands are full with her bible, her petit point and her purse, takes Elena's mail from him. On top of the usual pile of ads is a personal letter in a blue envelope. Elena's face brightens when she sees it. "Oh!" she exclaims. "A letter from my mother."

Sue examines the letter briefly, noting the foreign stamp.

"Your mother has an elegant, distinctive handwriting," she comments.

"Everyone admires it. She learned it at the convent in the old days."

But Sue is not listening. Her mind is racing, trying to make sense out of something else she has noticed on the blue envelope. The postmark is not Madrid as she had anticipated but is instead Alvarado

CHAPTER IX

Monsignor Fiedler is so happy to see Sue, all smiles and exclamations of delight, that her anger with him soon dissipates. In fact, she finds it something of a relief to pour out the whole story of Father Rossi's death to such an attentive and sympathetic listener. He leans forward in his chair, old eyes narrowed, a frown furrowing his forehead. Sue thinks a life of prayer has given him extraordinary powers of concentration. He does not miss the significance of a single detail. He asks a few questions but does not in the end question her conclusion of murder.

"Father Foley never mentioned the possibility of murder," he says. "I was already concerned for you knowing that Father's sudden death had to be a hard blow. And then you had so much work to do with all the arrangements for the funeral. I was impressed with the readings you selected and with the Gregorian chant. Do you remember, Sue, when we used to sing it every Sunday in the old days?"

"I loved it as a child growing up and I wanted the Mass to be very special. Father Foley was willing to go along with the music but he balked when it came to fresh flowers. He didn't see why the ones we had for the Cardinal on Founder's Day wouldn't be perfectly fine."

"Poor Father Foley. I'm afraid I left him with considerable debt to pay off. The archdiocese is so broke these days that they are calling for far more stringent payments on loans than was the case when I was pastor. And everything has become so expensive. Sometimes I think it would make Father Foley happy if I were to take my violin out on the street corner and set out a tin cup, a sort of just penance for the situation he inherited from me."

"He doesn't have to worry all that much. The finance committee has managed to increase our income to meet new diocesan requirements. All those niggling economies of Father Foley's are not as necessary as he thinks. Fred says he's that strangest of all anomalies, a tight Irishman. And I'm not surprised that he didn't mention murder to you. He has dismissed the idea out of hand and we are getting no co-operation whatsoever from him. He wouldn't even allow me to search Father's room."

Monsignor raises his eyebrows at this and offers Sue a welcome suggestion.

"Father Rossi's mother is coming on Monday to go through and dispose of his belongings. I would just guess that she might welcome some help from our Minister of Care."

"What a perfect opportunity!" exclaims Sue. "And Father was also no help when I asked him about Father Rossi's work at the Chancery. Do you know anything about it that might give us some clues?"

"He had an administrative job at the Catholic Missions Office. He didn't talk about it much except to fill us in on the Archdiocesan Partnership in Chilpaningo Chilapa in Mexico. That's a recent venture that interested him a lot. The Mission Office serves as link to some 950 dioceses throughout the world so it's not an unimportant job. Still, I was surprised when the Cardinal assigned him there some ten years ago now. He had been such a challenging and inspiring parish assistant that I would have expected the Cardinal to reward his pastoral talents by giving him a parish of his own. But I suppose that they need innovative men at the Chancery too."

Sue finds herself hungry for as much information about Father Rossi as she can gather. Anything she can learn about him might provide insights into possible motivations for his murder but beyond that, such late learning compensates a little for all she feels she missed when he was taken from them.

"Then you knew Father Rossi as a young priest?" she asks.

"I first met him when he was at St. Mary's Seminary. It was just after the conclusion of Vatican II and since I had worked on the preparatory commission on the Liturgy, I was asked to teach a course in it up there. Rossi was a student in my class and surprised me by asking if I would be his Spiritual Director. The Seminary usually provides directors, so it took a little arranging but I was happy to agree.

"He seemed to think I was of some help to him, but actually I simply provided a sounding board. He had very clear spiritual goals and was, at least at that time, spared the anguish and indecision that some young seminarians endure. I can remember only one crisis and he came though that with flying colors." Monsignor smiles, remembering this instance from the past.

"Can you tell me about it?"

"Well, I don't know why not. It was in the sixties, a time when a lot of educated young Americans sounding like Jeremiah the prophet (and looking like him too, with long hair and wild eyes and torn jeans) were condemning the Vietnam War, burning draft cards and making dire predictions about the death of the establishment. Of course all this agitation and unrest had repercussions in the seminary where emotional and divisive arguments sometimes erupted among students or between students and faculty. But Rossi kept his cool though all this excitement. He had an ability to see issues from both sides and to present his own convictions calmly so that people listened to him.

"Because he was so objective in various discussions we had, I think I had presumed that he was not deeply involved in the issues. But here I was mistaken. During one of our sessions he declared that it was imperative that he join a civil rights march in Alabama. The rector had refused permission for him to go and this presented a serious problem for him. He said that the injustice and abuse of the colored people in the

South could not be countenanced by any man with a conscience and he felt strongly—I would say passionately though he hardly raised his voice—that he must stand up and be counted as opposed to them. He absolutely had to be present at the next march. Although he had talked with the Rector several times, he was adamant in his refusal.

"Rossi stated in clear and unequivocal terms that he had absolutely no doubt about his vocation to the priesthood. However, if being a priest meant that he could not express his conscience in realistic and effective ways, then he might have to reconsider his vocation. He felt that being a true Christian came first and the priesthood, important as it was to him, would have to be secondary. He said he had prayed a good deal about the matter and was prepared to leave the seminary if the Rector insisted on denying him the necessary permission.

"Well, I reflected a lot on that conversation because so much of Rossi's character seemed to surface in it and it was my responsibility to guide him in spiritual matters. You could see clearly in this one situation qualities I had already recognized: the serious consideration he gave to matters of conscience, the quiet, determined way in which he translated ideals into action. His threshold between the ideal and the real was probably the lowest of any person I have ever known. By that, I mean whatever inspirations he received from the Holy Spirit, he put into immediate effect. He was never an ineffectual dreamer like so many of us."

"I know. It was something Fred and I really admired in him. But what happened about the march?"

"Oh yes, the march. Well, I remember another thing crossed my mind at that time. Once Rossi had asked me what I would have been had I not been a priest and I told him that probably I would have been an impecunious musician or possibly an impecunious fine arts professor and what did he think he would be if he were not a priest? He smiled and said probably a politician. He had a conviction that much could be accomplished through government and politics. And another facet of his character was that he was himself a pretty good politician. So in this situation about the march I had to take that into consideration. He certainly was in earnest about wanting to demonstrate for civil rights but was he entirely in earnest about leaving the priesthood in order to do it or was a bit of arm-twisting going on.

"When I inquired about this possibility, he simply crossed his arms and thrust out his underlip in a way he had when he was going to be stubborn. I see you smiling so you recognize that stance of his. And he simply said, I have to go, Father.

"So I decided to have a talk with the Rector. He said that the question of obedience was involved and that he didn't feel it was appropriate for him to backtrack on his decision. He suggested that if Rossi were to go over his head to the Cardinal, he would abide by his decision. The cardinal—it wasn't Cardone back then of course—didn't like the idea. What if all his seminarians took it into their heads to start running off to marches and demonstrations? On the other hand, vocations were already beginning to dwindle and he certainly didn't want to lose such a bright prospect for ordination. He gave his consent but he didn't forget the incident and when he gave Rossi his first assignment, he sent him to a very poor black parish on the south side.

"If Rossi recognized that he was being sent to Siberia, he never acknowledged it. He simply rolled up his sleeves and went to work. In addition to recruiting excellent black teachers for the school, he improved the discipline and curriculum and in a few years, had doubled the enrollment. He was instrumental in starting a gospel choir that became quite famous locally. But perhaps his most important contribution was helping his parishioners set up various advocacy groups that brought needed government help into the community. Until then, the church had had little experience or know-how in plugging the poor of their parishes into the political system.

"But none of this gives us any clues about the murder. All we really have so far is this puzzle about the young woman who claims to be from

Spain but whose mother writes her from Alvarado, an interesting lead since Father had those coins in his pocket. And then a pen we can't trace and the strange missing weapon—a hair dryer. I suppose Mike searched all the disposal bins in the area?"

"He was very thorough. He never turned up anything like that, but he did turn up a police record of Jens that we feel has to be taken seriously. The fact that he murdered his wife a number of years ago, that he was at the scene of the crime at the approximate time of the murder and that he responded to questions very evasively makes him our prime suspect at the moment."

"Jens? Oh, no Sue! No matter how incriminating the circumstances may be, I'm certain it wasn't Jens who killed Father Rossi!"

"But how can you be so sure? We know he was angry with Father Rossi at the time. If he actually murdered his wife, he must be capable of violence. And we all know what a queer duck he is."

"Odd, yes. One of God's more unique creatures. But a good man, and quite incapable of willfully killing anyone. Perhaps if I told you the story of his wife's death and the circumstances that led up to it, you would understand that it should not in any way incriminate him."

Sue looks at her watch, slips off her coat and settles back in her chair. Monsignor's stories usually began at the beginning and seldom omitted significant details. It is growing late, but after all, this is exactly what she had come to hear.

CHAPTER X

While visiting Jens in the Joliet prison, Monsignor had eventually been able to piece his story together. It had been difficult to make friends with the man. To receive communion each week seemed to mean a great deal to him but he was depressed, withdrawn, and not very trusting of anyone. It took many visits to put the scraps of his story together in any chronological order. When he had finally done so, Monsignor had presented it to the parole board. Possibly it won Jens an earlier release than he might otherwise have had.

Jens was born in the small agricultural town of Abstadt, Germany and had just turned fifteen when the Third Reich invaded Poland in 1939. He was one of five sons who up to that time had worked the family farm, enjoying a life of hard labor, prosperity and small town pleasure. But Hitler's campaigns had radically changed their lives. His father was killed in the invasion of Denmark, his oldest brother died in Yugoslavia. Jens himself barely survived the Normandy invasion at the end of the war. When he returned home in 1945, he discovered that, with the men away and money in short supply, his mother had found it necessary to sell a portion of their farmland. Even if it had been retained, it is unlikely that Jens, with three older brothers, could have made his living there.

His uncle, his mother's brother, lived in Chicago and was trying to arrange for Jens to emigrate to the United States. Monsignor had no idea what the immigration policy concerning German citizens was at that time but there seems to have been complications and delays in Jens' case. In the meantime, he went to work on the farm of a neighboring widow. She had only two daughters to help her and because Jens was such an industrious worker, she soon assigned full responsibility for the farm to him. He continued to live at home and to save every penny for his passage to America.

Today Germany is so affluent that it is easy to forget the bitter desolation that existed there following the war. Monsignor was convinced that in a different time Helga never would have married Jens. Helga was the daughter of the widow for whom Jens worked, a pretty, vivacious girl with a slender waist and page-boy hair which fell provocatively over one eye. She was sixteen when Jens came home from the war and there is no question that he immediately fell in love with her. He saw a good deal of her since he took his noon meal with her family and often ran into her in the vicinity of the house. He anticipated these contacts with delight and remembered them with something close to exaltation but it never occurred to him to initiate a courtship with her. She was a flirtatious girl, popular with the young men of the village and had suitors far more attractive than he. An intimate relationship seemed an impossible dream.

But it was a year when dreams sustained the spirit of the impoverished people of Abstadt. Jens' dream of adventure in a new land was hedged by reluctance to leave Helga but his mother's dreams knew no such restraint. Jens would have a fine life in America far from the mud and muck of their neighbor's farm where he broke his back for such paltry wages.

Of course the widow too heard of these bright prospects for Jens' future. Everyone knew that If you worked hard in America you could get ahead and she was quite aware that Jens was a steady, reliable worker. Jens never used the word "shrewd" to describe the widow but Monsignor felt that she had played her cards carefully. She encouraged

Jens to date Helga, she agreed eventually to an engagement but postponed the wedding until Jens had passport and papers in hand. The young couple had a week together before Jens sailed. The understanding was that when he had found work and established a decent home for her, he would send for Helga.

Even though parting from his new wife was painful, Jens could not get over his good luck in marrying her. His uncle Otto owned a comfortable home in an old German neighborhood northwest of the Chicago loop. He had several children and had no room to offer Jens but provided a cot for him in the basement. He was a ward committeeman with political connections and was able to get Jens a maintenance job at the Board of Education. Jens worked from five in the evening until one in the morning mopping marble floors and vacuuming offices. Because of his hours, he saw little of the family and rarely took meals with them.

It was an enormously lonely year for Jens. On his one night off, he took an English class at the local high school but it was a long time before he could master the language well enough to converse. He had no idea what to do with his daylight hours but eventually his uncle got him a second part-time job through the park district as a gardener in the Lincoln Park conservatory. This work he loved. He could hardly wait to show Helga the tropical trees and exotic flowers that he tended there, to take her to the splendid lily show at Easter or to see the glorious display of chrysanthemums in the fall.

In fact, Jens spent the entire year longing and waiting for Helga's coming. He was intent on acquiring enough money for a down payment on a house. He put aside every penny that he earned. In good weather he walked to work to save the carfare. His uncle was a big man, close enough to his own size so that Jens wore whatever clothes he discarded. When he had accumulated a sizable sum, his uncle helped Jens find a small frame house he could afford on a street of modest homes in his own German neighborhood. It had a brick foundation and was well constructed but was badly in need of paint and repairs. So now Jens spent all his spare time hammering and sanding and papering, getting everything shipshape as Helga would be coming soon. He had already sent her money for her passage and, at the widow's insistence, a sizable amount for clothes for the trip.

As time grew short, Jens spotted one last surprise for Helga that he was determined to get before she arrived. In the window of a North Avenue second hand store, he had seen an electric sewing machine. It seemed to him a miraculous escape from the drudgery of the treadle everyone still used in Abstadt and the perfect American gift for his wife who had been taking sewing lessons from old Hans the tailor back home. The machine was expensive but the storeowner agreed to let him pay for it in installments. Still, with the cost of the clothes for Helga, he was not going to be able to make the last few payments in time for her arrival. Although it humiliated him a good deal, he asked his uncle for a small loan to complete the payments. When he had installed the machine in the tiny upstairs dormer bedroom, he felt satisfied that at last everything was ready.

Sue could tell that Monsignor had been touched by the story of the sewing machine and she too found it a detail indicative of a loving man. But when Monsignor began to describe the young couple's meeting at Union Station, Sue was amused. He said that when Helga stepped off the train, she was wearing a fashionable summer suit with a peplum, a little pill box hat, tilted over one eye and shiny patent leather shoes with high, spiky heels. Did Jens ever describe these clothes or were they just what Monsignor imagined from Jens' remark that she looked far more beautiful and sophisticated than the secretaries he saw leaving the Board of Education each evening?

At first Jens felt like an utter oaf standing there in his uncle's suit with his sleeves and trousers much too short for him. The shyness and self-consciousness he had experienced in Helga's presence when he first returned from the war overwhelmed him. But Helga seemed scarcely to notice him. She was bubbling with excitement. The great height of the cavernous station, the tall buildings and glimpse of the river on the taxi ride home, all enchanted her. If the house seemed smaller and the street meaner than she had imagined them, she said nothing about it.

For a while everything went well. Between the evening classes she attended with her husband and the radio she listened to constantly, Helga quickly picked up the language, becoming far more fluent in English than Jens ever would. His Aunt Helen took a fancy to Helga and had them often for Sunday dinner. When Helga had mastered a minimum of conversational skill, Helen helped her find a position as a seamstress at Carson's doing fittings and hems in the dress department. Jens' uncle was trying to arrange full time work for him at the conservatory so that he could relinquish his night job, but in the meantime he continued with it. For one thing, Helga had set her heart on a refrigerator to replace the wooden icebox in their pantry. Everything took money.

To celebrate Helga's nineteenth birthday, Uncle Otto took them out for dinner at a German tavern on North Avenue where the bartender was a friend of his. It was an old-fashioned neighborhood place with a long mahogany bar, red check tablecloths and excellent food. The bartender gave them a royal welcome, the friendly waitress fussed over them, the savory lamb shanks were delicious. Helga was particularly pleased with the music. When the young accordion player discovered it was her birthday, he played all the songs she requested and soon the whole restaurant joined in the singing. It was a wonderful, festive evening. Jens enjoyed it immensely but his greatest pleasure was to see Helga so happy.

Knowing what happened in the end, Monsignor had discreetly questioned Jens about his relationship with Helga and about their social life together. It seems that Helga felt she was too young to start a family and rarely wished to make love. Jens reluctantly acceded to her wishes but he felt that they had good times together.

Sunday was their special day. Helga loved the grandeur of St. Michael's church with its long flight of steps ascending to the entrance and at noon they attended high Mass there. Then they were off on an outing. Sometimes they took a picnic to the lake, sitting on the sun-drenched rocks watching sailboats skid by in the wind or strolled through the Lincoln Park Zoo munching popcorn or took a bus in the evening to see Buckingham Fountain when the lights were playing on it. Jens remembered a boat ride in the park lagoons when Helga, trailing a hand in the water, laughed at the baby ducks following them and sang lullabies to them. How could Jens have guessed that anything was wrong?

It was his uncle who had to tell Jens what his bartender friend told him, that Helga was spending her evenings in the German tavern drinking beer and flirting with the men who gathered there. She and the handsome accordion player seemed to have quite a thing going. They enjoyed singing together and received a lot of applause for their performance. He often joined her at her table and walked her home when the tavern closed at midnight. On two occasions recently, an insomniac neighbor reported he had seen them enter Jens' house about eleven and the musician had not left until close to one o'clock.

Jens refused to believe these stories, stubbornly denying that there was any truth in them. But his uncle insisted that he must talk to his wife about the matter, that he must be very firm with her and that he must give notice at the Board of Education that he was quitting his night job. Surely full hours at the conservatory would be available soon. Still, Jens insisted that it could not be true, that it was all gossip, so his uncle suggested that he leave work some night soon on the pretext that he was ill and come home unexpectedly to see for himself what was going on.

Jens agreed to do this. When he arrived home about eight o'clock, he found Helga sitting at the kitchen table painting red polish on her nails. She was wearing a black-and-white dirndl dress with a tight fitting bodice and low neckline. Her black high-heeled shoes and black velvet band of ribbon in her blond hair completed her outfit. She looked lovely, Jens thought. She was humming happily to herself when he entered the room.

The rest of the story is ugly. Jens confronted her with the bartender's stories as his uncle had insisted that he must. She did not deny them but asked petulantly what she was supposed to do, sit in this dumpy, dingy little house all by herself night after night? A girl had to have some fun in life. When Jens brought up the accordion player, Helga did not have the grace to blush but smiled secretly to herself and refused to answer his accusations. She said the musician was a gentleman and she was going this very evening to sing with him at the tavern. He better not try to stop her.

Jens had felt less threatened on the battlefield in Normandy. He was certain that his marriage, his whole life and happiness were at stake. He stated in no uncertain terms that Helga was not to leave the house. He would soon be home in the evenings and everything would be all right again.

Screwing on the top of the nail polish bottle with a vicious twist, Helga said he had it all wrong, she was leaving for the tavern right this minute. She got up and tried to push past him at the doorway. He grabbed her by her upper arms and backed her up into the kitchen. "You must not go, you cannot go!" he cried. She fought hard to escape his grasp. She called him names, derogatory German names that were the equivalent of stupid ass and pig-headed moron. Jens began to sob great heaving sobs of distress and anger. He gripped her arms again and began to shake her.

"Helga!" he pleaded. "Helga! Please don't do this. Please come to your senses."

"They were struggling in front of the stove," Monsignor said, "one of those old-fashioned black stoves that you probably would not remember. It had a warming oven above the range and at the corner of this oven, an iron hook on which to hang potholders. Helga, who teetered at any time on her spiky heels, lost her balance in her effort to free herself. Her feet skid out from under her, she fell backwards against the stove, the hook cut deeply into the base of her skull. Jens had not pushed her. In fact, he thought it was just as he let go of her arms that it happened."

Well, Sue knew the rest of the story, the conviction of manslaughter and the incarceration at the Joliet prison. His aunt never forgave Jens and refused to visit him. Uncle Otto came to see him less and less as time went on.

Of course Jens must have been always a somewhat gross and homely man, but is it so hard to imagine what he may have been like when he was young, happily in love and full of hope? Monsignor felt that this tragic event had radically changed him, made him introverted and suspicious of everyone. It had taken much prayer with him to convince him that God had forgiven him. It is less certain that he ever forgave himself.

Just at the conclusion of Monsignor's story, the phone rings. It is Nora calling from the rectory to ask if she should be keeping his luncheon plate warm or had he been out on the town for his noon day meal? Monsignor assures her that he will be right over and Sue, suddenly realizing how late it has become, is about to depart in a hurry when Monsignor detains her.

"Sue? Can an old priest give you a piece of advice?"

"Of course."

"You look as lovely as ever, dear," Monsignor says, "but perhaps a bit hollow-eyed. I know you've been under a lot of stress and have had a lot of work to do. But promise me, Sue, that you'll try not to race your motor."

"Now you sound like Fred," Sue chides him. "A bit more secular than spiritual."

"Well, let me put it as St. Francis de Sales did in his *Introduction to the Devout Life.* Examine more than once during the day whether you have your soul in your hands or whether some passion or anxiety has not robbed you of it. I know from long experience that you'll find such a practice helpful."

"Could be just what I need. I haven't stopped to pray much lately."

Nevertheless, Sue's mind is still racing as she drives the short distance to her house. She had certainly been sympathetic to Jens' story but less sure than Monsignor that it eliminated him as a suspect. Who knew that he had not pushed Helga? Perhaps Jens himself couldn't be certain. And if he had become violent when he felt threatened years ago, was it not possible that he had done so again? The picture of the sharp kitchen hook penetrating poor Helga's skull haunts Sue, filling her with horror.

Ellen has been watching out the window for her mother's arrival. She meets her in the hall, greeting her in a sort of breathless frenzy.

"Mom, what on earth kept you so long? Dad got an emergency call from the hospital and he had to track me down to sit with Jennifer. Believe me, he wasn't very happy that you didn't come home when you said you would."

"An emergency?" said Sue. "Do you know what happened?"

"Some drunken driver ran into Cindy Downs on her bike on Trent Road. I guess he was breaking the speed limit by a zillion."

"Was she badly hurt?" Cindy is a friend of Sarah, a skinny, quick-witted girl whom they all love. Sue is alarmed and concerned for her.

"He ran into the rear wheel of her bike and she bounced off hitting her head on the pavement. It knocked her unconscious but they didn't know much when he called. Mom, do you think she's going to be okay?"

"Let's pray that she is. Where is Jennifer, honey?"

"She's in the breakfast room with Jens showing him the fish tank."

"Jens!" cries Sue. "For God's sake, what is Jens doing in our house?" The thought that he had been here alone with her children frightens her badly.

Tears sprang up in Ellen's eyes. "Now what have I done wrong?" she cries. "Can't I ever do anything right? He came to see you and didn't you always tell us all that stuff about whoever comes to the door is Christ and welcome them? So I said you'd be right back and would he wait and Jennifer said would he like to see the x-ray tetra so I don't see why you have to get so mad at me."

Time for one of Monsignor's pauses! Sue stops dead still for a moment until the silence of God seems to sing in her ears. Then she takes a deep breath and puts her arms around Ellen. "I'm so sorry, honey," she says. "You did just the right thing. I'll go see what he wants."

CHAPTER XI

"Fred, can you hang on a minute? Jens is here and I just want to see him to the door."

"What's Jens doing there?"

"He stopped by to bring me an absolutely heavenly hibiscus with huge orange blossoms. Wait 'til you see it." Sue smiles at Jens who stands awkwardly in the doorway. "I just want to say goodbye to him. I'll be right back."

"Well, make it snappy. I'm calling from the hospital."

When she returns to the phone, Sue immediately inquires about how badly Cindy Downs is injured. Fred says she had regained consciousness in the ambulance and while there were symptoms of a mild concussion, these had disappeared quickly. He feels she is going to be fine. However, her jaw is broken and he is now about to leave her in the care of Dr. Anderson who will do the setting and wiring. But Fred has something else on his mind as well. "Mike called from the police station to say that he is holding Tim James there on charges of theft, drunken driving and breach of separation contract. He's throwing the whole book at him trying to keep him there until…"

"Are you telling me it was Tim who hit Cindy?" gasps Sue.

"Well, yes, that's what I'm telling you. I guess he took a bus out from Evanston this morning and arrived at Jo's high as a kite. He's only supposed to come on Sundays and then only if sober so Jo called Mike to come and evict him. They had a prior agreement that she should do that in case of trouble. When Tim overheard this phone call, he ran out of the house and took Jo's car…"

"What about his own car?"

"I guess he'd sold it for cash. Anyway, he went tearing up Trent Road at an incredible speed and slammed into Cindy's rear bike wheel just as she reached the curb. He knew he had done it and came to a screeching stop. A neighbor who saw it all called an ambulance and the police. Mike was right on it and took Tim to the station. He's holding him until he will agree to go into the St. Luke Hospital Detox Center."

Sue listens attentively, trying to absorb this shocking news. "Sooner or later, something was bound to happen," she says. "Is there anything we can do to help?"

"That's why I'm calling. Mike has talked to Jo. He wants her and the boys to come down and have one of those family confrontations where they all gang up on Tim and tell him what his drinking has done to them, a hell of a business but I guess it brings reality home in some cases."

"I know," says Sue. "Jo has tried that before but Tim always threatened to go to the basement, go to the attic, go for a walk, always too slippery for them to hang on to 'til they got the job done."

"Mike is probably right, then. He seems to think they'd have a better chance and better control down at the station. Tim's been drinking up a storm ever since the separation three weeks ago and they are both scared he'll do himself in if they can't get him into the hospital soon. Anyway, I'm going to meet Mike at the police station and he hoped you could pick up Jo and the boys and bring them down there. He thought Jo could use your support."

"Of course," Sue agrees. "I'll stop by for them right now."

Ellen was at Sue's elbow waiting for news of Cindy. "Is she going to be okay?" she asks anxiously.

"She's going to be fine. She has a broken jaw but Dr. Anderson is going to fix that for her. But I tell you what, Ellen. I have to take the Jameses down to the police station to pick up Uncle Tim and I want you to stay with Jennifer. Sarah's not going to be home 'til five…"

"Was Uncle Tim the one who hit Cindy?" Ellen interrupts.

"He didn't mean to. It was an accident."

"And he was dead drunk," says Ellen bitterly. "He can be such a great guy. Why does he have to get blitzed all the time? I really feel sorry for Gerry and Timmy. But Mom, I forgot to tell you. Mrs. Bergman called and she wants Jennifer to play with Roger this afternoon so maybe she could go there and I could go back to Betsy's."

"Fine. I'll drop her off on my way. Remember, though, don't be late for supper."

Driving down Green Bay to the police station, Jo sits in the front seat with Sue, the two boys, very sober and quiet, in the back. In stressful situations, Jo assumes what Sue thinks of as her "white look." An extreme pallor robs her fair skin of all color, fine lines converge on her almond-shaped, sharply focused eyes, and a firm set to her small, delicate chin prevents it from trembling. Today, in spite of these signs of nervous tension, she seems steady, calm, resolute as, with an arm over the back of the seat, she turns to talk to her sons.

"I know you hate doing this," she says. "But you have to think of it as our one big chance. It may get Dad started on the right track and keep him there. Remember, all you have to do is tell the truth about what he's done when he's been drinking and how it has affected you."

"Sure," says Gerry. "And all he'll do is say the same old thing, that he never could have done anything like that. Not him, the perfect gentleman."

Gerry is a tall, skinny eighth grader whose arms and legs seem too long for his body and whose voice has grown husky overnight. He looks like his father, has the same curly hair, heavy brows, generous mouth, quirky smile and, until recently, the same light touch and quick humor.

But lately he has become sullen and often bitterly sarcastic. He is frowning now, thick brows drawn tight together.

"Gerry, please don't give up on him," says Jo. "This accident with Cindy must have brought reality home somewhat. It gives us an opening, an opportunity. Please try this one more time."

"But he'll get so mad at us," says Timmy.

Sue catches a glimpse of Timmy in her rear view mirror. He is sitting forward on the seat in nervous anticipation of the grim meeting ahead of him. Ten years old, just Sarah's age, he is smaller than she, a thin, frail child with hunched shoulders and a timid voice. He has luminously clear gray eyes and a generous sprinkling of freckles across his narrow nose, features which Sue finds immensely appealing. She knows that his excruciating shyness and faltering self-esteem break Jo's heart. No matter how hard she has tried, she has not been able to compensate for what his father's illness has done to this sensitive child.

"Yes," says Jo. "We know that he'll probably get very angry. But don't let that make you feel that you are doing the wrong thing. You've got to have courage to speak up, Timmy, to tell the truth about how things have been and how you feel about them. Do you think you can do that?"

"Even the worst things?" asks Tim. "I mean, do we have to tell him stuff that's really awful?"

"That's the idea, Tim. If he can be made to see how seriously his drinking impacts our lives, then he will have to stop denying that he has a problem. If you get a little scared remember that what you say may help him to get well. Just remember what a great father Dad is when he's sober."

"That's getting harder to remember all the time," says Gerry.

"Gerry, please."

"Okay, okay. We'll be the world's best witnesses, right Timmy?"

"I guess," says Timmy.

Sue has known Jo's boys since they were born, had in fact been pregnant with Ellen and Sarah when Jo was carrying Gerry and Timmy so that you could almost say since conception. She and Fred had been close to the family during the onset of Tim's alcoholism, a time when they had hatched many schemes to straighten him out. But none of these had worked. Gradually they came to realize how helpless they were, that there was nothing they could do but remain loyal friends. During rough periods when the boys were small, they spent considerable time at Sue's home and occasionally Timmy still stayed the night. They seldom discussed their problems with Sue nor did she ever refer to them. They knew she knew and this tacit understanding seemed to be exactly what they needed.

Sue longs to say something that will reassure Timmy but she feels it is best to let Jo handle the situation. Still, maybe she could help the boy focus on the fact that the ordeal, no matter how threatening, would soon be over.

"Listen," she says, "when you guys get through, maybe you'd like to come back to my house. We can order up some pizza for supper and watch the Bull's game, okay?"

"Sounds good to me," says Gerry.

But Timmy keeps biting his underlip and staring straight ahead as though he has not heard her. Sue can see that the thought of having to face down his bellicose father, having to challenge him in a way that is guaranteed to arouse anger and release a torrent of abusive language has caught Timmy in the grip of an overpowering fear. She wonders if it is really wise to place the child under such pressure even if the result should be favorable. She begins praying that God will give courage and strength to this poor little bruised reed. Jo is preoccupied with her own thoughts and Sue prays for her too and for Gerry as in tense silence they drive down the dreary winter road toward town. But the quiet is almost unbearable and she decides to break it, to try again.

"Timmy," she says. "You know this is all going to be over soon and then we'll go back to my house. What kind of pizza do you think you'd like for supper?"

Timmy does look up then but all he says is, "I don't feel much like pizza right now."

The young sergeant at the counter in the police station seemed to know Gerry and greets him amiably. He asks them to take seats while he calls Lieutenant O'Connor. Squeezing into a space next to Timmy on a long leather bench, Sue puts her hand on his shoulder. "Mike will be there, you know," she says. "It'll all go more smoothly than you think." She is pleased to see that his face brightens perceptibly at this assurance.

Before long, Mike and Fred appear in the doorway. Sue, who has been feeling apprehensive for the family and somewhat uptight about how this meeting may work out, is grateful for the solid reassurance of Fred's hug. Mike gives Jo a brief kiss in greeting and claps each boy on the back. He asks them to follow him to the conference room on the second floor.

"We'll wait for you here," says Sue.

Jo looks at her in a beseeching, almost apologetic way. "I'd love you to come too if you don't mind," she says. "Tim's used to turning us off, but if you and Fred had something to say, I think he might listen to you. I'd really appreciate it a lot."

"Anything we can do to help," says Fred.

The police station is one of the oldest buildings in Lakewood. It is a brick structure with large, square rooms, thick walls and walnut paneled dados. It is on the Historical Society's preservation list and there have been endless wrangles at village meetings about what remodeling should and should not be done. Perhaps to distract herself as they follow Mike, Sue keeps looking for the computer office. But then she pauses deliberately at the deeply recessed window outside the conference room to collect her thoughts. She had not anticipated participating in this meeting with poor Tim and feels totally unprepared for it. She wants to help but it is important to her that she not humiliate him. What could she possibly say that might make a difference?

She stands staring at the street outside with its double row of bare chestnut trees bristling in the gray winter air. In the long central island of the court, the brick paths of summer wind through dead garden beds. A cold wind skitters dry leaves along the walks and snaps the awnings of the shops. A few people hurry by, intent on the undramatic errands of everyday. The scene seems dismal, somehow distant and indifferent to the crisis the James family is facing. For some incomprehensible reason, it deeply saddens her. Then, by a subtle maneuver of her subconscious, a memory, clear in all its details, nudges its way into her mind, fitting itself into her melancholy like the missing piece of a puzzle. She knows now why she is sad and what she must say to Tim.

"Sue?" It is Mike holding open the door of the conference room for her.

"Coming," she says.

The family is seated around a rectangular oak table, Gerry slouched carelessly at one end and Tim sitting upright at the other. He is wearing a white shirt open at the neck and one of his expensive sports jackets. Except for a light beard and a somewhat filmy aspect to his eyes, he looks fine. Someone who did not know him might never guess he had been drinking. But Sue has learned from experience that his rigid, erect posture is a telling giveaway. A slim man, a natty dresser who often wears ascot scarves and tasseled loafers, Tim's ordinary posture tends to be casual, to have a languid grace about it. He only assumes this military bearing when he is trying to hold himself together.

"Sue darling," he exclaims jovially, "So you too have come to join the party. Do sit down and make yourself comfortable."

With a grandiose gesture of hospitality, Tim indicates the chair next to him, one which the children obviously have avoided. Sue had hoped to sit next to Timmy on the far side of the table but when she observes that Fred has an arm across the back of the boy's chair, she feels certain that his protective presence is all that Timmy needs. She slides into the chair next to Tim.

The century-old, ornate, iron radiator in the corner is hissing steam and the air in the room is close. She finds Tim's alcoholic breath, which smells to her like cantaloupe rinds rotting on a hot summer day, almost overpowering. She knows that Jo contends with a myriad of serious problems but she wonders how her friend could stand this minor detail, this foul scent of sweet decay, day in and day out. For a moment it distracts her from the task at hand.

Tim has turned to Jo who is seated at his left and, holding his head very high, peers down at her as though his haughty glance might further reduce her petite size. Jo has pushed her chair back from the table, crossed her legs and folded her arms under her small, firm breasts. She has a ballerina's body, slender, muscular, poised. Her back is very straight, her face taut and determined. She seems altogether resistant, Sue thinks, to her husband's withering gaze.

"Jo dear," he asks in a long-suffering, condescending tone, "Are these all the guests you have invited or are we to expect others?"

"This is it," Jo says. "and we aren't here for some kind of a party. Everyone at this table is concerned about you and wants to help you realize that you have a serious alcoholic problem and that you should go into St. Luke's detox to sober up and get a serious start on the AA program."

This seems like a clear, straightforward statement and, while possibly provocative, Sue is unprepared for Tim's violent reaction to it.

"I'm not going into any God-damned hospital," he shouts, slamming his fist down on the table. "I don't know who the hell you think you are to so grossly exaggerate the situation with our good friends here. It's true I may have a bit taken but you have to expect a guy to polish off a few drinks if his wife kicks him out of his home and refuses to let him visit with his own kids."

This last statement is burdened with so much self-pity and resentment that Sue finds it hard to tolerate. Jo, however, responds to it promptly.

"Tim" she says. "I want you to look at me and listen to every word I say. No, look here, right here at me. I want you to remember that the reason we agreed on a separation was not because you had a bit taken as you say but because you have been drinking heavily for eight years and have made life unbearable for all of us. You have lost your business..."

"If it weren't for that sanctimonious Charlie Phillips at the bank, I'd still have my store", interrupts Tim. "You do business with a man for years and then when you're a little behind in the game, he refuses to give you a loan to get started again. I'd like to blast..."

"Tim," interrupts Sue, putting her hand on his arm, "you know I've been thinking a lot about you and your store and what a terrific interior decorator you were. You always had such great respect for these old homes on the North Shore and a special talent for improving them in appropriate but innovative ways. Everyone agreed that you understood what the architecture of a house required, what colors or textures were needed to highlight the woodwork, what fabrics or designs would lighten up or give weight to a room. And you had a remarkable knack of combining your unerring instinct for the right thing with the customer's desires, sometimes a negotiated compromise worthy of a diplomat."

"No question," says Tim with inflated pride and arrogance, "no question but I am the best God-damned decorator in the whole area. Phillip's was a stupid ass not to make me a loan. I'll show him some day."

"I think you will," says Sue. "but only after you get into the hospital and make a good start on the AA program. I was just now looking out the window at Chestnut Court and it reminded me of an evening before Christmas when I ran into you there. Do you remember? You were walking from the station looking for your car. You couldn't recall where you had parked it so you were wandering up and down the street carrying a heavy book of fabric samples. You were obviously a bit stiff but still quite distinguished looking in that great coat of yours, the one with the cape."

"You like that coat?" inquires Tim.

"I love it," says Sue. "But somehow it just broke my heart to see you lugging that heavy book around months after the shop had closed. It was as if clinging to a remnant like that gave you the illusion that you were still in business, some sense of still being the man you once were."

"I think those textiles were reproductions of Italian tapestries," says Tim irrelevantly. "Very beautiful."

Was he listening at all or just plucking at little threads of thought to distract himself from what she was saying? At any rate, Sue decides to continue.

"I saw you give up the search for the car and plunk yourself down on a stone bench near the fountain. The trees were all strung with Italian lights and a flurry of snow was falling past the shop windows and to see you sitting there looking so tired and dejected in the middle of that lovely Christmas scene touched me deeply."

"So you sat down next to me," says Tim.

"You do remember then?"

"Not really but it would be like Sue to sit down next to the bum on the park bench."

"What got to me," says Sue, "was the way you kept hugging that book. Tim, I guess what I am trying to say is that there is no way you would have lost your business if you were not an alcoholic. Long before your investments flopped, way before Charlie turned you down on the loan, you were losing ground. There were complaints about late deliveries, slipshod work, mistaken orders. You simply were no longer able to do a good job. So what I hope and pray is that you'll get into the hospital and give yourself a chance to recoup your business."

"We had a lot of help problems," says Tim. "Remember Jo? People kept quitting or not showing up. You can't do a good job without competent help."

Sue sighs. She supposes that this is what people meant by denial. It is clear that what she thought might be an inspired approach has not made a dent. But it soon becomes obvious that they are going to play a game of keep the pot boiling. Without missing a beat, Jo picks up where she leaves off.

"No, Tim," she says. "It was really the other way around. The help left because you were drinking. So you've lost your business, lost your friends and caused your family untold grief. Just the anxiety we have suffered over your drinking and driving has been enough to give us a history of constant panic attacks. And now today the thing we all feared has actually happened. You mowed down little Cindy on her bike."

Tim seems to sober up at the mention of Cindy. "Mike says she's going to pull through, thank God for that," he says. But almost immediately, he eases himself into a defensive position. "I didn't exactly mow her down," he says. "Wasn't there going to be a village ordinance about kids not riding their bikes in the street?"

Mike has not joined them at the table but is standing near the door as though to guard against any sudden effort by Tim to depart. Sue feels that he has had no intention of participating in the conversation but now he firmly interjects a comment of his own.

"She was not riding in the street, she was crossing at the walk and had plenty of time to safely reach the other side if you had not been speeding."

"You might have been speeding too if your wife had called the cops on you."

Sue sees Timmy grasp the seat of his chair on either side and hears him clear his throat a couple of times.

"Dad," he ventures cautiously, "don't you care about Cindy? Cause I care a lot. I feel awful that she's in the hospital with her jaw all smashed up. She's Sarah's best friend and they're in my class and how do you think I'm gonna feel when I go back to school on Monday and all the kids know my father..."

"Toughen up, pipsqueak," snorts Tim. "For God's sake don't be such a wishy-washy worrying about what other people think all the time."

No one could miss the derisive put-down in the way his father dismisses the child's comments. Sue, who is watching him, thought Timmy received it like a slap in the face. He swallows hard a couple of times and then says in a shrill, angry voice, "Dad, you don't get what I said. I'm just plain tired of having to be ashamed of you all the time. And maybe I'm a lot tougher than you think."

Tim smashes his fist down on the table and roars, "Don't you *dare* talk to your father like that! I've brought you up to have respect for your parents and I will not tolerate any of this smart-ass talk from you, do you hear? You damned well better hear or I'll see that you get yours. Then we'll see how tough you are. And now you can get the hell out of this room. Get out! I won't have you sitting there looking at me with those damn big baby blue eyes of yours. Get out!"

"For God's sake, calm down, Tim," says Fred. "The boy's not going anywhere. He's staying right here with the rest of us." Fred puts his arm around Tim's shoulder for a brief moment and then on the back of his chair.

"Who the hell do you think you are telling me how to handle my own kids?"

"I'll tell you who I am. I'm a friend of yours, practically the last one you've got. If you could just get a start on your sobriety, you could have good times and good friends again. People really have an exceptional liking for you."

"A fine way they have of showing it," says Tim resentfully. "What's friendship without some kind of loyalty, but no, they all desert you as soon as you're down on your luck. Well, to hell with them, I say."

"Maybe you deserted them," volunteers Gerry. "That's the way I feel, like you deserted us."

"What do you mean, I deserted you? It was your mother who kicked me out."

"I don't mean that," says Gerry. "I mean that when you're drinking, you just aren't there. You just evaporate into thin air. I always know you're drinking long before I can smell it on your breath or catch you with a bottle because I sense that you are gone, absent, not there. I can tell you it's one hell of a feeling each time it happens and desertion is not too big a word for it."

"Now the boy thinks he's Eugene O'Neill waxing eloquent about his father's desertion." Tim addressees this remark to the group with cutting sarcasm and then, turning on Gerry with sudden and stunning viciousness, he yells, "I don't know what the hell you are talking about and I don't think you do either. You sound like a blithering idiot to me."

"I'm talking about you getting into the hospital and sobering up and being your real self again."

"Who knows what real is?" inquires Tim. His voice has dropped and taken on a dreamy quality. "All this airy fairy chatter about real is beyond my comprehension. If you have something to say, you better be concrete and specific because I don't get all this philosophical speculation about real and unreal and now you see him and now you don't."

"Okay," says Gerry. "I'll give you a concrete example. A few weeks ago, you drew all the money out of my savings account without even telling me. When I go to get it for my ski trip, there's this teller saying, 'We're sorry, Gerry, but your father closed out your account two days ago!' I just couldn't believe it! You knew I'd been saving up for months for that trip, raking leaves all fall and shoveling snow on every driveway on our block before Christmas and during that zero spell when it was cold as hell. And I had just got it all together."

"It's too bad we don't belong to the country club set and I could send you off on ski trips to Colorado whenever the spirit moved you," says Tim.

"Nobody's talking Colorado, and I wasn't asking you to send me anywhere. I'm just talking about you taking my money to lay in your supply of Jim Beam."

Tim has become very agitated. He stands up suddenly, knocking over his chair which makes a nerve-racking clatter as it strikes the floor. He begins pacing up and down the room in swift, unsteady strides. Sue thinks the family watches him with apprehension as though they anticipate a violent outburst of some kind. But Tim returns to the table, fumbles clumsily with the chair until he finally gets it upright, sits down and says very seriously to Gerry, "I'll pay you back as soon as I get things straightened out. I'll pay you back with interest."

"Dad," says Gerry. "The ski trip is over. There's no way you can pay me back. But you could admit you're an alcoholic or you never would have stolen my money."

Sue is uncertain about the dynamics of this meeting, exactly what it is supposed to accomplish. For sometime she has felt that Tim is being pushed further and further into a corner where he will only fight furiously to maintain his illusionary status. But she feels now that Gerry has struck home, that perhaps there is a chance that Tim will cave in. And for a moment she thinks she is right.

"Something's got to change for sure," Tim says. "But I can't do this thing alone. Jo, if you'll just let me come home, I promise to get on the wagon and do the AA bit or whatever you want."

The five-branched chandelier overhead with its shades of etched and frosted glass shed a cruel light on Jo's ashen face. Her pale blond hair, swept smoothly back into a classic bun, does nothing to relieve the lines of anxiety and fatigue which so prematurely age it. Is she hesitating? Sue knows that the worry of the last few weeks have worn her out, that not knowing where her husband is or what is happening to him had, in some ways, been more trying than contending with his drunken behavior. Watching her closely, Sue can see a characteristic compassion soften her delicate features and knows that what Tim proposed is a very tempting compromise for her. But then she straightens her shoulders and states her decision firmly.

"Tim, that's what you've been promising for years and it has not worked. You'll have to go into the hospital where they'll give you professional help and start you on a recovery program. I don't like this separation any better than you do, but I want you to win this time and I am going to stick it out."

"Jo" says Tim, "I don't think that's you talking. You got this bright idea about a separation from Father Rossi but you're not obliged to follow his advice. You could change your mind and give me this one more chance. Please, Jo. That damn priest had no right to interfere in our lives. We were doing just fine before he came along and put all these get-tough ideas in your head. It's not like you, Jo, and it doesn't become you. I hate that bastard for what he's done to my wife."

"We were hardly getting along just fine. The separation was my own choice, Tim, though I know that's hard for you to accept. And if I were you, I would speak with a little more respect for the dead."

"The dead?" Sue who is observing Tim carefully, sees a strange look of fear and concern flicker across his face and then vanish as he sits up very erect once more. "You mean Father Rossi is dead?" he inquires with a composure, which belies his initial reaction.

Timmy too is watching his father and now, grasping the seat of his chair as though the feel of the wood somehow gave him courage, he starts to say something, hesitates, and then in a thin, timid voice, shrill with anxiety, blurts out what is on his mind.

"You knew he was dead," he says. "I know you knew because you killed him."

Oddly enough Tim does not respond to the boy's accusation but sits in a sort of stupor staring at him while everyone else rushes to his defense.

"That's ridiculous, Tim," says Jo. "Your father may not have liked Father Rossi but he would never kill anyone. You know that."

"Father Rossi's death was an accident," says Gerry. "Why would you think Dad killed him?"

"Because he said he was going to and I know he meant it. He was very, very mad when we told him Mom was at a study group with Father, remember, Gerry?" Tim appeals to his brother as though he could use his help in what he has to say.

"He was mad all right," says Gerry. "He picked up a dining room chair and smashed the back of it against the doorway and he was cursing something awful."

"Jo," says Tim, "You know I would never do a thing like that, break one of your antique chairs."

"The chair was broken when I got home," says Jo.

"Anyway," says Gerry, "he was very drunk. He wasn't supposed to be there at our house so I went to the kitchen to call Lieutenant O'Connell because that's what Mom said to do. But he took off before I got back to the room."

"Before he left," says Tim, "he looked right at me and told me he was going to kill Father Rossi. He called him all those things like S.O.B. He was going right down to the baptistery and kill him with his bare hands, that's what he said. His face was scary, it was so full of…"

"Full of what?" encourages Fred.

"Full of hate, I guess," says Tim. "So soon as he left, I called Father Foley to stop him."

"Where was Gerry when you called Father Foley?" asks Mike

"He went out to shoot some baskets in the driveway."

"In that zero weather?"

"Yea," says Gerry. "It's a good way to let off steam. I can get pretty angry too."

"So you didn't tell Gerry or your mother about this threat of your Dad's?"

"I didn't want anyone to know," says Timmy. "I didn't think anybody had to know but today Mom said if we told the bad things it might help Dad."

"What did Father Foley say when you called?"

Father Foley had assured Tim that he was not to worry, he would take care of it. But the next morning when the boy went to serve the eight o'clock Mass, the pastor had delayed him in the sacristy to tell him that Father Rossi had died in an accident. He assured him that his father had had nothing to do with it, that Father Rossi had tripped on an electric heater and been electrocuted. Timmy had asked how he knew that his Dad had not done it. He said he was certain because his father had been with him at the rectory at the time it happened. He had come there looking for Father Rossi and Father Foley had made him stay 'til he had calmed down. He had Nora bring him some coffee before he drove back to the Y in Evanston.

"So," says Mike, "Why do you still think your father killed Father Rossi?"

"Dad wasn't headed for the rectory when he left our house. He definitely said he was going to the baptistery to kill Father Rossi with his bare hands. I guess maybe the heater came in handy. Father Foley said I shouldn't mention what Dad said to anyone, not even Mom. I wasn't going to tell anyone anyway, but Mom said telling awful things might help Dad get well."

"Gerry," inquires Mike, "do you remember what time it was that your father left the house?"

"I'm not sure. We must have got back from the gym about noon so sometime soon after that. But you don't believe any of this shit, do you? Timmy just got scared is all."

"I think that's right," says Mike, "but I still have to ask your Dad a few questions. Tim, where did you go when you left your house last Saturday?"

"Oh hell, Mike, how do I know? I don't remember going to the rectory but if Foley says I was there, I suppose I was. It was a rocky weekend and sometimes things escape my memory."

Sue knows this is true, that sometimes Tim's alcoholic amnesia could be absolute. Jo had mentioned sadly one time that there were large patches of their past that Tim could not recall, times they had experienced together that were totally lost to him. She said it was as if the history of their marriage was full of tattered holes.

"And you didn't know Father Rossi was dead until you heard it this afternoon?"

"Honest to God, I didn't. I've been a little out of touch you might say. God knows I didn't approve of the way he'd been advising my wife but I feel kind of rotten for some of the things I've said about him. He probably meant well and I'm sorry he's dead."

"And you can assure Timmy that you didn't kill him?"

"Of course he didn't kill him," exclaims Jo. "We all know Father's death was an accident. Tim's anger can be pretty frightening for the boys and I can understand why Tim's threat could seem real to Timmy, though I've explained to him often that his father is really only angry with himself. He simply finds some focus to vent his rage on when he can't acknowledge and accept his own problem. Father Rossi happened to be his current target. But at the worst of times, Tim has never injured any of us nor would he lay a finger on Father Rossi. You do understand that, Timmy?"

The boy nodded though Sue is uncertain that he is convinced. He is looking anxiously at his father.

"I was only trying to help," he says. In his timid way, he seems to be pleading with his father for forgiveness.

The recent course of conversation has sobered Tim considerably. He has abandoned his arrogant bearing and seems more aware of the boy and his feelings. Slumped in his chair, he is staring at him in sad bewilderment.

"Your mother, the psychiatrist has explained everything," he says. "Listen to me, Timmy. I don't want you to feel bad about what you said to me. I know you were trying to help but I can tell you, things have reached a sorry pass when your own son thinks maybe you murdered a priest. You're right, you are a lot tougher than I thought to accuse me of that. And you've convinced me that things must have been pretty bad last Saturday for you to reach such a crazy conclusion. So I guess you win, kiddo."

Tim pushes his chair back and stands up. He squares his shoulders and thrusts out his chin. Swaying a bit unsteadily but with dignity and an almost debonair demeanor, he says "Okay, let's get the show on the road." Watching him, Sue thinks there is something gallant about his surrender, that he looks like a battle-weary general who's spirit is unquenchable even in defeat.

Sue, who is enormously fond of this talented and exasperating man, finds herself wondering why she does not feel happy about this victory, does not experience great relief and gratitude that he has at last agreed to go into the hospital. Surely it is the result for which they had all prayed. Instead, the afternoon leaves a bitter after-taste, a persistent and troubling doubt in her mind. She realizes that Tim never really denied killing Father Rossi. Did he think he might have done it? And did Father Foley actually believe he had? If so, she is certain that they are both wrong, as wrong as poor Timmy who had been suffering his secret conviction of his father's guilt all week long. Still, a heavy cloud hangs over the day when she remembers the AA prayer card found in the baptistery.

CHAPTER XII

If only she could get to sleep! Sue turns over restlessly in the rumpled bed, attaching herself spoon-fashion to Fred's broad back. She winds her arms around him, hugging him close in the hope that the warmth of his body and the rhythm of his breathing might help her to drowse off. But it is no use. Her back aches as it has not done since her last pregnancy. The base of her skull seems tied in tight knots and behind her eyes a persistent pressure creates a bothersome headache. Images race through her mind. She can in no way control this rush-hour traffic although she has made an enormous effort to lie still and empty her intellect of all its preoccupations.

Finally, for the third time in the long night, she gives up trying to capture the sleep that eludes her. She plants a kiss on her sleeping husband's cheek and rubs her own cheek lovingly along the sandpaper contours of his day-old beard. There is little chance she will awaken him. Fred has always slept soundly through every nocturnal disturbance from crying babies to ringing telephones. But sometimes he senses her absence if she gets up in the night, is startled into consciousness by the emptiness of his bed and the silence in the room. She carefully tucks the comforter around him before slipping into her robe and stealing quietly down stairs.

She finds her appointment book and settles down in the wing chair in the library to make lists, to get a few things off her mind and on to paper. She begins with the supper party for parish newcomers that she must schedule soon. She has already mentioned it to Gabriel and Elena Esquivel, Bill and Pixie Bergman and a few other couples. Maybe it would be good to include Mike O'Connell since he wants a chance to explore the mysterious background of the Esquivels. And maybe Jo. It would be good for her to get out and these affairs seem to work best with a mix of old-timers and newcomers. Counting herself and Fred, the priests and the Deacon and his wife, there would be about twenty-two so three casseroles should do it.

Although matters relating to Father Rossi's murder keep crossing and recrossing her mind, she deliberately goes ahead with her plans for the party. Soundlessly in her slippers, she pads out to the pantry to find the new cookbook that the Women's Council had published at Christmas. With the heat turned down for the night, the house is cold, so she finds an afghan before thumbing through for ideas. A recipe for a chicken, artichoke hearts and bacon casserole catches her eye and also one for a hot Rueben dip which seems like it will go a long way in a crowd.

After tentatively making out a supper menu, Sue decides that a mystery story may distract her from the disturbing thoughts which keep intruding from the margins of her mind. As one of his presents for her birthday, Fred had given her several paperbacks written by women authors about women detectives and Sue selects one of these, confident that a good plot and a light, racy style will capture her attention. It doesn't work. Instead of becoming involved in the story, she finds herself thinking how her situation differs from those she has been reading about.

The heroines of these novels were usually professional detectives under a gun to prove how good they were. They often had legal backgrounds or legal connections, a familiarity with the criminal system, access to informants among gang members or in the underworld, a lot of street smarts and friends in right places. They tracked down their leads through an urban jungle that seemed utterly alien to her own peaceful suburban village. Although they might suffer some tension in terribly scary situations, they had the guts to place themselves in real and present danger in order to obtain some bit of information. Above all, they seemed to know what they were doing, to have clear goals and plans of action.

Sue sighs, thinking how little of their courage or their know-how she possesses. It had scared the hell out of her just to see the white Camaro parked in the driveway across the street from the Bergman's house yesterday. She is keenly aware that she is simply an amateur stumbling around in great confusion. It has been a week since Father's murder and she seems no nearer a solution than when she started. What bothers her most is that her only leads are not to some criminal element or to some ambitious loser coveting an inheritance but to old friends, to ordinary people in their own parish. Sue is not by nature a suspicious person. She likes to think well of others. The demand on her now to view them critically is difficult for her. It is probably why she is trying to distract herself rather than giving careful consideration to recent events related to the murder.

Sue tosses her book aside and finally allows herself to review her visit to the Bergmans. After Fred and Jo returned from the hospital where Tim had been safely installed, she had gone out to pick up Jennifer and shop for supper. The Bergman's house, a brick colonial with a circular driveway coming in off Forest Road, is very familiar to her. The previous owners had been friends of her parents with children her own age and she had often played there as a child. To see a swing still hanging from a high branch of a huge oak in the side yard gives her a pleasant twinge of nostalgia and she hurries up the walk curious to see what changes the Bergmans have made in the house. However, when Pixie invites her in and shows her around it is obvious that not much has yet been done.

"We had a sort of cottage-type house in St. Paul," explains Pixie, "and none of our stuff looks right here. I mean, you can't hang priscillas in a place like this."

They are standing in the middle of a large, formal living room with a central fireplace and French doors at the far end. A couch and small arm chair occupy the opposite wall. The rest of the spacious room is vacant except for a five hundred piece puzzle of Roger's scattered on the oak floor.

"It's a lovely room with wonderful possibilities," says Sue. "If you find you need some help with furnishing or decorating, Jo is awfully good at it. She's very reasonable as decorators go and might even save you money in the long run. So think about it. But I tell you what, Pixie, Jo is at my house right now, so I'd better pick up Jennifer and head on back."

They find the children in the basement rec room where a game of Ping-Pong is under way. As they approach, Sue finds the staccato sound of a prolonged volley somehow exciting and is pleased to discover that Jennifer is holding her own with Roger's father. Bill is wearing a navy turtleneck which accentuates his crisp, clear-cut good looks and is playing with the ease and athletic grace of an old-timer. When he spots Sue, he turns his paddle over to Roger and ambles across the room to greet her.

As she observes his unhurried approach and his laid-back bearing, Sue thinks that perhaps he is a courteous man who does the right thing without too much spontaneity or enthusiasm. Although she is aware of how attentively he is scrutinizing her, his face remains impassive. Still, when he takes her hand, the charm of his rather reticent smile is heart-warming. It is as if he reserves it for good friends and has decided to include her in that category.

"Jennifer is a good little player," he says "and she tells me her Mom is terrific. What if I take you on for a game?"

"Yes Mom!" exclaims Jennifer. "Mr. Bergman's awfully good but I bet you could beat him."

"I bet I could too!" says Sue, smiling at Bill. "But really, I've got guests at home and have to get back. Another time."

When Sue has found Jennifer's jacket and said goodbye to Pixie, Bill politely accompanies her to the car. As they cross the driveway, Jennifer looks longingly toward the side yard. "Could I please have one more swing before we go?" she pleads.

It is growing dark. A pale half moon riding high overhead sheds a soft light across the misty lawn. Suddenly this place, this yard with its long stretch of gray winter grass and its dense border of dark bushes stirs memories of a time when all was young, when birds sang in the green trees and clover bloomed in the green grass and children quarreled uproariously about whose turn was next.

"I wouldn't mind a swing myself!" exclaims Sue. "How about it, Bill?"

Sue knows that time can shrink a beloved scene of childhood so that an adult returning to it might look and look but never quite discover what had once so enchanted her. But her experience of the Bergman's swing on this twilit evening holds no such disappointment. It seems to her that the ropes suspended from the lofty limb of the ancient oak are longer now than then, that the tremendous tree with its stout trunk and tough bark has grown just as she herself has grown, that they meet again as remembered friends.

"Hang on!" exclaims Bill as he draws the seat of the swing back and then, pushing hard gives her a full running start. Soon she is skimming like a seagull over the dark lawn. Oh, the boundless reach and stretch of the swing, the clean sweep of it over the hedge climbing higher and ever higher 'til toes almost touch the sky! And the dizzying descent, down, down to earth and then beyond it, up, up to a high hesitation at the far apex of the arc the swing is slicing through the night air. And now forward again, gathering momentum, sailing swiftly and smoothly with the cold wind kissing her cheeks and Jennifer's laughter ringing in her ears and her whole being hurtling once more toward heaven.

"God, that was great!" Sue exclaims as the swing slows and she jumps off to give Jennifer her turn. "Exhilarating! A mini vacation from the adult world!"

A broad grin has dissolved the dead-pan composure of Bill's handsome face. It is obvious that he is amused and pleased with her joy in her ride, has shared in her moment of happy escape.

"I'll bet you really enjoyed your childhood," he says.

"My mother was afraid I'd never let go of it. How about you?"

"Mine was serious, very serious. Even baseball was a very serious game."

"But you're so good with kids. You play with them like someone who knows how to have fun. I remember Father Rossi was impressed with how great you are with Roger."

Bill starts to push Jennifer on the swing but she insists that she wants to pump herself so he moves out of her path and stands close to Sue.

"Speaking of Father Rossi," he says. "I'd like to ask you something but if I'm intruding in any way, will you just let me know?"

"Of course."

"I was just wondering if there was anything suspicious about Father's death."

"Why would you think that?"

"Well, the night he died, I met you in the parking lot, remember? You were coming from the baptistery but said nothing at all about Father Rossi. I thought maybe that was a little strange."

"Not at all," says Sue. "Father Foley asked us to say nothing until he announced the death at the Masses the next day."

"I see. But then a few days later, Mike called and asked me to look up the police record of the maintenance man here in the parish, a Mr. Jensladder. It struck me that there might be some connection, that he was suspicious of some wrong doing."

"You mean like murder?" says Sue. "I hardly think so. Jens was at my house just this afternoon. He and I are old friends. We both love to garden and he brought me a unique hibiscus which he had crossbred himself. He can be a little grouchy sometimes but if you knew him as well as I do, you'd know that murder was impossible."

Sue finds that she is grateful to have an opportunity to verbalize her confidence in Jens. The little time she had spent with him in the afternoon had restored her conviction of his innocence and made her ashamed that she had momentarily doubted him, even feared him. He had come to tell her that he had lied to her, that he had indeed seen Father Rossi's poor dead body lying on the floor. The sight had so shocked and scared him that he had run out of the baptistery leaving his boots behind him. Knowing his history she had no need to ask why he had been so frightened.

"What did the police record show that you were looking up?" she inquires.

"I guess I can't tell you that," says Bill. "Mike wanted it to be kept strictly confidential. But Sue, you know when I talked with Father Foley after Mass the morning following Father's death, the details concerning it sounded a little implausible to me. It seemed to me that he was over-insistent on the fact that it was an accident. I got the distinct impression that he was covering up for somebody."

"That never occurred to me," says Sue, wondering now why it had not.

"Anyway," he says, "I just thought if something were wrong, I'd like to do anything I could to help. It would be impossible for me to explain how badly I felt about Father's death. He was so understanding about Pixie's longing for another child and he seemed so certain that we would be the right parents for the little Mexican boy. I guess I've been trying to give Roger some of the fun I missed as a child and his confidence in me as a father meant a great deal to me. We became good friends practically over night. I'd never been close to a priest before and I think his concern and his friendship took me totally by surprise. It was something I never expected. And then quite suddenly he was gone."

Bill has not been looking at her but is staring at the ground where he is digging a little hole in the hard soil with the tip of his shoe. He looks up abruptly and even in the dim light, Sue cannot mistake the earnestness in his face nor the fact that his eyes are moist. This unguarded glance, vulnerable and sincere, is a revelation similar to Father Foley's when he patted the dead priest's cheek. Here, she thought is another man who loved Father Rossi. She would like to share the circumstances of his death with Bill but did not feel free to do so. Father Foley had been right about not letting a rumor of murder circulate in the parish. Still, he was a very smart man who had cared for Father and might be of great help in solving the mystery.

"Look," she says. "Mike O'Connell is a police officer and if anything were questionable, he would know about it. Why don't you ask him?"

"I think I might do that."

It is just as she and Jennifer are getting into the car that Sue spots the Camaro. It is parked facing the street in the long driveway of the mansion directly across Forest Road. The Bergman's front lawn slopes downhill to the street and from her high vantage point the car, like a white ghost in the misty moonlight, is clearly visible. It startles her when she discovers it and she hopes that the sudden shot of fear that runs through her is not noticeable to Bill.

"According to Pixie," she says, "your Mafia neighbors over there only ride in limousines. Fred tells me a Camaro is a very common car so what is one doing in their driveway?"

"Beats me," says Bill. "I've never seen it there before but maybe they've got one poor relative who doesn't own a stretch and only visits at night." He smiles as he closes the car door for her.

Sue pulls onto Forest Road and drives south toward the village when she spots the Camaro following her. This hardly surprises her and after a block or two, she decides to turn west on a side street to see if it will continue to tail her. When she again detects it behind her, a feeling close to panic possesses her. Her fear would have been difficult to define but she thinks it is exacerbated by the fact that Jennifer is with her, that, except for the child, she is driving alone on a dark street and the intent of her unknown pursuer might well be dangerous. At the next crossing she turns right and speeds north a few blocks in the direction from which she has come. Holding her breath and without looking back, she careens around a corner heading east to Forest and south again, circling finally into the Bergman's driveway.

Sue had been ignoring Jennifer's insistent questions but now by way of explanation, she says she thinks she has left her gloves at Roger's house. She repeats this to Pixie when she appears in the doorway wearing a white chef's apron with the inscription "Don't Expect Miracles" across the front of it. Sue smiles. How reassuring it is to find her friend, round cheeks flushed and sunny hair disheveled, going peacefully about the ordinary task of cooking dinner. Together they retrace Sue's steps through the living room, the deserted rec room and the kitchen, Sue finding this fruitless search an opportunity to calm her nerves and catch her breath. Bill joins them in the front hall just as she says that perhaps she had not worn gloves after all since the weather wasn't really cold.

"If they turn up, I'll drop them off for you," he says as once again he accompanies her to the car.

Just at the edge of the Bergman property, parked off the road and screened by shrubery except for the nose of the hood, Sue spots the Camaro lying in wait for her. She makes a quick spontaneous decision to share her concern about it with Bill.

"Your Mafia neighbor's poor relative followed me for several blocks when I was circling back to your house and now he's hiding down there behind the bushes prepared to tail me again," she says.

Bill glances quickly in the direction she has indicated. His expression when he spots the car is impassive and difficult to read, but Sue thinks she detects a good deal of perplexity and consternation in the way he frowns and narrows his eyes. Perhaps even some anger that this should have happened.

"But why?" he asks. "Why should he have followed you?"

"Your guess is as good as mine."

"You wait here." Bill's voice is firm and decisive. "I'll go down there and see if I can discover what he wants."

Sue watches him jog down to the road and approach the driver's side of the Camaro. In a matter of minutes, the car backs into the driveway of the Mafia mansion and then drives rapidly north on Forest Road. Sue is relieved to see it disappear in the opposite direction from the one she will be taking.

"What did he have to say?" she inquires when Bill returns somewhat breathless from his uphill run.

"He said he got lost looking for Greenbridge Lane. He wanted to ask you for directions. It is hard to find. You know how it comes in at such an odd angle and the woods there are so dense."

"You believed that?"

"Not entirely but it's the only explanation we have."

"What did he look like?"

"Black, fairly young and rather aristocratic, I'd say. My guess, he is a bartender or caterer engaged for a party in that fancy subdivision across the bridge."

Sue recalls the sharp features and polished shoes of the man she had encountered on the steps of Adele Adabeau's south side home. Involuntarily, she shudders slightly as she opens the car door and slides into her seat. Although Bill's impassive face has betrayed no particular worry or anxiety, he seems sensitive to hers. "I'd be happy to follow you home," he offers as he is closing the door for her.

"That's nice of you," says Sue. "But no thanks. I have to stop on errands and I'm sure he's gone for good now."

Recalling this unsettling incident in the middle of the night, Sue realizes that there is something else about her role of detective that she dislikes. When she and Jo were cleaning up the kitchen after their pizza supper the night before, she had been dying to tell her about her scary experience.

She was accustomed to sharing everything with her and the restraint, discretion and secrecy which are required of her now seem burdensome and unnatural. Instead, as she shoved a fistful of silverware into the dishwasher, she told Jo about the opportunities for decorating that might open up with the Esquivels and Bergmans and asked her if she would be interested.

"I think maybe I could handle it," Jo had said. "Maybe I could work it in on Wednesdays and Sundays and hang on to the Thrift Shop job until I see how it develops."

Jo seemed tremendously relaxed and relieved now that Tim is safely in the hospital but she expressed some anger at Mike O'Connell for his treatment of Tim during the session at the station.

"What was that all about?" she had demanded. "He was cross-examining Tim as though he were a suspect in a murder. How could he even think something like that?"

"I guess Timmy brought it up," Sue had reminded her.

"Well, his father scares the wits out of poor Timmy sometimes and to tell you the truth, Tim can be pretty violent on some occasions. But murder? For God's sake, come on!"

Pretty violent on some occasions! This is the part of the conversation that Sue would like to forget. And the AA prayer card. Wasn't it she who had said that details were important in a case of murder? Sitting there in the library listening to the foreign language her house seems to speak at night, the fitful whisper of the fish tank filter, the rasping hum of the old refrigerator, she tries once more to bury her concern. Lines of dawning light appear on the half-closed mini blinds and outside a mourning dove is cooing. She finally goes back to bed thinking that it has been a long night and that, thank God, there is nothing she has to do on Sunday except bring Communion to the old invalid, Kathy Kennedy.

CHAPTER XIII

Sue finds regretfully that her Sunday leisure, the time alone with her family that she had anticipated with so much pleasure, is drained away by one interruption after another. First, Monsignor Fiedler detains her after Mass, asking her to find Mike and to meet him in his apartment. When they arrive he produces a paper grocery bag from which he carefully withdraws a pile of clothes: a pair of jeans, a sweat shirt, several well-worn T shirts all carefully folded, and on top, a pair of men's leather gloves. He lays these carefully on his couch.

"Look!" he exclaims "I've discovered the murder weapon for you!"

With a man's handkerchief wrapped around the handle, he extricates a small, hand-held dryer from the pile and holds it up for them to see. The front of the plastic cover had been smashed so that a metal fan protrudes from the end of the dryer. It looks wickedly sharp and Sue shudders when she sees it.

"For God's sake, where did you find that?" asks Mike. "I went through every bin and trash can in the whole neighborhood looking for it or something like it and found nothing."

"It was in the St. Vincent de Paul drop box for the poor," explains Monsignor. "I don't believe we have a key to it so yesterday I kept an eye out for the driver when he came for the Saturday pick-up. He let me go through everything, which I did very carefully. I didn't keep anything else because these things seemed to be in a distinct pile all tied together with the arms of the sweat shirt. Everything else was in plastic bags. Afterwards I had a little chat with Sister Thomasita. Her study window at the Convent overlooks the box and I thought she might remember seeing someone who dropped clothes into it on the Saturday in question. It wouldn't do to arouse Sister's curiosity, so I simply told her we had discovered a valuable broach pinned to a giveaway dress that we thought was probably not intended for the poor and we were trying to trace the owner."

"Pretty inventive," says Sue. "How did you come up with that one?"

"There really was a broach. And value is just a relative thing, is it not?"

Sure enough, after the scripture meeting, Sister had lunch in the Convent refectory and then settled down by the window in her study to say her rosary. She got no farther than the first decade when a snappy red Toyota drew up and Winnie Harris slid out of the front seat. Climbing through a knee-high pile of snow, she quickly shoved something into the poor box. When Monsignor asked if it had been a batch of clothes, she said she didn't know. Winnie had looked so angry that Sister had failed to notice what she was managing to part with for the poor. She thought Winnie was probably upset because the snow was too deep for her fancy high-heeled leather boots. Still, Sister thought you could bet your bottom dollar on it that the pin was Winnie's. She had been certain from at least the fifth grade on, that Winifred was the valuable broach type. Sister had seen no one else that day but, of course, she wasn't stationed at the window long.

Something like a silent movie runs through Sue's mind as she examines the pile of clothes. She can see Winnie with her Sierra Club canvas bag (Winnie is an avid environmentalist) over her arm pounding on the baptistery door. When Father Rossi lets her in, they move to the table for a few minutes, consulting about some papers Winnie had brought with her. Although she can't hear them or guess the gist of the conversation, Winnie seems to be talking in her exaggerated, enthusiastic way. Then both figures rise from the table and start toward the rear of the room.

Here the action picks up. Winnie sets her bag on the counter. Suddenly, without warning, she pulls a heavy object from it—a silver candlestick? and wheeling around with the ferocity of a tough tether-ball player, strikes Father on the temple with it. He falls and loses consciousness. Wasting no time, she fills the coffeepot with water, pours it over his legs, places the heater and plugs it in. A tremendous tremor convulses Father Rossi's body and then he lies absolutely still. But Winnie is not convinced that he is dead. Drawing the hair dryer from her bag, she smashes the case on the counter, connects it, and then, looking aside with a grimace of distaste, applies it to Father's temple and the calf of his leg. The body does not even twitch.

As Sue watches the final frames of her silent movie, she sees Winnie, a meticulous person, carefully pick up the broken pieces of the hair dryer and put them in her purse. She adjusts Father's trouser over the bruise on his leg, turns his head facing the counter so that his hideous wound is no longer visible and then stands back to survey the scene.

Her attitude is critical but approving. She looks as though she is about to show a client an interesting room in a beautiful home. "Here," Sue can hear her say, "we have the perfect murder scene. The victim is someone whom no one on earth would want to kill. Please note that there is no gun, no blood, no apparent motive. The details are interesting but rather inconclusive, especially if we place the coffeepot here as though it spilled by accident.

Winnie collects her belongings, (would Winnie forget an expensive pen?) smoothes a few stray hairs into the brick-colored edifice of her perfect bouffant and, leaving unseen, drives down to the poor box near the Convent. It would be like Winnie to tie the bunch of clothes in a neat bundle.

Her anger, which Sister noted, may have been with Father Rossi whom she has just killed: but perhaps she is very angry with Boyd too.

Sue is quite certain that the gloves which topped the pile were his old ones to which he was attached. Good leather, soft and pliable with age, warmly lined, a little soiled in the creases and exactly the same size as the ones which had been left in the baptistery. Too shabby for Winnie's taste. Sue can see her pitching them into the poor box, an angry gesture. He wouldn't get another chance to reject her Christmas present of expensive new ones.

"The trouble is," Sue says "that I can visualize Winnie killing Father. I can't possibly imagine any other woman, not Jo or Elena or Pixie or anyone else but somehow I can see Winnie doing it." And she ran through her scenario for Monsignor and Mike.

"I always wondered what women carried around in those bags," says Monsignor dryly. "I never would have guessed that they were keeping a candlestick handy for murderous emergencies."

"Well, it is unlikely," admits Sue. "However, Sister may have detected a venal love of jewelry in Winnie in the fifth grade, but I never heard anyone else who did. She was ahead of me in school and had a reputation as a killer athlete, very competitive and very tough. You were smart to stay out of her way on the basketball court."

"She still serves a mighty mean tennis ball," says Mike. "She's famous for smashing short shots over the net."

"She often strikes me as angry," says Sue. "You know what a great social manner she has, very friendly and out-going, but underneath it all, I sense something brittle. I don't mean she's a hypocrite exactly but just that she sits on some well-stoked anger."

"It's interesting you should say that," comments Monsignor. "I've always had the impression that Winnie is angry with God and perhaps not for some trivial reason as some people are."

Mike has placed the hair dryer in a plastic bag, promising to get prints if possible. Sue refolds the clothes, putting them back in the paper bag. "I have some questions about these," she says. "The sweat shirt looks too big for Boyd and the T shirts look like they belong to a young boy."

"Wouldn't one of Winnie's college kids be about the right size for that sweat shirt?" inquires Mike. "And as for boy's T shirts, everything is unisex these days. Perhaps they belong to her girls."

"Maybe," says Sue, holding a shirt against her own chest. "But they're a bit skimpy for high-schoolers, I'd say."

"I'm glad you've raised some questions," said Monsignor, "because I find the evidence inconclusive. I'm quite convinced that Winifred Harris did not kill Father Rossi."

Later, in her kitchen where Sue chops celery for tuna sandwiches, Fred agrees with Monsignor. "Win's a big, tender-hearted baboon," he says. "She'd never hurt a flea. You're getting so you're suspicious of everyone, Sue."

"I know," sighs Sue. "But you've got to consider the evidence. Sister saw her put something into the poor box and Monsignor subsequently found the hair dryer there. You can't just ignore that."

"I can," said Fred. "Can't you turn this matter over to the police? I really don't think it's been good for you to be so involved. It's beginning to take up all your time and to keep you awake at night."

"Just understand," says Sue stubbornly. "It's something that I have to do."

They have scarcely finished lunch when Jo calls. Tim had had a bad night with DT's and constant vomiting but his nurse had assured her that he had pulled through all right. There were to be no visitors. Jo is grateful beyond measure that he is in the hospital where he is receiving proper care and medication. She feels great relief about this but also feels restless. She needs to be doing something. Did Sue think it was possible to see Elena Esquivel about her interior decorating that afternoon and, if so, would Sue be free to go with her? She didn't feel up to going alone.

Although Elena had responded enthusiastically to Sue's phone call, she seems quiet and withdrawn when the women arrive at her home. It is Gabriel, dressed rather formally in a beautifully tailored business suit, who welcomes them cordially and proceeds to show them into the living room. It is an enormous room running the full width of the house with windows at both sides. At the far end, set in a recess of the plain, plaster wall, a cavernous fireplace yawns ominously. Grouped in front of it is a collection of antique, carved furniture that Gabriel had bought from the previous owner. Winnie had assured him that the price was too good to pass up. The heavy armchairs are cushioned in a faded red velvet. At the windows, drapes of the same red velvet hung by brass rings from thick brass rods.

Sue sighs. Everything seemed impossibly ponderous, oppressive, shapeless, ungainly. How could such a room ever be converted into something attractive and livable? She thinks Winnie has done Gabriel a disservice on the furniture, but Jo, who is immediately interested in the project, thinks otherwise.

"The furniture will be good in this room," she assures Gabriel. "It needs weighty pieces to anchor it. But I think we should begin by separating them, using them sparingly in far corners of the room, perhaps this library table against the entrance wall."

As they are moving furniture, Jo notices a collection of large oil paintings in substantial gold frames stacked against a wall. "What have we here!" she exclaims, lining them up face forward. "These look like originals and they are wonderfully charming!"

Elena perks up then and seems to take an interest for the first time.

"They belonged to my aunt who died shortly before we left home," she says. "They were painted by Teijido, an artist who was a friend of my mother's family. In fact, he painted many portraits for them and my mother has a few of her own so she said that I might keep these. This is one of my mother and her sisters when they were young and Teijido too was a very young man. Perhaps it does not have the finish of the later ones, but I am very fond of it. It was painted in the parlor of our city house. The girl who is playing the piano is my mother, the youngest. They all seem so joyous and carefree, don't they, though their lives became difficult later on."

Sue examines the painting attentively. Through an open window in the background, one can see an impressionist spring, sunlit trees in tiny leaf. There is an impressionist influence too, perhaps Renoir's, in the luminous texture of the girls' white dresses but the portraits of the dark, handsome young women gathered there are more reminiscent of Rembrandt: faces of distinct character and subtle smiles. Elena's mother seems the least attractive, a little thin-lipped and intense, concentrating on her playing.

"And this," says Elena, "is my brothers and me playing in the park when we were children. The boys remember how they detested posing in their sailor suits. I don't recall that but I do remember Mr. Teijido with his pointed beard and his magic brush. See how the poppies sway in the breeze and the fountain splashes in the sunlight? He has caught it all."

"The boys look playful, even mischievous, but you seem so sober," remarks Sue. "Were you always such a serious little girl?"

"Perhaps," says Elena. "I was a late child and the only girl. My mother never allowed me to have the fun the boys did."

Elena moves quickly to the last picture. "This is my aunt as a young woman in her riding habit. It was done at our coffee plantation where my aunt and uncle live and where Teijido often came to visit so that he could paint the countryside and the peasants picking beans. He has captured my aunt's buoyant, blithe spirit very well. She was a wonderful, warm-hearted person and sometimes I wonder if Teijido was in love with her. I think this may be his masterpiece. Mama was very generous to let me have it."

"It is remarkably good," says Sue who finds the paintings a fascinating diversion from the decorating project, and studies them carefully to see what she can learn from them. Taken all together, they convey an impression of wealth and aristocratic background, of a culture quite foreign to contemporary America, a feeling of a bygone era. Still, some of them were done less than twenty years ago when Elena was a child. There seems nothing in them that gives an unequivocal sense of place. Are there coffee plantations in Spain or is this mountain rising majestically behind Elena's winsome aunt really in Alvarado?

Her thoughts are interrupted by Jo who has discovered a large painting of the Madonna of Guadeloupe which Teijido had copied on wood. She seems stunned by it. She has Gabriel carry it to the fireplace and, leaning it against the wall, she stands examining the serene face with its delicate features and downcast eyes. Finally, she turns to the Esquivels and asks, "Do you both like this painting? Would you think of hanging it here above the fireplace? As you can see, it's the perfect rectangular shape for this recessed wall, but we must be certain that you both like it."

Gabriel and Elena assure her that they do. This Madonna who had appeared long ago to a little Mexican peasant boy was much revered in their country. Teijido's copy had hung in the dining hall of Elena's aunt and held precious memories for both of them. If Jo thought a place of honor above the fireplace was appropriate for it, they agreed it should be placed there.

It is obvious that the painting has inspired Jo. She asks Gabriel to remove the velvet drapes from one of the windows so that she can better see the shape of it without such heavy camouflage. She begins pacing the room in some excitement, her high heels tapping briskly on the bare floor, her almond eyes narrowed in intense concentration. The others watch her silently, careful not to intrude on what they recognize as a creative moment.

Gabriel, leaning his slight frame against the fireplace wall, watches Jo with interest and amusement. His dark, wide-spaced eyes and well-defined brows give his thin face a decided distinction but it is this intensity of observation and underlying humor that most attract Sue.

He is enjoying himself. Elena, on the other hand, is obviously bored. She sits in one of the carved armchairs, her shoulders slumped, her eyes strangely opaque and inward looking. The degree of her dejection and withdrawal frighten Sue. She touches one of her hands which lay listless in her lap.

"Are you okay, Elena?" she asks softly.

Elena seems to resent this intrusion on her reverie. It startles her into an upright position and an attitude of huffy ill humor. "Why wouldn't I be okay?" she asks petulantly and continues to sit sulking while Jo finishes her inspection of the room.

Finally Jo says "I'll tell you what I'd like to do and you can tell me what you think. I'd like to pick up our decorating scheme from this magnificent Madonna: do the walls in an antique white to set off the old furniture, refinish the floors in a dark walnut which will give depth to the room and use a rug in the soft ivory tone of Our Lady's face to define a congenial sitting area in front of the fireplace. These tall, narrow windows are a unique feature: I'd like to eliminate drapes and simply paint the deep recesses of these arched windows in the teal of the Madonna's veil. This fabulous blue-green color. Then we could stencil a fine leaf border around the windows to emphasize their lovely shape. Maybe in this bronze-gold of the background."

Gabriel seems interested in the geometry of the scheme. Would a rectangular rug diminish the boxy, square look of the room? Would the rug create a sort of aisle or avenue along the south wall where they might place tropical plants? Would the windows as she describes them add height to the room? Jo is delighted that he understands so well what she is trying to accomplish.

Sue marvels at how well organized Jo seems. She leaves the names of two painters with the Esquivels so they can start getting estimates on the work immediately. She invites them to luncheon at the Merchandise Mart on Wednesday when they can select rugs and furniture. In the car driving home, Sue expresses her admiration.

"I could almost see the room taking shape as you described it," she says "and I think it will be lovely but are you sure Jo, that it's not going to look like a chapel?"

Jo smiles. "I expect that it will have a sort of serene sanctuary ambiance," she says, "but the oils and the accents will make it very livable. I want a little different theme for them and I think it will be just right. They are sort of old-world religious people."

"You think so? I can see Gabriel as a devout Catholic gentleman but Elena puzzles me. Sometimes she seems so sullen and hostile that I think of her as quite capable of sinister plots. You don't get that feeling?"

"No," says Jo. "I think she's just a homesick little Convent girl still mourning the death of her favorite auntie. Speaking of plots, Sue, I did want to sew things up with the Esquivels but I guess I'll have to ask you to subsidize my Merchandise Mart lunch until I get paid."

"Of course," Sue fishes for her checkbook in her purse. "Buy them wine. Live it up."

That evening, after dinner, Sue makes the remaining phone calls on the newcomers party scheduled for the following Sunday. She had decided to include the Harrises and when she reaches Winnie, she is puzzled by a morose, monotonous quality to her usually vibrant voice. What is happening here?

"I suppose you want Boyd too, both of us?" Winnie asks.

"Well, yes, of course. Our guests will be mostly young couples and I could use your help in entertaining them."

"Oh well, I'd love to come but I can't be sure about Boyd. He seems very fond of you and might say yes, but actually we haven't been going anywhere together lately."

Sue senses something so subdued and sad, so different, in Winnie's tone of voice that she is slow to respond. She decides that she can't ignore either Winnie's statement or her obvious depression.

"Winnie." She says. "We're old friends and go back a long way together. Do you want to tell me what's going on?"

"Well, actually we're talking about a divorce. Sue, I know I can trust you not to mention this to anyone?"

"Of course."

"Well, Father Rossi thought a divorce in our circumstances might be good for both of us. I was absolutely furious with him when he suggested this but I've been giving it some thought since he died and it's just possible that he was right."

"But Winnie! You've been married so many years and there are your four children! I can't believe Father Rossi would…"

"I know. Look, Sue, I can't talk about this on the phone. Maybe we could have lunch sometime soon and I could fill you in on the whole story. Okay?"

After Sue hangs up, she sits for several minutes trying to understand her own response to this conversation. Her most immediate and spontaneous reaction to the subdued, almost pathetic pitch of Winnie's voice is one of deep sympathy. But very quickly questions arise. Under what unusual circumstances might Father Rossi have recommended a divorce? What about the hysterical outburst she had overheard when Winnie was in his office on the day before his death? What about the hairdryer in the poor box for that matter? But no. Only a crazy person would kill a priest for recommending a divorce. Whatever else she might be, Winifred Harris was not crazy.

Chapter XIV

Nora answers the door when Sue arrives at the rectory on Monday morning, a welcoming smile warming her wrinkled Irish face.

"Our Eyetalian Mama is in the parlor with Father Foley," she announces. "For the life of me, I don't know what she ever did to deserve the likes of our dear Father Rossi."

Whenever she wasn't too pressed for time, Sue enjoyed visiting with Nora whose gossip was usually charitable and often punctuated with charmingly expressed insights. But when the conversation turned critical, she had learned simply not to respond. So she said nothing in reply to Nora's comment although she knew exactly what she was talking about.

On the first night of Father's wake, her own disappointment in meeting Mrs. Rossi had been extreme. She wasn't sure what she had expected but certainly not this short, stocky, overweight woman whose broad hips and heavy thighs were encased in tight-fitting black pants and whose T shirt sported a large sunflower which blossomed incongruously on the shelf of her matronly bosom.

What's more, she had been a complainer. God came in for his share of blame. And then nothing was right about the wake. She seemed to despise the lovely arrangements of shaggy, winter-white chrysanthemums that Sue had procured at her own expense. Why weren't there roses? Shouldn't there be roses for a funeral? And where was a comfortable chair? Her feet were killing her but these kinky chairs were hardly worth sitting on. And who were all these people streaming into the baptistery? She seemed to resent the large crowd of strangers who kept pressing her hand and murmuring sympathy, all these well-dressed parishioners and diocesan priests and Dominicans (Sue wondered at the number of Dominicans) and school children who thought so highly of her son. She told Sue she wished the funeral could have been in her own parish where her family and neighbors could have laughed together at old memories and wept if they wanted to.

Sue was not unsympathetic to her feelings and after a little time had elapsed, arranged for the family and their friends to gather together in the priests' dining room where she served coffee and some hastily purchased cookies. But the rectory surroundings seemed to make this a less than successful gesture. The group stood around stiffly and soon decided to go home. As she was leaving, Mrs. Rossi patted Sue's cheek.

"Pauley sometimes says to me how you are a good girl, always doing a kind thing," she said. "He liked you and so do I."

Sue smiles now remembering this rather patronizing expression of gratitude. It pleased her to know that Father Rossi had mentioned her to his mother. But she has something else on her mind right now.

"You know, Nora," she says, "there's something I want to tell you because I know how relieved you'll be. Tim James went into the hospital last Saturday where he's getting good care and a fresh start on the AA program. You were so kind to give him coffee the day of the Cardinal's visit, trying to sober him up before he left the rectory."

"Where would you be hearing such a story?" says Nora. "I haven't set eyes on poor Mr. James in a month of Sundays. Of course, we all know the dear man has a bit of a problem, and it's mighty glad I am if they've found a way to cure it. But I never brought coffee to Tim James any time lately nor has he been near the rectory to see his friend Father Foley.

So much for the alibi Father Foley had given young Timmy concerning his father's whereabouts at the time of the murder. When Mrs. Rossi emerges from the parlor and is laboring up the stairs to her son's bedroom, Sue follows with a heavy heart. It would have been a wonderful relief to have eliminated Tim from suspicion but the fact that he had not been at the rectory on the day of the murder seemed to confirm that Father Foley's story was a cover-up.

Father Rossi's room seems devoid of anything personal. It has the bare, spare Spartan look of a monastic cell or a room in a retreat house: a bed, a desk, a chest of drawers, a crucifix over the bookcases. It does not take the women long to go though and sort out his few belongings. Mrs. Rossi takes underwear, socks and sport shirts for her grandsons but spurns the handsome sweater Sue and Fred had given their friend for Christmas.

"Joey and the others wouldn't be caught dead in a classy item like that," she says, "But maybe, Sweetheart, you'd like it for your hubby."

Reluctantly, Sue takes the sweater. Although she knows she could never bear to see Fred wear it, she feels that she is being offered a gift that she should accept.

Father Rossi's library interests her. There is a fine collection of spiritual classics, a large selection of liberation theology, some biography and history and several hefty volumes on constitutional government. She and Mrs. Rossi agree that any spiritual books should be donated to the parish library and the rest given to Brandeis. Sue asks if she might keep the stack of magazines on the floor under the window. They were the only untidy note in the neat room and it seems to Sue that they must have been saved for a purpose. They are her last hope of finding anything of significance. She empties the contents of his desk into a carton and says she will ask Father Foley if she should go through to see if there are matters that need attention. Then she takes down the crucifix, a contemporary one with a simple metal figure of Jesus mounted on fine-grained, polished wood.

"Here," she says, blowing a little dust from the thorn-crowned head and the narrow cross bar. "I knew we would find some lovely memento that you would like to have for yourself."

But Mrs. Rossi shakes her head vehemently. "Who needs another cross?" she asks. "I've got enough crosses. My mother's hand-painted crucifix from Bologna is right now hanging over my bed. Why should I want another cross?"

Sue finds herself exasperated by this negative response to her offer.

"I thought because it was his," she says.

"I know you think that, and you don't know me so well and don't know what I am saying. I am saying that you were Pauley's good friend and maybe you should have his cross. I would like you to have the memento."

Sue looks at Mrs. Rossi then, at this corpulent woman whose thick gray hair falls in heavy waves to her plump shoulders and whose surprisingly light blue eyes are sunk deep in the flesh of her fat, olive face. And she is caught off-guard by a sudden glimmer of resemblance; found in those eyes, half-buried, a dear familiar kindness which brought sudden tears to her own eyes.

"Thanks," she says. "It would mean a lot to me."

The gift of the crucifix makes lunch a lot easier for Sue. She has taken Mrs. Rossi to the Dickens café; a place she realizes is a poor choice as soon as the menus are brought. A half-sandwich and a cup of homemade soup are not apt to satisfy her guest's appetite nor will the attractive décor impress her much. Still, this is her opportunity to find out what she can about Father Rossi's childhood and she is pleased to find his mother responsive to her questions.

Paul was the oldest of her five boys. She and her husband had only been a year in this country when she became pregnant with him and he was the first child in the history of their family to be born in a hospital. Mrs. Rossi would never forget the wonder and joy of his birth. All night long in her hospital bed, she kept waking, her heart singing with exhalation at the thought of her own baby son lying in his crib just down the hall from her room. And, although her other sons followed swiftly on his heels, he had remained her favorite. Still, it seemed to Mrs. Rossi that he had not belonged to her long, that he had been snatched from her in early childhood.

Sue can see bitterness and pain in Mrs. Rossi's pudgy face. Very gently, she asks her what she means.

"You know how Pauley walked," she asks. "With his toes pointing east and west?"

Sue smiles remembering well how he had toed out a little, how his body swayed slightly from side to side as he walked.

"Well, I can see him still setting off for school on his first day, can see him walking away from me, walking down the sidewalk toward Notre Dame with that independent little strut of his as though it were yesterday. And I can't tell you what sadness overtook me when I watched him go. How could I know that he was leaving me? How could I possibly know? But my heart knew what would happen. My heart knew that he would never really be my boy again."

It was Mrs. Rossi's impression that the school had swallowed up her son, had robbed her of his primary affection. He never said anything bratty like the boy Jesus had done to his mother when he was found in the temple, but something of the same kind had happened. Sister Angela, the Principal who found him so bright, had adopted him as her own. She took a personal interest in his preparation for First Holy Communion. As he grew older, she allowed him to use her office for his homework as home was too crowded and noisy for concentration. He was a good athlete as well as a good student and she arranged for him to coach the younger children and to do some tutoring for which she paid him a reasonable pittance. He was seldom home: his whole life revolved around the school and church where he went to serve Mass early in the morning. And when he graduated, Sister saw that he got a scholarship to St. Ignatius High School.

Who could blame Sister Angela? She was this skinny saint who worked herself to the bone for the children, a little toothpick of a nun whose loose habit flapped behind her as she raced from place to place. Still, it seemed to Mrs. Rossi that the Church had stolen her child.

The whine, the complaining, self-pitying whine, had returned to Mrs. Rossi's voice so that Sue found herself resisting any sympathy she may have felt for her.

"Perhaps we all lose our children a little when they go off to school," she says.

"If you are just learning to speak the language when your boy already is reading it, you lose him a lot."

Sue looks at her watch. "I'm due down at Community Hospital in a while," she says. "I have time to drive you home."

Mrs. Rossi lived on the near West Side just down the street from old Notre Dame Church. Sue watches her as she waddles up the narrow sidewalk to her small, flat-roofed red brick house. She sits in the car for a few minutes looking at the humble home in which Father Rossi had shared a room with four younger brothers and at this tired, shabby neighborhood in which he had grown up.

What had she learned from his mother? That the lovely church and old school at the corner had been an oasis in the intellectual dryness of his early life; that in high school he had a steady sweetheart named Anna Maria but that he had broken up with her when he transferred to the junior seminary; that his father, who worked at a local nuts and bolts factory had been very proud of his choice of the priesthood but that his mother always wished he had married Anna Maria and lived close by as Joey did; that once he had gone to the seminary at Mundelein, his parents had really kissed him goodbye.

When he was ordained, he was assigned to a black parish instead of being sent to his own people. The Cardinal was an ass to do things like that. Later, he was always sending postcards with no news on them from Central America. He had presided at his brothers' weddings and been dutiful about remembering birthdays and Mother's day and even came to see his parents some Sundays but who wanted duty? His heart was always elsewhere. And when his father died a few years ago, where was he, his father's pride and joy? He was in Alvarado somewhere. Of course he flew in to offer the funeral Mass but what good did that do for poor Anthony who was already gone?

As she starts back for Evanston driving along Ashland Avenue toward Armitage, Sue spots the Camaro behind her. In broad daylight and on a crowded street, it frightens her less than previously. She tries to go on reviewing Father Rossi's early life, savoring the sense of it and wondering if somehow the seeds of his death had been planted there.

CHAPTER XV

The admissions clerk at the hospital is a pert, homely woman with a double chin and horn-rimmed glasses. She greets Sue in her usual jocular way.

"You're late," she says. "Don't you realize that you're holding the whole world up? Dr. Young has been leaving messages for you to see her in her office as soon as you arrive. Something about a new patient from your parish."

"Who could that be? I just stopped by to bring a couple of Sarah's books for Cindy Downs."

"Cindy was discharged this morning with her jaw all jammed up with wire. Her poor Mom is going to have to puree her food for weeks on end. Why don't you park the books with me until you leave? I comprehend exceptionally well at the fifth grade level."

"Okay. Any idea who this new patient is?"

"Name's here somewhere. Ah, here it is. Elena Esquivel. She's in psychiatric."

Elena! Sue wastes no time finding her way through the labyrinthine corridors of the hospital to Dr. Young's office. The reception room serves several doctors and is crowded with patients in casts, in wheel chairs, with eye patches or simply sitting dejectedly in hospital gowns thumbing old magazines. The receptionist says Dr. Young has a patient with her but has left instructions for Sue to knock on her door as soon as she arrives. Sue thinks that whatever is wrong with Elena, she couldn't have a better doctor than Joan Young. She knows her well both through the parish and through consultative contacts in the hospital. She is a comfortable, middle-aged woman with a stocky, solid build, short steel-gray hair and a plain, kind face. Her perception, diagnostic skill and common sense are legendary. She is highly respected by the hospital staff and is so much in demand that there is often a long wait for her services.

When she comes to the door of her office to talk with Sue, Dr. Young explains that Father Foley had pleaded with her to take Elena's case since she was a foreigner with no family or friends in the area. Elena had been brought into the hospital in an ambulance early that morning after a violent attack on her husband. She had been taken to the psychiatric ward and was heavily sedated so that she was now resting peacefully. Joan had arrived at the hospital only at noon and had not yet had an opportunity to examine her as she had a couple of urgent appointments to keep first. Elena's husband was in the waiting room down the hall near the elevators. Would Sue be kind enough to keep him company until she had a chance to examine the patient and get back to him?

"Of course," says Sue. "But what do you think is the matter with Elena? I had noticed some mood swings but never anticipated an episode like this."

"Off hand, I don't know. It may be something situational and non-recurring or it may be something serious, schizophrenia perhaps. We'll need a while to evaluate it. In the meantime, I think both she and her husband could use your friendship."

Sue detects genuine concern in Joan's attentive, somber eyes and assures her that she would be glad to help out. She finds Gabriel, hands in pockets and shoulders hunched, looking out the window of the waiting room. He is obviously relieved to see her and approaches her in his own upbeat, humorous way. His right hand is bandaged and, with a small shrug, he shakes her hand with his left.

"Well," he says, "we had a little soap opera scene at our house this morning. I suppose they told you?"

"Just that it happened. Do you want to fill me in on the details?" Sue settles on the sofa and indicates to Gabriel that he should sit next to her.

"Well," he says, "this morning in the kitchen I am being the chef. Elena has found it difficult to adjust to a life without servants so here I am whipping up these delicious oeuves rancheros for breakfast."

Gabriel kisses his fingers and holds them high to indicate how exquisite these eggs were that he was preparing.

"And then, Elena, the lady of the house, appears in her peignoir in the doorway. I don't look at her because I am very preoccupied with my heavenly creation but I say to her, 'Elena, put on the coffee, will you?' That is all I say to her but you should know that Elena has resisted mastering the simplicity of the Mr. Coffee Maker as she has resisted almost every other household chore and responsibility since we arrived. I have helped her out but I also am trying to be firm that she should learn the American way of doing everything for yourself. I remind her that it is her own choice that she came to this country. She says she had no idea that Americans were so poor they had to do their own cooking. So we have been having this tug of war with me saying 'Elena you must learn' and Elena saying 'I can't' or 'I won't.' and somehow this morning when I say this ordinary thing, Elena will you put on the coffee, that is the straw to break the donkey's back."

Gabriel pauses, perhaps reluctant to continue. She waits patiently but as the silence grows, lays an encouraging hand on his arm.

"That's how things often happen. Some little thing cracks open the dam and suddenly there is a flood."

"More like an electrical storm," Gabriel smiles ruefully. "Elena began by shouting at me to let her alone and I, stupid fellow, shout back that it won't kill her to put on the coffee. I am not looking or I would realize that she is not merely angry but furious and out of control. Then suddenly she is pounding on my shoulders with her fists and screaming

'Stop it! Stop it!' and it sinks into this thick skull that something serious is happening. When I wheel around to face her, she snatches up the sharp knife from the kitchen counter. You can see it does not pay to chop peppers for the rancheros before breakfast."

Gabriel grabbed Elena's wrists and attempted to take the knife from her but discovered that rage had released great strength into her trembling body. In the struggle, his hand was cut between the thumb and forefinger severing sinew and creating stunning pain. He realized immediately that with his right hand so impaired, he would be unable to wrest the knife from her and so he fled from the kitchen. Remembering his flight, Gabriel smiles a sad, mocking smile that seemed to say, can't you see how ridiculous all this is?

Gabriel went on to give a farcical account of Elena's relentless pursuit of him through their house; the overturned furniture, the near collision in the pantry, his final escape to the second floor enough ahead of her so that he could grab the phone from the hall table and lock himself in the bathroom with it. He had called Father Foley explaining that Elena had flipped her lid and was out of control and asked if he could recommend a good psychiatrist who would come to the house.

Father Foley told Gabriel that doctors didn't make house calls these days. He said that he would phone the paramedics and explain the situation to them. He was certain that they would be there in no time flat and would know exactly how to handle Elena. He recommended Dr. Young as an excellent psychiatrist and offered to call her himself as she was usually booked months ahead and perhaps he could be influential in getting her to take the case.

Gabriel recounts all this with the excitement and verve of a seasoned Hispanic storyteller. One eyebrow is comically cocked and a self-deprecatory amusement lights his dark eyes. His whole attitude seems to indicate that the incident was absurd and one might as well shrug one's shoulders and smile at it. But just beneath this droll disinterest, like a pulse beating wildly beneath the thin skin of one's wrist, Sue senses apprehension and deep anxiety. Another time she would respond with humorous banter of her own but not now.

"You do know that when someone is disturbed they tend to attack the person they most love and are dependent on?" she says.

"That's what the doctor who admitted Elena told me."

"Dr. Young thinks it may be only a situational reaction. Perhaps if Elena's been under a lot of stress adjusting to life in the U.S., it's just a temporary aberration which won't recur. Do you know if she has a history of episodes like this?"

"In an odd way," Gabriel says, "Elena's had a tough life, the poor little rich girl, you understand? But no. I don't think there have been occurrences of violence before. Growing up she was often moody and sometimes angry with her mother but never anything like this."

"You knew her growing up?"

"I knew her very well. You see Elena is my sister. I think, Susan, it is time to drop this whole charade that she and her mother invented when we were coming to America. We are not husband and wife and we do not come from Spain but from Alvarado. I had been involved in giving testimony to the UN Truth Commission on war crimes there and my family considered it dangerous for me to remain in the country."

"But I thought the war was over, that there was an end to the oppression and the killings in Alvarado."

"True, a treaty was signed and there is progress toward achieving the solutions that were agreed upon. But some important changes in the army have never been implemented and there are still incidents of retaliation against those who have been working for reform. Bishop Aguilar calls it an epidemic of selected violence.

"Just a few years ago a friend of mine, a journalist, discovered that the Alvarado army was selling arms to guerillas in Guatemala and Honduras and were also in the business of selling drugs in Mexico and the United States. When he threatened to reveal his finding, the army arrested him and eighteen days of torture began. They make a truly delicate art of torture!"

Gabriel is trying for a light touch again, but there is no possibility of camouflaging the bitterness in his tone. Sue could hear an angry hammer in his voice.

"This man's hands and ribs were broken. Torturers applied electric shock to his genitals and dug into his teeth with an ice pick. He was held in solitary confinement for eighteen months before being released to the general prison population. He went to trial several times because jurors who had been threatened would not appear at his trial. Eventually he was found innocent and is now living in Mexico but always in constant fear.

"My parents have not forgotten what can happen to someone who reveals incriminating evidence and they became concerned for me. My usefulness seemed to have reached an end so I agreed to come here where my father arranged a position at Citibank for me. Elena was dying to come along. Living in Alvarado has been an intolerable situation for her. We belong to an old Alvarado family which settled in the country way back in the 19th Century but we are one of the few such families that have been committed to reform, especially to reform of land tenure. This does not make us popular with the people of our own milieu.

"Elena feels that she has been spurned by her young contemporaries, that whole group of government and military families with whom she would normally associate. My mother was always concerned about Elena and in her sophomore year sent her to boarding school to the Sacred Heart Convent in New Orleans. She made close friends there. It was a good experience for her although she was often homesick. But whenever she returned, I think she felt more out of it than ever. I would guess that the climate of ostracism in which she was living badly affected her self-esteem. In any case, maybe because she was desperately seeking love and acceptance, Elena has had two illegitimate pregnancies."

Gabriel hesitates a moment, looking quizzically at Sue. "It is right that I should tell you all this, yes?"

"Absolutely. I am Elena's friend and I want to understand. But much as I hate to interrupt your story, I am wondering if you have been waiting here for hours and if you ever had any lunch?"

"They told me the doctor would be in at noon. I've only been here since then. And to tell the truth, Susan, I'm not very hungry."

"That's good. The sandwiches in the Auxiliary Shop are excellent but hardly hefty. They know me down there and I can give you express service. You'd better wait here in case Dr. Young comes to find you."

After slight protest, Gabriel agrees to let Sue bring him a BLT. Hurrying along the hospital corridor toward the restaurant, she feels a little guilty to find herself once again considering Elena as a serious suspect in the murder of Father Rossi. She was sincere in saying that she wanted to be her friend but the violent attack of the morning opened the door to second thoughts about her possible involvement.

Sue has a clear intuitive feeling that at last she might be on the right track, that Father Rossi's death was somehow connected to Elena and the violent country from which she came. It was as though the piece of the puzzle she held in her hand was the right color, had the proper design on it but that the shape refused to fit in place.

If the cord Sue had glimpsed in Elena's sewing bag on the day of the murder had indeed been connected to the weapon hair dryer, how had it wound up in the poor box? She had dropped Elena at home. How would she have known there was a drop box and why would she have walked all the way back to the church complex to get rid of the dryer? The clothes in which it was wrapped presented a problem also. Although they might well have fit Gabriel, they were hardly his style. Things do not add up very well, but the hunch that she is on to something goes right on humming in her head.

When she returns with the sandwich and a cup of coffee, Sue is relieved to discover that Gabriel is still alone in the waiting room. From time to time, people pass through to use the elevators but no one remains long enough to destroy the privacy of their conversation. Gabriel proves to be hungrier than he had thought. Taking quick bites of his sandwich and swift sips of coffee, he seems eager to respond to Sue's questions and to resume his story.

"Elena's first pregnancy had occurred when she was very young, only fourteen. The father had been a childhood friend, the son of the plantation manager. Fortunately, it had resulted in an early miscarriage and it had not been difficult to arrange distance between the young people. The other pregnancy had been just a couple of years ago and in some ways had been far more shattering. The father was a professional man, a friend of the family, and this time Elena carried the baby to term. She was very romantic and emotional about the whole affair for which you could hardly blame her. She was desperately in love with the man and would like to have married him and kept the child but this was never a possible solution."

"He was already married?"

Gabriel nods. "A man with many responsibilities. My father never blamed him too much. He had just endured an enormously shocking experience and was under great stress and fatigue at the time. And we all knew that Elena could be very seductive and aggressive about getting what she wants. No one ever said as much, but I have wondered if Elena had not hoped that her pregnancy would somehow trap this fellow into a marriage. She kept persisting in her hope that somehow that would be the outcome although it was impossibly unrealistic."

"Poor Elena."

"Yes. You can see she has had a troubled background. All this was hard for Elena but equally hard for my mother. My mother is the saint, you know, a gentle lady whose halo is maybe a little tight. She spends her days telling her beads for our poor, war-torn country and depriving herself of candy, wine, even of reading favorite authors, making bargains with God to keep her children out of trouble. For such a holy woman, Elena's pregnancies were traumatic. She tended to think of them as terrible moral transgressions instead of understanding them in simple, human terms.

"Of course in our social milieu, it would not have been possible for Elena to remain at home while she was pregnant. On both occasions, she was sent to stay with my aunt in the country. Although my mother wrote her frequent, loving letters, I think Elena felt deserted by her. And although mother had her best interests at heart, I think being sent to the States to school after her miscarriage may have seemed like punishment or banishment to Elena.

"In any case, she became very attached to my aunt who was wonderfully kind to her and always managed to make light of her situation. I think when Aunt Maria Luisa died just before we left for the States, Elena felt that she was losing the only person who ever understood her. And then Father Rossi's death was a terrible blow too."

"Father Rossi? Did Elena know Father Rossi?"

"She must have known him from the time she was a child of nine or ten. He was very fond of her and I think the attention he used to pay to her was very important in her life."

Thinking about Father Rossi's relationship with her own daughter, Jennifer, Sue understood how much his affection must have meant to this little left-out girl in Alvarado.

"You knew Father Rossi too, then? How did you happen to know him?"

Gabriel remembered very well when he first met Paul Rossi because it was just at the time of the Assante massacre in December of '86. Rumors of this tragedy in which the army killed more than one thousand campesinos had reached San Christobal but were not generally believed. Gabriel's father contacted a friend, the pastor at Maryknoll's Good Shepherd Parish on the northern outskirts of San Christobal, to see what he might know. The missionaries too had heard only rumors. However, they had a priest visiting them from the United States who felt compelled to investigate the matter for himself and to see what had really happened. The priest was, of course, Father Rossi from the archdiocesan mission office in Chicago. It was agreed that he and Gabriel would go together on this trip of investigation.

"Do you know about Assante?" Gabriel inquires.

"I'm sure I read about it but my recollection is pretty vague."

"Well, what we discovered was horrendous. Assante was a poor village in which there had been close-knit families, small shops, a school, a church in which Mass was celebrated with great zeal. The people had high hope that their situation of misery and repression would improve, that one day they would win their freedom. And then came this cruel massacre. The men were gathered into the church and shot. They brought the women together, young and old, and raped and killed them. One hundred children were shot or bayoneted to death. By killing the whole village, the army tried to do away with the social base of the guerillas, to scare the hell out of all the villages so that none of them would support the rebels. Actually, I think it galvanized support for reformation and change. It certainly affected my own life and Father Rossi's too. We became good friends and often worked together although he became much more involved than I. It was about Assante that I gave testimony to the UN Truth Commission.

"Anyway, when we were leaving for the States, my mother was worried about Elena and thought that if she arrived as a married woman, she was less apt to get in trouble again. Elena loves to play a role so she decided to represent herself as my wife. I agreed to this silly arrangement to keep the women happy but I told Elena that the idea that we are from Spain is ridiculous and bound to backfire. Everyone at the bank knows I am from Alvarado. But Elena is romantic, you know. She wanted to have a new life and thought that having a Spanish background was far more interesting than a Alvarado one."

Sue remembers how insistently Elena had informed Father Rossi that she was from Spain on the day of the first Scripture meeting.

"You knew Father Rossi was in our parish when you moved here?"

"Actually no. We knew he was in the Chicago area and planned to look him up but it was pure coincidence that we landed in his parish. I had a good visit with him at the rectory before the accident. His death hit us both very hard and perhaps the shock of it is part of what has derailed Elena."

Thinking of the theory that people who are disturbed sometimes attack those on whom they most depend, Sue begins wondering what Elena's relationship with Father Rossi had been.

"I remember well how distressed she was," she says. "Had he been her spiritual director or her counselor in some way?"

"No. I think she only remembered him very fondly from the old days. Actually, she had not seen him in three or four years until we moved here."

Not much of a lead there. Sue looks at her watch. She would just make it home in time for the children if she left promptly. She invites Gabriel for a pot roast dinner but he says he has to return to the office to finish up pressing business and asks if he can have a "check for the rain." She assures him that they will make it another time soon and that she will come to see Elena the following day if visitors are allowed.

Sue had left her car on the third level of the hospital garage. As she emerges from the elevator, she sees the white Camaro pull out of the slot next to the one in which she had parked and speed down the circular ramp. It is well out of sight by the time she reaches her automobile. Glancing in the back seat where she had left a plastic yard bag full of things she had taken from Father Rossi's room, she discovers that it has been emptied pell-mell onto the floor. Checking carefully, she decides that everything is still there, the cross buried under the disorderly pile of magazines, the sweater tossed carelessly on the seat. She finds this invasion of her privacy distressing and frightening. What could it mean

and how had it happened since she is absolutely certain that she had
locked her car?

Chapter XVI

"Bentley," Fred says. "Representative Dick Bentley, a Democrat from Massachusetts. He set up his own investigation into the murders of the four Dominicans at the University of San Christobal. So the growing information we have about the situation in Alvarado isn't all from idealistic Catholic missionaries."

Sue is glad Fred has arrived home in time for this part of her conversation with Bill Bergman. Her knowledge of the brutal twelve-year civil war in Alvarado is meager but she knows Fred had often discussed it with Father Rossi and would be able to supply Bill with the information he is seeking about Father's political convictions concerning that small Central American country.

Bill had arrived at the front door just as Sue was shoving her pot roast, liberally smothered in mushroom and dried onion soup, into the oven. It was still early, a little after five. She was not expecting Fred until later although she was impatiently waiting for him to come home. The invasion of her car had left her tense, edgy. If the enigmatic black man could get into her automobile without a key, might he not be able also to enter her home? Her drive from the hospital had been punctuated by alternating bouts of fear and frustration. A winter storm had set in, a high northwest wind slashing gritty, fine snow against the windshield. Streets were slippery and traffic slow but in the end, thank God, she had made it home before the children. Now when the doorbell rings, it sends tingling alarms through her entire body. For one panic-stricken moment before she can summon reserves of courage and common sense, she almost decides not to answer it. Her relief to find Bill Bergman waiting on her stoop is enormous. God, how good he looks to her standing there with his coat collar turned up against the wind and snow glistening in his crisp, crew-cut hair! Next to Fred, no one could have been more welcome.

Bill has stopped by on his way home to tell her that he had talked with the personnel manager at his law firm about a possible position for her Haitian friend. He had received a satisfactory answer and wanted to let her know right away. The firm would need a couple of secretaries soon and the French language skill would be a great asset. Bill suggests that Sue tell her friend to call for an interview within a week or two.

Other events had temporarily crowded out Sue's concern for Adele Adabeau but she is impressed with Bill's promptness in tracking down a job for her and very grateful to him for his interest. She adds "reliable" to her growing list of positive adjectives to describe him. She tells him that she has to finish paring vegetables for supper but invites him to join her in the kitchen and have a beer while she finishes up.

Bill declines the beer but says he would like a few minutes to review the material about Father Rossi's murder that Mike has run off on his computer for him. At Sue's suggestion, he had cornered Mike after Mass the day before and talked with him about his suspicions of foul play. Mike had hedged a bit at first but in the end seemed happy to accept an offer of help. He found he no longer had much time to work on the case. In fact, he was due to go on duty shortly but had a few minutes to drive down to the office with Bill and give him a printout of the information they had so far collected. He had suggested that Sue could fill him in on details and perhaps answer any questions.

In the kitchen Bill snaps open his brief case and begins lining up papers in a deft, precise fashion on the table. Sue puts down her carrot peeler for a moment to observe him. She realizes immediately that this is not to be the casual conversation she had anticipated, that he approaches it in an authoritative, business-like way. She senses some real significance in his attitude, some seismic shift for the better in their haphazard investigation. She hastily checks the freezer to verify that there is frozen spinach for last minute cooking, then returns the raw vegetables to the crisper and sits down opposite Bill.

He rewards her with one of his rare, reticent smiles.

"Sure you got time for this, Sue?"

"Quite sure."

He places charts in front of her which seem to outline the information he has obtained. She is impressed with how they immediately clarify what they know about clues and access to the baptistery.

"Let's run these over," Bill suggests. "Mike says this Elena is Spanish and acts oddly but not enough is known to consider her a suspect."

Sue hesitates only a minute. She has already completed a mental screening of the Esquivel situation in preparation for a report to Mike and quickly decides to stick with it although she feels that it might be possible to share more information with Bill. She has an instinctive trust in his discretion. She thinks it wise not to mention the hospital at all since it would inevitably lead to questions about Elena which Sue considers absolutely confidential.

"Jo James is doing some interior decorating for the Esquivels," she says. "And we were up at their house on Sunday so I've had a chance to find out more about them. I've had a long conversation with Gabriel and discovered that our impression that they are a Spanish couple is mistaken. Actually they are siblings and come from Alvarado. They belong to an old wealthy family there. The father is in the banking business and owns a coffee plantation. They both knew Father Rossi since the early eighties. Gabriel and Father met when he was staying at a Maryknoll missionary parish in Alvarado. They evidently went together to investigate the El Assante massacre and became good friends after that working on projects for reform."

"I remember the so-called Assante massacre," says Bill. "The whole thing was a big myth propagated by the Communist guerillas to discredit the army. I think our government checked it out pretty carefully."

"Gabriel claims it was a grim fact. He has recently testified about what he witnessed to the UN Truth Commission. Anyway, about Elena. She had the opportunity, but I cannot for the life of me dream up a possible motive for her to want to murder Father. But I'll tell you what, Bill. I've got this huge hunch that Father's death is somehow connected to Alvarado."

Bill's reserved face with its subtle, fine print expressions is hard to read and Sue finds herself scanning it for reactions. Now, at the mention of the intensity of her intuition, he narrows his deep set eyes and looks at her attentively.

"You might be on to something," he agrees. "What about this Gabriel? It's hard to believe that the son of one of those coffee kings is really interested in land reform. And if Father was lined up on the left, it's possible that this man was his enemy."

"I told you, they were friends. I gathered they saw things in the same way."

"You believed that?"

"Yes, I believed that."

"Okay, let's leave the Esquivels aside for a moment. Mike is convinced that Tim James is responsible for the murder. He evidently told his young son that he planned to kill him and he was undeniably out of control that day. Still, there is no real evidence that he was ever at the baptistery."

For a moment Sue wonders if she should mention the AA prayer cord but decides against it.

"Mike may not be very objective in his judgment," she says. "He's an old friend of Tim's wife and resents what his alcoholism has done to her. I may not be very objective but I'm sure he didn't do it. We just have to track down the real murderer so there won't be any doubts about his innocence."

"An open question, I guess, but the murder seems too planned to have been executed by a man in Tim's condition. And then there's Winnie Harris. I know there's this business about finding the hair drier but I spent some time with Winnie house hunting and she certainly didn't strike me as a murderer."

"There is something about Father giving her some advice which infuriated her but that hardly seems like a strong motive for murder."

"But Mike says you could visualize her doing it?"

Sue smiles and quickly relates her ridiculous fantasy about Winnie knocking Father out with a candlestick. She had meant to illustrate that of all the women under suspicion, Winnie was the only one with the physical strength to actually murder Father. The hair drier was not conclusive. Someone else might have dropped it in the box but gloves which were found with it looked like some which belonged to Winnie's husband, Boyd.

"What about Boyd?"

"Can't come up with anything. He and Father were old friends. But I'll keep trying for more information."

"And then there's Jens. With a prison record and an expressed grievance against Father Rossi, he seems the most likely suspect to me. Also, he admits to having been at the baptistery in the right time frame. Here, have a look at this."

Bill hands Sue a copy from the page of an encyclopedia. In the left column is a paragraph entitled ELECTROCUTION. Sue scans it quickly, noting particularly the lines that Bill has highlighted.

> The criminal to be electrocuted is strapped into a specially constructed chair. One electrode is applied to the scalp, the other to the calf of one leg. The electrodes are moistened with a salt solution to ensure adequate contact. Death ensues within two minutes after the current has started to flow through the body.

"I called Mike this morning and asked him to check the hair dryer to see if any salt solution had been applied but if so, it was carefully wiped off as were the finger prints. But obviously the murderer was familiar with the process of electrocution. Perhaps Jens picked up that information in prison."

"If it's in the encyclopedia, anyone might have picked it up."

"You don't suspect Jens?"

"I did briefly but I had a long talk with Monsignor about the death of his wife and I'm convinced that it was accidental. I honestly don't think Jens is our man."

"Well, maybe not. I think that we have to track down more information about who was at the baptistery that day. We don't know that Tim James was ever there or even Winnie for that matter. And, maybe more important, we don't know who else may have had access at the approximate time of the murder."

Bill slips another paper across the table to Sue.

"Here," he says. "I sketched this plan of the church property. It's not exactly a professional architect's drawing but I think it will serve our purposes."

"The church and the school are a little skinny but it looks pretty accurate to me. I see you drew in my magnificent blue spruce in front of the baptistery."

"*Your* blue spruce? I thought it was *my* blue spruce?"

"How about our blue spruce?"

"Agreed. Our blue spruce."

How to describe Bill's smile? Engaging, playful, amused. But there is another quality more difficult to define. Perhaps confidential, a very entre-nous smile. Like the one at the swing in his side yard, it seems to bond their friendship.

(map)

"Now," says Bill. "If you'll look at this sketch, you'll see that the only place from which one can see the front entrance to the baptistery is the school. Do you know if anyone was in the school that morning?"

Sue shakes her head. "We had the meeting at the baptistery because the school was closed. Father Foley doesn't like to heat it for just one meeting."

"Well, how about across the street? Do you know anyone who lives in any of the houses opposite the entrance?"

"We just might be in luck. There's an old invalid, Kathy Kennedy, who lives in the second floor apartment across from the baptistery. Someone brings her Communion every morning. I'm scheduled for Sundays but I can trade with whoever is on the list for tomorrow and stay on for a visit. We all try to do that anyway. The fortunate part for us is that she's in a wheel chair and spends a good deal of time looking out the window."

"Of course it's getting to be a while since that Saturday. It would be a miracle if she remembered."

"But the big snow that morning may have made it eventful for her. And the fact that Father Rossi died that day. Maybe those things will help her to recall."

"Good. Will you give it a try? And then the poor box, both the Convent and the rectory have windows facing it. Would any of the nuns besides Sister Thomasita possibly have seen someone make a deposit? Pixie and I were with Father Foley just about noon getting registered in the parish and he was going to have lunch when we left so I doubt that he was looking out any windows, but might his housekeeper have seen someone?"

"The Convent is now a retirement home for a few old nuns but I'll check it out with them. The rectory kitchen is here in the rear of the building with windows overlooking the garden toward the parking lot. Nora has sharp eyes if she happened to be looking out."

"I hope it turns up something. Now, back to our chart. The next thing we have is clues. Mighty little there. As far as I can see, the only items found on the scene of the crime were a pair of gloves which Boyd Harris claimed and which presumably were left after the scripture meeting and a pen found on the table with the name of Bennington Insurance Company engraved on it. I thought I recalled that name from back home so I phoned St. Paul to check it out and discovered that Bennington has offices in St. Paul and Minneapolis."

Bill has become so serious and business-like again that Sue cannot resist teasing him.

"You know who that makes a suspect," she says.

Bill's smile is swift and appreciative. "How sharp you are!" he exclaims. "See that you keep that in mind."

The next thing on Bill's list is the profiles of suspects Mike has compiled from Sue's reports to him. She is amused to see how brief and cryptic Mike's notes are compared to the descriptive ones she had been keeping in her own notebook.

"I can give you more details on these people if you like," she offers.

"Maybe the most important profile is Father Rossi's. I was interested in his dedication to the civil rights movement and his community work in the inner city but we seem to lose track after that."

"Well," says Sue, "I learned just today that he spent a good deal of time in Central America, maybe mostly in Alvarado, while he was working at the Propagation of the Faith office down town. And from what Gabriel said, he seems to have taken an interest in reform in Alvarado. When I talk with Gabriel again, I'll try to find out more. I also learned a little about his childhood from his mother. I saw his home today when I drove her there. I can't get over what a humble piece of real estate it is. It's hard to imagine raising five boys in such small quarters."

"They all slept in cots in one bedroom which was known as 'the barracks,'" says Bill. "Mr. Rossi came to this country after serving in the Italian army in World War II. He tended to rule the roost with harsh, military discipline. It amused me to learn that because Pixie calls my own father 'the general.'"

It turns out that Bill knows a great deal more about Father Rossi's childhood than Sue does. Early in their acquaintance, the men had discovered that they both came from immigrant families and had grown up with excessively autocratic fathers. Exchanging humorous stories about their boyhood had quickly cemented a friendship between them.

Their fathers were actually quite different. Mr. Rossi was often loud and demanding and certainly tolerated no back talk from his sons but he was also a passionately affectionate man. Father Rossi had said that the noise, the decibels of discord when his brothers were in trouble, had been intolerable but on the whole anger and love had been equally and vociferously expressed. Sound seemed to resonate in his memories of home, a roller coaster of rowdy racket sometimes strident, sometimes joyous, not unlike the opera which blared on the radio on Saturday afternoons filling the house with powerful and dramatic emotions.

"When he got to the seminary in Mundelein and had a room and bath to himself, he thought he had died and gone to heaven," Bill says.

Bill's father on the other hand, was silent and stern. As a member of a solitary Catholic family, he had developed a fierce fighting loyalty to his own faith which he had passed on to his children. He was a very patriotic man. In World War II he had served in the American army against Germany, his native country, with an absolute conviction of the necessity for saving the world for democracy. He had been appalled by what had happened under Hitler and had taken every possible occasion to impress on his young son the necessity for constant vigilance and willingness to fight for the rights and liberty of his fellow citizens.

As an adult, Bill was grateful that his father's patriotism had been inculcated in him as a basic value in his life. It stood him in good stead. Nevertheless, he had found his father difficult. He was a perfectionist who had made constant demands on his family which they found almost impossible to meet. With his three daughters, he was sometimes sentimentally affectionate and indulgent but with Bill, the oldest and the only boy, he was curt and strict. He had deeply ingrained German traits of order and propriety and held absolutely rigid ideas about how and when everything should be done. From Bill he exacted respectful and prompt obedience. Always uncertain where he stood with his father and eager to please him. Bill had complied with his commands. But within himself he reserved a private terrain that was off limits to his father's dominion.

Father Rossi had done this too, preserved a part of himself, which was free and independent of his father's constant strictures and the limitations of his dreams. Mr. Rossi fully expected Paul to follow him into the hardware company where he had struggled for years to build up status and seniority. He anticipated that his son, with his bright mind and better education, would quickly mount the ladder to executive positions, would succeed in ways he could not himself achieve. He often talked about how, through his own reputation for steady and reliable work, he would be able to procure a good entry-level position for Paul.

Paul understood how useless it would have been to argue with his father over his plans for his future. He nurtured his own dream of a vocation in private until he made up his mind to transfer from St. Ignatius High to the Junior Seminary. It took courage to approach his father with his decision. He expected all hell to break loose. He thought there would be tirades and shouting and perhaps weeks of contentious wrangling.

Mr. Rossi, however, received the news with uncharacteristic calm. Perhaps he had suspected all along that his son was cut out for a life quite different from his own. Or perhaps he had an intrinsic admiration for his boy who could so quietly and certainly defy his father's dream in favor or his own. And perhaps too, although he himself seldom attended Mass, he had a deep respect for the priesthood. In the end, he supported Paul enthusiastically and was proud of his choice.

"He was only sixteen when he took his father on," says Bill with obvious admiration. "I was finishing my sophomore year at Guelph Agricultural College in Canada when I finally got up enough nerve to tell my father that I had no desire to take over the farm. That was his big plan for me. When I told him that I had decided to become a lawyer, he didn't exactly take the news as easily as Mr. Rossi had taken Paul's."

Sue feels that Bill's story has not been shared widely with others and gives it the careful attention a confidence deserves.

"What happened?" she inquires with interested concern.

"Well, for an unbearably long time, he gave me the silent treatment. Even Father Rossi admitted that this cold lack of response might be harder to take than the hot-headed yelling to which he was sometimes subjected. When Dad finally talked about it, he said that he was willing to invest in an agricultural education but that financing the several years it would take to become an attorney would have to be up to me. How, he asked, did I expect to pay for it?

I told him I would find a way. I did manage to get a working scholarship to St. Thomas College in St. Paul for the remainder of my undergraduate work and later to make a loan to attend the University of Michigan Law School."

"The law must have meant as lot to you."

"Have you ever thought of how important the law is? It was the best way I could think of to fight injustice and, strangely enough, it was my father who had inspired me to do that. He was a man of strong moral principles and convictions."

Although she is aware of Bill's ambivalence towards his father, Sue decides to take a long shot.

"You loved him a lot, didn't you," she says.

"God, yes. The question always was, did he love me? I still find myself trying to live up to his expectations, doing extraordinary things sometimes to win what I imagine would be his approval. Anyway, Father Rossi and I enjoyed reminiscing about our run-ins with our bossy fathers. My childhood was so serious that I found it wonderful to be able to laugh at it with someone who understood what it was like. Actually, it wasn't until Pixie came along that I learned to see things in a humorous way. She was the best thing that ever happened to me."

It was when Bill and Pixie were discussing their ideals of parenting, how they hoped to retain old-fashioned discipline but also to fold in plenty of fun and friendship for Roger, that Father Rossi brought up the possibility of the Bergmans adopting the abandoned Mexican child.

"Has Monsignor Fiedler called you about that?" inquires Sue.

"Yes. I had a long visit with him Friday night. He's a great old gentleman, isn't he? I felt that you could tell him anything so I confided in him my reservations about raising a Mexican child, how that might affect Roger and how it might be for the boy himself growing up in an all-white community. Monsignor said he thought both Roger and the community would adopt my own attitude toward the child, so it might be best to examine carefully what that attitude was. He hit the nail on the head, of course, because I am a little prejudiced. To tell you the truth, I would prefer a child with German-Irish background and blond hair like Pixie's."

"Mr. Gung Ho America."

"Something like that. Still, I realize this is a unique opportunity to get a child and I don't want to disappoint Pixie or let Father Rossi down on his desire for us to raise Juan. Monsignor suggested that we take the boy on an outing, that perhaps meeting him would help to resolve my problems and to make up my mind. He thought you might be willing to come along to ease the situation a bit."

"Of course," says Sue, reaching for her appointment book. "When were you thinking of?"

"Perhaps this weekend? The paper work is moving rather rapidly on the adoption and Monsignor thought the sooner the better."

"Well, things are somewhat tight. On Sunday we have the newcomers party. And on Saturday morning I have the Scripture meeting but I tell you what, I'll ask Monsignor to take that. I think he might enjoy doing it. Let's bring Jennifer and Roger along and go to the Shedd Aquarium. That would be exciting for all ages."

"Sue, speaking of Monsignor, I don't understand why the priests are not more involved in Father Rossi's murder. You'd think they'd have asked the police to make an official investigation."

"I know, but Father Foley either really believes it was an accident or he is protecting Tim who is a close friend. Monsignor says he doesn't want to go over Father Foley's head since he's in charge of the parish unless we have the solid evidence Mike thinks necessary to approach Captain Vogel. Monsignor has been helpful though and Mike is doing his best."

It is then that Bill asks a curious question. "Sue," he says, "Do you really believe in the Communion of Saints, this business about how the dead still live and are united with us in some sort of spiritual way, that they're interested in us and pray for what is happening in our lives?"

"Don't we all believe that?"

"I guess. I've rattled that off in the Creed every Sunday of my life—I believe in the Communion of Saints, the forgiveness of sin—but I've never had an opportunity before to experience it as real. But since Father Rossi's death, I've had this sense of his nearness, his friendship, his understanding of hard choices I've had to make in my work. Do you feel that too?"

"I wish I did. That's the way it was after my parents' deaths, that sense of their closeness and complete comprehension of my problems, but since Father died, he just seems gone, missing, no longer there. I keep thinking that if I could solve his murder, I would be more at peace, more aware of his presence."

"Then you think he wants us to find his murderer?"

"I don't know. The truth is always important isn't it? I just know that when we found him dead, I promised him that I would discover the person who had done this to him and I intend to do that even though I'm finding it harder than I might have guessed."

"Hard in what way, Sue?"

"Well, the thought that the murderer might turn out to be someone I know, some good friend like Tim for instance, makes me sick. I can hardly bear the thought of it."

"Maybe you'd better prepare yourself for that."

"Yeah, I know. And then there's this man in the white Camaro who keeps tracking me down and scaring me to death. Just today he broke into my car in the hospital garage."

When Bill hears her account of the break-in, his reaction is very subdued. He acts as Mike and Fred so often did, as though the whole episode might be a figment of her imagination. He asks a lot of questions. Did she see the man enter her car? In fact, had she actually seen him when he drove away? Could she be sure it was the same car as the other night? Had he stolen anything from her car?

Sue lifts the yard bag that she had deposited on the kitchen floor and places it on the table.

"Incidentally," she says, "here is a nice sweater that we gave Father for Christmas and I'd like you to have it. People differ a lot in their feelings about dead friend's belongings. Would you like it or would you feel funny about wearing something of his?"

Bill seems touched by her offer.

"Fred wouldn't like it?" he asks.

"I already gave Fred a very similar one. I remember how excited I was when I found them on the New England pre-Christmas sale last year. It would look nifty on you, Bill."

"I don't exactly need anything to remind me of Father, but it would be nice to have something of his. Thanks a lot, Sue."

"And then there are these magazines. Maybe you could help me with these. I'm quite sure he was saving them for a purpose and they might give us important leads. Some of them are back issues of *America* and

Commonweal and *the National Catholic Reporter* but some are Spanish: a scholarly looking magazine called *ECA* and *Processo*, a sort of news update thing, and this, *Cartas a las Iglesias*. You don't happen to know Spanish, do you?"

"I only speak tourist Spanish but I can read it well enough to scan these and give us a summary."

Bill sorts through the magazines with obvious interest. Sue is impressed with how quickly he separates the English from the Spanish, how neatly he stacks piles for each of them. The swiftness and decisiveness of his actions gives her confidence in his intelligence.

"Maybe we can find out more about his interest in Alvarado," he says. "Did he talk about it much with you?"

Fred arrives and gives Sue a homecoming hug and Bill a warm welcome. He insists in his hearty, boisterous way, that Bill have a beer, that they move into the living room and light a fire. He brings Sue a glass of Chablis before settling down to answer Bill's questions about Alvarado.

" 'I don't put a lot of trust in Congress,' Bill says about Bentley's investigation. I think our President had it right all along. We had to support the army against the Communists. I know Roberto D'Astici is a bastard and nobody ever approved of his death squads, but I think the army improved after we began training them at the School of the Americas in Fort Benning."

"Father didn't think so," says Fred. "He always claimed that they desisted from their atrocities just long enough for Congress to vote them more funds. He used to say that more than 15,000 civilian deaths could be attributed to government military and security sources. I found that hard to believe but it's now beginning to be verified."

"Well," says Bill, "War is war. The guerillas were certainly responsible for their share of the killings. The tragedy is that we spent some six billion in aid, sometimes as much as one million a day and in the end, the Communists are taking over anyway. But maybe there's still hope of salvaging some of the damage if we keep the army strong."

As the conversation continues, Sue is amused to note that Fred, always conservative and a staunch anti-Communist, has now assumed a defense of Father Rossi's liberal views while Bill is holding fast to Fred's former ones. She finds herself drifting in and out of the discussion.

Sipping her wine and listening to the men talk, she feels all her earlier uneasiness drain away. The winter wind lashes at the house, whining at the windows, shaking and banging a loose shutter. The fierceness of the storm outside increases a sense of her home as a safe haven shielded from all harm. Soon, she feels, very soon, with the competent help of Father Rossi's friend Bill Bergman, they are going to solve the mystery of his death. Relaxed by the wine, warmed by the fire, comforted by the presence of the men, a kind of contentment that she has not experienced in many days wells up in her heart.

Chapter XVII

Shadow, Kathy Kennedy's elderly cat, is an appropriate accessory to the oriental décor of her small apartment. Her glistening charcoal coat perfectly matches the ebony window blinds and the dark frames of the Japanese prints which adorn the grass-papered walls. Curled comfortably on the pale silk sofa or stretching sensuously on the teakwood table, tail lightly touching a lovely Chinese bowl, she seems to be yet another piece of precious Eastern art. Sue watches her stroll languidly across the intricate Tabriz carpet. Ears perked, jade-green eyes sleepy and inscrutable, she strikes a statuesque pose in front of the folding screen at the entrance to the dining room.

"She looks like she belongs in that mystic landscape," Sue remarks.

"She's getting old," Kathy says, "Gravity is beginning to take over. Her tummy almost touches the floor these days. But we're content, she and I."

The strange truth is that Kathy does seem content. At the time of the automobile accident in which her husband was killed and she was left a paraplegic without use of her legs, no one guessed that she would make an easy adjustment to the limitations of her condition. People said it was a tragedy that never should have happened to such an animated, active woman.

A tiny person, very bright, tense, energetic, Kathy had for years taught Scripture and English at Lakewood Academy, an elite Episcopalian school for girls. Her reputation for scholarship and for rapport with her students was extraordinary. Since her retirement, she had conducted writing seminars at Community College and had served on every civic board one could think of; the Historical Society, the Botanical Garden Association, the Public Library. How could such a woman with her extensive contacts and endless activities settle for life in a wheel chair?

That she had done so with relative ease was a mystery most villagers could not comprehend. Sue's mother, however, a close friend and contemporary, had held a theory that made sense to Sue. She said that Kathy had been on stage all her life and was grateful for a legitimate excuse to retire from it. She need no longer make an enormous effort to be forever clever, to project the strong, opinionated personality that belied her diminutive size. Relieved of the burden of maintaining her public persona, she was free to read and research to her heart's content and to see only those people who cared enough about her to visit regularly.

But is she relaxed in her retirement? Sue never finds her easy to be with. She is too intense, too fervent in her convictions, too eager to escalate ordinary conversation into an occasion for a lecture. And then there is her compulsion to look things up. An unabridged Webster's and an overweight Jerusalem bible lay open on a low, lacquered chest. Often a casual chat is interrupted by a request that Sue check the precise meaning of a word or find an obscure passage from Deuteronomy. Her patience is sorely tried by this intrusion of scholarly pursuit into a social visit and she usually arrives with her exit excuse ready.

Today, however, she is prepared to stay awhile. Maria, the Hispanic nurse, has just finished brushing Kathy's deeply dyed, jet-black hair into a sophisticated knot at the crown of her head. A less severe style might soften her seventy-something features but she obviously prefers distinction to a more youthful look. Even at this early hour, she is wearing carved carnelian earrings. The wide sleeves of her silk kimono flutter when, with quick, bird-like gestures, she expresses her excitement at the idea Sue has just proposed.

"I agree that a person's final words take on great significance after his death," she says enthusiastically. "And interviewing parishioners who last saw Father Rossi is an interesting project. I did happen to be watching out the window that day and I think I would remember any car that drove up after the scripture meeting."

Sue is standing at the window looking across the street. Because of the incline on which it is built, the baptistery is almost level with Kathy Kennedy's second floor apartment. Although the spruce tree blocks a view of the entrance, the driveway on both sides is clearly visible. Maria had brought a luncheon tray to Kathy at the window on that fateful Saturday noon so that she could enjoy the winter scene outside. And Kathy, always curious and observant, remembered well who had come and gone at the baptistery.

"Perhaps ten minutes after you drove off," she says, "a dark car pulled up and parked for a few minutes."

"A dark car?"

"Yes, either black or navy, I couldn't be sure which."

"Do you know what kind of a car it was?"

"It was a four-door, dear, I'm quite sure of that. But to tell you the truth, I'm not very up on cars. I can't say I know one make from another."

Sue smiles thinking that this was very typical of Kathy. Practical, everyday knowledge was not her specialty. People said that although she knew the geography of the Holy Land in great detail, she could easily get lost in Lakewood.

"I'm quite sure there were two people in the car, a man driving and a woman in the seat next to him. When they left, they circled around into the parking lot for a few minutes and then drove south past the church. A bit later, a red Toyota came charging up the driveway. That car I did recognize because it belongs to Winnie Harris and is often parked across the street for daily Mass. Winnie keeps promoting a first floor apartment for me, but actually, Sue, I have no desire to have anyone carting me in and out even at a first floor level. And I would find the move difficult. I love it right here with all our things that Dan and I picked up when we were in the orient."

"Winnie means well," Sue says, "but don't let her talk to you into anything you don't really want to do."

"She's very persistent but you know, dear, that I can be equally obstinate. Anyway, after a brief stop at the baptistery, Winnie too circled into the parking lot. I couldn't figure out what great attraction an empty parking lot had for people that morning."

"Maybe they were dropping clothes off at the Vincent de Paul poor box."

"Of course. Why didn't I think of that."

"And there were no other automobiles? Not Tim James' flashy, low-slung sports car for instance?"

"No, I would remember that one for sure. I'm afraid I'm not much help to you but if you talk around, I'm sure you'll find other people who had contact with Father. I myself had a wonderful visit with him just the night before he died. He came over to check out his introduction to St. Luke's gospel with me. He was flattering that way, always assuming that I knew more about scripture than he did. We were talking about Luke's gospel when Father asked if I could verify an interesting notion he had come up with. He thought that perhaps forgiveness of others was Jesus' unique contribution to religion. He said that while the Old Testament often speaks of God's forgiveness of us, only in the New Testament do we find an emphasis on forgiving each other; forgiving brother, friend, enemy. I couldn't say off-hand that he was right but I have decided to research an article on the subject. I think *Cross Currents* might be interested in it. It seems strange to me in retrospect that what we spoke of that night was forgiveness. I have thought and prayed a lot about it since. Some things are so impossible to forgive."

Kathy is silent for a moment and Sue waits patiently for her to continue. She feels that this is the most genuine conversation they ever had. There was none of the usual husky, theatrical quality to the old lady's voice. She seems on the verge of simply and sincerely sharing a problem she has experienced. It is easy to imagine that she had been unable to forgive the driver of the car that had crashed into the Kennedy's killing her cherished husband. Was that the problem?

But Kathy only said, "I truly hope, dear, that you never have something so inextricable to forgive that whenever you think of it, it sticks in your throat, choking you and robbing you of your peace. But if that should ever happen to you, I want you to remember that forgiveness is God's business. He will give you the grace to do what you thought was impossible. That is what Father spoke so beautifully about the night before he died."

"I'll remember," Sue promises, although she thinks to herself that she never has much of a problem forgiving people. She finds anger and resentment so irksome a burden that she always wants to shed them as rapidly as possible. She feels a momentary twinge of jealousy that Kathy's farewell conversation with Father Rossi had been meaningful to her while her own had been so casual.

She knows that a close friendship had existed between Father and this frail, eccentric old woman who lives near the edge of death. Kathy has somehow survived many health problems, had a triple bypass several years before, suffers frequent angina attacks, needs sometimes to have oxygen for her emphysema. She makes light of her ailments, joking about her 'green moustache' when the oxygen tubes are inserted in her nostrils. Now observing her bright, brave on-stage cheeriness, Sue feels a new affection and admiration for her and rather than envy, gratitude that Father Rossi had left her a gift of peace.

Glancing out the window one last time, Sue notices a white Camaro parked directly in front of Kathy's apartment building. She reminds herself that Fred had said there were many such cars in the village but she knows with certainty that this one belongs to the black man who manages to follow her wherever she goes. She tries to keep her composure, to behave as though its presence has not struck terror in her heart.

"I have to go now," she says. "Dr. Young wants me to visit one of her patients at Community Hospital. But I'll be interested in seeing your article on forgiveness. Maybe you'd let me read parts of it as it develops."

Too breezy and brittle to accept affection graciously, Kathy is not someone Sue normally kisses goodbye. But today she risks giving her a quick embrace, touching her forehead lightly with her lips. She is surprised at the old woman's response. Tears well up in her eyes as she takes Sue's two hands firmly in her own.

"You are so like your mother," she says. "If she had to go, I'm glad she left you behind. Come back soon, dear."

As Sue rounds the stairway at the landing, she comes to an abrupt standstill. Her sudden intake of breath expands her throat painfully. Her heart pounds with alarm. There at the foot of the narrow stairway stands the black man, the driver of the Camaro. His right hand rests on the same banister as her left one. Without letting go of it, he backs deferentially against the wall to let her pass. But Sue, first frozen by fright and then pausing deliberately to compose herself, to draw strength from a quick prayer, maintains her position on the landing. She scrutinizes the man warily. She is acutely aware of everything about him; his thin face shadowed with melancholy, his neat appearance and courteous attitude, the expensive, somewhat worn brief case that he carries.

Danger accelerates Sue's mental process. Thoughts race through her mind. Perhaps she is not this stranger's target at the moment. He seemed as surprised to run into her, as she had been to see him. Since he is mounting the stairs and there is only one second floor apartment, he obviously intends to call on Kathy. Was her old friend somehow threatened? In the brief moment that she stands there, Sue makes one absolute resolution. She is not going to let this man anywhere near

Kathy Kennedy. She decides too that she will approach him in her usual friendly manner, as though she suspects nothing.

One of her legs is quivering uncontrollably but steadies as she starts slowly down the stairs. Her mouth is so dry that she is surprised at how normal and firm her voice sounds when she speaks.

"Good morning," she says. "Can I help you in some way?"

"I am looking for Mrs. Daniel Kennedy," he says.

"I have just left her and I don't think she was expecting anyone. Did you have an appointment with her?"

"No, not really. I was hoping that I could interest her in an up-to-date set of the Encyclopedia Britannica."

"Well, I can save you some time. Within the last year, our Women's Council gave her a new, complete set through some deal at Dominick's. You know, you get a volume for practically nothing with each load of groceries. That must be tough competition for you."

"But none of those sets offers the quality that Britannica does. I really would like to show Mrs. Kennedy our excellent illustrations and the marvelous maps that have been developed to clarify economic and political realities."

Sue pauses on the stairway just a step or two above the one on which the Camaro driver stands. She does not take her hand from the banister but firmly confronts him, blocking his way to the second floor. She still feels nervous and frightened but is amazed at how spontaneously she can play the role of her own friendly self. She is also impressed with how convincingly he is acting the part of a salesman. He makes an effort to speak enthusiastically about the encyclopedia but also seems sad, quietly despondent, a man who suffers daily rejections. Almost automatically, as though the situation were real, Sue finds herself responding to this sense of his discouragement.

"Look," she says. "I know Mrs. Kennedy is not in the market for an encyclopedia and you would be making a mistake to intrude on her at this early hour. But you are in the right village for possible sales.

Children's education is a high priority around here. Why don't you try your luck some place where a sale is more likely?"

But the man holds his ground stubbornly. "I'm working from a list of teachers and professors," he says. "My boss wants to experiment with giving them precedence. I would really like to show Mrs. Kennedy how our encyclopedia has been revised for easy access to quick information and easy reference for more in depth research. I think she might be very interested."

Why is he so insistent? What possible interest could he have in Kathy Kennedy? Is it possible after all that he is just a salesman? But Sue remembers with a sharp intake of breath the many times he has followed her and knows that such a simple answer is not feasible. His intention in calling on Kathy had to have some relationship to Father Rossi's death and had nothing to do with selling her an encyclopedia. It is obviously a ruse to get him into her apartment and Sue is determined not to allow him entrance.

"You really shouldn't try to see Mrs. Kennedy," she says. "She's not very well and she's definitely not in the market for your books. But I tell you what. You might want to try Monsignor Fiedler who is retired and lives at the second entrance in the rectory just around the corner. He is very definitely a scholar and a much better bet for a sale."

Sue continues to stand directly in front of the man, obstructing his passage to the second floor. He hesitates a moment longer as though searching for a reasonable excuse to pursue his objective. Then, nodding politely and gripping his briefcase, he turns toward the door.

"Thanks for the tip," he says.

Well, she has met the enemy face to face and he appears to be an inoffensive, mild, harmless and rather ordinary man. Far from finding this reassuring, however, Sue stands shivering in the vestibule as she watches him get into his Camaro and drive off. He made no pretense of going in the direction of the rectory but continues south at a good clip. As she steps outside, Sue takes a deep breath of the crisp winter air. God, what a relief to have him gone! She jaywalks across the street to the church corner and strides briskly to the rectory. Father Foley answers the door.

"Good morning, Sue," he says. "Are you okay?"

"Of course I'm okay." She wonders if her recent experience has left her pale and shaken.

"I missed you at Mass. I thought maybe you'd come down with the flu or something."

"No. I just took a pass this morning and brought Kathy Communion early so that I could get on down to the hospital. But I thought she didn't seem too well and I was wondering if Nora could stay with her this morning while Maria goes out to do the shopping. She usually leaves around ten o'clock and is never gone for more than a half-hour or so. Somehow, I'd rather Kathy wasn't alone today."

"Nora's sister is in town from Ireland and she's taken the train downtown to show here the sights, the Sears Tower and Marshall Fields and all that. But I'll look in on Kathy around that time. She's been editing the Sunday bulletin for us and I have to bring it over some time today anyway."

"Good," says Sue. "I'd appreciate that. And could I use the phone in the office for a moment?"

As soon as she is alone, Sue calls Mike O'Connell at the police station. She quickly recounts her encounter in the Kennedy hallway and asks Mike what he makes of it.

"God, Sue" Mike says. "I don't know. Are you sure this was the same guy? I mean, maybe he really was just a salesman."

"Mike, I'm telling you it's the same man and he's up to no good."

"Okay, okay, I'll see if I can track him down but I can't figure him in the picture because I really think Tim James is responsible for the murder. All we need is a little more evidence."

"You can forget Tim James. I was up at Kathy's to check what cars were at the baptistery early that Saturday afternoon and she definitely did not see Tim's sport car. The important news is that she spotted another car, a dark four-door with two people in it. I don't know how we're going to track it down, but it has to belong to the real murderer. You know, Mike, none of our suspects ever made much sense. It surely would make me happy to be able to let them off the hook."

"Aren't you jumping to conclusions, Sue? As far as I'm concerned, they're all still suspects until proven otherwise. Did Mrs. Kennedy see any other cars that day?"

"Yes. Winnie was there. Both cars drove around to the poor box."

"Winnie was there for sure? That's interesting because I have something strange, something really weird, to tell you. I think I mentioned that my little daughter will be spending next summer with me while her mother moves to the Berkeley campus to take some graduate courses. Well, I asked Winnie to let me know if a good bargain came up on a small house because my current bachelor's studio wouldn't take care of the situation. So yesterday morning before that big snowstorm blew in, Winnie took me to see a ranch house that hasn't been on the market for long. In fact, she first showed it on the day of Father Rossi's death. She said I'd better snap it up fast as some black man has been through a couple of times and seems serious about wanting to purchase it. Winnie says she's not prejudiced herself but she'd like to keep the neighbors happy."

"Anyway, as we were leaving, I was looking back at the house trying to take everything in and just then I spotted something gleaming in the sunlight in the bed of myrtle close to the doorway. I was curious and stopped to investigate. Now, are you ready for this Sue? Can you guess what it turned out to be?"

Mike has a tendency to create a detailed story out of all the incidents he relates and Sue is growing impatient with how he is dragging this out.

"How could I guess," she says. "You'd better just tell me."

"It was a heavy antique silver candle stick hidden in the foliage."

"What do you mean, a silver candlestick?"

"I mean just that, a sliver candlestick. I have it right here."

"But that's absurd. The candlestick was never a real weapon. It was just a figment of my imagination."

"Maybe you're a psychic," says Mike. "I wouldn't be surprised."

Chapter XVIII

Joan Young said that it was too early to diagnose Elena Esquivel's case with certainty but her early guesses were either a manic depressive psychosis or, perhaps more seriously, schizophrenia. In the first case, one would expect recurrent attacks of depression or elation or both. Attacks could be preceded by emotional upsets or great stress involving intense feelings of guilt, remorse or painfully wounded pride.

"I really think it is manic depression," Dr. Young told Sue, "and that some intense stress brought about the episode yesterday. She is very withdrawn and so far is not inclined to talk with me. When I suggested that you visit her, I got my first and only positive response from her. Perhaps she will share what's troubling her with you, but even if she does not, I know your visit will be good for her."

Great stress involving intense feelings of guilt and remorse? Sue thinks about the possible implications of this in Elena's case as she stands in the doorway of the hospital room. She has never visited anyone in the psychiatric ward before and, not knowing what to expect, is feeling somewhat apprehensive. She is relieved to see that it is a single room, that they will be alone. Elena, lying on her back, is sleeping soundly. Her dark hair plaited into a heavy, shining braid, hangs over the shoulder of her cotton gown. Her dark, delicate brows are clearly defined in her pale face. Without make up, with one arm flung back on the pillow and her lips slightly parted, she looks defenseless and innocent, like a child sleeping there in the white hospital bed. Sue pulls up a chair and takes one of her hands in her own.

A black nurse, thin as a blade of grass, comes briefly into the room. The sharp, sculpted bones of her hips are visible under her tight-fitting uniform. Her narrow, mahogany face is carved with kind lines.

"You family?" she asks.

"She has only a brother in this country," explains Sue. "Dr. Young has elected me next of kin."

"Well, if you like, you can wake her up any time now. She's been sleepin' like a newborn all mornin' long. I guess she had her a mighty restless night. Nurse comin' off duty says she was moanin' on and on about someone takin' her baby."

"Taking her baby?"

"That's what she says. She says sometimes she's cryin' and sometimes she's angry as a cougar and just as hard to quiet down. But now the doctor's got her medications figured just so and you'll find her peaceful as a lamb. Best not let her nap too long, turnin' day into night."

The nurse departs as quietly as a shadow, her white rubber-soled shoes making not the least sound. In the absolute silence she leaves behind, Sue gazes for a long time at the sleeping girl. She is reluctant to disturb her. She feels hesitant about her ability to handle this situation which so exceeds her normal experience. Still, all she can do is approach it as lovingly as possible. With a little sigh, she squeezes Elena's hand and gently strokes her arm until she finally opens her eyes.

At first Elena seems happy to see her, smiling at her in sleepy surprise. Then abruptly her attitude changes. Deliberately turning her back to Sue, she flounces over in the bed and, facing the window, assumes a defiant fetal position. Sue tries some casual, reassuring conversation but this has no effect on Elena who remains stubbornly silent. Finally, Sue decides on a bolder approach.

"Elena," she says, "You know I'm your friend and you can talk to me about anything that's troubling you. Maybe you'd like to tell me who took your baby?"

"What do you know about my baby?" Elena's voice is edged sharply with suspicion and hostility.

"Very little. Gabriel told me yesterday that you had a child a few years back and just now, a few minutes ago, the nurse told me that you were angry during the night about someone taking your baby. If that really happened, if someone took your child away from you, that must have been heartbreaking. It's no wonder you are still angry about it."

"He did it," sobs Elena, her voice trembling with sorrow and anger. "It was all his fault. He's the one who talked me into it and now he's gone and the baby's gone and I will never ever find him. He took my baby."

Elena is still facing the window and on impulse, Sue picks up her chair and carries it to the other side of the bed. She sits a little distance from the girl, afraid that if she comes too close she might once more roll over and withdraw into her cocoon. But Elena, engrossed in her grief, hardly seems to notice her.

"Maybe you'd like to tell me who did this to you, who took your baby?" Sue suggests softly.

"It was Father Rossi. I remember how he admired the baby when he came to the hospital to see me. 'Imagine being two days old,' he said. 'Just imagine that!' But then he sat by my bed just like you are sitting there and he told me I should give up my little son, it is for the best. I know my mother sent him to talk me into it."

"You had decided to keep the baby?"

"I never wanted to give him up, never, but everybody told me I must. My mother and father said that adoption was the only right thing to do for the child who needed two parents to raise him up. They insisted that I must not think of anything else, that it would be an impossible situation. When I am staying with my auntie during the pregnancy, I told her that they just didn't want the disgrace of an illegitimate child in their household. She said that wouldn't embarrass her at all and if I wanted to keep the child I could come live with her and Uncle Rafael. But later she changed her mind. My uncle thought that adoption would give me a better chance for the future and my aunt came to agree with him. But I still said I was going to keep the baby. I told everyone all along that I never would give him up."

"Then how did Father Rossi talk you into it? Did he know how you felt about it?"

"He knew. When I became pregnant, my mother wanted me to go to confession to the parish priest because she had already spoken to him about my problem. But I said I would go to Father Rossi. I was not sorry for my sin and if I could not have the child's father, at least I would have the baby to always remember him by."

"What did Father say to that?"

"He said that perhaps the sin was largely the man's fault but that I must have sorrow for any part I played in it that may have offended God. But I said it was not the man's fault or mine, it was just something that happened. He insisted things don't just happen, that we must be responsible for what we do, but, Sue, it *did* just happen and I cannot feel it was a sin."

Perhaps this unacknowledged guilt is part of Elena's problem and Sue decides to give her an opportunity to talk about it. "How did it just happen?" she inquires gently.

Elena needs no urging to tell her story but her recounting of it is so ragged, so emotional and without logical sequence, that it is difficult to follow. Sometimes Elena cries and becomes almost incoherent. Sometimes she raises her voice in anger about apparently irrelevant details. Sue finds herself listening intently, straining to get the gist and significance of what she says so that she can recreate it for herself in some comprehensible form.

It had all happened in mid-November in the Esquivel's city house in Alvarado. Elena had had a mild case of mononucleosis and had been so homesick that the nuns at her Convent school in New Orleans had allowed her to go home early for the American Thanksgiving holiday. It was her first day home and she was already bored when news reached her family of the murder of several priests at the Dominican University early that morning. All day long there was distress and speculation about the tragedy but only that evening did they learn all the details concerning it.

The family was at the dinner table, Isabella just passing around the dessert plates, when the man in question arrived. Throughout her story, Elena referred to this man as "he." Only later did Sue fully appreciate the discretion both Gabriel and Elena exercised in never mentioning his name.

"He" was a friend of her father and brothers who came often to their home for meetings. Although he was considerably older than she and paid only kindly attention to her, Elena imagined that she was deeply in love with him. She liked to anticipate the maid in answering the door for him and, although she found political discussion tedious, often remained in the parlor so that she could be near him. A smile in her direction was reward enough for her patience. To some extent Sue could identify with Elena's feeling for this man. She could remember the intensity of her own first love at sixteen and the ridiculous amount of time she had spent imagining romantic encounters. Still, in Elena's story, there was a quality of passionate dreaming and unrealistic expectation which removed it beyond the realm of normal teen-age infatuation.

Elena's brother, Aloysius, drew a chair up to the table for their visitor and her father fixed him a strong whiskey and soda. He was obviously distraught and shaken by the Dominican murders. He had arrived at the college for his early morning class only to discover that four of his colleagues had been executed on campus. Evita, their cook, and her teen-age daughter were also dead. The women's bodies were discovered in the Dominican residence with their arms wrapped around each other.

Felix Rodriguez, the rector of the university, had been one of the victims. Elena said this news brought tears to her father's eyes. He spoke sadly about what a brilliant social critic and political analyst Father Rodriguez had been, how hard he had worked for his dream of a negotiated settlement of the war in their country. The family knew him well. All of the dead priests were friends who had come occasionally to their home for dinner.

There was little doubt in anyone's mind that the army was responsible for this terrible atrocity. In fact, Celine, the housekeeper had spotted soldiers on the grounds. There was angry speculation at the table about who might have ordered the brutal attack but Elena's mother interrupted this indignant discussion to suggest that they drive out to the college. If Isabella agreed, they would bring her along to cook for the faculty until they could find a new domestic to replace Evita. She thought of this and other arrangements which might relieve the burden of the bereaved priests. When they were ready to leave, she took the face of their visitor between her two hands.

"Such a terrible shock," she said. "You look absolutely exhausted. You've been through such a hard and harrowing day, why don't you stay here and rest a bit? I know you haven't taken time to eat and Elena can bring you a little dinner."

"It has been a long day," he admitted. "A little time out would be welcome."

"He was a professor at the university?" Sue inquires.

"No, he just taught a law course there, I think."

"He was an attorney?"

Elena hesitates. "My father said he was an expert on constitutional law so I guess he was an attorney but I think he held some other important post."

Sue gets the distinct impression that Elena is uncertain what the man's profession was, that her interest in him did not include his work. She is sorry that she has interrupted Elena's story and tries now to get it back on track.

"So after the family left for the university, you were alone with this man."

"Yes, I was so happy to have this time together with him."

Elena went out to the kitchen and heated up some dinner for him but he was not hungry and only toyed with his food. He went over to the sideboard and fixed himself another drink and brought it back to the table. He was very quiet, preoccupied with his own thoughts and Elena could think of nothing to say to him.

"I am so sorry about the priests," she ventured finally. "It must have been awful finding Evita and her daughter in each others arms like that."

This image had haunted Elena. The girl had been exactly her own age and her death seemed more real to her than that of the others.

"God, yes!" he said. "The bastards! There's no way they could claim that those women were Communist agitators."

Following this outburst, they fell silent again. After a few awkward moments, he had excused himself saying if she didn't mind he would phone home to let them know where he was and then stretch out on the couch in the library until her parents returned. There were still details he must discuss with them. Elena was bitterly disappointed by this turn of events. Although she had suffered acute embarrassment at her inability to carry on a conversation with him, she had treasured the precious opportunity to have him all to herself. This had ended abruptly, unexpectedly, and she had no choice but to say of course, it would be good for him to rest.

She cleared the dishes from the table and, knowing that Isabella would not be back, made some effort to rinse and stack them. All the time she was working, he was on her mind. Her sense of his presence in the house was achingly acute and after several minutes, she crept into the library to see if he were resting well. It was dim in there, the book-lined walls in deep shadow. Only the small tiffany lamp on her father's desk shed a subdued light at the far end of the room. Still, she could see that he had kicked off his shoes, hung his suit coat on the back of a chair and had already fallen asleep on the couch.

Elena begins to cry again. Sue pushes the button to raise her bed so that she can sit up a little while they visit. Now, reclining against her pillow, the girl reminds Sue of a tragic heroine in a classic film, tears sliding silently down her chalk-white cheeks. A familiar sullen look has returned to her face. She seems passive, pathetic, abandoned to grief. Sue, hoping to break into this introverted mood, pulls a Kleenex from the box on the bedside table and hands it to her.

"Here, Elena," she says. "Would you like to tell me what is making you so sad?"

Elena responds despondently and as though from a great distance. "My mother was so angry with him. She said he had betrayed her trust and should never come to her home again. My father was very upset too. He could not understand how it was possible that this had happened. He took me alone into the library and asked me many questions. He was very stern; it was like an inquisition of his own daughter. I know that he thought I had been seductive. But Sue, I loved him so much. All I wanted to do was to comfort him, to stroke his cheek and hold him in my arms. Was it such a sin to kiss him while he slept? And then, well, then it all just happened. Do you think it really was wrong?"

Sue was slow to answer. She knew that many of her contemporaries would have hastened to assure Elena that the incident was nothing, that it happened every day. After all, it was merely a one-time affair in which, unfortunately, she had become pregnant. Just forget it. But obviously Elena had been unable to forget it. Even after years, she was still questioning her own behavior. Sue understands that she and Elena share a religious culture which transcends borders and bonds them close together. In this milieu, conscience plays a delicate role which should not be ignored. Still, what she had to say must be said with infinite kindness. She pulls her chair up to the bed and lays her hand on the girl's shoulder.

"Elena, we both went to convent schools. We know that adultery is wrong."

Sue is unprepared for Elena's reaction to this simple statement. Her composure crumbles absolutely. She sits bolt upright in bed and begins rocking rhythmically back and forth. Her weeping takes on a new character. Convulsive sobs rack her body and her face becomes red, anguished, contorted. She seems so out of control, so close to hysteria, that Sue wonders momentarily if she should ring for the nurse.

"I am so wicked," Elena wails. "I know that I am very wicked and everyone is angry with me. Jesus will never forgive me."

"Elena, you are not wicked," Sue assures her firmly. "And as far as I know, no one is angry with you, Jesus least of all. I am absolutely sure that when you went to confession to Father Rossi, he never gave you that impression."

"No," Elena admits. "He spoke about how gentle Jesus was with the woman taken in adultery, how he wouldn't let anyone throw stones because they were all sinners too. He said Jesus loved me and would forgive me. Father Rossi was very kind and gave me absolution but it didn't wash my sin away because I was not sorry. I didn't want to be sorry for it."

Sue considers this a moment, making an effort to understand the complicated knot Elena had constructed to block the flow of contrition and forgiveness. She is not at all certain she can unravel it but she spots one strand which, if she toys with it, might help to loosen things up.

"Elena," she says, "Maybe you don't want to be sorry for your sin because it is precious to you. You want to hold on to it, to remember it as something beautiful and good. Is that right?"

Elena nods. "It was so wonderful, like heaven," she says dreamily.

"I can understand that but I guess maybe your love was wrong, Elena, because it was a stolen love. I t didn't belong to you."

"I stole it from God," Elena says, crying more quietly now. "He took my baby to punish me."

This sounds like Elena, a little dramatic and extreme but Sue decides to let it pass. She senses a quagmire quality to Elena's conscience, a morass of denial and scruple, that needs Dr. Young's expertise or that of an experienced priest. She makes an effort to get the conversation back on a more realistic track.

"Elena," she says. "It's hard for me to see that either God or Father Rossi took your baby. Father recommended that you give up the baby for your own good. He probably said all the same things your family had been saying to you, but he was more persuasive and you trusted him, right?"

Elena nods. "He promised that if I would let the Guardian Angel Orphanage have my baby, he would see to it personally that he was adopted into a loving, Catholic family."

"And you agreed to that?"

"I believed that he wanted what was best for the baby so I said he could make the arrangements. He came over to my bed and gave me his blessing and then he picked up my little infant in his arms and took him to the nursery to tell them what I had decided. I can still see him going through the doorway carrying my little son. He took my baby away."

Sue can understand how this traumatic parting with her newborn had frozen forever in Elena's mind the image of Father Rossi carrying him away from her. Still, after expressing her sympathy, Sue feels compelled to try and straighten things out.

"You know, Elena," she says, "It seems to me that everyone who loved you wanted what was best for you and that goes for Father too. They may have been wrong, but if you agreed to do what they advised, then you have to be responsible for that decision. You can't go on blaming Father Rossi for it. I am trying to understand why you are so angry with him. I remember the first day you saw him at the scripture meeting in the baptistery, you seemed to have a chip on your shoulder."

"I was annoyed to find Father in this wealthy suburban parish in the United States. I wanted to tease him about it. My father was always saying how dedicated he was to the poor in Alvarado, how important his work was, so why had he deserted us to come here?"

"You missed him?"

"We all missed him."

"But Gabriel said you hadn't seen much of him in recent years."

"That's true. I guess he was travelling a lot."

"Perhaps you are angry that as soon as you found him again, he died and left you."

"I don't understand why God took him."

Sue, who has become personally involved in Elena's story, sits back now and looks at her more objectively. It is hard to believe that this sad, mixed-up girl had possibly killed Father Rossi. But it is also hard to remember that only yesterday she had threatened her brother with a knife. Is the conviction that Father had taken her baby from her sufficient motive for murder? How reasonable or strong need a motive be in the case of a girl as disturbed as Elena?

As she is leaving, Sue helps Elena make out a list of things she might want from home: bathrobe, slippers, make-up, needlepoint. Then, giving her a farewell kiss, Sue stands back and, observing the girl's tear-stained face, carefully asks if perhaps she might also want her hairdryer?

"Hairdryer?" Elena looks a little startled and bewildered.

"I think you'll be here for several days," Sue says. "I thought your hairdryer might come in handy."

"If you think so," Elena says.

At home, messages have piled up on Sue's answering machine. Taking a sandwich and a coke into the breakfast room, she spends a few minutes checking them out. Jo had heard that Elena was in the hospital and wondered if her date with Gabriel at the Merchandise Mart was still on. Winnie Harris wanted to have lunch with Sue tomorrow, Wednesday. Father Foley wanted her to call back as soon as she got his message. He needed help with something. And Bill Bergman said if it was okay with her, he'd stop by after work to discuss the Spanish magazines he had read the night before.

Sue returns all the calls except Father Foley's. She is sure he wants her to serve as a sponsor in the RCIA program of preparation for adult baptism and she wants to avoid taking on any new tasks if she possibly can. She needs time to think up a convincing reason to refuse. Reminded of the magazines by Bill's call, she piles a stack of them on the table and begins reading through, highlighting passages as she goes. The most relevant articles on Alvarado in the American publications were written by an Ignatius Lopez, and she begins to look for these as her research continues. She finds the material engrossing and only when Jennifer comes home does she put the work aside. Then, ready with a firm excuse for turning down Father Foley's probable request, she dials the rectory.

"Sue!" Father Foley exclaims. "I'm glad you finally got back to me. I'll never get over how sensitive you were about Kathy Kennedy. Maria said she hadn't noticed anything at all."

"Kathy Kennedy? What are you talking about, Father."

"When I went to call on her this morning, there was no answer although usually she buzzes me in without any difficulty. So, not knowing how soon Maria would be back, I called the police. Sure enough, when we went up we found the poor woman dead in her wheel chair. Heart attack, the doctor says. I think you were the only person who saw this coming."

"I didn't exactly see it coming."

Sue feels shocked and alarmed by the news, her mind racing over possibilities that would never occur to Father Foley. Finally she asks if there is anything she can do.

"Her sons are flying in tomorrow," Father says, "Bob Casey has taken her down to the funeral home and he'll wait to see what they want by way of a funeral when they arrive. Maria is getting the apartment ready for the family and then would like to go home but she doesn't know what to do with the cat."

"Doesn't the rectory need a cat?"

"No," says Father firmly. "It would just be an unnecessary expense."

"You aren't serious."

"I'm serious about no cat."

"Okay," said Sue. "I'll take her. Tell Maria I'll be right over."

Giving Shadow a home seems like the least she can do.

Chapter XIX

"You like pretzels?" Bill inquires, tossing a big bag of them on the kitchen table. "These are supposed to be extra-special."

"Love them," says Sue. "An old-time favorite and they'll come in handy because Mike is stopping by when he gets off work and Fred should be home soon. Let me put them in a basket and get you a beer. Then we can take these magazines into the breakfast room as soon as I feed this cat."

"I didn't know you had a cat."

"A new acquisition. An old friend of my mother's died today and Shadow is my inheritance. She came with a litter box and a dozen cans of Fancy Feast. Do you suppose I should serve it up in a sherbet glass?"

"Absolutely. Anyone can tell she's a sophisticated member of the aristocracy."

When they settled at the breakfast table with stacks of magazines lined up between them, Sue announces that before they begin exchanging notes, she wants to tell Bill about the death of her mother's friend. She begins at the beginning with her morning visit to Kathy Kennedy and the discovery that there had been another car at the baptistery at the time of the murder. She goes on to tell of her encounter with the Camaro driver on the stairway and her request to Father Foley that he stop in to check on Kathy while Maria was shopping. She winds up with the stunning news that Kathy was found dead when Father went to call on her during Maria's absence.

Bill listens attentively but his reaction is so reserved and non-committal that Sue can not figure out what he thinks of her story. Then, as though he read her mind, he asks her the same question she had for him. What does she make of it all?

"I think the man intended to call on Kathy before I got there," she says. "I usually arrive after the eight-thirty Mass but skipped church this morning to save time for the hospital. He somehow knew I was going to question Kathy and it was important to him that information about a new suspect not get out. For all he knew, Kathy might have been able to identify the car and the couple in it."

"But how would he have known you were going to interview Kathy?"

"That's a real puzzle. Do you suppose someone has bugged this room?"

"God, I wouldn't think so, but we could have Mike check when he comes. But another question, Sue. You say she died of a heart attack but I gather you are thinking this man may have been responsible for her death. Do you have any evidence of that?"

"None," admits Sue. "Maria saw no one when she left and Father met no one when he arrived. But it seems possible to me that he did get into her apartment and scared the hell out of her so that her poor heart gave out."

"But if he knew you had already seen her, why would he have gone through with a murder?"

"Witnesses don't always remember things on the first round."

"Or he had an assignment to bump her off and wanted to report that he had done it."

"You think it's possible then?"

Sue had been scanning Bill's impassive face for a clue to his reaction to her story. It registered little emotion but she was aware of the narrowing of his eyes and tightening of his mouth which she had come to associate with his careful calculation of the facts. When he spoke, it was with an authority and earnestness that she found reassuring.

"Possible, but just barely, Sue. I can't assure you that nothing happened but my guess is that it is extremely unlikely. I think you can safely put it out of your mind unless some corroborating evidence should turn up. I know this man has given you a hard time but it's a wild leap of the imagination to conclude that he would murder an old lady or, for that matter, harm you in any way. I think it's all scare tactics and this morning was just another incident of the same thing."

"I hope you're right. I'll try to see it that way. Mike is going to renew his effort to track this guy down and we'll see what comes of that. So let's move on. I think you must have been up all night getting through that pile of magazines."

"Well past midnight. I'm better at speed reading English than I am Spanish. But I promised you a summary and I'll do the best I can. These ECA magazines are a random selection made over a number of years. In each issue there are a number of articles by an author named Ignatio Lopez, so I have concluded that it was for his work that Father Rossi saved them."

"I kept running into that name too, only anglicized to Ignatius."

"Interesting. So I was probably right. These articles are all scholarly and carefully researched. I would find them hard to argue with unless I knew a lot more than I do. They deal with various aspects of the Alvarado problem with each issue dedicated almost exclusively to one subject. There's one on the history of the land tenure from the time of the Spanish conquest to the present with an update on the failure of government agrarian reforms. This one here is a comprehensive review of the recent political history, the Aleda party and all that. There is one that I found particularly helpful because it examined all the reformist parties and organizations, their founding and philosophy and the ways in which they have united for common objectives. Until I read this, there were all a maze of initials to me; the NFL, the PDC and so on ad infinitum."

"Do me a favor. Make me a list. I never could keep them all straight."

"I'd be glad to if you'd find it helpful. It would be a good review for me because, to tell you the truth, I had no idea that so many professional people, worker's unions and whatnot, were involved in the reformist movement. I'd like to go over it again. I had a much more black-and-white picture of the conflict. You know, Communist guerillas against government army, maybe not all good guys but at least not Communists. Didn't you see it that way?"

Bill had been doodling a row of rippling American flags across the top of a Spanish newspaper but now looks up earnestly at Sue.

"Not exactly," she says. "I tended to believe what our missionaries reported in the Catholic press."

"Well, I tended to believe what our government told us. Back in the eighties, President Reagan and Jeanne Kirkpatrick and Henry Kissinger were all convinced that the Soviet Union was exporting revolution to Alvarado via Cuba and Nicaragua. There were white papers and testimony before Congress about Communism spreading through Central America and threatening our southern borders. There's an article here refuting that theory, claiming that the influx of arms was negligible, with documentation to back it up. But our country must have had some documentation too, don't you think?"

"For a long time Fred was convinced that they did but they may have overblown what little information they had to gain support for their cause."

"Well, I have to admit these articles are persuasive and I can't just write them off as leftist propaganda. I'm interested in finding out more. Today I phoned down to the San Christobal University to see if this fellow Lopez had written any books and if I could get in touch with him."

"You phoned Alvarado?"

"On the office phone," says Bill with one of his engaging between-us smiles. "Anyway, I found out that Ignatius Lopez was a pseudonym and that the man who had written under that name died recently."

"You might have saved yourself a phone call. I could have told you that."

"You mean you figured that out from reading his articles? You're even smarter than I thought you were!"

"I know. Nobody ever guesses how truly sharp I am. But actually it didn't take much brains to come to the conclusion that the articles were written by our friend, Father Rossi."

"Father Rossi! What makes you think that?"

Sue wonders briefly if she can share with Bill the experience she had while reading a long article in the *National Catholic Reporter* about a young American doctor serving in the Puaraza Front, a 200-square mile rebel-controlled area northeast of San Christobal. Although this man had community health "responsibles" to assist him, he was the only qualified physician to care for 10,000 compesenos. The hardships, hunger and military assaults these people suffered were harrowing. Sue became absorbed in accounts of surgery by candlelight without anesthesia, of skin grafts performed with razors and wounds sutured with dental floss, of malnutrition and disease among children surviving on one tortilla a day, of recurring 'guidos' when an entire village had to bury its few belongings and flee up the side of the volcano to escape indiscriminate bombing by army helicopters.

As Sue grew increasingly engrossed in the story, she became aware of the voice of the storyteller, the author of the article. There was something curiously familiar about the calm cadence of that voice, the objectivity, humor and compassion which informed it. She could hear in it swift sympathy for the small boy whose foot was severed by a land mine, quiet admiration for the woman who cared for thirteen orphaned and widowed members of an extended family in a two-room house. Only gradually did she identify the speaker, then suddenly found herself in tears. As she read on, it was almost as though Father Rossi sat there with her at the table telling her about his friend, this remarkable young doctor in Puaraca. The sound of his voice and sense of his presence were overwhelming.

"I recognized some tell-tale tag words," she says, "and then I could hear him talking. Read this article in NCR and you'll see what I mean. Besides, he was human, you know. It's more likely that he saved his own work rather than that of a friend."

"Of course you're right. I can see it now though it never crossed my mind. I never particularly thought of him as a scholar, did you?"

"He used to give some mighty lean and learned homilies but he always spiced them up with human interest anecdotes. I certainly didn't think of him as a dry academic."

"Neither did I. I wish I had read all this work before he died. It might have made some kind of difference in our friendship if I had understood how he thought about things."

Sue can identify with the regret she detects in Bill's voice as he contemplates lost opportunities in his relationship with Father Rossi. She often felt the same way, that well as she had known him, she had been ignorant of whole areas of his life.

"I think the friendship you had was very important to him," she says. "He probably shared things with you that he never did with anyone else."

"Maybe."

Although he was looking directly at her, Sue feels she can not adequately interpret the introspective sadness in Bill's deep-set, deep-blue eyes. God, he is a handsome man, and probably capable of deep feelings which he never can or will articulate. He is silent for such a long time that she begins studying his face again to see if she can figure out what he is thinking. No luck with that. His expression is inscrutable. Then, maybe conscious of her curiosity, he drains the last bit of beer from his glass and reaches for a couple of pretzels.

"You realize, don't you," he says, "that it may well have been this literature that cost Father his life."

"Someone caught up with the true identity of Ignatius Lopez?"

"Something like that."

Before they can discuss this possibility, they are interrupted by a great hullabaloo in the hallway. Jennifer is greeting her father with excited squeals of delight and Fred is responding in his usual booming, buoyant voice which carries clearly to the breakfast room.

"A cat? Not for keeps, I trust. What about the Mommy law that says no pets that can't be kept in cages or tanks?"

"She's our inheritance from Mrs. Kennedy going up to heaven so it's a distinctly different case, Mom says. Mom says a cat doesn't need a kitty sitter. She can take care of herself when we're not here. Her name is Shadow and she's totally all black."

"She looks to me like she has on her Halloween costume."

"Oh, Daddy! That's just plain silly. But I tell you what. Mom's doing some work with Roger's father and do you think maybe he could bring Roger over here to see Shadow? I just can't wait for him to see her."

"Well, we'll see what we can do about that. If there's enough food on hand, maybe the Bergmans could come for supper."

Sue smiles across the table at Bill. "Once in a while my family comes up with a really good idea. How about it?"

"I'd like to say yes, Sue, but to tell you the truth, I'd rather not involve Pixie in all this murder stuff. Maybe another time?"

"I understand completely about Pixie, but Mike won't be staying long. What if I call Pixie and have her come with Roger about six-thirty?"

Sue is congratulating herself on how readily she is able to respond to one of Fred's spontaneous suggestions of guests for dinner. Early in their marriage his custom of inviting people on the spur of the moment and without consultation had driven her up a wall. Put on the spot, she'd had to deal with irritation for most of any evening.

Sue had grown up in a family which planned parties carefully, selecting guests who enjoyed each other's company, shopping judiciously for a menu of special dishes, setting a beautiful table with cloth and crystal and flowers. Sometimes, for special occasions, she still creates such a gracious dinner but inevitably their entertainment has drifted in the direction of Fred's less formal style. This is partly because his habit of hospitality is irreformable and partly because eventually Sue had to admit that such unpremeditated evenings could be a lot of fun. If Fred's grandmother, as she was often told, had kept a ham hanging in the pantry for unexpected guests then she, Sue, could learn to stock her shelves with cans of cranberry and jars of pickled peaches which might add last-minute interest to an ordinary meal.

"I've made a big meat loaf which will easily serve us all," she says. "We'd love it if you'd stay."

"I will if you'll tell me what you were thinking a moment ago with that enigmatic, Mona Lisa smile on your face."

"I was thinking that it's lucky we grow more flexible as time goes by."

"Flexible is a good word?"

"Marriages depend on it. The first year can be like trying to mix two blocks of cement, don't you think?"

Pixie is delighted with Sue's invitation and says she will bring some early Mexican strawberries which she had picked up at the market that very afternoon. Mike arrives just as Sue hangs up the phone. He and Fred join them at the breakfast room table. Mike is excited as he tells them that he has just agreed to buy a two-bedroom ranch house.

"The back yard borders on the bluff overlooking the railroad tracks," he says. "That won't bother me but it helped to make the price plausible. I have to give Winnie credit for finding it for me but I do keep wondering about that candlestick. God damnedest thing! Winnie seemed as surprised as I was when we found it there but of course she could have been feigning that reaction. She readily admitted that it looked like her own candlesticks and later reported that one of a pair was missing from her dining room. I checked that out. There are sliding glass doors in that room looking out on the lagoons but I could find no sign of anyone tampering with them or of making entry anywhere else. I don't know what to make of it. I must admit Winnie seemed pretty uptight when we met about the house this morning."

"Why wouldn't she be a little nervous if someone has broken into her house," says Sue. "I find the candlestick an unsettling mystery but I think we ought to concentrate on the four-door sedan Kathy Kennedy saw at the baptistery that morning. I think my encounter with the Camaro driver in her hallway lends credence to the possibility that the people in that car might be serious suspects."

"Some murderer," remarks Mike. "Brings his wife along for company on the job."

"She might be good camouflage," says Bill. "A couple could look more innocent than a man alone."

They discuss how they might track down the car. On the supposition that it may belong to a parishioner, they decide that Mike should check the licenses of all navy and black sedans parked in the church lot at all four Masses on the following Sunday. He could get Jens or Gerry James to help with the job. Sue thinks dark cars are not popular and that the survey will not turn up a long list. She will then call on the owners using the pretext of writing an article for the Sunday bulletin on Father's last conversations. Did the pretext sound reasonable? They agreed it would have to do since there seemed no alternative approach.

Mike reports that he had impressed his boss, Captain Vogel, with the fact that the Camaro driver, although they couldn't prove that he had broken any law, was harassing a Lakewood resident by following her wherever she went. What could he do about it? Vogel had leaned on a Chicago cop friend to track the man through the last place where he was known to have rented a car. He was able to procure his name: Victor Place. Mike had then phoned Britannica saying that he had given an order for an encyclopedia to a salesman and would like to talk with him about it. A secretary informed him that Mr. Place was not in the office but if he would leave his name and number she would have him return the call.

"So he works there," says Mike. "Maybe he's just a legitimate sales-man going about his business."

"I think you might be right," says Fred.

"Yeah, he just follows me around so he can sell me some encyclopedias." There is a sharp edge of sarcasm in Sue's voice. She finds it frustrating that no one seems to take the Camaro driver seriously.

Bill places his hand on Sue's arm. "Don't kid yourselves," he says. "He may be employed by Britannica but he's also hired to shadow Sue and has been doing a professional job of it. She thinks her kitchen may be bugged and we were going to ask you to check it out, Mike. You've got to take this man seriously."

Fred brings more beer while Mike makes a thorough but fruitless search for bugs in the kitchen and breakfast room.

"Boy, am I glad you didn't find anything," says Sue. "The idea that someone might have been in our house in our absence really had me scared."

Fred tilts back in his chair and with his hands in his pockets surveys the team of amateur detectives skeptically.

"I can't believe you guys are serious about bugs in the house or about Winnie Harris as a suspect for murder. Winnie, of all people! Quite often I think this whole business is a sort of group hysteria created by the death of a friend, that no one has given enough credence to the pos-sibility that it really may have been an accident. I'm getting a little tired of it taking up all my wife's time and attention"

Sue watches the color in Fred's freckled face mount like a barometer of his disapproval toward the roots of his sandy hair. How frequently he airs some irritation with her in company which he has failed to express in private. Still, she can hardly pretend she isn't aware that her preoccupation with the case has been bothering him. The fact that he keeps discounting the Camaro driver might even mean that he feared for her safety but was refusing to acknowledge it. He is an expert at burying anxiety. Well, she isn't going to address all this right now.

"Look, Fred," she says. "I wish you wouldn't tilt back in that chair. You know that drives me crazy. It's not as if you hadn't gone over a couple of times."

Bill, however, responds directly to Fred's comments. He regards him closely, his intensely blue eyes narrowed, sharp, concentrated.

"An accident? But how do you account for the wounds on Father's head and calf?"

"Well, yes, there is that," admits Fred. "But somehow it doesn't seem real to me. I can't believe that any of these people could possibly have killed Father Rossi. I guess what I really think is that we should back off and leave the whole investigation to the police."

Bill's face is without any definable expression as he continues to give his assiduous attention to Fred. Never in her life has Sue found it as difficult to interpret a person' reactions as she does his but as she watches him observing her husband, she has the distinct impression that he is not interpreting Fred's reluctance to face up and come to terms with Father's murder as she does. He is thinking rather that Fred wants them all off the trail and computing in his keen mind what that might mean. Was it possible that he seriously considers Fred a suspect? But no, he is too smart to come to such a ridiculous conclusion.

"Look," Bill says. "Except for Mike, the police are not handling this case. And I'll tell you something. When this murder gets solved, it probably will be your wife who solves it. She has a remarkable gift for talking with people, for receiving their confidences and one day someone is going to tell her something that will make the whole puzzle fall in place. You wait and see. We need her to work on this investigation."

"Okay, okay," says Fred. "Not that I could stop her if I wanted to."

"I appreciate that we have to keep some local suspects in mind," says Bill, "but Sue and I are becoming more and more convinced that

Father's death is related to his work in Alvarado, that perhaps it was politically motivated." He elaborates on this possibility filling the others in on all they have learned from reading Father's many articles in a variety of Catholic publications. His summary is succinct and clear and certainly not dull so that Sue is surprised to find that Mike who is sitting next to her is writhing restlessly in his chair. His squirming is light, a mere vestige of the wriggling he used to manage in religion class years ago when Monsignor Fiedler was introducing his eighth graders to the social doctrine of the church. Still, it indicates the same recalcitrant boredom. His eyes have the same glazed-over look. It occurs to Sue that Mike thinks he has the mystery solved, that he is not interested in a new theory.

"You don't think that's all a little far-fetched?" Mike inquires when Bill has finished. "You think that military down there has an arm long enough to reach into our baptistery and do Father in with a hairdryer? I thought their style was bullets in the back while a priest is saying Mass."

"I thought the cold war was over and there was a negotiated peace in Alvarado," says Fred. "Isn't the timing for your theory a little off base?"

"I find it a plausible angle," says Bill. "We know that the death squads down there are still bumping people off, that they haven't really given up. And Father's advocacy for change and for the poor would surely have made him a subversive Communist in their view. Haven't we been saying all along that we don't know who would want to kill Father Rossi? Well, maybe he did have some real enemies."

They continue talking about this possibility as Mike stands in the hallway struggling into his winter jacket.

"Sue, gotta be sure we don't get diverted from our own backyard," Mike says. "I could see a danger in that. But, God, if you seriously think it was some kind of a political assassination, we're into something way over our heads. Maybe I should get Captain Vogel to inform the CIA of the possibility and have them check it out."

"What makes you think the CIA is not involved?" Bill asks quietly, so quietly that it made all of them stop dead still for a moment. The CIA? But they have no time to think about this as Pixie and Roger are skipping up the walk toward the house.

Sue thinks afterwards that their arrival was a blessing., a welcome relief from the intense speculation about the murder in which they were engaged. Roger was delighted with the cat. Pixie, with her enthusiastic small talk and her joyous exclamations reminded Sue of the bubbles one used to blow through a circular wand at children's birthday parties. Ellen was enchanted with her and Fred too seemed to enjoy her airy levity. It turned out to be just the sort of light-hearted dinner that he loved, wine, candles, a lot of laughter, a chance to tell his best jokes to a new audience. Keeping close to the wall, well out of the children's reach, Shadow explored the room, rotating several times around the dining table.

"See!" exclaimed Pixie. "She's weaving a magic circle around us."

"I'll buy that," said Bill. "I can feel it."

They did seem to be bound together and lifted up, adults and children alike, by some miracle of grace. There had been no evening approaching this one since Father Rossi's death. If only, Sue thought, if only he could be with them now. Or was he, after all, not far away?

Chapter XX

Although it is a Greek restaurant, the waitress is an Hispanic girl with limited English and so slender in her bolero vest and black pants that she scarcely makes a dent in space. A slim, supple stem, all grace and gesture, bearing a flower-head of heavy, dark hair. Delicate dangling gold earrings swing in her effort to communicate. She is obviously new on the job. Sue gives her an encouraging smile.

"A glass of Chablis would be nice," she says.

She would prefer to skip the wine but Winnie insists that she have some. Winnie is definitely in charge of the day. She has selected this place, the River Lodge, because she says they can have privacy here. It is out on Rosewood Road far enough from the village so that they are not apt to run into customers or parishioners. Also, no one will rush them through lunch. They are seated at a table in a far, dim corner of the bar which, with glittering glass and shining chrome, slices the room in half. In their deserted section, the undercurrent of conversation from the crowded dining room barely reaches them.

"I'm glad you can come to the newcomers party on Sunday," Sue says. "I'm sure you've sold half of the guests their homes and they'll be happy to see a familiar face. I've asked Monsignor to bring his violin so that he can entertain us."

"You don't think that classic stuff will be too heavy for a mixer?"

"I suggested something brief and light. I think it'll be fine and new-comers should know what a dear and talented Pastor Emeritus we have."

"Well, you're undoubtedly right. We can always trust our care minister for the thoughtful touch." Winnie says this in her emphatic way which sounds less than sincere to Sue but her follow-up question seems genuine enough.

"Sue, does your hair and your marvelous skin color just happen naturally or do you have some fabulous beautician who creates this casual, real-life look for you?"

"God's gift," says Sue. "Just wash and wear. But I keep wondering as I get older if maybe I should think about a more sophisticated hairstyle, something better groomed and more elegant like yours. I have a friend who says that as middle-age approaches, we need all the help we can get."

"Don't believe it. You look like a Cover Girl ad. You're perfect just as you are. Now if you were me with this carrot-colored hair and the washed-out complexion that goes with it, you'd know you had to do something about yourself. I remember when Boyd and I were engaged, I felt it would be deceptive to have him marry me thinking I had eyebrows and lashes like the rest of the world when actually they are non-existent without makeup. So one day when we were swimming down at the lake, I came up out of a deep surface dive and let him see me stripped of my mascara. With my hair slicked back like a seal and my face left behind in the water, I felt absolutely naked and perhaps pretty scared. I said, 'Here you have the real me, old fellow. Do you still want to tie the knot?'"

"And of course he said yes."

"Of course. What else could he say? And believe me, I never gave him another chance to slide off the hook. But now…"

Winnie pauses, taking sips that are more like miniature gulps of her Chardonnay. Not looking at Sue, she becomes preoccupied with the menu. She seems relieved when the waitress comes to take their order.

"Yes," she says. "I think we're ready. Sue, I'd recommend the spinach pie. It's got a light, flaky crust and a faint fennel seasoning that's out of this world. You really ought to try it."

"Sounds good to me."

"Soup or salad?" Inquires the waitress. "The soup today is split pea."

"Salad, I think," says Winnie, apparently deciding for both of them. "With the Greek house dressing. And please bring us each another glass of wine."

"Not for me," says Sue. "I have a way to go on this one."

When the waitress departs, Winnie drains her glass and, leaning forward confidentially, seems ready at last to talk about the divorce which Sue knew was on her mind. Her usually cheerful face—firm, round cheeks, plump pudgy chin—sags suddenly. The amused glint in her aqua eyes under their lidded load of blue shadow grows dimmer as though someone turned off the light switch. The change in her countenance is so dramatic that Sue feels a mask has been removed revealing a sadder, older Winnie no one would quite recognize. This Winnie reaches across the table and lays her hand on Sue's.

"I wouldn't tell this to anyone else," she says, "but I'll tell you because I know I can trust you not to repeat it. Maybe you'll even understand it."

"I'll try," promises Sue. Her interest and sympathy are immediately aroused by the other woman's unexpected vulnerability.

"When Peter came home at Christmas," confides Winnie in a subdued tone decibels removed from the bravado of her ordinary voice, "when he arrived from Notre Dame for the holiday, he was wearing a gold ring in his left ear."

"Peter!" gasps Sue.

This revelation came as such a surprise that she has no time to minimize the shock in her voice. Peter is a lanky, lovable fellow with an open, freckled face and a remarkable friendly manner. Everyone likes Peter. He is Winnie's fair-haired child, the apple of her eye, her pride and joy. He had graduated from the Jesuit academy with honors and had been accepted for college at Princeton, Yale and Notre Dame. There was a ripple of excitement in the parish when the news went round that he wanted to turn down all three and enter the seminary college at Niles in the fall.

But Boyd had reservations about his son's vocation. He had no objections to it on a religious basis but thought the boy was still very young and should take advantage of a top-grade education before making life decisions. At Boyd's request they consulted his friend, Father Rossi, at the Chancery office. His impression was that Peter was exceptionally bright and spiritually on track but socially very immature. For instance, although he was popular in mixed groups, he had never dated anyone. He thought a year away at college might be a good thing. Boyd was pushing hard for Princeton but Father suggested a year at Notre Dame as a compromise solution. Peter agreed.

"Maybe the ring wasn't significant," Sue says. "Men seem to wear all kinds of things these days." Sue thinks that if Peter wanted to attack his mother's formidable authority, he had picked a perfect weapon. She could think of no one for whom respectability, conventional behavior and social acceptance were more important.

"Maybe it was just a delayed adolescent rebellion. I didn't think Peter ever gave you the trouble in high school that Ellen is already giving me."

"Oh no," says Winnie sadly. "It was serious all right. I don't think I handled it too well. I really was furious. I told him if he thought he was going to wear that thing to the Christmas Eve Mass, he had another think coming. If he had a problem, there was no need to flaunt it in public. He insisted that if the parish couldn't accept him as he truly was, then it wasn't much of a Christian community. He said he had complete confidence in people's lack of prejudice. I said he was living in a dream world, that that was far too much to expect of ordinary people. I'm afraid we got into a pretty loud and contentious argument. It became clear that he had every intention of wearing that damn ring to Mass. I finally said that was up to him but I certainly was not going to attend Mass with him if he insisted on wearing that earring. It wasn't a very happy Christmas."

"How did Boyd take all this?"

"He was far more reasonable than I. Maybe he had suspected something of the kind previously, although I can't imagine why. Peter was such a normal kid, a great athlete and all that. Why would anyone suspect that he was gay? When he announced that he had invited his live-in lover to visit us over the New Year's weekend, I really hit the ceiling. Boyd had a hard time calming me down. We began to have some pretty bitter arguments. He said my attitude was demeaning to Peter, that if I kept up my caustic remarks the boy was apt to leave home. I said morality was involved, I couldn't just shut up about it. The whole business was wrong, wrong, wrong. Finally Boyd suggested that we talk with Father Rossi about it. Maybe he would have some ideas on how we should handle the situation. Very reluctantly I agreed to go up to the rectory with him. Sometimes I wish I had never seen Father because it was then that my whole life began to unravel."

The waitress has brought Winnie's wine and now places salads in front of them, plates of crisp mixed greens with a marvelously light oil-and-vinegar dressing. Winnie immediately reaches for her glass and then attacks her salad, viciously stabbing a cherry tomato with her fork. Her face looks like doomsday has struck.

"Everything is okay?" inquires the waitress anxiously.

"Couldn't be better," Sue assures her. She is grateful for the interruption, which gives her time to consider a response to Winnie's overboard statement about life coming apart at the seams.

"Look, Winnie," she says. "All the information isn't in on homosexuality yet but it certainly looks like it's a genetic inherited condition with no onus attached to it. Besides, you can't make Peter the measure of your own success and acceptability. You have a separate life of your own."

"I guess my own life is the problem," says Winnie enigmatically.

"Wasn't Father Rossi any help?"

"You'd have to say he was. There was something very reassuring about how calmly he accepted what had happened as though it were an everyday occurrence. You know how priests are about sin. You could tell them you'd just committed murder and they wouldn't flinch. They're a hard lot to shock. Anyway, Father said that one of his reservations about Peter entering the seminary had been the fact that he had never fallen in love. He considered it important that a young seminarian know what he was giving up when he chose a dedicated celibate life. He thought maybe there were hidden pluses in what had happened to Peter. He seemed to think that if he had a real vocation, it would survive this heady, off-beat affair. He was willing to bet that it would. I found it hard to see it that way but it did give me a measure of hope."

"What did you do about this visiting lover?" Sue wants to give Winnie every opportunity to talk this difficult situation out.

"Well, Father advised us to go easy on Peter. He suggested we handle the affair just as we would if it were a heterosexual relationship. We should make it clear that we did not condone live-in arrangements but that we would like to meet and welcome his friend who meant so much to him provided they slept in separate bedrooms. Peter resisted that but eventually agreed to move into the den. It worked out all right. The man was older than Peter, a shy, quiet intellectual. He was only with us a couple of days. They didn't hold hands in public for which I was grateful. But in the meantime, my own life began to go down the drain."

Sue watches Winnie sip the last of her wine and, setting the glass down, twirl the stem between her thumb and forefinger. She seems lost in thought, to have reached some hurdle in the conversation that she can't surmount. Sue waits patiently through a moment of awkward silence, then decides to give her an opening.

"You mentioned divorce the other day. I know that's one hell of a thing to be going through, Winnie."

"You don't know the half of it. It's really been a nightmare. It all began with this thing about Peter when we went to see Father Rossi. At the end of our visit, he said Boyd had told him that we had some serious marital problems. He wondered if we would like to discuss them with him or if he could recommend a marriage counselor for us. I remember that I just stared at him in disbelief. 'Serious marital problems?' I said."

"You didn't know there were problems?"

"There are always problems, aren't there? I guess I didn't think they were serious but Boyd had concluded after all these years that they were. I think he's been going through some kind of crisis. He's been out of work, you know, and we've been getting on each other's nerves.

'Well, I certainly didn't want to start going to some counselor that neither of us knew, so we agreed to see if we could work things out with Father Rossi. He gave us all kinds of time over the holidays and for a while afterwards. In retrospect, Sue, I think I would have been better off with a trained therapist but I had no idea I'd be getting in over my head. Father was kind enough but a therapist might have eased me into recognition of how things really were. But then it might have taken years to dredge up from the unconscious, things that Father Rossi managed to unearth in a few weeks. I think he didn't fully appreciate how successfully they had been buried or understand the emotional trauma I went through in having to face them. He was as direct and honest person himself and possibly never guessed what facades a manipulator like me can manage to construct."

Winnie said this last with a degree of self-loathing that surprised and startled Sue.

"We all do some bubble building," she says. "It couldn't have been that bad."

"Bad enough so that I became totally exhausted trying to deny the truth. I couldn't sleep. I think I lost ten pounds. This matter with Peter triggered the hardest thing I had to face. Maybe you can guess what that was. Maybe it was perfectly obvious to everyone but me."

Winnie raises her carefully stenciled eyebrows anxiously.

"I don't know what you're talking about," says Sue.

"I mean that I too am a homosexual."

Something ignited in Winnie's pale eyes as she made this announcement, some challenging meteor-flash of anger and defiance. Was she saying, I dare you to be my friend now? Heaven knows Sue had seen pain before but nothing as bitter and sharp-edged as this. She felt ordinary reassurances would be totally inadequate. A genuine reply would take time and commitment Sue was already resolving to expend. For now, she kept her voice level and matter-of-fact.

"You didn't know it before these sessions with Father?"

"You find that hard to believe? I suppose the evidence was there all along but I simply refused to look at it. More than anything else in the world, I wanted to be normal, to have a normal life. You can't imagine how threatening a suspicion of sex-deviance was to me, how truly frightening I found it, how I caulked all the cracks through which it might reach my conscious mind: But when Father asked questions about our marriage, I began to see things as someone else might, not as I rationalized them. For instance, he started out by saying that Boyd had told him it had been a long time since we had slept together. Father said he knew this sometimes happened in a marriage, that intimacy lapsed and the couple drifted apart, but could we explain how this had happened in our marriage? He was gentle in his approach but Boyd was not. Boyd immediately asserted with an intensity that took me by complete surprise that there never had been any intimacy in our marriage."

"But that could hardly be true. You had the four children after all and you always seemed to get along exceptionally well. You've always been a popular couple invited to just about every party that happens in the parish."

"Social life is not intimacy, though I suppose to some extent it compensates for a lack of it. It was terribly important to me that we be included in everything and I worked hard to accomplish that. I needed social acceptance and I do enjoy people provided they don't get too close. But Boyd could take or leave a party: he just went along to accommodate me. No, he was right about the intimacy. There never really was much of it."

The waitress removes the salad plates and now sets their entrees before them. Winnie takes advantage of her presence to polish off her glass of wine and order a third for herself. This time Sue agrees to have another.

"I'm not really a wino," Winnie says when the waitress departs, "but I find it hard to talk about all this sex stuff. Sue, you can have no idea how difficult intercourse was for me. I tried hard our first year. I really wanted our marriage to be a success, but I was totally without inclination or desire. We treated what we called my frigidity with humor and hot baths to relax me. Boyd was always reading sex manuals trying to figure out some way to arouse me but his efforts only made me nervous. I began to dread bedtime. I always remained a very passive partner waiting for the ordeal to be over with."

"Maybe you're over-reading all this," suggests Sue. "A lot of couples have a tough first year. Maybe it's only on TV that a woman climbs into bed and has an exalted orgasm on first try."

However, as Winnie's story unfolds, there is more to it than a difficult adjustment in the first year of marriage. She presented her history clearly, concisely as though she had rehearsed it in preparation for their luncheon. She often interjected bitter sound-bites of self-derision which were meant to be humorous but which Sue soon latched on to as keys to the emotional content of her tale.

Winnie was the only child of a couple who were devoted to each other and whom she tended to idolize. Her mother was exceptionally beautiful, a dark, willowy woman who dressed like a model and entertained with the graciousness and know-how of a Washington hostess. Winnie thought she was pretty close to perfect.

"Can you imagine an attractive couple like my parents getting stuck with me as their only child?" she inquires.

Of course, Winnie says, people in their state of life were terribly preoccupied with their own affairs. Her father, an international lawyer, frequently traveled abroad and liked to take her mother with him. In grade school Winnie was often placed in the Convent boarding school for long stays and was enrolled there permanently in high school. She really didn't mind that, it was a lot of built-in company for a child without siblings. She had an undying crush on the young Mother Superior, a strict but loving nun with whom the students had regular, private visits. Sue guessed that these provided more quality time than Winnie ever had with her parents. However, she was allowed home periodically for dental appointments and to go shopping with her mother.

"Can you imagine trying to find the right clothes for a hulk like me?" says Winnie. "But my mother was an expert at it. She talked me out of the feminine fluff I liked to dream that I could wear and taught me to buy only expensive, perfectly tailored clothes."

"You always do look stunning."

"You mean my clothes do. You know, Sue, those shopping trips were very two-edged. The time alone with my mother was precious. She was frivolous and fun and I loved being with her. But these visits also were lessons in the fact that I could never be like her. It wasn't just that I couldn't wear the glamorous clothes she did but that I was somehow different. I knew it even then."

Winnie took a sizable bite of her spinach pie, murmured a few mmm's and said, "Marvelous stuff, isn't it?" and then related an anecdote that must have been crucial in the development of her personality.

The nuns were forever saving on electricity. One evening in her junior year when her parents had dropped her at the Convent after one of these shopping adventures, Winnie had climbed the waxed, wooden stairs into the gloom of the dimly lit front hall and walked into what she described as a dark womb of depression. This return to school proved numbing, paralyzing. She grew listless. This went on for some time until it became apparent that her grades were plummeting. Then Reverend Mother called her into her office for a talk.

"Winifred dear," she said. "You seem so sad lately. Would you like to tell me what's been troubling you?" Her small, pale face sandwiched narrowly into her starched bonnet was so full of concern and compassion that tears sprang up in Winnie's eyes.

"It's just that no one is ever going to love me the way my father loves my mother. He adores her, you know, but no one is ever going to want to marry me."

"Is that what you want in life? You want very much to be married?"

"God, yes! I want to have a husband and a home and a family. I really love kids and I'd like to have a whole bunch of them. But no one is ever going to marry me."

"Why not?" said Reverend Mother. "I think every young girl should expect to be married if that is the vocation to which God is calling her. But of course you'd have to prepare yourself for a vocation like that. You can't expect it just to happen to you."

"Prepare?" A wild new hope awakened in Winnie's heart. She had been slumped in the office chair with her arms crossed under her breasts, a habit she had contracted so no one would notice how mature they had become. Now she sat up straight and looked intently at Reverend Mother.

"There! That's much better, sitting up like a lady. Maybe we should begin with posture. You know God has given you an agile, athletic body, a real gift. When you are playing on the basketball court, anyone can see how beautiful it is, how graceful and supple and strong. But the rest of the time you tend to stoop and slump and to lope down the corridors as though you were ashamed of your body. That's no way to treat a gift of God."

"But I am so gross. You can see for yourself what a mess I am."

"Well, let's presume your husband is going to be a tall man. There'll be no need for you to keep trying to shrink into yourself. Let's practice a posture that says I am proud of the way God made me."

Preparing for marriage became a purposeful pursuit for Winnie. Reverend Mother also said she must learn to stop mumbling. She spoke as though she expected no one to listen. She must project her voice more forcefully and use more expression in her speech. A monotonous monologue was never going to catch a future husband's attention. She suggested that she join the drama club. Winnie swore that theatre wasn't her thing but surprised herself by assuming roles that required serious acting. Reverend Mother was pleased with her progress but warned her that moderation was a good virtue to practice. She need not overdo the acting in real life.

"Just wait and see," Reverend Mother said. "You'll make your place in the world, Winifred."

"I suppose in a way I have and it never could have happened if she had not had confidence in me. You know, she never once called me Winnie until the day I graduated, but I could believe God loved me because I knew she did."

There was a while in those high school years when Winnie became involved in what she referred to as "hanky-panky" with one of her classmates. A case of puppy love. She said you could never learn from her what Lesbians do, that it was a simple matter of sneaking into her friend's bed after lights out and nuzzling around under the sheets: exciting touches that never went too far but still had to be processed through the Confessional on Saturday afternoons.

"Sue," she says, "do you remember confession with your laundry list of sins of impurity? God, it was so humiliating! I used to get so uptight I was sure I'd wet my pants. I know I suffered far more guilt than the girls who had been out on a date and done a little heavy necking. I knew what I had done was an aberration, a crime against nature. My shame was overwhelming."

"I don't think experiences like yours are uncommon among adolescents," says Sue "I don't think they prove anything."

"Hey, I'm trying to be honest here and I think in my case it was significant. I was hopelessly hooked. My firm resolutions of amendment were never firm enough. I was terribly addicted to the friendship involved. I dreaded more than anything breaking up that relationship. But Reverend Mother, in her Friday talks to the high school students, used to present the ideal of chastity in such a positive light. I suppose Aids is a strong motivation for chastity these days but it couldn't hold a candle to the motivation Reverend Mother presented to us: how having a clean heart kept you close to God, how we should preserve ourselves for the true and permanent love of our lives in marriage. She talked about heroic virtue in a way any athlete could understand: the challenge and the discipline and the victory of it. She got through to me. It took all the grace one gets in the Sacrament of Reconciliation but I did break out of it. It gave me great self-respect to do that, Sue, and when I look back on it, maybe heroic virtue wasn't too strong a phrase. I did give up something important: the only bit of real lovemaking I would ever have in my life."

"Not that I didn't fall in love later on, when I was married and had three young children. This love was so full of respect that, dream as I might, I would not have laid a finger on her. Do you remember Elaine Veil or were you living in Boston when she was here?"

"I remember her," said Sue. "A beautiful blond. Wasn't she president of the Council for a while?"

"Yes. God, she was a fabulous woman, so intelligent and witty and clever. I really adored her. She had this way of listening to you with such attention and amusement in her eyes, always ready to laugh as though you were the most humorous person in the world. She was so much fun to be with."

"She was a hard worker too in the parish, heading committees for the Mistletoe Market Christmas Sale and stuff like that. I became involved in sewing and crafts and Mother Club meetings and things that would normally have bored me stiff just because Elaine was involved. I never missed a chance to see her, to be with her, and for a number of years I was really very happy. I think some of my joy spilled over into our marriage. I may not have been good in bed but I felt loving in a very upbeat way and Boyd was the beneficiary of that mood. I never kidded myself that Elaine felt about me as I did about her, but I knew that she enjoyed my company. That had to be enough."

Winnie's face had brightened when she talked about Elaine but now became sober again.

"It broke my heart when Elaine moved to Detroit. She wasn't a letter writer. We talked sometimes on the phone but less and less as time went on. She made a new life there, of course, and we're pretty much down to Christmas cards now. The last time she was in town to see her mother, she had lunch with Jo James but she never even called me. She couldn't get in touch with everyone, of course, but I won't pretend that I wasn't hurt."

"No wonder," says Sue.

"I don't know when things began to fall apart with Boyd. Maybe earlier than I realized. When the children were little they created some bond between us. We both enjoyed them. You know, Sue, I don't think there can be any more wonderful feeling in the world than your own small child's hand in yours as you walk to the store or to kindergarten. But kids grow up. They become more interested in their friends than they are in you. They begin giving you difficulty and back talk so that the interest and amusement, Boyd and I once shared began to frazzle. He objected to the criticism and discipline I thought necessary. He was always being the great defender. There was a lot of friction and tension over how to handle situations with the kids, a lot of quarrels, I guess. Life became more and more unpleasant so that by the time he started working late hours at the airport and sometimes staying overnight, I couldn't have cared less."

"To tell the truth, Sue, I was relieved to have him gone and certainly relieved that he no longer seemed interested in love-making. I may have suspected from time to time that there was someone else but I desperately didn't want to know about it. I never asked questions. I just wanted my life to go on as it was. When I got into real estate, I found that I loved it and I gave it all my time and energy. We were able to buy our home out on Lagoon Drive. It was my dream house come true and we've done a lot of entertaining there. Boyd always cooperated by making it home for important parties. Things didn't seem too bad to me.

"But it all was very different from Boyd's perspective when we had our counseling sessions with Father Rossi. Boyd felt that he was just a prop for the life I wanted to live: the necessary husband for social occasions, the necessary father for the children I insisted on raising my way. The trouble is, I could almost see what he meant. Not since early in our marriage had there been any love between us and for me there had never been any physical attraction or closeness. I had wanted it to work but I had given up working on it. Something very essential was missing but honest-to-God, Sue, I'm not sure it was my fault."

"Anyway, Boyd wants a divorce. The most startling discovery was that he has a child by some woman, a seven-year-old girl. Father said he found it hard to believe that I didn't know something serious was going on, that surely a wife would have sensed the distance such an affair would have created between her and her husband. I found that hard to explain. Or how to explain that I failed to recognize that I was a lesbian. I never once used the word even to myself until that last day with Father."

"Last day?"

"Yes, the day before he…died."

Sue notes the hesitation before the verb. It makes her heart skip a beat but she keeps her voice calm.

"You had a visit with him that day?"

"Yes. Boyd and I had an appointment with him that night but he called in the afternoon to say things had ganged up on him and he had to go in the evening to prepare his talk for the Saturday scripture group with Kathy Kennedy. That was sad about her death, wasn't it? She was a rather special lady. Anyway, Father asked if I'd like to see him in the afternoon and I agreed to do that. I was having a very rough time and hoped for some spiritual direction that might help to get me through it. I thought this might be possible if I went alone without Boyd.

"I told Father that I had been unable to pray, that I knew I needed to pray but that I simply couldn't. Every time I tried, I seemed to be up against an iron wall. He said that an experience like that could indicate that I was very angry with God. Did I think there might be some truth in that? I said I didn't think so. Why would I be angry with God?"

"Well," Father said, "It might be because your life as you have known it for a long time is threatened by the possibility of a divorce. That might make anyone angry with God."

"I don't think so," I said. "That's really not God's fault."

"Or maybe," he said, "Maybe you should ask yourself why you are so angry with Peter. Maybe you are angry with God because Peter is gay."

"I thought about that, about how furious I had been with Peter over something he probably could not help. Finally, I looked up at Father and said, 'Perhaps I am angry with God because I too am a homosexual.' Sue, I had never admitted this to anyone before, not even to myself. Perhaps I had hoped Father would deny the possibility as you have been doing off and on through lunch. But he accepted my statement calmly as though I had said nothing out of the ordinary."

"If that's the reason for your anger," he said, "You must tell God exactly how you feel about it. I think if you do, that you'll find you are able to pray once more."

"But I didn't wait to tell God how angry I was. I let loose at Father instead. This sudden recognition of my status seemed to have erupted from my subconscious with the suddenness and fury of a volcano. His acceptance of it as though it were a fact infuriated me. I really went berserk. I was seething with anger and resentment as though confession of my condition were his fault. I was in a terrible state and I don't know what I may have said to him. I was still in a rage the next morning when I went to pick up Boyd's gloves at the baptistery.

'I was angry because he was recommending a divorce, saying asinine things like I might be happier in a more honest life. I was angry that he knew about me what no one else in the world knew, that I was a queer. I kept pounding and pounding on the baptistery door because I wanted to kill him. I wanted to tell him to buzz off my life. Well, when I found out later that he was dead, I felt like children sometimes do, that somehow I was responsible. I was overwhelmed with guilt and regret."

"When did you find out that he was dead?" inquires Sue.

"I'm not sure. Maybe it was at the Cardinal's reception or maybe the next morning at Mass. Anyway, since then I have come to my senses and have been grateful for his advice. I have been able to pray again and some kind of load has been lifted since I've told Boyd he can have his damn divorce. I was sorry that there was no chance to apologize to Father but I sometimes feel that he is close and has forgiven me. But lots of problems remain, like how do you explain to your children that your marriage never existed and what do you tell your parents?"

Winnie looks at her watch.

"Sue," she says. "I have to run. I have an appointment to show a house on Lawndale at one thirty but I'm hoping we can talk again soon."

"Of course. Next time lunch is on me."

Driving home, Sue thinks of Winnie's problems with great sympathy. She is resolved to support her in any way she can. But inevitably questions crowd into her mind. Was it strange that Winnie had not mentioned the theft of her candlestick? Why couldn't she recall when she had heard of Father's death? Of course he wasn't JFK but you'd think she'd remember, unless she already knew that he was dead. And since her habit of coping was to bury unpleasant things, could she have buried her murder of Father Rossi? She'd have to ask Dr. Young if that were psychologically possible for someone to do.

Chapter XXI

Sue glances out the window at the brutal winter day, at the stiff, snow-burdened oaks so starkly white against a pewter sky, at the abandoned bird feeder swinging in the frigid off-lake wind, at glassy icicles, thick, treacherous daggers dangling at the dining room windows. For a moment she shudders and then, smiling to herself, remembers that winter is supposed to be a challenge to true Midwesterners. Farther south and out west, whole cities shut down after storms like this but here people laugh at such timidity. St. Felicia's is open and the main roads are clear so she plans on going to the south side.

Sue keeps an eye out for the Camaro on the drive to the inner city. Only two other women have elected to go, so Sue has the back seat to herself and, with papers spread out on it, is engrossed in mapping out a lesson plan. Every time a white automobile passes her window or appears to be following them, it triggers alarm signals in her body, tingling in her throat, tension in the pit of her stomach. But only one car is actually a Camaro and it is driven by a woman. As they pull into the school parking lot she gathers books with a feeling of huge relief. Maybe the man has given up.

Sister Teresita greets her in the corridor. This remarkable black principal reminds Sue of a fifteenth century sketch of the Oba or King of Benin which had been sent by the school as a Christmas card. She has the same proud, prominent mouth and blossom-shaped lips, the same royal lift to her rounded jaw. The whites of her eyes are as clean and clear as her immaculate turtleneck as though both had been freshly bleached that morning. Her only adornment is a small, silver cross, which hangs just above her ample, oval breasts. A simple statement of her dedicated status.

"Susan," she says. "I'm so glad I caught you. I want to ask you about the encyclopedia."

"The encyclopedia?"

"The Encyclopedia Britannica which you recommended for the school. The salesman was here this morning about it."

"I recommended? I don't remember recommending any encyclopedia."

"Well, this man, Mr. Street or Mr. Place or something like that, said you had recommended the encyclopedia to Monsignor Fiedler at de Sales and that you were sure we'd be interested too. The one we have is pretty dog-eared and dated and this one is a beauty, no question about it, but it costs an arm and a leg. I wasn't just sure what you intended."

"Sister, I don't even know this person. I met him on a stairway the other day and told him to try Monsignor so that I could get rid of him. I didn't want him disturbing a sick neighbor. If a new encyclopedia is high on your list of priorities maybe I can see if the Women's Council would be interested in donating one. But I'll tell you something, I'd definitely prefer that we not order it through this pushy salesman."

Sue is aware that anger has crept into her voice, that it even trembles a bit. She finds it frightening to discover that this man is still on her trail, knows her name and knows where she is, and has put her in this embarrassing position with Teresita who obviously thought she was offering to purchase a set for the school.

A puzzled frown frets the smooth surface of Sister's broad forehead.

"He seemed pleasant enough but obviously there's been some mistake. I know your students are waiting for you so maybe we should discuss it another time."

Actually, her kids are just arriving when she reaches the cafeteria. As they pull out their chairs from the table and prepare to sit down, Sue spots Lamont transferring something from one pocket of his black slacks to the other. He does this swiftly and her vision of the transaction is partly obscured by the back of his chair, but she knows what she has seen and it shocks her to the core. Only last night in a TV movie, the police had discovered the trunk of a car loaded with small white packets exactly like the one the boy had just shoved out of sight. She is uncertain how to approach this problem and decides to give it time. At least for the moment, Lamont is not going anywhere.

Her lesson plan concerns cars. She takes out flash cards with the names of automobile parts printed on them: fender, wheel, tire, door, etc. She then spreads pictures of car parts clipped from a magazine on the table and asks the children to sound out the words and match them to the pictures. This takes better and goes faster than she had anticipated. When they review the flash cards and the ad she has created, she wonders what to invent next and how to involve Lamont who is edgy and not participating. Just at this point, he interjects one of his sidetracking remarks.

"There's this dude who drives a white car," he says.

If he wants to grab his teacher's attention, he has succeeded. Sue looks up just in time to see him pull a twenty-dollar bill out of the pocket of his shirt and quickly tuck it back in. "This dude ain't up to no good," he adds. His smile in her direction is sly, self-conscious.

Possibly this comment is the hooker to one of Lamont's imaginative tales. But is it? Lamont is no dummy. It dawns on her that he has deliberately shown her the drugs and the bill, that he is trying to tell her something.

"Isn't up to any good," she says, trying for a little time.

"That's what I just said, ain't it?"

"Lamont, I want you to pay strict attention to this game. You'll be good at it. I'm going to show you a way to extend your reading vocabulary. If you can read these few words, you can read lots of others that rhyme with them. Take car, for instance. If you run through the alphabet one letter at a time, you'll find lots of rhymes for it: bar, far, jar, star, tar. Okay? Now let's try it with the word 'hug.'"

"Bug" shouts Jimmy. "Dug, mug."

"Drug?" suggests Lamont.

"Right. Now let's try it with a two syllable word. How about socket?"

"Locket" shouts Jimmy. This kid is displaying an unexpected talent for rhymes.

"Pocket?" suggests Lamont.

"Right," says Sue.

"Let's try the word 'part.' Like car part." proposes Lamont.

"Okay," Sue agrees hoping he isn't going to pull a fast one with the letter F.

"Smart," says Lamont. "Like some teachers are mighty smart."

"Some kids too."

She continues the game briefly and then passes out work sheets. This is something she rarely resorts to but she feels a need to put the class on automatic pilot while she tries to figure out what Lamont is up to and what, if anything, the dude in the white car has to do with it. She comes up with no plausible explanations. She is tremendously troubled by the presence of drugs, possibly heroin, in her little group and anxiously reviews possible approaches to the problem. She finally decides that it is too serious a matter for her to handle alone. Even if he thought of it as betrayal, she is going to march Lamont to the principal's office as soon as class lets out. She is relieved when at last the bell bleats through the halls.

"But she might call the cops," Lamont protests when she puts her hand on his skinny shoulder and steers him down the corridor. "Can't me and you figure this thing out?"

"No, we can't," she responds firmly. "This one goes to the top."

Sister Teresita is patrolling the hall ahead of them, moving majestically through a swarm of children like a ship through a sea of agitated gulls. In her stout, black shoes she plods inexorably forward like some unstoppable force of nature. Her broad back is absolutely vertical, her head held high on the smooth, round pole of her neck. How rigid, how formidable and unforgiving, this rear view of the principal must appear in the eye of a child culprit. Sue reaches for Lamont's thin, grubby hand but he wrenches it away angrily.

"Sister, can we see you in your office for a moment?"

"Something serious?"

"Yes, very serious."

Sister's office looks like she could use a full-time secretary which she certainly doesn't have. Files are stacked on the floor, reports piled on the desk. Letters spill down the hill of mail in the in-box. Sister sits serenely behind this mess and asks calmly what the matter is.

"Lamont has something in his pocket he wants to show you."

"I have?" says Lamont.

"You have."

Reluctantly, Lamont produces the white packet and places it on Sister's blotter. Slowly, deliberately, she reaches over the chaos of her desk, picks it up, takes a letter opener to slit a corner of it and, dampening her finger tip, touches a little of its contents to her tongue.

"Lamont," she said. "I was hoping this was some kind of a joke but Mrs. Carney's right. We can only regard this as very serious business. I want you to tell me right now exactly where you got these drugs."

Teresita has ironed most of the drawl out of her speech but a few wrinkles remain in times of stress. Otherwise, Sue would never guess that she was in any way perturbed. Lamont seems to have some kind of lump in his throat which he can't quite swallow but eventually he speaks in a high, nervous voice.

"This dude with the shiny shoes give it to me out on the parking lot. He wants that I put it in Miz Carney's pocket when she ain't lookin. He says she have deep pockets in her jacket and to shove it way down so she not notice nothin."

"Was this gentleman someone you knew?"

"Never know'd him in my whole life."

"Lamont, I want you to explain to me why you would take drugs from some absolute stranger. You'd think you'd never heard that famous line about just say no to drugs."

"He give me big bucks to do this job, but that ain't why I took it. I figgered it like this. Lamont, I sez, if you don't take these here drugs some other sucker's goin' to take 'em. And this other sucker, he might really put it in Miz Carney's pocket. And then Miz Carney, she might get in a heap of trouble."

"I see. Well, it makes me proud to know that a second-grade student of St. Felicia's school is smart enough to protect his teacher in this manner. But I think you'd better give me the big bucks while we see how to straighten this matter out."

Reluctantly, Lamont lays his twenty-dollar bill on the desk. "This dude, he sez he'll know if I planted the drugs in Miz Carney's pocket so don't try no funny stuff like trying to sell 'em on the street. He sez when he find out I done it right he give me another twenty bucks."

"That complicates matters a little," says Sister. "Before we formulate plans, I'd like to hear from Mrs. Carney on this subject. I presume this dude with the shiny shoes is our encyclopedia salesman? Wearing a black coat and carrying a brief case, Lamont?"

"That the geezer."

"Mrs. Carney?"

"I truly don't know him, Sister. But he has been tailing me lately and I have to admit it looks like he has it in for me."

"Can you tell us why this person might be giving you trouble?"

"I really don't know. I think maybe I've been trying to track down some information he doesn't want me to find. That's only a guess."

"Do you see any reason why I should not call the police?"

"Sister, please don't call the police," pleads Lamont.

"Lamont, if you just tell your story as you told it to us, you have no reason to fear the police."

"That what you think, Sister. You jus' say drugs and them there cops, they got it in for me. This here dude, he one mighty smooth operator. Comes up his word 'gainst a black kid like me, guess who goin' to win. 'Sides, he prob'ly done call the cops already to tip them off 'bout Miz Carney havin' possession. Seems like to me we all get in trouble if Miz Carney can't do no 'splainin' why this geezer set her up."

"Susan?"

Sue is impressed with Lamon't street smarts in this situation. She is also touched by the risks he has taken to protect her. If she has one priority at this point, it is to be sure that the boy will not get in trouble.

"It would be impossible for me to explain why he set me up because I don't really know the answer myself. I think Lamont's story is going to be hard to sell to the police if we can't supply a motive for the man to do such a thing. Do you think we have to call them, Sister?"

"We could consider alternatives but I'm not sure you'd like the consequences, Susan. If this man has tipped off the police, then they may stop you on the way home."

"But would I be in any trouble if they didn't find anything?"

"If they don't find nothin," says Lamont, "I'm gonna be in big trouble with this dude. He sez he know if I don't deliver."

Tapping a pencil against her spiral calendar, Sister ponders the situation briefly. Then, picking up a sharp letter opener, she made a decisive announcement.

"This is what we're going to do. Lamont, I'm making a fine slit in this bag and I want you to take it in the wash room right there and flush the contents down the toilet."

"You can't mean it," gasps Lamont. "That there stuff might be worth a thousand bucks!"

"Were you thinking of selling it to the pastor?" inquires Sister wryly.

A few minutes later, driving Dottie's car through the ice-rutted streets to call on Adele Adabeau, Sue finds herself hoping that Sister's solution has been the right way to go. Perhaps she should have called Bill Bergman for advice, but she somehow trusts Sister's judgment and Lamont's acquiescence in it. They both live in this projects area of crime and drugs and seem capable of figuring the angles.

Hampton Court sleeps under a counterpane of fresh snow, a charming, dead-end enclave in a dreary and dangerous world. Although her visiting time has already been shortened by the consultation in the principal's office, Sue parks the car and sits quietly for a moment trying to calm the turmoil of her thoughts. She closes her eyes and makes an effort to place herself in the presence of God as Monsignor had suggested. At first a mottled red suffuses the darkness of her vision, then recedes leaving a black, empty screen. The distant sound of an approaching train accentuates the quiet. Whenever images of Lamont's face, pale and panicky at mention of the police, or of Victor Place and the puzzles he presents cross her mind, she gently lets go of them, lets them float away like debris on a swiftly moving stream. At last a great stillness possesses her. Her sigh is deep-rooted, elemental. She feels restored, ready to give her full attention to her new friend.

Sue had called before she came so Adele has coffee and blueberry muffins ready when she arrives. She serves them with the quiet graciousness which had so enchanted Sue the week before. She expresses gratitude and delight that Sue had been able to find a job opportunity at Bill Bergman's law firm. Together the women review Adele's resumé and then at her request Sue approves the suit she plans to wear to the interview. Now Sue give's her friend an opening to talk about her personal life if she should so wish.

"I hear Boyd Harris, your landlady's nephew, is getting a divorce," she says.

"Yes?" responds Adele. "I hope it is the best for him. He is a good man."

Obviously she does not wish to discuss it and Sue takes the opportunity in the silence which follows to invite Adele and Twinkie to join them the next day when the Bergmans take Juan to the Shedd Aquarium. She explains that Bill and Pixie hope to adopt the boy and want to meet him before plans are finalized. Sue thinks that Juan will feel more at home if the Adabeaux whom he knows are with the party. Adele agrees that this might be so and says that she and Twinkie would love to go along. It is agreed that Sue will pick them up at ten and they will meet the others at the aquarium.

She is driving carefully along a side street approaching Michigan Avenue when she hears a siren screaming behind her and sees in her rear view mirror the flash of a revolving police car light. She pulls closer to the curb to let it pass and then realizes with a shock that she is being stopped. Somehow, she and Sister had presumed that this would happen, if at all, on the way home when the other women would be with her. She feels suddenly extremely isolated and alone.

There are two policemen, one middle-aged with strong Slavic features, possibly Polish, the other young, black, sharp looking. The white officer politely requests her license and when Sue produces it, asks her to step out of the car for a moment.

Sue, too, is polite.

"Officer, would you please tell me what this is all about?"

"You must admit it is suspicious for a young lady like yourself to be driving alone in this neighborhood. Would you mind explaining what you are doing here?"

"I was visiting a friend on Hampton Court. But actually I come out here to tutor at St. Felicia's School."

"That's not the way we heard it. We had a report that you come into town regularly on this pretext to pick up a supply of drugs for the north suburbs."

"That's crazy. Do you believe that?"

"Ma'am, I must insist that you step out of the car."

The street is icy and Sue slips as she steps onto it. The officer takes her elbow to steady her. As soon as she moves from the car door, the black policeman proceeds to search the front seat, rummaging through the glove compartment, feeling along the floor under the seat, proceeding quickly and thoroughly.

"It's not my car," Sue tells the officer. "It belongs to my friend, Dottie."

"He won't harm anything," the officer assures her. "Now you must permit me to search your person."

This doesn't take long. He pats her across the shoulders and down the back, then reached in her pocket and pulls out the white packet.

"Ah!" he says. "Look what we have here!"

"Powder for my baby," says Sue.

"You carry powder for your baby in a package like this?" The officer takes a small penknife from his pocket and punctures the top of the bag. He sniffs the contents and then passes it to the other man who also takes a sniff and then throws back his head and laughs. His laugh tumbles up from deep inside him as though he has never before found himself in such an hilarious situation.

"Johnson's ain't it?" he says. "Same brand we use at our house. Someone must have spotted you putting that in your pocket and called the station."

But the officer in charge evidently thinks this might be too easy an explanation. He orders the black man to continue his search of the car. He asks Sue to unzip her jacket and proceeds to pat down her pockets and her slacks. It is starting to snow again, fine gritty flakes defining the direction of the bitter wind. Whether from cold or from fear, Sue begins to shiver. What, she is thinking, what if they find another plant in the car? She knows from previous experience that Victor Place has no difficulty entering a locked car. Her teeth begin to chatter.

"Look, Mrs. Carney," the officer says, "why don't you get back in the car and we'll continue the search in there."

Sue squeezes into the driver's seat and he drops heavily into the seat next to her. He is a big man. Courteously enough, he asks her to remove her boots. She struggles out of them while listening to the policeman in the rear continue his relentless search. She hears him slam the car door and swing open the trunk. Oh God, please, she prays. The officer probes the fleece lining of her boots and, finding nothing, returns them to her.

"Good warm ones," he comments.

"Yes, they're great."

They sit in silence for a moment, the motor throbbing, the wind whinnying outside her window. Then the other policeman appears beyond the glass grinning, teeth even and ivory-colored in his black face.

"Clean," he reports.

"I'm sorry about this, Mrs. Carney," the white officer says. "When I first set eyes on you, I was sure that there was a mistake but I have to report a thorough search. Do you mind if I take this packet with me?"

"Not at all. There's lots more where that came from."

Bingo! If Place called the police to check things out, he would know that Lamont had delivered the goods which was the main point of Sister's plot. But a nice side effect was the fact that he would also know that she had foiled him.

As soon as she gets home, Sue kicks off her boots, drops her jacket in the front hall and hurries into the library to call Bill Bergman. She wants to tell him that Adele will be calling his firm for an appointment and to explain the arrangements for the visit to the aquarium. She is relieved to find him in his office and soon after delivering these messages, finds herself telling him in detail about the drug incident. She realizes then that this was really why she has called him. After all, she could have left the other messages with Pixie.

She tries to make her account funny and lighthearted. She says the police had not roughed her up and even omitted searching certain areas of her body. If she ever decides to be a courier, she thinks she might be able to carry drugs in her bra with impunity. When she finishes, there is a prolonged silence at the other end of the line. Was he listening? Was he still there? Finally she says, "Bill, did you hear me?"

"Yes." His voice sounds tight, angry. "I thought this guy had stopped following you."

Had she told him that? "He hasn't been following me for the last couple of days, but how did you know that?"

"I called Mike this morning. I wanted to know when Winnie had shown a black customer the house where the candlestick was found."

"You think there might be a connection?"

"Possibly. Anyway Mike said this guy seemed to have stopped trailing you. Now it looks like he's upped the ante. We can't let him get away with that."

"Look, Bill. It may sound crazy, but I really don't want to report it to the police. This little guy, Lamont, means a whole lot to me and he may be right that he would get in trouble."

"I wasn't thinking of the police. We know where he works and I'm going to confront this damn bastard myself. I'll scare the absolute hell out of him."

"How are you going to do that?"

"I'll threaten a law suit that'll make him think three times before he pulls a fast one like this again. This is serious business, Sue."

"I know. I've been thinking it over and I've decided not to tell Fred about it. He already objects to my going into town each week and you know he wishes I'd leave this whole investigation up to the police. This would only add fuel to the fire. Beside, it really might worry him a lot."

"Are you sure you don't want to drop out, Sue?"

"Just when we're on to something with Alvarado? Don't be silly."

"Good. You don't have to tell Fred or anyone else about this business if you don't want to. I promise, I'll take care of it, okay?"

"Okay. Thanks a lot." Sue was about to hang up when she thought of something she would have told Fred if she were telling him anything.

"Bill?"

"Yes?"

"I can't get over how easily I lied to the police. I mean details like diaper rash!"

There was a little pause at Bill's end during which she could imagine his amused, reticent smile.

"Danger makes us all inventive," he says. "See you tomorrow."

CHAPTER XXII

In winter they seldom lower their window shades. On a clear night, they both like to lie in bed and gaze up at the few stars caught in a tangle of black tree tops or to watch a plane moving like a magic meteor in the night sky on its way to O'Hare. But days are growing longer now, dawn comes earlier each morning. On Sunday they awaken at first light and after making love, linger a long time in each other's arms while an albine sun spreads pearly light on the winter scene outside their windows.

Sue doesn't want to stir, to break up the indivisible, inseparable closeness of their clinging bodies, the wonderful warmth and mystery of it. How to describe this belonging, this unfathomable connectedness? She thinks of the biblical term "cleaving." A man shall cleave to his wife. But the moment cannot endure forever. The back yard is coming to life. A squirrel scampers along the fence top scattering clumps of snow, doves peck at crumbs in the driveway. Fred's shoulder is beginning to cramp her arm and she can postpone the bathroom no longer. Still, she feels like she is ripping something apart, tearing along a dotted line, as she throws back the covers and gets up.

"Time to rise and shine," she says to Fred.

He brings coffee up for the two of them. The house is quiet, the girls still asleep. Time alone together is precious even when they use it simply to outline plans for the day. Fred has to meet Mike at the church parking lot during the eight o'clock Mass to get the license numbers of dark sedans. It shouldn't take too long, he says, and he'll be back to do any chores for the party that she wants to line up for him. But he has already accomplished every task she can think of. He had opted out of the aquarium visit the day before to stay home with Sarah who didn't want to go. In Sue's absence, he had plowed the driveway, built fires in the living room and library, picked up beer and wine at Berry's where they loaned him glasses with his order, taken platters down from a top pantry shelf too high for Sue to reach and vacuumed the entire downstairs.

"God, you were wonderful yesterday," she says. "Every liberated woman should have a husband like you. I think there's nothing left to do except cooking and table setting. I'm glad you're working on those licenses, though. I'm convinced the murderer was driving the car that Kathy Kennedy spotted at the baptistery."

"It's crazy to think we can identify that car. In fact, this whole investigation is kind of nuts if you ask me. The sooner we get through with it, the better I'll like it."

Sue decides to change the subject.

"I'm really sorry you didn't come with us yesterday. The architecture of the addition to the aquarium is terrific. There's a marvelous view of the lake and we saw some fantastic specimens of sea-life. But the great thing was that Bill and Juan got on so well together. At first they were both a bit shy but Juan is a bright, curious kid and pretty soon he was asking Bill all those why questions that make an adult feel like God all-knowing. Why do fish live in water? Why do they have fins? Why doesn't water get in their eyes? He was impressed with the whales but perhaps a little scared too, so he began to hang on to Bill's hand and after that, he never let go. I knew we had won the day when Bill told Pixie they'd have to get an aquarium like ours for him.

"You know Bill was such an ass, hesitating because the boy was Mexican. But at one point he said to me, 'he looks pretty American, don't you think? He could easily be Italian.'"

Recalling this conversation reminds Sue of the moment when she had crouched down in front of Juan to let him blow his nose on her handkerchief. This close up view of the child's face revealed familiar features that did not entirely surprise her. The boy's forehead was broad, his eyes set wide apart. Rubbing her thumbs along his well-defined brows which extended in straight lines to meet his hairline, she said, "You know, Juan, you look a lot like a friend of mine."

Her discovery raised all kinds of questions that would never be answered now that Father Rossi was dead. It made sense that he had not wanted the child adopted by a wealthy Alvarado family whom he might consider an enemy of the people or to leave him to grow up in such a poor and violent country. Why he had taken great pains to erase all trace of the boy's origin was harder to fathom but in view of the Esquivel's unanticipated arrival in Lakewood, perhaps it was wise that he had. He had made a solemn promise to place the boy in a good, Catholic home and he had gone to great lengths to keep his promise.

"I'm really going to miss Father Rossi at the party tonight," Sue says.

"Me too."

That evening, as she waits for some egg rolls to heat up in the microwave, Sue becomes aware of the rising volume of voices drifting in from the living room. She has an experienced ear, a sort of inner-audio thermometer, that can accurately measure the degree of sociability achieved in a crowd and is reassured now that the party is off and rolling.

Winnie appears in the doorway carrying an enormous wooden bowl of salad, her contribution to the supper. She is wearing a sophisticated bronze silk pants and tunic outfit that flatters her figure and blends beautifully with the color of her hair. The effect is artistically pleasing. One feels satisfied that the very best had been done with the materials at hand.

"I'll just shove this in the fridge," she says.

"Winnie, what a beautiful salad! Enough to feed an army! I don't think there's room for it in there. Maybe in the back pantry where it's pretty cool."

"I guess it'll keep fresh there all right. Sue, shouldn't you be putting those casseroles in? And what about these rolls. Have you got a baking sheet for them?"

Sue sighs. The last thing she needs is to have Winnie second-guessing everything that has to be done. "Don't worry," she assures her. "I think I've got it all under control."

"Boyd is coming later. He hasn't gone anywhere with me since Christmas but he didn't want to miss your party. He's enjoyed that Scripture group of yours and I think he's very fond of you. I've noticed that men always like you."

"I guess it's mutual. I like men too."

Sue is busy placing appetizers on a large glass platter, concentrating on an attractive arrangement.

"He's taken a job teaching at a city college and he's moving out on Wednesday. That can't pay anything, do you think? His father was Harris Hang-Ups, you know, those great picture hooks everybody uses. He made good money but he left it specifically for the education of his grandchildren. Didn't trust Boyd with it, I guess. Anyway, with college tuition taken care of, I told Boyd that if I could just have the house, he could forget the rest, I'd manage just fine."

"Sure you will."

Sue is breaking off a clump of parsley from the crisper for a finishing touch on her platter. "There!" she exclaims admiring her handiwork.

"But God, Sue. I don't want to be alone."

Sue glances up swiftly at the sound of Winnie's voice. What had she heard? Not exactly depression or despair, maybe something closer to the plaintive cry of a child. And when she looks at Winnie leaning against the island counter, her shoulders slumped, her arms folded under her breasts, her lips pressed tightly together creating little ceramic pleats around her mouth, she wonders if this was how she looked to Reverend Mother all those years ago, like someone very close to tears for want of love.

Sue checks the oven heat, sets the timer and puts the casseroles in while she tries to think of some hopeful response.

"Look Winnie, you're going to be fine. Of course it's one very tough adjustment, but remember what Father Rossi said, that maybe in the end you'd be happier this way."

"Damn Father Rossi! What the hell did he know! God damn him anyway!" Winnie lets this expletive loose under her breath but with such impassioned fury that Sue immediately realizes this is not the time or place to continue the conversation.

"Winnie, let's get together sometime tomorrow and talk about it, okay? Right now, you could do me a big favor by circulating with this wine to see if anyone needs a refill."

This request seems to be exactly what Winnie needs to regain her composure. She enters the dining room, decanter in hand, almost as if she were going on stage. Her party manner is so habitual that she has resumed it without any visible sign of struggle.

"Sue, your table is absolutely gorgeous!" she says in her exclamatory way. "Those spring flowers are stunning with your green cloth! Where did you find iris this time of year?"

"Gabriel Esquivel sent them. A very thoughtful gesture."

"Don't miss the sweet-sour dip," Sue says to Mike as he samples an egg roll. When they are alone, he reports on the sedan survey.

"We came up with thirty cars all told. One snazzy Cadillac Seville turned out to be Joan Young's. Then there was a snow-covered Ford looking like an auto igloo that we recognized as Father Foley's with his St. Christopher statue on the dashboard. I guess he had to leave it in the lot all night because Jens ran the plow right past the rectory garage and left a mountain of snow blocking the door. I don't know how he happened to do that but you can bet he'll be hearing about it. Foley cares for that car like it was his only child. And then, just as we finished getting all the licenses at the noon Mass, Pixie came strutting out of church in those nifty high-heeled boots of hers and got into a navy four-door infinity—her status symbol. I guess Bill does pretty well for himself. She was shepherding that little Roger guy like he was the proverbial lost sheep or something. It's good they're thinking about getting another child or God knows what over-parenting might do to the kid. So that leaves us with twenty-seven car owners to check out. Hey, can I have another egg roll?"

"Sure. Help yourself."

"Anyway," Mike goes on, "that's a hell of a lot of calls to make so I think we'd better split up the list as soon as we get the names. I had an idea for an approach. I thought we could say we were soliciting funds for a Loyola scholarship as a memorial for Father Rossi. What do you think?"

"It's a great idea! I'll talk to Father Foley about it. He could put a notice in the Sunday bulletin. It's a very plausible excuse for the calls and maybe it'll really raise something for a scholarship. I like that."

Sue spots Father Foley talking to Jo on the fringe of the crowd in the living room. Jo looks very modish in an ice-blue satin blouse which enhances her delicate coloring. Relieved by Tim's entrance into the hospital and stimulated by her interior decorating assignments, she has been acquiring a new wardrobe, finding great bargains in petite sizes at her resale shop. To Sue, this revival of her friend's interest in her appearance seems a sure sign of her general well being.

Still, she realizes as she approaches them that neither Father Foley nor Jo are in a party mood. Some anxiety or apprehension has knit Jo's brows tightly together and Father too appears distressed. He is rubbing the side of his neck, a gesture with him of perplexity and worry. They are talking so seriously together that they fail to see Sue coming toward them and when she joins them with her platter, they abruptly drop their discussion. Sue is embarrassed that she has intruded on a private conversation but she is also mystified. Surely these are two people who share their every problem with her. What concern are they now keeping secret?

To relieve an awkward silence, she says "I asked Pixie to bring cheese and crackers but she made these stuffed mushrooms instead and they're heavenly. You'll have to try them. Father, have a couple. I hear Jens blocked you out of the garage with his snow plowing last night. Why would he do a thing like that?"

Father samples one appetizer and quickly selects another.

"Beats me. I called him this morning and asked him to come dig us out but he refused. He said he didn't work on Sundays. I assured him that it would be permissible, that it would be getting an ox out of the pit to just clear the garage entrance but he insisted that he didn't believe in all these new fangled Vatican II rules. He believes in keeping holy the Sabbath. 'We aren't talking about oxen,' he said, 'we are talking about shoveling and I'm not going to do any shoveling on a Sunday.'"

Father is sipping his scotch and venting his irritation with Jens by making a funny story of his stubbornness. He is a man for whom a drink works wonders and already he seems to have forgot whatever worry was troubling him.

"I don't know what's gotten into the man since Paul's death," he said. "He's been consistently obstinate and sullen, very hard to deal with."

"You trace this attitude to Father Rossi's death?" Sue is listening attentively

"Well, Jens has always been a character. We all know that. But I would say he's grown considerably worse in the last few weeks. This snow deal seems pretty deliberate, doesn't it? His animosity and lack of co-operation is definitely on the increase. Maybe he's just getting older as Rossi used to suggest. Or maybe Rossi took the brunt of a lot of his ill humor and now its all being dumped on me."

"Does he seem depressed to you or like he has something on his mind?"

"Could be something is bothering him. 'Tis a black mood he's in' as we Irish say."

"Timmy would be glad to shovel you out," suggests Jo.

"Too big a pile for a little fellow. It can wait 'til tomorrow."

"How are the boys doing, Jo?"

Jo's report on the boys and on her recent visit with Tim yields no clue as to what might have been the subject of her worrisome conversation with Father. Tim was taking the AA program very seriously and had asked to see Father to make a general confession.

"I went down yesterday," Father says. "The guy's really got religion in an impressive way. I think for sure he's going to make it this time."

So what had been their big concern, the subject of their anxious conversation? After explaining Mike's idea for a scholarship for Father Rossi, Sue moves on to visit with other guests. She enjoys meeting new people, making new friendships. She is standing in the bay window chatting with an older couple who have moved into de Sales parish to be near their son's family when she hears voices raised in a far corner of the room. It is difficult to see through the crowd but it sounds as though a heated argument has erupted in the vicinity of the aquarium. When she passed there a moment ago, a group of young men, beers in hand, had been admiring a blue-and-black striped fish and laughing at the name Jennifer supplied for it. "A pseudotropheus zebra," one of them had said. "Are you sure?" Now the conversation seems to have taken an ugly turn.

"If you'll excuse me," she says, "I'll be right back."

As she draws near the discordant discussion among the young men at the fish tank, she observes that Fred and Bill Bergman are with those waging war, passions high, voices strident. Fred's face is red with indignation. More reserved, Bill seems to be drawing fire by shooting sharp, caustic questions into the fray. She picks up a few key words: Vietnam. Cold war. Damn draft dodgers. God, she thinks, aren't we ever going to put all that behind us?

"Hey guys," she says, "Lighten up! This is supposed to be a party. Finish up these appetizers and I'll get us some more,"

Her intervention succeeds in snapping the thread of the dispute. Arguments sputter out, voices drop to a conversational level. Satisfied that peace is restored, she has started for the kitchen when Bill says, "Hey, Sue, let me carry that out for you." and takes the platter from her hands.

As soon as they are alone he apologies for the disruption.

"I'm sorry. It just makes me so damn mad when one of these bleeding heart liberals acts as though the cold war never existed. They're like those neo-Nazis who deny that the holocaust ever happened. They suffer from some radical lack of historical reality."

"I hope Fred didn't start the whole thing. I know he feels so strongly about Communism. Did he bring up Vietnam?"

"I guess that man who moved here from New York started it. He was defending the President's position in ducking the draft. He claimed that the domino theory was a lot of hogwash and maybe that's what lit the fire. Do people like that really believe that communism was never a serious threat? What do they think we were fighting for all those years?"

Although he has not raised his voice, Sue can hear anger evolving in it again, can see it glitter in his eyes.

"But isn't the cold war over?" she asks. "Do we have to go on fighting it forever?"

"I guess it's not over until we've stamped out all the embers. Who knows what will happen in Russia, for instance and there's still Cuba. But you're right. It was a ridiculous argument. None of us are old enough to have been involved in the Vietnam War, yet everybody was hotly claiming what they would have done had they been around for it."

"You would have gone?"

"You bet. Fred too."

"I have very mixed feelings about it. I was very young at the time. My oldest brother Peter became a helicopter pilot and was shot down in his first year of service in Vietnam."

Sue feels this past memory move sharply and vividly into the present, feels herself stumbling over its hard edges. Tears well up in her eyes.

"I'm so sorry about your brother's death, Sue. He was a brave man and you can be sure he died in a worthwhile cause."

"I've never been sure of that."

Just then Pixie comes rushing into the kitchen, breathless, eyes bright, cheeks flushed, blond hair shining under the florescent ceiling light. She is wearing a princess style ankle-length print dress and does a few pirouettes in it, skirt swirling above her T-strap sandals.

"I'm having the best time," she exclaims. "Big Bucks here insisted that I get a new dress for the party. How do you like it?"

"Perfect on you," said Sue. "You look like a slim, sophisticated six-teen-year old. How do you manage that?"

"Gotta stay young for the children, you know. Don't you just love the word 'children' as in two of them? Juan is absolutely adorable. I can't tell you how excited I am about him. Even old William here is pretty excited, aren't you?"

"He's a great little guy," Bill bestows a smile of benign and loving amusement on his wife. She really is the light of his life, Sue thinks as she checks the casseroles and puts the rolls in to warm.

"I came out to help," Pixie says. "What can I do?"

"I set a table for the older people in the breakfast room. How would you like to fill the water goblets in there and then we can get the salads on."

When everything is ready and the candles lit, Sue finds Gabriel and, linking her arm in his, brings him into the dining room to see how beautiful the buffet table looks with his centerpiece of fresh spring flowers gracing it. They stand a moment in the doorway talking before she announces that supper is served.

Elena has been diagnosed with schizophrenia but there are excellent medications these days to control her symptoms and Dr. Young is pleased with now well her therapy is coming along. Gabriel had thought that perhaps he ought to take her back to Alvarado for a while but the doctor suggested that the new environment here might be beneficial for her after her initial adjustment to it. She thought de Sales was an unusually warm and welcoming parish and that Elena might thrive in it. At least they ought to give it a try. She would allow her to return home as soon as the decorators had finished.

"You and Jo have been so good to Elena," Gabriel says. "And if this party is a sample of how friendly the parish is, I can see why Dr. Young thought it would be good for Elena. I wish she could have been here tonight."

"I do too, but there'll be lots of other occasions."

After supper is over, after the living room has been cleared and the dishwasher stacked, after Monsignor finishes playing an unaccompanied violin sonata and has received enthusiastic applause, Sue follows him into the library where he is fitting his violin into its case.

"You must have been practicing all week," she says. "That was really beautiful."

"Not too long I hope?" His endearing smile lifts all the little lines that web his old face.

"Just exactly right. How did you come up with such a perfect piece?"

"I have memories of happy parties in this house. So it was easy to select something in the right mood. I was glad to see you included Winnie among your guests. She's been going through a pretty rough time."

"I know."

"I've been thinking that maybe I made a mistake about the package of clothes I found in the give-away box. I'm not sure that the gloves you thought were Boyd's were tied up with the other things. Just possibly, they may have been tossed in on top."

"I don't think Winnie's a very serious suspect anyway."

Sue takes this opportunity of a few minutes alone with Monsignor to fill him in on recent developments, to tell him about the Alvarado articles and the possibility of a political murder, about the dark sedan and how they planned to track down the driver. Monsignor listens attentively, his head cocked to one side like an alert little bird, his eyes never leaving her face.

"You know, dear," he says kindly, "I dislike venturing so hackneyed a phrase, but it sounds to me like you're looking for a needle in a haystack."

"I know, but it's our only chance, don't you see? We have to follow every possible lead."

"Sue dear, I have a feeling that you've become much too tired and tense over this situation. Maybe you should give it a rest and leave it to the others."

"I guess I'm a little tired all right. I've reached something I recognize as my 'near-tear' point, a sure indicator of fatigue. So I'll try to pace things better. But believe me, I have absolutely no intention of giving up."

"Desperate dedication to a questionable cause?"

Sue feels offended and betrayed by this description of her position.

"Questionable cause?"

"Don't you have questions about it? I surely do. I wonder if Father Foley isn't right and that after all, it was an accident. I wonder if it's really possible that anyone in our parish would murder a good priest like Rossi and in my heart it seems very unlikely. And I wonder, if it were a political assassination, what chance there is of amateurs tracking down the offender. Wouldn't he be long gone from here?"

Monsignor's questions are not unreasonable but Sue finds them puzzling and a little strange coming from him. There is something evasive, uneasy and not quite convincing about the way he presents them, something she can't quite put her finger on.

"You didn't feel this way earlier," she said.

"Well, time has a way of giving us fresh perspective. I wish, Sue, you'd consider letting Mike and this smart chap, Bergman, pursue the matter if they want to. I'd love to see you let go of it and get back to your parish work which you do so well."

"But I've been doing the parish work," protests Sue. "I haven't slipped up on anything, have I?"

"I think that's just it. You've been carrying an awfully big load. I'm not so sure Father Rossi would like to see you under so much strain on his behalf."

"I promised him," Sue says stubbornly.

It is close to midnight when the last guest departs and Fred and Sue are finishing the clean up in the kitchen. Fred, in his vigorous and efficient way, washes pots and pans, trays and platters at the kitchen sink. He enjoys his role of host and loves to rehash a party afterwards.

"You know who had a really good time?" he says. "Gabriel. I saw him engrossed in some interesting conversation with Boyd Harris and I was glad of that because Boyd was just hanging around the edges for a while."

He chats on, rinsing and wiping rapidly until he becomes aware that Sue is not responding. He glances toward the counter where she is measuring off strips of Saran wrap, covering dishes of leftovers to store in the refrigerator.

"Hey! You're six miles up in outer space. What are you thinking about anyway?"

"Oh, just about some of our guests." Sue proceeds to mention them, carefully editing her thoughts as she goes along. "Jo who says Tim is doing fine (and has possibly upset her and Father Foley by confessing a crime of murder to them?) and Gabriel who says Elena can come home soon (and is a schizophrenic capable of violence) and Father Foley who was telling us how Jens blocked his entrance to the garage with his snow plow (and possibly has been bearing a burden of guilt and remorse since Father Rossi's death) and Winnie who is lonely even before her divorce begins (and has made Father Rossi a prime focus for her anger.) I know it was a parishioner who killed Father Rossi," she says.

"How did we get on that subject?"

"Somebody has confessed the murder to Monsignor."

"Did he tell you that?"

"Of course not. And he'd never lie you know. But he's not very good at dissembling either and that's what he was doing when I was talking with him. Suddenly he's lost all interest in solving the mystery and wants me to drop the investigation."

"I wish you would too."

"He kept looking at the fire, never looking at me and it was such a switch from his previous attitude. I think he knows who did it and would rather it was never discovered. What do you think?"

"I think we should let these casserole dishes soak all night and go to bed. You gave a great party, sweetheart."

CHAPTER XXIII

Later, when she looked back to the time following the newcomers' party, Sue realized that the investigation started to collapse soon after and was dead in its tracks long before Easter. For a week or two there was a flurry of interest over the calls on the dark sedan owners but when they met to discuss the results, they turned up nothing of significance.

Mike had made one call on a Guatemalan family living in the small enclave of humble homes originally built along the tracks for railroad construction workers. This visit aroused his suspicion. He thought an Alvaradan could easily represent himself as a Guatemalan and that the man living there looked like a thick-necked thug quite capable of murder. But when he checked this family out with Father Foley, he said they were Guatemalan refugees whom Father Rossi had brought into the parish through the Sanctuary Movement, and that the father was an excellent worker whom he'd like to hire to help Jens with the maintenance work.

This brought Jens center-stage in Sue's mind and she began to seek him out for casual conversations. One day when they are alone in the sacristy, Sue folding Father Foley's vestments and hanging them in the closet, Jens polishing the waxed hardwood floors with a machine Sue thought she'd like to borrow sometime, she waits until he has unplugged it and is winding up the cord.

"Father Rossi had a habit of hanging up his own vestments," she says. "But Foley is always in such a hurry. I miss Father Rossi a lot, don't you? I feel so badly about his death."

"Yah. He vas a good man, a good priest of God."

"Did what happened ever seem strange to you, Jens? Did you ever wonder if maybe it wasn't an accident after all?"

Sue is watching Jens face and sees him suck his lips into a straight, stubborn line. He becomes mute and mulish, rolling his machine with deliberation toward the door as though he intends to leave without the courtesy of a reply. But then he changes his mind, props the handle of the waxer against the closet door and turns to face Sue uncertainly.

"Missus," he says, "Vat happened vas the work of the devil."

Sue feels her heart beat a little faster but she keeps her voice gentle.

"What do you mean by that, Jens?"

But Jens has changed his mind again, grasps the handle of the waxer and propells it rapidly out the door and down the hall toward the rectory office. Sue follows. She stands facing him directly as he stows his machine in the utility closet.

"Jens, what do you mean, the devil?"

"It vas an evil person vhat did the father in. God vill punish."

Although she asks him questions trying to draw him out, Jens refuses to say anything further. His homely features and grim face look wooden and gray as though carved from a piece of driftwood. A dour, obstinate dinosaur, he stands waiting for Sue to move out of his way. She feels exceptional sympathy for Father Foley who has to deal with this stubborn man on a daily basis. But she is not without sympathy for Jens. She is sure it is fear that has locked his lips.

"Look Jens," she says, "You know we're old friends. If you ever feel like talking about Father Rossi's death, you know where to find me."

When Sue says this, Jens manages to stretch his rigid mouth inter a rubbery semblance of a smile. He likes the idea that they are friends.

"Maybe I should bring the geranium for the kitchen window?"

"I'd really like that!"

This conversation is so inconclusive that Sue doesn't bother to report it to Mike or Bill. Once the calls on the cars were completed, they ran out of projects and had not met in a couple of weeks. Bill Bergman stopped by occasionally to run over some of Father Rossi's articles with her. He had talked with Gabriel Esquivel about the possibility of having them published and had had little encouragement from him. He said that journalist friends of his had never been able to find a market in American publications for articles which presented similar views of the conflict. But Bill is interested in pursuing it anyway.

"I think Americans deserve to know what a mistake our country made about Alvarado," he says. "I can't believe there wouldn't be an interest in these papers. They are written so clearly and persuasively and are so well documented. What I'm thinking about is a book with a considerable prologue explaining our country's policy because we certainly thought we had substantial reasons for supporting the Alvarado army. Then we could introduce Father's material to demonstrate that there was a lot we didn't know and a whole different way to look at the situation."

"But isn't it all just about over? I would think such a book would have to be more timely."

"If we don't examine our mistakes, we're very apt to repeat them. Anyway, I feel that I owe it to Father to give it a try."

Bill says this with a degree of seriousness that impresses Sue. They are sitting at her breakfast room table having a coke and she glances up at him just in time to catch the gravity of his expression. In his deep-set, extremely blue eyes, there is a look of earnest resolution which she thinks she understands very well.

"I feel exactly the same way about finding his murderer," she says.

"Sue, do you think you could help with the editing of these papers? Fred tells me you're an English major and I assure you, I'm not. I could use your assistance with organizing the material."

"I'd love to help."

Sue means this. She finds reading Father's articles brings him back to her in some almost tangible way, that she can hear again the cadence of his calm voice, catch the sparkle of his subtle humor. She would enjoy a careful rereading of his work. Already a plan for alternating his human-interest stories with more analytical articles is evolving in her mind. She is enthusiastic in agreeing that Bill should stop by any evening he has spare time to work on an outline for the book.

The dreary winter dragged on without record cold or spectacular snow. For a while, Sue saw a lot of Winnie who complained immoderately about the melancholy weather, the leaden skies and lack of sunlight. Aware that the dismal atmosphere aggravates her depression, Sue made an effort to have lunch with her whenever she could squeeze it in. Winnie's schedule is busy too but Sue soon learns that her only fixed and unbreakable appointment is with Julius, her hairdresser. This was her anchor in an otherwise fluid week filled with real estate customers, bridge games and shopping expeditions.

Winnie liked to drive, to select the restaurant, to pay the bill. Her choice of place alternated between the elegant and the ethnic, between the Lake Shore Club where an enormous crystal chandelier lit the two-story entrance hall and the homely Greek or Italian restaurant where the food was superb. But once seated, Winnie was oblivious to their surroundings. She talked dramatically and incessantly about the details of her divorce, about the difficulties of living alone, about how the children were coping. Only once did she need a second glass of wine to fortify herself for the conversation. This was the day after her daughters had had Sunday brunch at the Raddison Hotel with Boyd and his girl friend.

"You won't believe this, Sue. I don't even know how to tell you this except to come right out with it. This woman of Boyd's is black."

Would it be less damaging to Winnie's pride to know that the woman was an intelligent and acceptable person than to think she had been rejected for some stereotypic black of her own derogatory imagination? Sue decided to take a chance on this.

"I happen to know her. Her daughter Twinkie attends St. Felicia's where we go to tutor. She's a Haitian woman with a background very similar to ours. She graduated from a Convent school in Port au Prince and emigrated to this country several years ago. What did the girls think of her?"

"They didn't say much of anything except that there was a lot of fresh shrimp on the buffet. They thought the little girl was cute but you know, Sue, it's going to take time for them to get used to an instant step-sister. Anyway, this woman is a Catholic and wishes to be married in the Church so Boyd wants an annulment. Monsignor says that means raking over the marriage or lack of it at the Chancery, a painful process. I'll have to think about it."

Obviously there were still problems to discuss and Sue continued to see Winnie at least once a week. Then, one unseasonably warm day in March, she sensed that some corner had been turned. She had insisted on taking Winnie to lunch at Murphy's Tavern where the charcoal-broiled hamburgers were the best on earth. Sue picked her up at the beauty parlor at noon. They were hurrying across the restaurant parking lot so that Winnie's coiffure would not be ruffled by the mad March wind when she put her arm through Sue's and confided two important things: that she had agreed to the annulment process and that she had told Julius, the hair dresser, about her impending divorce.

"No better way to announce it to the whole village," she says.

When they settle into a booth and give the waiter their order, Winnie snaps open her purse and fishes around for her compact. Peering critically at herself in the tiny mirror, she continues the conversation in a breezy, offhand manner.

"I told Julius that Boyd's girl friend is going to get tired wiping up the coffee rings he leaves all over the house. God, he is such a messy person! Does my hair look okay, Sue?"

"Perfect. Julius does a nifty job for you. I don't suppose you ever do it yourself? I bet you don't even own a hair dryer."

"Well, actually I don't. I've never needed one and the girls are swimmers, you know. They have these sharp-looking short cuts that they just towel dry."

So much for that. The mystery of the candlestick remained but without the dryer connection, Sue felt she could safely scratch Winnie from her list of suspects. In the meantime, Elena returned home from the hospital. Soon after her arrival, Sue and Jo dropped in to help her with the final details of interior decoration. They spent a pleasant if exhausting afternoon hanging pictures and arranging décor. When they finished, they stood in the door of the living room admiring their work. Sue was amazed at the sense of quiet elegance and old world charm that Jo had managed to create. Elena was effusive in her praise of it.

"I never dreamed it could look like this!" she exclaimed. "I love it. And now if you'll show me how to make the coffee, I'd like to serve you some."

Because of her visits with Elena in the hospital, Sue had expected her to be somewhat vulnerable and dependent when she returned home. She had anticipated shepherding her through a tenuous recuperation. Actually, this was the only time she asked for help of any kind and perhaps even this request about the coffee maker was in a sense symbolic, a small but special hurdle in her recovery. In the following weeks, Sue was many times reminded that Gabriel had described his sister as strong willed and self-assertive. With modern medications holding her schizophrenic symptoms in check, the determined and resolute young woman who emerged astonished Sue.

The first thing Elena wanted to do was to learn to drive. After a few weeks of lessons from Mike whom Sue had recommended as the best possible instructor, Elena was driving herself everywhere. She attended early Mass each morning, was faithful to the Saturday scripture meetings, took a course of cooking lessons at the Community House, went with a group of new young friends to the Friday concerts at Orchestra Hall, joined the De Sales Women's Council and even offered her home for the March book review and tea.

"You're not trying to do too much?" Sue inquires anxiously.

"The ladies bring everything. All I have to do is provide the beverages. I love how informal everything is in America."

"She does seem to have found her milieu," Dr. Young told Sue when she stopped in her office to discuss Elena. "She's really very sociable but never had much of a chance to make friends in Alvarado. I'm pleased with how she's coming along."

"I guess I was wondering if we should expect symptoms of her problem to recur. I feel sort of responsible being her only friend who is aware of her illness."

"I've impressed on Gabriel how important the medications are. Often as time goes by, patients like to think they no longer need them. But I think that is all you have to worry about."

"I guess what I'm wondering is whether Elena's violent episode with Gabriel was unique or whether there were other incidents, perhaps a pattern of violence."

"Sue, I think I am free to assure that as far as I could determine, this was a singular event brought on by rather unusual stress. I don't think you have to be concerned about recurrence."

"She seemed so angry with Father Rossi when I talked with her."

"Her anger at Father about the loss of her child was rather easy to resolve. I think he was a temporary focus for a lot of underlying anger which we're still trying to untangle. That will take a good while longer."

"I suppose it takes time to come out of one of those violent attacks. A patient couldn't just walk away from an attempt on a person's life and act reasonably calm and collected?"

Dr. Young had been listening attentively to Sue, trying to understand her concern. This last question seemed to puzzle her but she answered it without inquiring about its relevance.

"An attack of this kind is certainly not like some cold-blooded attempt to harm someone. The emotional upset and agitation would certainly persist and be very discernable afterwards."

"I see."

"Sue, you've found Elena's problem pretty troubling, haven't you?" There is sympathy and concern in Joan's amber eyes as she says this.

"I must admit it's been a little over my head."

"Maybe you are feeling more responsibility for Elena than is necessary. Your friendship is very important to her but she'll be in my care for some time to come and besides she has a very reliable brother and a very committed spiritual director in Father Foley. I think she sees him once a week. So, Sue, don't worry too much about her. Just be a good friend to her, okay?"

If, in Joan's professional opinion, there would be great emotional turbulence persisting after an act of violence, this let Elena off the hook on Father Rossi's murder. Sue remembered clearly their calm conversation about the girl's needlepoint when she drove her home that day. Also if the murderer had confessed his crime to Monsignor, as Sue was convinced he had, the fact that Father Foley was Elena's confessor also exonerated her.

Driving home, Sue drew a deep sigh of relief. Not only was it a good feeling to have Winnie and Elena cleared of suspicion, but is was also marvelous to be free of the fear she had experienced while the white Camaro had been following her. She had not sighted it in several weeks, in fact not since Bill Bergman reported that he had taken care of the matter. But fear was not far off, was even at that moment waiting for her as she pulled into her driveway.

Jens was trudging up her front steps and turned to greet her as she got out of the car. He was holding a pot of bright red geraniums that he carried to the kitchen and placed on the wide windowsill for her. She was enthusiastic in her admiration of the plant. Running her thumb over the dark, velvet leaves, she said that she didn't know how he managed to grow such full, beautiful, healthy geraniums. Everyone else's got as rangy and scrawny as adolescents over the winter.

But Jens was not responsive and it soon became obvious to Sue that he had something on his mind. She asked him to sit at the kitchen table while she poured coffee. When she joined him, he picked up his mug eagerly but still said nothing. She decided to give him an opening.

"Jens did you come to talk about Father Rossi's death?"

"Yah, Missus. I haff to tell you because I just saw him again yesterday."

"Saw whom, Jens?"

"I saw the man vhat was leaving the baptistry just vehn I vas coming in and found the poor father's body lying dead upon the floor. I saw him again last evening."

"You didn't see him kill Father Rossi?"

"No, Missus, but he must haff done this dreadful thing. He vas just leaving by the front door vhen I came valking in through the chapel. Vhat vas he doing there if he did not murder the poor father?"

"What did he look like, Jens? Can you describe him?"

"He moved fast like lightening out the door...but I could see he vas tall and young, maybe the age vhat your husband iss. He vas vearing a blue vinter jacket like all the men folk vear."

"Could you tell if he was heavy or thin, dark or blond?"

"Not heavy. Vehn I saw him again last night, it vas dark already but I could see he vas thin and tall and dark. He vas looking in your vindow. I come to tell you, Missus, as fast as I could find you home."

Sue realized that they had scarcely been home at all the previous evening. The whole family had gone to MacDonalds to celebrate Sarah's eleventh birthday. Sue shivered involuntarily at the thought of the murderer peering in their window during their absence. She appreciated that Jens was only telling her about this person because he feared for her safety. Previously he must have reasoned that because this stranger had seen him on the scene of the crime, it might mean trouble for him. But his silence had troubled him too, resulting in his taciturn and surly behavior. He had not been having an easy time of it.

"Thank you so much for telling me, Jens. Do you mind if I ask you a few more questions?"

Jens shifted uneasily in his chair.

"I vill answer vhat I can, Missus."

"Did you happen to see the car this man was driving?"

"No, Missus. I vas so scared, I run out the back door without the boots. I see now maybe I should look for license but then I only hear the car zoom down the driveway."

"Was he someone in our parish do you think? Have you ever seen him again?"

"Vonce I see him. I go on Sunday to first Mass. So early not many people. But on Ash Wednesday, I go to evening Mass for the ashes and the dust to dust. Now iss big crowd of people. I see this fellow stand in vestibule to talk with the Monsignor. He is vearing the vinter coat. Here iss Satan dressed up in fine coat for Church like he vas not the evil one. He hass big smudge of ashes on the forehead. Everyvone think a penitent, huh? But he iss not penitent. He hides vhat he hass done."

The mention of the coat shocked Sue. Not Tim. Oh, please God, not Tim!

"Did his coat have a cape?"

"Cape?"

"You know, an extra piece of material across the shoulders."

"Don't know if cape. Very fine gentleman's coat. Like Paul Newman in the show."

"Curly hair, Jens?"

"Dark hair. Maybe curl, maybe not. After barber shop, vhat can tell?"

Well, she was never going to get precise descriptions from Jens. After he departed, the thought that it might be Tim lingered on. Mike had always had a conviction that Tim was the murderer but she had never wanted to consider the possibility. Still, she remembered Jo and Father

Foley consulting seriously and surreptitiously at her party. What had they been concealing?

When she told Fred about her conversation with Jens, she omitted her suspicion of Tim. She wanted to check it out firSt. Fred, who had failed to get alarmed about the Camaro, was indignant at the thought of the murderer looking in the window of his home. He called Mike and asked him to stop by on his way home. Mike promised to have the house kept under surveillance.

After supper, Sue left Fred to whop up the pots while she went into the library to phone Tim at the Y. She was lucky enough to find him in. She asked if by any chance he had stopped by to see them the night before. He hesitated before replying that no, he had not been out that way but would like to stop in some evening. He wanted to thank her for suggesting that he try the big stores on the highway for a job. He was now employed at Whickles helping fat, middle-aged women select materials for their new overstuffed sofas. Sleazy furniture, cheap yard goods, tasteless customers, but it was a job, a regular paycheck. Jo was pleased, he said.

Sue was sensitive to his slight hesitation in replying to her questions. God, how she loved this man with his devotion to excellence, his fierce loyalty to family and friends, his ironic humor, his sense of style. But she knew that when he was drinking he was a master at deceit: inventive, brash, convincing, looking you right in the eye without flinching. Often he had been able to cover his tracks for weeks before anyone knew that he was hitting the bottle again. Could she trust him to be telling the truth now?

When she hung up, she told Fred she was going to drive over to see Jo for a few minutes. They had both been terribly busy and hadn't talked to each other in days. She found her friend padding around in ankle-high, elkskin eskimo slippers she had picked up brand new at the resale shop. She happened to know that if you ordered them from Alaska, they cost sixty dollars and she had paid only six. Jo was always elated about a good bargain but the really exciting news tonight was that the Family Service Board had offered her the management of the shop at a quite reasonable salary. They had been impressed with her attractive window displays and her merchandizing ideas and were urging her to accept the position. What did Sue think?

Out of long habit, they gravitated toward the kitchen to have a cup of coffee. It was a country kitchen, very simple, with a Mexican tile floor and a conservatory window where herbs grew in blue-and-white cache pots. They sat at the old pinewood table where for years they had hashed over the problems of their lives.

"I guess the job would provide a stable income you could count on, but I wish you could somehow get into decorating full time. I'm thinking about how much the Bergmans liked your choices for their living room, the Impressionist chintz drapes and the apple green carpet. How you managed to make that formal room look as light and airy as Pixie herself, I'll never know!"

"It was something of a challenge," Jo says. "Bill is so reserved and conservative that it had to be traditional to satisfy him. But Pixie is a blithe spirit. She reminds me of spring somehow and when I saw that material, I knew that was it. Tim says compromises don't work, you have to find a real solution. For the Bergmans, those April colors proved to be the answer."

"Some one said they saw Tim at the evening Mass on Ash Wednesday talking with Monsignor in the vestibule."

"Yes, I saw him too. I think he was stalling around back there hoping we'd come out and invite him to the house for supper. But I've been very firm about our arrangement. Sundays only."

"Is he doing okay, Jo? I saw you talking so seriously with Father Foley at the newcomers party a while back and I couldn't help wondering if Timmy's accusation at the police station were troubling him."

"I don't think he remembers much about that. Mike keeps wanting to bring it up with him but I told him if he valued our friendship, he better not do that, I would never speak to him again. The poor guy has enough to face up to without raising unfounded doubts in his mind about a murder which everyone but Mike thinks was an accident. Actually, Father and I were talking about Timmy who had skipped school for three days running. We didn't want to worry you in the middle of festivities but I told you later, remember?"

True, she had.

CHAPTER XXIV

"To forgive a friend for killing your friend…" Bill leaves his sentence suspended on a note of Shakespearean sadness as though the drama and dimensions of her problem with possibly having to pardon Tim were completely comprehensible to him. He has been listening to her attentively. His responses are always studied, careful. When he speaks again, it is with quiet deliberation.

"Sue, I really trust your instincts but this time I think you are jumping the gun. You can't connect Tim to the murder by a simple thing like a winter overcoat that may or may not have had a cape. He isn't the only man in the parish who owns a well-tailored coat."

"And wears it to a week-night Mass? That's Tim. Everyone else turns up in jackets or trench coats."

"Maybe not if they were coming directly from downtown. Remember, Tim's car was never spotted at the baptistery and some unidentified dark sedan was seen there. Besides, have you forgot about all this literature here? I think you were much closer to the truth when you had a hunch that the murder was political, that it was connected to Alvarado."

Had she forgot that theory or had she just pushed it to one side to allow herself for the first time to think of Tim as a real suspect? Somehow the overcoat had made this plausible. Who else owned a coat so remarkable that it would impress Jens? And who else, for that matter, had vowed that he would kill Father and been enough out his mind to do it?

"Look," Bill says, "I'd be careful not to get sidetracked by Tim. I've always thought it was too premeditated a job to have been perpetrated by someone who was blind drunk. We've learned a lot from Jens. He has confirmed your suspicion that the murderer is a parishioner and now we know his approximate age and social status. We're getting closer all the time."

Closer to whom? For some incomprehensible reason Sue finds she can feel fear, a pervasive, inchoate nervousness, taking possession of her. A dread such as she suffered as a child alone at night in the dark back bedroom of her home where undefined dangers lurked in blotches of black shadow. Because, if it had not been Tim, then what sort of murderer had been peering in her window when she was not at home?

Still, when nothing happens in the next few weeks, when the police report that they have seen no one in the vicinity of the house, her fear begins to abate. Most of the time, she is too busy to think about an intruder. She likes her work; likes arranging flowers in the quiet church, likes the good-humored camaraderie of the rectory office, likes daily contact with priests and parishioners. She is good at and enjoys organizing whatever comes her way: the schedule for Eucharistic ministers, the calendar of parish events, the windfall of books which Kathy Kennedy had left to the library. Most of all she takes pleasure in being of service: assisting brides with wedding arrangements, helping a grieving family plan the liturgy for a funeral Mass.

Tim often crosses her mind. The thought of him brings a feeling of acute discomfort; deep suspicion and anger at war with long-standing affection. She is aware that she has mixed motives when she invites him for dinner. She is genuinely concerned for the loneliness of his present existence but she also hopes to find out something, anything, which might resolve the doubt and mistrust which Jens has aroused. She can see at once when he enters the door that he is not his usual self, is less arrogant, more diffident. He lounges with his customary languid grace in the library wing chair, stretching his long legs toward the fire but it seems to Sue that his personality is suppressed, on hold. His attempt at amusing anecdotes about the people with whom he shares life at the Y lacks his usual ironic edge, in fact is so muted as to blunder across an invisible line into pathos. Sue is picking up a picture of Tim as he sees himself; a failure among other freaky failures.

"It's not your natural habitat," she says lightly. "You won't be there for long."

"God, I hope not."

Sue enjoyed preparing dinner for Tim, an appreciative gourmet. She has concocted a pork tenderloin and mushroom dish seasoned liberally with fresh rosemary, has whipped up genuine hollandaise for the artichokes. It might all be wasted on the children but she and Fred decided to include them in the dinner hoping they might ease the conversation. The girls are always their brightest and best when there is company. You could pretty much count on them. So when Ellen, looking innocently across the table at Tim, says she understands that after all this time Cindy Brown finally had the wires removed from her jaw, Sue is furious. How could a daughter of theirs be so cruel, so rude?

"I know," Tim says. "Timmy and I went to see her last Sunday."

With a defiant toss of her ponytail, Ellen is intent on pursuing her persecution of their guest.

"I'll bet that was Timmy's idea," she says.

"You're right. It was. Timmy knew how badly I felt about Cindy and suggested that it might be nice to tell her so in person. I was very glad I went."

Sue thinks it is doubtful that Jennifer knows what this conversation is all about, but the child is sensitive to the silence that sets in after Tim's humble rejoinder. She rushes breathlessly to fill the vacuum.

"We've got a new cat named Shadow," she exclaims. "Shall I get her to show you?"

"Not until after dinner," Fred says. His sense of hospitality had been offended by Ellen's behavior and Sue can see that he is grateful when she begins chatting about Kathy Kennedy's death and the sale of her belongings which Jo had conducted.

"The family insisted that I have one item of my choice," she says. "I picked this lovely Chinese screen because Shadow looks so neat when she poses in front of it."

"It's truly elegant and perfect where you've placed it between the two rooms." Tim's approval is genuine and gratifying to Sue. Her trust in his aesthetic judgment is absolute.

After supper, Fred commandeers Ellen's help in the kitchen and sends Sarah upstairs to do her homework. Sue and Tim are alone in the library when Jennifer brings the cat in to meet him. She dumps her unceremoniously into Tim's lap where Shadow seems immediately at home, stretching herself for a nap on the slope of his chest. Sue watches him stroking the sleepy animal, softly massaging the supple structure of her bones, fondling her silky fur; observes his pleasure at this tactile exploration. As he draws his knuckles gently down the length of Shadow's spine, Sue thinks his art is not all in his eye. His hand knows a lot; knows the rough or ribbed texture, the satiny or gossamer feel of myriad materials. Those hands with their long, light fingers and well-kept nails strike her as benevolent, utterly innocent of harm.

"You can keep Shadow while I go finish the scrap book I'm making for you," Jennifer says. "It's all about cats."

"Okay, sweetheart." Touched by Jennifer's obvious affection for him, Tim's smile is weary, almost tearful.

"What do you do in the evenings after those AA meetings," Sue inquires. "Do you have a TV in your room?"

"There's one in the lounge but I've never watched much anyway. Since you've asked, I'll confide in you what my present occupation is. I spend my time recording my resentments in a notebook. Tonight, for instance, I'll note that I resented Ellen's comment about the bike accident and then I'll have to acknowledge that I have disappointed Ellen, that I've really let her down and that I'll have to make an effort to win her friendship back. If you're as proficient an alcoholic as I am, you can fill a notebook with far more serious resentments than that one."

"Like your resentment of Father Rossi?"

"God, Sue, sometimes I think you're clairvoyant. Maybe you're just the person I should talk to about Father Rossi."

"Go right ahead. I'm listening."

"Well, I've had to face the fact that it was Jo's decision, not Father's, that I get the hell out of her life until I had a stretch of sobriety behind me. That took some doing because I'd like to think Jo would never kick me out, that she'd be loyal to me no matter what."

"It doesn't mean she isn't loyal."

"I know. I know. But even when my resentment against Father Rossi began to dissipate, I was left with a terribly troubling doubt about his death."

"Doubt?"

"Oh, come on, Sue. I know you were there in the police station when Timmy accused me of killing him. I've asked Father Foley if there were some questions about his death. He told me that Mike had some unfounded suspicion that it was not an accident. He said he had carefully examined all the details of the situation and concluded that obviously Rossi had tripped on a cord and electrocuted himself. He had absolutely no reason to believe that anyone had murdered him. He advised me to put it out of my mind but I'm having difficulty doing that. Sue, I know you've got an ear to the ground on everything that happens in the parish. Have you heard anything about it?"

"I was at the baptistery on the night of Father's death, Tim, and I've been convinced from the start that it was a murder."

"God, you really think so? Sue, you don't think I might have done such a thing, do you?"

The anguish in Tim's voice strikes deep into Sue's heart. God, how she hates this whole business, how she wishes she could assure him that, of course, he had had nothing to do with it. But she knows if she is to get to the bottom of the mystery, she can't back off now.

"There's no evidence that you did," she says. "Your car was not seen near the baptistery that day. But one person has said that he saw the killer wearing a distinguished winter coat and I guess you know who owns one. That doesn't prove anything of course."

"Damn it all, I wish I could remember anything about that day! The kids say I was at the game. Jo claims I broke a chair at the house. I can't recall any of it. You'd think I couldn't forget something as violent and shocking as killing a priest but I know there are other unhappy incidents in my life that have been lost forever. Still, sometimes one of these comes back to me when I return to the location where they occurred. A face or a tune or a scent can trigger a memory for some people. For me, it's place, the special architecture and ambiance of the scenes of my crimes. Look, Sue, maybe you could help me out. Do you think we could drive up to the baptistery and let me have a look around? Would Fred have to come?"

Sue smiles. "He'll want to stay home with the children. Even though Ellen is old enough to sit, we don't leave them alone since the night the murderer was seen peering in our window."

Scrutinizing Tim's face as she said this, Sue notices a look of concern, which is difficult to interpret.

"How awful!" he exclaims. "But doesn't that let me off the hook?"

"Maybe. Unless you happened to be in the neighborhood that night."

"What's that supposed to mean?" Tim's look of hurt dismay is so profound that Sue wishes she could take back what she has just said.

"Nothing, nothing at all. I was just joking."

But she is not joking. She remembers Tim's hesitation on the phone when she asked him if he had called on them that evening. What had been the meaning of that pause? She knew that whenever he climbed on the wagon after a period of drinking, Tim's self-esteem plummeted to zero. He may have been embarrassed to admit that he had dropped by uninvited. He may even have wondered if he would be welcome. And now he might feel obliged to continue concealing his presence at their home. As for being hurt, Jo said it was characteristic of him to act deeply offended when accused of something he wished to deny. He is a very complex person with ingrained habits of deceit and, much as she loves him, Sue is determined to remain open to his possible guilt.

When they switch on the chandelier at the baptistery, Sue's own memory is cruelly jogged. She has been back there for many meetings since Father's death, in fact, had been cataloging books there every morning recently, but she has had no occasion to return to the baptistery in the evening. She remembers now the strangeness of the room when she and Fred left the Cardinal's reception and went up to look around: recalls vividly the dark, dead windows, the light falling on the bruised body lying so still on its side near the counter. For a moment she is overcome with the shock and sadness of that night.

Tim is pacing off the room, walking back and forth despondently with his hands in his pockets.

"God," he says. "They ought to do something about the lighting in here. I remember how impressive this place was when the family gathered for Timmy's christening. At night you lose that whole wonderful sense of spatial elegance."

"I know. Are you getting any vibes?"

"The thing I keep remembering is that day of Timmy's baptism. You've got to remember it too, Sue. You were his godmother. He was such a small, fragile baby and Monsignor was so sweet with him. In fact, it was such a sweet time in our life. Camelot. Before I fell from grace."

Sue knows what he is thinking: that he has betrayed the innocent little infant he so clearly remembers, that he has let him down miserably, has sown almost iradicable seeds of fear and distrust in his psyche.

Sorrow for sin might win God's pardon and a measure of peace but the past could not be so easily undone.

"There's no going back to Camelot," she says. "But look, Tim, believe me, there's a whole life of loving ahead of you. Timmy will thrive in it."

"Even if he discovers that his father is a murderer?"

"You aren't picking up any crucial memories, are you?"

"No, not a damn thing. In fact, I could swear that I have never been in this baptistery since whenever the table was moved to the center of the room. At the baptism, it was over there against the wall. Jo laid the baby on it to remove his carrying blanket. She had him all dressed up in her family's long, embroidered christening gown and I can remember how beautifully that yard of fine baptiste cascaded over the edge of the table."

Sue smiles. What other man on earth would recall a detail like that?

"The Good Shepherd nuns used to make those gowns," she says. "They were lovely. And you're right about the table. It was moved to the center of the room when Father Foley became pastor and refused to heat the school for weekend meetings."

"When Foley told me that Father's body was found on the floor, I imagined it lying right here in the center of the room where the table is. Sue, I may be reaching for anything which might let me off the hook, but wouldn't you think that if I had actually killed Father, my subconscious would come up with the right location for the body?"

"Probably," Sue says, but she thinks that the function of Tim's subconscious or his memory, for that matter, were beyond her comprehension.

As she is locking the baptistery door, Tim suggests that they stop in church "for a visit." Sue smiles at the old-fashioned phrase. Still, it seems in character. Jo said that Tim had a simple faith unclouded by the doubts that troubled many of their contemporaries. To him God was the great fact of the universe revealed in all places and in all things. His religious practice had changed little over the years except that his

renewed dependence on God for his sobriety had given it greater aware-
ness and depth.

The vigil light is a distant red flicker at the side altar as they enter the
church. Tim slides into the last pew where he kneels with his head
buried in his hands. Next to him, Sue bows her own head in earnest
prayer. She senses that God draws near to them in the shadowy silence
of his house.

"I wish I could pray with the ease and intensity that you do," Tim says
as they are driving home. "I could feel how focused you were. What if
you tell me your prayer and I'll tell you mine."

"Okay, you go first."

"Im so damn ashamed about everything that I can't quite speak to
God yet. So I've been praying to Father Rossi. It's like having a friend at
City Hall who will present your problems to the boss."

"You think of him as a friend?"

"Of course. I would never have been so damn mad at him if I hadn't
considered him a good friend. I always sensed that he respected me even
when I was making an ass of myself. So I was deeply offended when he
sided with Jo about a separation. I honestly don't think I would have
killed him but I certainly was enraged that he had betrayed our friendship and was depriving me of my wife. So I keep begging him to forgive
my anger and to please clear up this mess about the murder, to resolve
it, if that's possible."

"My own prayer exactly. With God's help, I keep hoping I can turn
up the real killer and relieve you of this anxiety."

"Are there other suspects?"

"They've really all been eliminated. There is, though, a theory that it
may have been a political murder. According to a Vatican City report in
the Catholic newspaper, the Dominicans at St. Christobal University in
Alvarado have received death threats and warnings to stay out of
politics from a group called the Domingo Monterros Commando, so
danger continues in that country. Father Rossi was involved in work at

the University and I have a friend, Bill Bergman, who's convinced that it cost him his life."

"Bergman? Jo introduced him to me at church. I guess she'd been doing some work for him. What do you think of his theory?"

"He's smart. He may be right. It's just a very difficult thing to nail down. It may take a miracle to exonerate you."

"But miracles do happen."

"I guess."

The miracle occurs the very next day. In the morning, a social worker from Catholic Charities arrives at Sue's front door, a short, chatty woman with disproportionately big buttocks and sharply clipped bangs. She introduces herself as Cynthia Collins and sits down in Fred's deep armchair where her feet do not quite reach the floor. Sue pulls up a foot stool for her.

"My mother was a petite person too," she says. "We always kept this handy for her."

"I won't take long," Miss Collins says. "We have to interview a few people before placing Juan in the care of his adopting parents, William and Patricia Bergman. In a way, it's simply routine, as Father Rossi recommended them before he died and Monsignor Fiedler has also vouched for their good character and reliability. But we would like your name on the record too if you are willing to be interviewed."

"Of course."

"How long have you known the Bergmans?"

"It feels like forever although I guess it's only been since January. We have become very close friends and see a great deal of each other."

"Do you know any reason why they would not be acceptable parents for this child?"

"None whatsoever. If their love and care for their son, Roger, is any indication, they will make terrific parents for Juan. I know how much they both want another child."

Miss Collins has some concern that Mr. Bergman has expressed prejudice against a foreign child and if this truly exists, there is no way they can allow him to adopt Juan. Without hesitation, Sue assures her that she thinks Bill's feeling is less a prejudice against Mexicans than a strong preference for all things American. She says she thinks he had already accepted Juan as his own son and would never allow prejudice to adversely influence the way in which he would raise him.

"Monsignor's opinion is much the same as yours," observes Miss Collins, "and Mr. Bergman himself assures me that he will respect Juan's heritage."

The interview turns out to be thorough and takes longer than Sue anticipated. When it is over and Miss Collins begins to expostulate about the Pope's reiterated condemnation of artificial birth control, Sue's patience begins to wear thin. She is already behind schedule and tired to death of the subject anyway.

"If you'll excuse me," she says. "I'm running a little late. Were there any other questions about the Bergmans?"

"No, I think that wraps it up. As I said, this interview is just routine."

"Well, it's necessary to check things out, I'm sure. What if I had turned up something crucially wrong with the Bergmans?" Sue says this lightly but the woman takes it seriously.

"You can be sure we would have investigated the matter and if you turned out to be right, we would never place Juan with them. As it is, they'll probably get him very soon."

When Sue finally gets in her car, she observes that the gas is pretty low. She debates about whether to pick up some here or to wait until after her visit to the hospital. But she likes to give her business to Tom Barocci, a parishioner who's station is on the main road just south of the village, and decides to stop there on the way down.

"Long time no see," Tom says pleasantly when she pulls in and asks him to fill her up. He looks like an Italian Santa Claus, all crinkles and good cheer. His thick, well-trimmed beard has grown white in recent years. Tom has been around for as long as Sue can remember.

"Incidentally," he says. "I've been hoping to run into you. I keep wondering how your friend Tim James is making out. He drove in here several weeks ago three sheets to the wind and I haven't seen hide nor hair of him since."

"He's finally on the wagon and doing very well. We all feel he's going to make it this time."

"God, I hope so. Such a nice guy. That day he wanted to charge some gas and I refused him at first because number one he looked like he shouldn't be driving anyway and number two he already owed me a couple hundred. But he insisted that he just wanted enough gas to drive out to McKean's to sell his car, that jazzy Jaguar of his. In the end, I put it on the cuff for the poor fellow and haven't seen him since. That's a while back. I remember it was the day the Cardinal was coming and I'd switched schedules so I could make the big do at the church. How long ago was that?"

"Quite a while. Do you happen to know what time he stopped in here?"

"Must have been noon. Old Fiedler's Folly was playing the Ave Maria and Mr. James was crying in his beer about how some soprano sang that hymn at his wedding and now his wife was kicking him out. He was in pretty sad shape and I couldn't help wondering how he made out."

"I guess he did sell his car so maybe that's why he hasn't been by. I'll tell him you were asking for him. When he remembers it, I know he'll catch up on the debt."

"I wasn't worrying about that, just about him. Fella you can't help liking."

It is less than a forty minute drive out to McKean's where pennants are flying in the breeze but business is less brisk than it looks in the TV ads. Sue talks with several salesmen before she discovers one who remembers Tim, or more exactly, remembers his car which he says was a real beaut.

"I paid him plenty for that Jaguar," he says. "I kept trying to wheedle the price down but he insisted on getting his own figure and then wanted two hundred dollars cash as well as his check. It took us a while to unload that car. That's how I remember it so well."

"Do you happen to recall how he left here? I mean, if he sold the car..."

"Now you mention it, I do remember. He kept dropping his coins in the phone booth in there and finally he asked me would I call a taxi for him. He had a bit taken if you know what I mean. With all that cash in his pocket he was feeling like a lord. Ordered the driver to take him to the Y in Evanston as though he were on his way to a banquet at the Palmer House."

The receptionist at the Y is a lumpy looking matron of uncertain age. Sue thinks that there had to be a more subtle hair dye than whatever one she uses. She takes a motherly interest in Sue as soon as she mentions Tim's name and, luckily, she has no difficulty remembering the day of the big snow in January.

"Lordy," she says "it was something awful the way the traffic got tangled up that day. But look, dearie, as for Mr. James' comings and goings, I can't tell you anything about that. We don't give out that kind of information except to relatives and then only in special circumstances. You don't happen to be his wife, do you?"

"No. I'm just a good friend and all I want to know is what time he arrived at the Y that day and if he went out again in the afternoon."

Sue thinks she detects a protective fondness for Tim in the woman's attitude and a good deal of curiosity about her inquiry.

"Let's call Mr. James at work," Sue suggests "and get his permission for the information that I need. I assure you it is for his own good."

Sue is informed that Mr. James is with a customer and will be right with her. She grows impatient as she is left for a long time holding the receiver, listening to Japanese flute music intended to soothe the waiting customer. When he finally comes to the phone, Tim sounds harassed. Sue comes to the point quickly.

"You sure you want all the sordid details?"

"Come on, Tim. I'm a big girl."

"Okay, let me talk to her and Ill get back to you tonight. We have a three ring circus of a sale going on here."

When she hangs up the phone, the receptionist pretends to be peeved with Sue.

"You might have told me you were his sister in the first place. Of course you know then that your poor brother has a bit of a problem with the bottle and I can tell you I was that worried about him on the day we were talking about. He arrived here I'd guess a little before two o'clock coming through the door there with a big Polish taxi driver holding him up. When I saw the shape he was in, I insisted that the cabby help him to his room. I went along just to be sure the driver didn't roll him for his money and just as well I did because he had a fat wad of bills in his wallet. So after this fellow got him laid out on the bed, I have him a generous enough tip and sent him on his way. And then I pulled off Mr. James' shoes and put a blanket over him so he could sleep it off."

"Do you know if he stayed in his room all afternoon?"

"I'm certain of it. You see, his wife is always worrying about him and calling up to check with me to be sure he's still alive, I guess. I'm never supposed to tell Mr. James that she's been inquiring for him and I haven't said a word about it, though I think it would please him to know she cared enough to call. Anyway, she phoned about five o'clock and asked would I look in on him and be sure he was okay. Well, he was still sleeping the sleep of the dead. When I call his wife back, she leaves the number of the school up there at de Sales where she'll be in the evening and also the number of his AA sponsor. Just in case he gets the DT's, she says. The DT's mind you! I wouldn't forget that day for the worrying was in it. But close to eight o'clock, just before quitting time, who comes walking through the lobby looking the proper gentlemen with his tie straight and his hair combed but Mr. James. Going out for a bite to eat, he says. Eat, indeed! It took another couple of weeks before he sobered up for good."

"God, Sue", Tim exclaims when he calls that evening; "what an angel of a sleuth you turned out to be! That's absolutely spectacular news. I feel like I can breathe again, like maybe I can get on with my life after all. Don't you think its fascinating that Father Rossi picked Tom Borocci to pull off his miracle for us? I always thought he looked like the merry old elf of Elsinore. He's going to believe in miracles too when I turn up with his two hundred!"

Chapter XXV

When Juan was finally placed in her care, the first thing Pixie did was make an appointment for him with Fred. He is amused with this office visit and recounts the details of it to Sue that evening as she is cooking dinner.

"The kid's in perfect health and bright as a light bulb", he says. "He's bilingual and surprisingly articulate for one so young, full of intelligent questions about everything. Pixie wanted me to determine his age as nearly as I could so she could pick out a date for his birthday. What could I say? I examined his teeth and gave him a few motor control tests. Then I looked her right in the eye and said "He's going to be four years old on May 15th."

"Great! We'll give a birthday party for him. We could have Monsignor and maybe Adele and Boyd could bring Twinkie since she's the only child we know he knows."

"Aren't Adele and Boyd stretching it a bit?"

"I'd really like to have them and I can't think of another occasion where it would be so appropriate."

Although it is still some time off, Pixie is very receptive to the idea of the party.

"I'd like to give it myself," she says, "but somebody here has his nose out of joint about all the attention Juan is getting. Maybe it's best that you have it and I'll bring the cake. And Sue, do you think you could include the foster parents he's been staying with? They're a nice young Hispanic couple and he's been missing them."

"Of course. I was just trying to think who else we might have."

"Another snowballing party?" remarked Fred. "Not that I mind. The more the merrier."

Ever since Tim had been cleared of suspicion, Sue felt that she was operating in a vacuum with no further leads and nothing to work on. Except one thing. Jens had mentioned that he had seen Monsignor talking to the murderer in the vestibule of the church on Ash Wednesday. She had little hope of obtaining information from Monsignor, but at least she could try.

"Sue," he says, "It would be impossible for me to remember who stopped to talk with me that day. People are so kind. Whenever I say an evening Mass, so many of them pause for a word or two."

"But this man is about Fred's age. He has dark hair and was wearing a handsome winter overcoat. Jen's description makes him sound like a stand-out, like someone you might recall."

Monsignor smiles and shakes his head.

"Sue dear, I'm afraid I can't help you. I'm happy for you that you've eliminated so many of our friends from your list of suspects. Did you ever consider that maybe that's all you have to do? I really wish for your sake that you could lay the whole problem aside."

"You know I can't do that."

Sue came away with one firm conviction. Monsignor did not want her to find out who had murdered Father Rossi. Was that some kind of lead in itself?

One day soon after, Pixie called and asked if she could come over to see Sue.

"You won't believe what's going on here," she said. "My big-time attorney husband is thinking about moving back to St. Paul. His old firm up there has made him some kind of irresistible offer."

"Oh no! You can't think of leaving us."

"I know. Just when I've come to love this place. But Sue, that isn't all. Can I come over and talk to you?"

"Of course."

Sue finds an old set of tinker toys for Juan to play with while she and Pixie carry coffee into the library for their visit.

"Thinking of uprooting us again is bad enough," Pixie confides, "but something else happened that has me upset. I mean really upset. You know Bill drove up to St. Paul last weekend to check out this offer and while he was gone, a man called him on the phone. He said it was very important that he get in touch with him. I said he'd be back about two o'clock Sunday afternoon so he left a number for Bill to call the minute he came in. Sounded urgent, you know. He didn't leave a name. He just said tell him the boss called.

"Well, Bill phoned Sunday morning to say he couldn't make it home until after dinner and I hung up before I remembered to give him this message. I had absolutely no idea where I could reach him, so I thought I'd better phone this guy because he had made such a big deal about Bill getting back to him promptly. I mean, you would have returned the call too, wouldn't you?"

"Probably."

"Then Bill had no reason to get mad at me for butting into his business. Anyway, when I punched that number, you'd never guess who answered the phone."

Pixie pauses for a long, dramatic moment.

"I can't imagine," says Sue. "I think you'll have to tell me."

"Well, the man who answered the phone said, CIA, Mr. Norton speaking. Of course I thought I must have the wrong number, so I said 'Is this 285-4466 or whatever the number was and he said, 'Yes it is, can I help you?' So I said I was calling for Mr. Bergman, that someone there wished to speak to him. He put me on hold and pretty soon Mr. Important is on the other end of the line and I give him the message about Bill being later than I thought. Well, there was a long silence, I mean this real long kind of sinister silence, and then he says to me, 'Did your husband tell you to phone me?' I explained that no, but I just thought and all that. So he says thanks, but he'd appreciate it if I did not mention this call to anyone but Mr. Bergman. Did I have that straight? Kind of upset and persnickety, you know!"

The CIA! Sue's mind is racing. Hadn't Bill once said, "What makes you think the CIA is not involved?"

"Anyway," Pixie goes on, "I spent all afternoon trying to figure that phone call out. I mean, if Bill had some case involving the CIA, wouldn't he have told me? One of the rewards of being married to a hot-shot lawyer is you get to hear about some pretty interesting cases but he never mentioned anything about the CIA to me. And that man sounded like I'd broken some taboo phoning down there. Anyway, to make a long story short, I insisted Bill tell me what it was all about the minute he got home. Sue, It's awfully hard for me to get across to you what that conversation was like."

Tears spring up in Pixie's wide blue eyes.

"Maybe he was just trying to spare you some worry or concern." Sue is presuming that this was all somehow connected to Father Rossi's murder.

"Spare me is right! You know what I discovered? I found out that my very own husband whom I though I knew through and through has been working for the CIA ever since he was a student at St. Thomas College. Odd jobs, he says. Not like he isn't really a lawyer, he says. Secret undercover stuff, he says, not anything he was in a position to tell me. He's quitting now so he guesses maybe it's all right for me to know but he doesn't want anyone else to know. He swore me to absolute secrecy so this is just between us, Sue. I had to talk to someone, didn't I, and I knew I could trust you not to mention it to anyone else."

Everyone confides in Sue, Bill had once said. She may be the one to solve the mystery because everybody talks to her. Some day, someone will tell her something and suddenly all the pieces will fall into place.

Sue tries to remain calm. She is aware of a tingling in her throat, a tightening in her stomach, the sudden coldness of her hands. She wants desperately to be alone, to shrink far inside herself, to somehow ward off the psychic blow which threatens her. Instead, she makes an enormous effort to focus her attention on Pixie.

"You can't imagine what it's like to discover that your husband is not exactly the person you always thought he was. I mean he's had this secret life I knew nothing about. Sue, I'm having a very hard time with this."

"Believe me, Pixie, I understand. You must feel deceived and betrayed and hurt that he didn't trust you with his secret. But it's not as though he'd had another woman on the side. He's always loved you and been faithful to you. It may be that he simply did not want to worry you."

Sue was thinking how easily she had gone along with Bill in keeping Father Rossi's murder from Pixie. Something about her excitable, girlish personality seemed to demand protection. Still, Sue had learned that far from being the dumb blond Fred had first assumed her to be, Pixie was a bright, insightful and very perceptive person. Maybe she had misjudged her. Maybe she would have got to the bottom of the mystery far sooner than Sue had. She watches Pixie now, poised as if for flight on the edge of the desk chair, legs crossed, nervously swinging one foot back and forth. Although winter is gradually turning into spring, she still wears her handsome, high-heeled boots.

Mike? Yes, it was Mike who had said that they had eliminated three dark sedans in the parking lot that Sunday. One was Father Foley's covered with snow, one was Joan's and Pixie had strutted out of church in her nifty high-heeled boots and climbed into the third. "An Infinity status symbol," Mike had said.

"He's always been this big patriot," Pixie is saying. "Hanging the flag out every chance he gets. And kind of a conservative nut, seeing Communist conspiracies in every headline. Well, I'm not exactly the political type and I decided early in the game that I wasn't going to let that bother me. You have to admit Bill's got a lot of other things going for him. But the CIA! I'm not so sure I'd have married him if I knew things went that far!"

Just then Juan, making loud motor noises, came running over to Pixie to show her his tinker toy construction.

"How neat!" she exclaims. "An airplane! But where are the wings?"

"Not an airplane," Juan explains patiently. "It's our car."

"Of course. How stupid of me not to see that. Juan's been helping Bill polish up our automobile and his new Dad really appreciates that a lot. One great thing is how well they get along together. You like your new Papa, don't you, sweetheart?"

"Yes!" Juan says very seriously. "I love him."

Sue is already fond of the little boy and regards him attentively when he makes this declaration of affection. She thought later that the seed of a scheme was planted at that moment but she had no time to consider it then. There was something else she wanted to check out.

"Pixie," she says. "I've been meaning to ask you. Remember the day we bought our hair dryers? I was wondering if your old one ever turned up? Mine is on the fritz and I thought I might borrow yours if you had two of them."

"No, it never did turn up. There was a whole carton of things missing when we moved, some shirts of Roger's and whatnot that never did surface. But I can lend you my dryer if you like. I could drop it by this afternoon."

"Oh, never mind. It's not important. I got along for years without one and I can manage 'til I get this one fixed."

At the door when Pixie is leaving, Sue says to Juan, "How about a hug for your Aunt Sue? You'll come back soon and play with the tinker toys again, okay?"

"And see the fish!" exclaims Juan enthusiastically.

With her arms around the boy, Sue says "Gosh, Pixie, you were lucky you didn't have to wait very long for this little guy. Just a few months, wasn't it? Don't I remember that your application for him was found in Father Rossi's coat pocket the day he died?"

"That could be. We dropped it off for him that day of the Scripture meeting right after we registered at the rectory with Father Foley. I guess we were the last people to see Father Rossi alive."

"You both went into the baptistery to deliver the application?"

"Well, no. Bill had the papers in his briefcase and I'd already signed them so I waited in the car. You remember how absolutely frigid it was that day. I should have said Bill was the last person to see him. He felt just awful about his death. I mean, he was like what you might call grieving for days afterwards."

"I'll bet," Sue tried to suppress the bitterness in her voice.

Later, when Pixie, holding Juan's hand, had smartly click-clacked her way down the walk to her car, Sue slams the front door with a ferocity that takes her by surprise. God, how angry she is! How could he possibly have done such a thing! How could anyone in his right mind commit such a terrible, treacherous murder! What a crafty, cunning, double-crossing son of a bitch he had turned out to be! A hot hatred burns in her throat. Her arms tremble. She picks up the coffee mugs in the library and, carrying them to the kitchen, bangs them down on the counter.

"Odd jobs!" she mutters. "Just you wait, you son of a gun, you'll pay for this."

She spends the rest of the day cleaning the kitchen, viciously scrubbing the crusted oven with a matted piece of chore girl, windexing the windows, the toaster, the micro, the glass in the fridge with an incredible and venomous vigor. Premeditated, he had said. Too premeditated for some poor drunk to have pulled it off! Damn, what a credulous, gullible, stupid sucker she had been! Sprinkling cleansing powder onto a scouring pad, she tackles barely visible scuff marks on the black-and-white floor she had mopped only yesterday.

In her progress across the room she comes across a pen that had fallen from the counter and kneels for a moment holding it in her hand. Bill had traced the company name engraved on the expensive pen found in the baptistery to St. Paul. "You know who that makes a suspect," he had said with his engaging entre-nous smile. How very cute! What a damn, deceitful, dissembling bastard he was! Well, she'd caught up with him now and he was going to get his. With a violent swing of her arm, she pitches the pen across the kitchen. The flying missile narrowly misses Shadow who had slithered in from the dining room. The cat streaks across the checkerboard floor and begins rhythmically rubbing against Sue's leg, against her hand which tightly clenches the abrasive sponge. Purring softly, she nuzzles her nose against Sue's cheek.

"Cut that out, Shadow," Sue says hoarsely, pushing her aside. "If you're too kind to me, I'll cry and that's one thing I am absolutely not going to do." Still, she could feel the pressure of angry, unshed tears behind her eyes. Soon her head begins to pound.

When Fred comes home, she announces that she isn't feeling well and is going to bed. There is a casserole on the counter that Ellen can shove in the microwave. No, she is not hungry, she doesn't want any supper. No, she is okay, she just has a perfectly ordinary Advil headache, nothing to be concerned about. Everybody gets headaches once in a while.

"But Mom never does," she hears Jennifer say as she climbs the stairs. "What's wrong with Mom?"

"Probably just that time of the month," speculates Fred. "She'll be fine in the morning."

"Maybe she's pregnant," suggests Ellen. "I hear old Moms get very upset if they discover they're going to have a late child."

The next morning, Sue cancels all engagements and wanders restlessly through the house tackling routine jobs. She works in choppy fits and starts, her anger creating an agitation so foreign to her that sometimes she tears into tasks with a feverish frenzy and sometimes slows to an absent-minded halt, standing confused and muddled in the middle of a room wondering what it was she had intended to do.

Her disquiet is profound and makes it difficult for her to come up with any clear plan of action. Her thoughts are fragmented, thrashing wildly in the turbulent wind of her emotions. She tries to elaborate a scheme for reporting the murder to the police. She dwells on scenes of the trial in which Bill would be convicted and given a life sentence. Life is hardly long enough but she hesitates at hoping for the death penalty. Yet, this scenario is so hemmed in with problems that it ties knots of frustration in her stomach. Is there sufficient evidence to convict him? Would anyone believe her story? Wouldn't the CIA deny any connection to the crime? And what about Pixie and her children?

When the phone rings, it startles her. She resents what seems like a rude intrusion into the privacy of her thoughts and she lets it ring a long time before answering it. Still, it had not occurred to her that it might be Bill and when she hears his voice a sob shudders through her body leaving her shivering and speechless.

"Where did I bring you from" he inquires. "I just had to let you know that we've got some good news. The Paulist Press would be very interested in publishing Father Rossi's papers. I'd rather have some prestigious secular press do it because they would get wider circulation that way but at least it's an ace in the hole....Sue, are you there? What do you think?"

"I think you can go to hell," Sue says savagely. She bangs down the receiver in an attempt to convey her utter contempt for him.

Being the sole possessor of the key to the mystery of Father Rossi's murder gives Sue a peculiar sense of power. She is unwilling to share her knowledge with anyone else until she has determined what she wants to do with it. The fate of Bill Bergman's future is in her hands. One way or another, she is going to see that he is punished; punished for the horrendous crime of murdering a good priest who was supposed to be his friend, punished for robbing her of a unique and precious relationship which had given joy to her life, punished for the phony fraudulent friendship he had formed with her and her family.

She feels uncomfortable with the turmoil of her feelings and wishes she could calm down, could think things through rationally. She knows it would help to talk it out with someone but that isn't going to be Fred or Mike who might question her conviction that Bill is the murderer or might want to pursue some plan which did not meet with her approval. She wants to hang on to the reins. After some consideration, she phones Monsignor Fiedler and asks if she could come over to see him.

Walking to the rectory, she prepares for her visit by lining up the evidence against Bill in consecutive order beginning with her first meeting with him in the school parking lot the night of the murder. She remembers this encounter clearly: how handsome he looked in his beautifully tailored winter coat, how he had inquired about the lights in the baptistery. As she presents her carefully constructed story in the dimness of Monsignor's little parlor, she is aware of the hammer in her voice. She tries to modify her tone, to give her account with a degree of clarity and objectivity. This effort is not always successful. Whenever she recounts some particularly poignant piece of treachery like the night of her ride on the Bergman's swing when Bill had professed his distress at Father's death and wormed his way into her confidence, tears invade her tale.

She detects earnest sympathy and concern in Monsignor's expressive face as he listens her out but when she has finished he gently protests her case.

"Isn't it all pretty circumstantial evidence?" he asks. "I'm not certain that it's very conclusive, Sue. All the usual proofs of guilt are missing. There's no smoking gun, no finger prints, no blood trace to run through a DNA test. Can we be sure it really was Bill?"

"Jens can identify the killer."

"But he never witnessed the actual murder."

"Look, Monsignor, I understand your position on all this. I realize that you're probably trying to protect a confidential confession but I'd rather we not play games. I know Bill did this awful thing and I know that you know it too. I'm not here to discuss whether or not he's guilty but what I should do about the fact that he is. I need you to level with me and help me figure it out."

Monsignor looks at her thoughtfully for a moment and then, leaning affectionately toward her, inquires in his most amiable and mild manner what she is thinking of doing.

"Well," says Sue, "I feel very fenced in and frustrated by what you just mentioned, the fact that the case would be difficult to prove. The CIA would probably deny everything including having me followed by the encyclopedia salesman. If we were to pursue it, I'd have to talk to a lawyer first to see what our chances of success would be. But Monsignor, I'll tell you one thing, Bill's not going to get away with this. One way or another, I'm going to see that justice is served, that he gets punished for what he has done."

"You have something else in mind?"

'Yes. I've been thinking that I could see to it that he doesn't get to keep Juan, the little boy they've just adopted. He got that child through Father Rossi and he doesn't deserve to have him."

"Hasn't the adoption gone through?"

"It isn't final until August. They have to wait a year to be certain that no one claims him. When the social worker called on me recently, she mentioned that if I had any serious objection to the adoption, they would certainly look into it and deny custody of the child to the Bergmans if it should prove true. I figure his being a murderer is sufficient cause to deny him custody."

"Have you thought what that would mean to Patricia."

"Yes, I've had to think about Pixie and I'm well aware that it would break her heart. But I guess the wife of a murderer can't expect to get off Scot free."

"How would Catholic Charities go about investigating your charge?"

"That's where I'd need your help. You would have to affirm my charge. I think your word would be sufficient for them to take it seriously."

"You really think Patricia should know about the murder? And what happens to little Juan? You've thought about that?"

"Naturally, that's the most important thing of all. I've been thinking that maybe Fred and I could adopt him. Like all the males in the world, Fred has always wanted a son and I would truly love to have this boy. Of course, I'd have to talk to Fred first and I'm not sure how much I want to tell him. I don't know exactly where to begin. I thought maybe you could help me figure it out."

Monsignor is silent for a moment, his head slightly inclined so that Sue gets the impression that perhaps he is praying. Then he smiles at her in that benign, beatific way of his that always warmed her heart.

"Sue", he says, "I appreciate how painful this whole matter is for you and I'm grateful that you came to me to talk it through. You want to know where to begin. I have a suggestion to make that I want you to consider seriously. I think you should begin by forgiving Bill."

"Forgive Bill!" Sue exclaims. "I could never forgive him for this! Are you crazy?"

"No crazier than any Christian must be. We have to be careful not to let the sun go down on our anger. We must forgive our brother before we can bring our gift to the altar. We have to find it in our heart to forgive the most unforgivable crimes as Christ did when he forgave those who had scourged and humiliated him and hung him up to die a criminal's death on a cross. If you can begin by forgiving Bill, then whatever actions you decide to take will be done for justice sake and not for revenge."

"But I can't," Sue says miserably. "I can't do it. I don't even want to try."

"Sue dear, you've often told me that all the wonderful things you do for people in the parish come very naturally to you, that it requires little effort, that you enjoy your work. That doesn't make your charity less charitable but it might mean that God would someday ask something far more difficult of you. You have to consider carefully what your answer would be."

"But I can't," Sue repeats. "This was not a little picadillo he committed. He killed Father Rossi! How can I possibly forgive him for that?"

"Forgiveness is never easy. Often it takes considerable time. I don't expect some miracle to immediately lift the burden of anger from your heart. But I would hope that you would begin by praying about it and then when you are more tranquil, you might consider talking to Bill. He may be unable to deny your accusations but at least he deserves a chance to explain his behavior."

"Talk to him! I'm never going to talk to him again in my whole life."

In some dim way, Sue is aware of how childish this sounds but she means what she says. She would never speak to him again. She finds herself building a wall of resistance against Monsignor's advice and decides to leave before he becomes more persuasive.

At the door, Monsignor takes both her hands in his.

"I am so truly sorry for your trouble, Sue," he says. "I know how badly you've been hurt. I wonder if an old priest who loves you could ask two small favors?"

"Of course," What else could she say?

"I want you to promise me that you'll pray about your problem and also that you'll take no action until we talk again."

"I promise." Sue kisses him lightly on the cheek as she leaves.

CHAPTER XXVI

Sue stayed home for the next couple of days. A dense late-March fog hugged the house erasing the outside world and creating a sense of isolation which she cherished. She wanted to be alone, to be left alone. She went nowhere and talked to no one. For long stretches of the morning, she sat in the breakfast room staring out the window at the flurry of wings where sparrows sparred for space on the barely visible bird feeder. When she and Fred watched the evening news, she resented the attention it demanded of her. Did she really have to care about one more famine in Africa? She wandered off to the kitchen and absentmindedly stirred the stew she had left simmering there.

The phone rang several times during the day but she refused to answer it. When Fred came home and played back the answering machine, he announced that Bergman had called her several times.

"What's that all about?" he wanted to know. "He says he really has to talk to you. Maybe you should get back to him right away."

"Nothing important," Sue said. "Just something about a publisher. It can wait."

Sue, what's wrong. I've never seen you so apathetic. Are you feeling okay?

"I feel fine."

"Not nauseated maybe? You haven't been eating enough to keep a bird alive."

"No, not nauseated."

"I thought maybe Ellen was right, that maybe you are pregnant."

Sue did not immediately deny this. "How would you feel about another child?" she asked.

"You are pregnant?" Sue noted the caution and concern in his voice.

"No and I certainly don't want to be, but I was thinking it might be a good idea to adopt a little boy. You always did want a son."

"Sue, are you out of your mind? I had the distinct impression that you were housebound enough years of your life with babies."

"Well, I didn't have an infant in mind. I thought maybe a child about Juan's age. What would you think of that?"

"Sue, I'll tell you what I think. I think something is happening to your hormones that has temporarily deranged you."

Fred tended to come up with a physical explanation for everything. This comment was so typical that Sue managed a smile.

"You don't have to shut out the idea so absolutely," she said. "You could think about it a bit, visualize the possibilities."

That's what Sue herself had been doing, imagining what it would be like to have Juan as her own child. She thought about taking him to the lake in the summer. She would teach him to swim, holding his hard little body above the waves while he gleefully kicked and splashed. When Father Rossi had arrived in the parish last August, he had taken up swimming regularly and she remembered how his sallow skin had gradually become a handsome ruddy bronze. She pictured herself rubbing sun screen lotion on Juan's face; on his skinny arms and slender shoulders and then watching him romp on the beach day after day until a healthy glow invaded the pallor of his dark complexion. Somehow this dream melded with the happy memory of Jennifer's birthday beach party when Father had held her in his arms while the sunset dabbed delicate pastels into the sky. Father was somehow close, present in her dream of Juan.

The fantasy gave her some relief from the debilitating depression that had overtaken her. She was experiencing an oppressive sadness, a heaviness of heart which made it impossible for her to return to work. She felt listless, tired, unable to think clearly, to plan. For a day or so she moped around the house allowing the constant thought of Bill Bergman's treachery to overwhelm and immobilize her. Eventually her anger, returning in full force, rescued her. She would not allow him to cause this paralysis, this constriction, in her life. She would find a way to break out of the melancholy trap in which he had imprisoned her.

She needed to accomplish some routine, undemanding work and decided it was the perfect opportunity to copy her old beat-up address book with its broken spine and multiple corrections into the beautiful new one that Jo had given her for her birthday. The names in her book also constituted her Christmas card list. There were over three hundred entries so transcribing was a task for which normally she did not have time. Now, as she worked through the cluttered pages of the C's, through the many crossed-out and rewritten addresses of the Carneys, her dejection dissipated and the affection for her family which these names aroused began to heal the hurt in her heart.

Under the dining room table, Shadow persisted in brushing against her ankles, not letting up when she stamped her feet or pushed her aside. She grew impatient with her. She knew she had been fed so she tried opening the back door to see if she wanted to go out. The cat looked disdainfully at the cold misty weather and retreated rapidly into the dining room where once again she began her rhythmic rubbing. Sue finally put down her pen and picked her up, stroking her affectionately for a moment. "What are you trying to tell me?" she asked.

Shadow jumped from her lap and struck a pose in front of the Chinese screen that made Sue smile. She looked, as she often had in Kathy Kennedy's apartment, like an oriental statue Sue had seen advertised in the Metropolitan Museum catalogue. She would have to scratch Kathy from her Christmas list she thought, remembering sadly her visit with her on the day of her death. Suddenly, quite spontaneously and with no effort on her part to recall their final conversation, she remembered what Kathy had said to her that morning. "If you ever have something so difficult to forgive that it sticks in your throat robbing you of your peace, just remember forgiveness is God's business. He will do for you what you cannot do yourself."

She returned to Church the next morning and knelt well behind the little congregation of faithful parishioners who gathered there each morning. She allowed the momentum of the Mass to carry to heaven for her the prayers which she had been so unable to articulate in the last few days: pleas for mercy, songs of praise and thanksgiving, petitions for peace and loving union. The haunting melody of the responsorial psalm—"If today you hear his voice, harden not your heart"—sang on repeatedly in her soul long after the liturgy was over and the others had left. "Please, God!" she begged, knowing that her own heart was still a block of cold cement.

"I didn't receive Communion this morning," she told Monsignor when she stopped by to see him on her way home. "I'm still so damn mad."

"You thought our Lord would not understand your anger? Sue, I know you are under the impression that Bill killed your dear friend Father Rossi in cold blood, that he deceived and manipulated and betrayed your friendship. Why wouldn't that infuriate you? Anger is an understandable and healthy reaction to such a traumatic experience. Believe me, it can be a helpful emotion when it is rooted in justice and self-esteem. But you have to watch out for vindictiveness, Sue. And you have to be careful not to nurture your anger or it will devour you. Sooner or later, you have to move beyond it."

"You say forgiveness takes a long time. How long?"

"I guess that's up to you."

"I've started to pray about it. I don't know what else I can do."

"You could talk to Bill. I think that might help."

"Monsignor, I honestly don't think I can do that."

"It would take considerable courage, I know, and maybe hope that something would be accomplished by a meeting with him."

"Like what?"

"Sue, I know Bill's friendship with you and Fred has been very precious to him. He's an extremely reserved man and does not have many close friends. I know he wants to talk to you and I think it might be helpful to listen him out. Do you think you could find it in your heart to call him?"

"Call him? The hell I will!"

When Sue met Bill at the River Lodge for luncheon the next day, she was amazed that he looked exactly as he had the last time she had seen him. The evil she had discovered in him was in no way visible, was hidden like a malignant cancer that only shows on x-ray. He had come from the office and was wearing a business suit but had left his tie in the car as his concession to suburban living. She had almost forgot how extraordinarily handsome he was. Perhaps he appeared a little more diffident than usual but if he felt uncomfortable, he was very cool about it.

"Some wine, Sue?"

"A glass of Chardonnay would be nice."

"You picked a good spot to meet."

He had suggested coming to her house but when she would not allow it, he had invited her to lunch.

"It will do. Winnie always liked the privacy here and the food is good if you enjoy Greek."

"Sue, I'm really grateful that you haven't told Pixie about Father Rossi. She's having enough trouble with the idea that I worked for the CIA."

"It was no favor to you. I just haven't told anyone yet. How many 'odd jobs' have you pulled off for the CIA I wonder?"

"If by odd jobs you mean executions, I assure you this was the only one. When they first hired me back in college, I was asked to audit the class of a professor, a diocesan priest, who had previously led peace marches through the streets of St. Paul. They suspected that he was a Communist and perhaps a popular rabble-rouser. He was teaching a course on the Social Doctrine of the Church, a history of the encyclicals beginning with Leo XIII and while some of that stuff always seems to me to lean a little left, I had no trouble exonerating him. He was not a Commie, in fact was quite a loyal American. That's what I usually did for them, check out people with whom I had some more or less natural contact."

"Sometimes these people are actually dangerous, a threat to our country?"

"Occasionally yes. Far more often they are just opinionated demagogues incapable of much harm."

"But you considered Father Rossi dangerous?"

Bill's face was seldom very expressive but the anguish and dismay he registered now were very apparent to Sue.

"Look," he said. "I didn't do the research on Father Rossi but if you had seen his file you might have thought of him as a threat too. You must remember that it was our policy to oppose a Communist takeover in Alvarado. We were trying to discourage the death squads but to back the military wholeheartedly in fighting off the guerrillas. Father Rossi was no innocent bystander in that long war down there. We had pictures of him meeting with guerrilla leaders. The university where he had connections was considered a hot-bed of Communism. He taught an evening course in Constitutional Law there which was attended regularly by rebel intellectuals, and was actually geared toward helping them draw up a new constitution in case of victory or strategies for negotiation in case of a peace settlement. In the end, the New York Times called the Peace Accords a negotiated revolution. Father was considered to be the most intelligent and influential witness to affairs in Alvarado by some key members of Congress. Although he had left the country, his work in Washington was creating havoc with our hope of keeping the army strong in Alvarado. It was an impressive file."

"I don't know how any rational Catholic could think of a Dominican University as a hot bed of Communism."

"I assure you Sue, I'm not the only Catholic who did. Church opinion in Alvarado itself was very divided on the war. The work undertaken by priests committed to the poor had no official sanction and often came under fire from political and ecclesiastical corners. They were branded as the 'popular' church or the 'parallel' church with the implication that their commitment was more Marxist than Christian and their loyalties more to revolution than to the Church. They were rejected by the Episcopal conference and tolerated with varying degrees of tension by the Archdiocese. It would be a mistake to think that there was no plausible case against them."

"Look, Bill. I don't give a damn how logical your case against him was. You knew Father Rossi, you were supposed to be his friend and I will never understand in a million years how you could possibly have killed him."

Sue had intended to play it cool, to remain calm and was surprised at the venom with which she now lashed out at Bill. She could see that he was stung, pained by her anger. For a long moment, he did not respond.

"Sue, I always knew you'd catch up with this some day and I certainly knew how hard it would be for you. It may seem odd to you, but I have felt from the beginning that Father Rossi himself understood and forgave me and Monsignor too knew that my motive was for a cause that I felt obliged to serve. Maybe it's something only a man would understand."

Sue resented this implication that women were less comprehending than men, that she might be unable to grasp his point of view.

"You could try me," she said. "I guess that's what we're here for."

"I don't know where to begin so that you'd really get the idea of what a bind I was in."

"How about at the beginning wherever that was."

Neither of them had touched the gyros they had ordered but Sue now picked up her fork as she prepared to listen. She made an effort to give him the open-minded attention she would have given to anyone else.

"I remember telling you about my father."

"Yes. The general who was hard to please."

"Exactly. I guess that's where it begins."

When Bill was first interviewed for work with the CIA, he consulted his father before accepting the job. He was supposed to tell no one that he had been contacted but he felt safe in making this one exception. He told himself that he was seeking advice but actually he was eager to impress his father, to tell him something that would win his respect. This worked miraculously. His father regarded him with a new deference and leveled with him in a way quite different from his previous critical attitude. He also supplied him with a lot of advice which Bill had not really been seeking.

He admonished Bill to do his work bravely and courageously even if assignments should prove dangerous or onerous. He was to remember that his country was engaged in a very serious cold war and that the outcome was important not only to the U.S. but to the world at large. He should be honored that he was asked to serve. He said they both knew that the CIA sometimes had to play hardball and he should be prepared to do what was necessary with loyal resolve and a clear conscience.

"Look, Dad," Bill had said. "They only want me to obtain a little information for them. They're not asking me to assassinate Castro."

Still he remembered this conversation when the unexpected happened and he was given the Rossi assignment. Father had been a prime target of the Alvarado army. They had narrowly missed him in their early morning raid on the Dominican University. Both the CIA and the former government considered it imperative that he be put out

of commission. In a sense, it was the most important thing Bill had
been asked to undertake and might make a significant difference in the
final outcome in that small, troubled country. He was a natural for the
job since he was moving to the Chicago area anyway and could easily
buy a home in the parish where the priest was stationed. Even if he were
unsuccessful in making the murder look like an accident, no one was
apt to suspect him. In spite of all this, he was reluctant to accept the
assignment until he recalled the things his father had impressed on him
when he first joined the CIA.

"Are you trying to tell me that you killed Father Rossi in order to
please your father?" Sue suggested bitterly.

Bill was obviously offended by this question.

"Sue, that's not fair. Are you listening to me or not? What I'm trying
to tell you is that killing Father Rossi became a matter of principle to
me. No matter how difficult and distasteful the assignment was, it was
something that I had to do to fulfill the obligations I undertook when I
joined the CIA. I couldn't just back out when the going got rough. Can't
you understand that?"

"No, I can't understand that. When you met Father Rossi you
must have realized that he wasn't the country's number one enemy,
that he was just as dedicated to the poor as you were to your war on
communism."

"Meeting Father sure made it tough. The last thing I expected was to
have him call on us to welcome us to the parish and to take a personal
interest in us. His offer to see about the possibility of adopting Juan was
so thoughtful and meant so much to Pixie. She insisted on inviting him
to dinner and a friendship that I never anticipated began to develop.
There was a lot about our childhoods that we had in common but we
never discussed politics. I didn't understand his viewpoint on Alvarado
until we read those articles you found in his room."

"They would have made a difference?"

"I know now that the CIA viewed Alvarado through a very narrow lens. All they saw was a black-and-white picture of Communist guerrillas fighting to take over a legitimate government. Father's view was much wider and more comprehensive. Actually the situation down there was very complex. He was much more interested in recognizing and rectifying historic injustices. I also learned that you didn't have to be a Communist to fight for a better break for the poor."

"But after you knew him, how could you possibly have gone on planning to do away with him?"

"Sue, can't you see what an awful dilemma I was in? Liking Father didn't at that point make him any less the enemy, but it certainly made it harder for me to get on with the job. I struggled with a lot of second thoughts and temptations to back out of the deal. The boss kept urging me to get it over with but I kept finding excuses to delay. Finally, the perfect situation presented itself when Pixie mentioned that Jens had brought a heater into the baptistery for the Scripture meeting. Electrocution was something I had been considering; in fact, I had been carrying Pixie's dryer around in my brief case for a couple of weeks. The timing was so right with the reception for the Cardinal coming up to keep everyone distracted. I knew it was now or never, so somehow I managed to get up guts enough to do what I thought had to be done. I'll understand if you never forgive me. I've been having a hard time trying to forgive myself."

"You'd never know it by the way you infiltrated our little group and deceived us into trusting you."

"Sue, look. If it hadn't been for you and Mike the incident would have been written off as an accident. If Foley had found the body instead of you, we would have been home free. But when the boss discovered that some amateurs were poking around, he instructed me to get on the inside of the investigation so we would know what was going on. I could see the wisdom of that and it was relatively easy to do. But Sue, I never once tried to deceive you. When I told you how awful I felt about Father's death, believe me I was telling you the truth. I couldn't betray the CIA by revealing what actually occurred, but in some sense I kept hoping you would discover it. I tried to supply you with whatever evidence I could, the pen from St. Paul, for instance. It became important to me that no one else be blamed for the murder and I kept steering you away from Tim who seemed a likely suspect without an alibi."

"You didn't steer us away from Jens. I think you were trying to frame him."

"Just the opposite. I knew if you pursued and questioned Jens, you'd eventually find out that Jens had seen me leaving the baptistery, that he might well identify me."

"Bill, there's one thing I've got to know. Was Kathy Kennedy killed by that encyclopedia salesman in order to protect you?"

"God, Sue, I sure hope not. It may be something we'll never know. Actually Place is some nut they hire to discourage investigations and create distraction. Dumb diversions like planting Winnie's candlestick in the bushes are more in his line. When he pulled that off, I stopped reporting information he could use in further games. And from the start, I tried to get him called off from shadowing you. He did let up on it from time to time but it wasn't until I raised absolute hell about that attempted drug planting deal on the south side that the boss withdrew him permanently. He too thought that was way overboard, completely out of line."

Bill had been doing most of the talking and had barely made a dent in his lunch., He'd given up trying to eat his gyros as a sandwich and was approaching it in an absent-minded fashion with his knife and fork. He continued to talk, going back over old ground and filling in details. Sue, who was accustomed to his taciturn manner and abbreviated comments, found herself wondering if this was how he came across in court: quietly articulate, earnest, persuasive. Little was added to the substance of what he had already told her, but she began to get a sense for the frame of mind in which he had murdered Father Rossi, to find it almost comprehensible.

Still, when the little Hispanic waitress came to ask if they wished desert, Sue told her that she thought not and asked her to bring separate bills as she wished to pay for her own lunch. She could tell that this hurt Bill as she had intended that it should. She carried away the wounded expression on his face as a sort of trophy, but it soon began to backfire, to haunt her instead.

Chapter XXVII

"How did your meeting with Bill go?"

Sue looks up from the stack of Father Rossi's books she has been cataloguing to see Monsignor coming across the library to join her. He takes a seat across the table from her. She notices in the strong morning light that the skin of his thin cheeks looks like finely creased parchment.

"It went all right I guess. He said you could understand why he had to do it. Is that true?"

"I understand that he is sincere in what he tell us. I think he was caught up in the cold war very much as the Reagan administration was when they tried to illegally fund the Contras."

"He talked about being committed on principle. Isn't that some kind of insanity?"

"More like some rigid code of honor. He was raised to see things through no matter what."

"But murder! What a terribly immoral thing to do!"

"Pretty extreme, I admit. And I won't pretend that I wasn't shocked to the core when I first heard it. But I'm glad I don't have to judge the morality of it. I think war is seldom justified but to kill in a war one considers important to the salvation of the world might be rationalized in some subjective way. I'm content to leave judgement to God."

"You look at everything so kindly."

"Well, remember what St. Francis de Sales says about judging our neighbor. 'Were there a hundred different ways of looking at an action, we should choose the most favorable.' Poor Bill is doing the best he can to rectify his tragic mistake. He's been making every effort to see that Father Rossi's papers are published so that his work lives on."

"But Father himself is gone. There is no way he can rectify that."

"Sue, I sometimes recall what you said about Paul Rossi shortly before his death—that your deepest sense of him was of a Christian who would be willing to die for his faith. I think you were prophetic in saying that. He was certainly a priest who took serious risks to his life in pursuing justice for the poor. Maybe it would ease the pain of your loss if you were to think of his death less in terms of murder and to view it more in terms of martyrdom: that in God's providence he died a martyr's death."

"I could try. But I think there has to be some justice. This is America. You can't just knock someone off and get away with it. I promised Father Rossi that I would see that his killer got what was coming to him."

"You think Bill is paying no penalty for his crime? He fully appreciates that he made a grievous mistake and he has to live with that for the rest of his life. And he knows that he lives in some danger. The CIA rarely if ever executes someone in the United States and they will do whatever is necessary to keep the murder from being discovered. Bill feels that he is under constant surveillance. Sue, you might ask yourself what Father Rossi himself would want in these circumstances."

During the next several weeks, Sue frequently asked herself that question. In her morning prayer to the Holy Spirit, she dwelt on a final phrase—to cherish what is right and just. But what was right and just? Monsignor had said that she would know better once she had forgiven Bill, but how could she possibly forgive him? After making her bed each morning, she stood beneath the cross Mrs. Rossi had given her and begged God to enlighten her. Over and over again, she reviewed the possibility of going to the police. It became a mental treadmill from which she could not escape. Still, she took no action.

The erratic Lakewood spring seemed interminable to Sue. In late March crocus crowded the parkway and soon forsythia splashed vivid color throughout the entire village. In April, jonquils, fluttering and dancing in the breeze, spilled down the steep incline east of the garage. After a brief spell of cold nights and quickly melting snow, a mass of early Emperor tulips raised their scarlet cups to the warming sun. But the beauty and excitement of her awakening garden failed to wipe winter from Sue's leaden heart. She went dutifully about her daily work feeling listless, dull, distracted. Fred, obviously worried about her, insisted that she have her thyroid checked.

Grace is not always sudden or amazing. Sometimes it is as subtle and imperceptible as the slow ripening of the lilacs along Sue's driveway. When at last they were a sea of purple blooms filling the air with delicate fragrance, she finally internalized the spring. One morning with some of her former exuberance, she called Jo at work.

"Guess what?" she exclaimed in some excitement. "I just saw my first robin!"

"Sue, where on earth have you been?" Jo replied. "I saw a pair hopping on the lawn weeks ago."

Only days later, Monsignor called, his voice sounding a little anxious. "Is the party still on?" he inquired.

"Party?" Sue was momentarily confused.

"The party for the little Bergman boy on the fifteenth. Do you still plan to have it?"

"I guess so. I wouldn't know how to call it off. We can't disappoint Juan."

"Well, Sue, I was wondering if you could help me with an idea for a birthday present. I'd like to make it something special."

"I know just the thing. Pixie told me they are giving him a fish tank which they plan to stock gradually to keep the interest going. If you could pick out some exciting specimen, maybe a paradise fish or a marbled hatchet, I know it would make a hit."

It pleased Sue to contemplate the enjoyment Monsignor would take in the village pet shop when he went on his errand.

A bouquet of bright balloons floats above the fish tank on the night of Juan's birthday party. In the dining room, Fred, whose grandmother always said "Will you is a poor fellow" insists that his guests have a second piece of Pixie's delicious cake. Sue and Juan have slipped away to have one more look at the pair of banded gouramis swimming in a plastic water bag on the surface of the tank. A number of oblique reddish stripes mark their flanks. Their gill cover sports a bright blue pattern and their fins are mainly orange. Quite spectacular. Monsignor had said that a paradise fish was too aggressive for a community tank but these gouramis were very peaceful and suitable for a beginner. Juan, with nose pressed against the glass, is obviously mesmerized by them.

"Do they close their eyes when they go to sleep?" he wonders.

Although she had been avoiding him for weeks, Sue is not displeased when Bill, in his laid-back way, ambles over to join them.

"I hear you had a terrific job offer in St. Paul," she says. "Are you going to take it?"

"I haven't decided yet. The position's not that great, not really as good as the situation here, but I thought maybe it would be best for us to clear out of town."

Sue hesitates for only a moment.

"We would miss you," she says. "Fred and I both hope you'll stick around."

"You really mean that?"

"Yes, I mean that. After all, we have Father's book to complete and besides, I wouldn't mind watching this little fellow grow up."

"I suppose Juan is important to you."

At the mention of his name, Juan turns to look up at them. With tender affection, Sue touches his pale, off-olive cheek and runs her finger down his not quite perfect Roman nose.

"He is rather special."

Bill bestows one of his rare just-between-us smiles on her so that Sue remembers now what an easy, understanding rapport had always existed between them.

"I realized who he was the moment I saw him at the aquarium." Bill says. "His eyes are different but everything else about him is so familiar. I was sure you caught the resemblance too."

"I suppose I did. I guess I don't always allow myself to know what I know."